Candy & Flowers

Candy & Flowers

Chad Moore

Money on The Books North Carolina

www.moneyonthebooks.com

ISBN# 0-9821770-9-7

First Edition: (Date)

Author's Note

This is a work of fiction; neither the characters portrayed here nor any of the events that take place in this story should in any way be understood or construed as real. Rather, they are the products of my imagination.

ACKNOWLEDGEMENTS

First of all I wanna shout out my family.
  Starting with Ms. Ann Allen, the woman who
brought this Immaculate Conception into life (you
did good Ma!)
My sisters, Michelle and Mary Moore; my brother,
Mark Moore (I know you fed up with doin Fed time
lil brah but hold yo head and be easy, either that
or you can tear down the whole facility and make
em regret they ever put yo ass in the system. Either
way hold yo head !) My Uncle Cameron Moore,
my daughter Celeste Moore, my nephews D.J.
and Xaviar, my niece's Tyeisha and Muffin.

My man Nut
(through thick and thin, like next of kin). You been
ridin hard wit me homeboy - "birds of a feather".
The game is to be sold not told but even the
wealthiest man got a benefactor; Ghetto Legacy
get passed down from generation to generation -
if they don't get what I'm sayin it's cause they
can't get what I ain't gave em - game recognize -
play hard and disregard, cause if they ain't
countin they don't count, it's self explanatory.

Get 2 Da $
  Shouts out to Big Chuck, Big E, Richy Rich, K.D.,
Jim Diamond and Aunt Judy.

Also
  Travis Littles, Darren, and Darryl, Pookie, Ray, Bo
Bo, Sean Moss, James Dozier, Jamar, Fame,
Christina, Enoch, Chill, Ty, Kool-Aid, P, Matt AKA
(Shaft),Belly, Keith, Supa-Dave, and my man
Rodney (Toolbox) Searcy AKA Short Dawg.

And of course my State Prison Family
Sean Payton, Derrick "Dizzy" Fitzgerald, Victor
Wilson AKA "Victor Newmoney", B-Lo, Myreon
Bennet AKA "Double Edge", Chedda Man (Shine
time), Jinx, Mohammed, Marlin Berry AKA "Marley
Marl", Carlos Hall, Big - E, Tone, Antoine Lockhart,
Goldie, Lil Tonio, Rodney Monteith, Vinnie,
Tobacco Red, Shawn Cannon AKA "Black", "O"
AKA "Osama", Antonio Shine, Cash (from "wide
awake Wilson"), Blue, Tony Scott AKA "T-
Dot"(Olmerta Ent.), Lil D, Dontavious Drummer AKA
L.D., Nick (The Mayor) and my old bunkmate Mark
Bassett for tellin me "to stop procrastinating wit this
book". And everybody else at Brown Creek (Too
many to name!)

Acknowledging those who've acknowledged me
in my absence!
Tori Briggs AKA "Jazzy", ("Look at you can't let go!)
Love a two way street though it's all good. And of
course Miss Ebony - "hindsight 20 X 20"! And I can't
forget, Treneice Mackey, Granny, Kim King,

Tanisha McGriff, Dameka Dykes, Shakkia Redfern, Tiffany (Ms. Redbone), Tequita Bean, Toni Boss, Season's, Kelli Griffith, Crystana Lattimore, and Jen Villalpando. The letters, phone calls and visits, all are highly appreciated. I hope they continue through the duration of this bid. (Especially # 27).

And to all those who read this before it reached print
Robert Moore AKA "Sonny", Lil Mike (from Hickory), Butta, Tony Boone, Black, Reginald Bruce AKA Squeaky and Tanisha Barrino. Thanks for your honesty and criticism.

And a special thanks
To my mom, Ann Allen AKA "Ms. Ann" for all of her hard work - typing, research, running around etc. etc., and to my man Charles Harris AKA B-Lo for all your help editing, proofreading, motivation etc. etc. - (I'll see you at the release party-drinks on me!)

To all those not mentioned
It's still love but this print don't come free, every word cost.
Don't worry after this one sells, maybe I'll have a lil more $'s to splurge on shout outs.
  But, until then it is what it is and I am who I am.

Love is Love/ Choo AKA "Ghetto Legacy"

R.I.P.
Doris Moore (Grandma), Tony Moore (Grandpa),

Jerome Briggs, Dwayland McDowell (Rowdy), my man "Big" who passed in prison and never got to see the streets again and my man Marquise - no longer with us but always with us. Gone but never forgotten.

CHAPTER 1

Strobe lights flickered on and off as Mystical boomed throughout the almost empty club "shake it fast-show me what you working wit", as the main attraction for the night worked the stage in a bright yellow G-String and knee high boots, which were now pointed in the air toward the ceiling. The inexperienced dancer flipped upside down on the pole and slid face first toward the stage, but not slow and graceful like the veterans who shake their asses off every night in Club Fantasy to make a quick buck; but instead slid clumsily to the bottom of the pole, slamming head first into the stage, with a loud thump. "Boo!", a voice yelled from the table closest to the stage. "Come on Bitch, you can do better than that, show me what you workin' wit! Let me see you handstand or something, back dat ass up Bitch!"

The voice continued to blurt out obscenities as coins bounced and rolled across the stage, one landing right beside the frustrated dancers face. Coming to a brief spin, it stopped on heads, only to reveal the face of 'Old honest Abe'. And, as the dancer glanced at the face of Abraham Lincoln, embedded in copper, thoughts of being freed from this degrading slave ritual were starting to look more like fantasy than reality. Because, this dancers chances of being freed didn't seem too likely.

"Come on Bitch get up, put yo wig back on ", the voice in the front of the stage yelled, "hop to it, the show ain't over".

"Come on baby, let's go" a soft spoken, but deep, voice whispered in the loud spectator's ear.

The loud, rude, spectator turned around and faced the man with the husky voice and smiled. She licked her wet, shapely, lips. Then, she poked them out, as she began to pout like a five year old who was just told to go to bed. "Come on Marcus", she said in a now sweet and soft tone, "I was just startin to enjoy this, let me get one more song baby", she pleaded while battin her puppy dog eyes.

Marcus was cold-hearted by nature, but Candy Brown was to him what kryptonite is to Superman. So, like always, he melted like putty in her hands.

"Alright Candy, one more song, but that's it. We got to get this shit over wit and get the fuck up outta here."

"O.K., daddy", Candy said in a sweet, seductive voice. She reached out and rubbed his crotch, while whispering a soft "thank you" in his ear, letting her lips barely caress his earlobe; but not once removing her eyes completely from the stage. "O.K. mufucka, get up!" She screamed as she turned to face the dancer, who still laid on the stage, sweating and out of breath, and left with no dignity.

Doing as he was told, he began to stand up, revealing his muscular build as he grabbed the pole for support. Biceps flexing, he pulled hisself to his feet. He struggled to stand in the high heel boots he once so much admired from afar, due to the way they seemed to jack the dancers asses up in the air, making them look more enticing. These were the same boots that he now despised, just as much as the predicament he was in.

He almost hated those boots, and his unfortunate predicament, as much as he hated the pecan brown beauty, who sat in front of him, facing the stage, with a large handgun pointed in his direction.

She had a devilish grin on her face. But the beast standing behind her, had an innocent face that nowhere near matched the evil, distant eyes embedded into his head. Then, the beast spoke,.

"You heard her. Get yo ass up and entertain the lady." It was then that Leon, the manager of Club Fantasy, began to stroll toward the front of the stage, as Candy motioned for him to come closer.

"Now turn dat ass around Bitch!", she spat, slapping Leon on the ass as he turned around slowly.

"I'm gonna kill this Bitch" he thought to himself "her and that Bitch nigga of hers". But, little did he know, Marcus had no intentions of letting him live to see another day.

"Drop it like it's hot", Candy yelled, slapping Leon on the ass again, as Ludacris came through the speakers, "p-poppin' in a handstand".

Marcus shook his head as he proceeded toward the bar. Pouring himself a shot of Gin, with a drop of grapefruit juice, He took a seat on the barstool. He took small sips, as he watched Candy continue to degrade Leon, having him perform as many tricks as she could think of. All of the tricks she herself had used so many times, in so many cities, to make ends meet.

"Marcus baby", Candy whined as she looked over her shoulder towards the bar.

"What is it Candy", Marcus answered as he walked towards her, drink in hand.

"Daddy he's not entertaining me anymore, I'm gettin bored with him", she said sounding like a spoiled child.

"Yeah, me too baby" Marcus stated, in a grim tone, as he took one last sip from his drink and handed it to Candy.

It was then that Leon realized that these two had more planned for him than humiliation and robbery.

"Come on bruh", Leon pleaded as Marcus walked toward him, with gun in hand. "Marcus man, please bruh, you got the money, why don't ya'll just take it and go. Come on dawg, I won't go to the police, I promise!"

Leon continued to plead. Dropping to his knees, he began to cry, begging for his life, while snot bubbles formed on his nose and grew to the size of small marbles, before popping and oozing down towards his lip.

Sweat dripping from his forehead, and foam building up in the corner of his mouth, he continued to plea.

"Come on Candy, talk to him!", Leon screamed as he looked at Candy, with one last bit of hope in his eyes. But that bit of hope left him when Marcus grabbed him by his neck, with his left hand, and pressed the barrel of the fifty caliber, held tightly in his right hand, against Leon's stomach and pulled the trigger.

There was a loud boom, followed by a ringing noise, which seemed to drown out the music momentarily. Then, the music faded back in, it was Jay-Z's ninety-nine problems.

"If you havin girl problems I feel bad for you son, I got ninety-nine problems but a Bitch ain't one."

Marcus turned around slowly, facing Candy, who was now standing on the table dancing seductively. Staring at Marcus, she began to raise her shirt up slowly, revealing her small waist, picture perfect abs and perky breast, as she pulled the shirt over her head and throwed it to Marcus.

"Candy get yo ass off that table and put this shirt back on, it's time to get outta here."
"Oh Daddy, you no fun sometimes", Candy whined but quickly did as she was told once she looked into the very serious eyes on that innocent face, that face that she loved so much, the face of Marcus Flowers, her friend, her guardian, her everything.

Candy put her shirt on and looked at Marcus with that child like smile and said, "piggyback."

Marcus shook his head and smiled, then turned his back to Candy. She stuffed her pistol in the back of her jeans, then wrapped her arms around his neck and hopped off the table, onto his back.

Marcus took one last look at Leon. He lay face down on the stage, in a yellow G-String, and a puddle of blood, with a bright red wig lying to his side.

He snatched the wig off the stage and reached over his shoulder and placed it on Candy's head, which was corn rowed and covered with a stocking cap.

"Get yo'self together lil mama" Marcus said.

Walking towards the door, with Candy hanging onto his neck, her legs wrapped around his waist, and tucked under his arms, he stopped only long enough to grab the book bag full of money from the bar.

"I love you Marcus Flowers", Candy whispered into his ear as they made an exit and stepped out into the cold winter air.

The music from inside faded, as they got further away from the building and closer to the car, which was hidden on the opposite side of the street, behind a small body shop.

Marcus put Candy down and handed her the bag. Then, he opened the driver's door and hopped in, right behind her, as she slid in, crawling over the seat to the passenger side.

Marcus, catching a quick glance of her rearview, thought to himself, "we gone go to the tattoo shop tomorrow and put my name across that in big letters".

"What you smilin for Marcus?"

"Nothin baby, jus a lil inside thing."

"Yeah I bet nigga.... keep grinnin like you know something I don't, I saw that red Bitch all in your face earlier tonight before you left the club, what she do blow you off before you doubled back up in there."

"Candy don't start that shit", Marcus drawled as he crank up the car and pulled off into the quiet, empty street.

"Don't you start nigga", Candy was saying as Marcus leaned forward and popped in a C.D. to drown her out, because he knew there was no win when it came to an argument with the lil ball of fire sitting next to him.

Candy leaned back in her seat, arms folded and lips poked out, as they drove off, barely beating sunrise and getting as far away from the crime scene they left behind as they could, before Leon was discovered and the police began looking for suspects.

CHAPTER 2

That was Then

"Strawberry shortcake, cream on the top, tell me the name of your sweetheart", Candy and Felicia chanted as they turned the rope for Tiffany. Going through a list of names as Tiffany continued to skip over the rope with a big grin on her face and pigtails bouncing up and down.

"J.R., Tyrone, Eric, Marcus."

"Ooh, you landed on Marcus", Felicia screamed at Tiffany.

Marcus stood on the sidewalk with his friends, all too occupied with a Nerf football to pay the girls any attention, but upon hearing his name he looked up and smiled at Tiffany.

"Tiffany and Marcus sittin in a tree K.I.S.S.I.N.G., first come love then comes..."

"Shut up Felicia", Candy screamed at the top of her lungs, it's my turn to jump you wastin time, here get the rope Tiffany", Candy said with a look of disgust on her face.

Tiffany grabbed the rope and began to turn as Candy jumped, all the while, facing Felicia and rolling her eyes. Felicia stuck her tongue out at Candy in response.

Then the girls continued to chant, "strawberry shortcake,

cream on the top, tell me the name of your sweetheart",
Felicia and Tiffany sang as Candy bounced, the whole time
staring at Marcus and buggin her eyes out at him when he
returned her stare, never missing a beat as the rope went over
her head and under her feet.

Felicia and Tiffany commenced to call out names, "Tyrone,
Jerome, Keith, Lamont, Jerry, Ricky", the girls continued to
call out names as Candy bit her bottom lip and looked at
Felicia as if she wanted to choke her to death.

Felicia only smiled in return and continued to call out a
long list of names, "Patrick, Tyler, Marquise", Felicia
blurted out almost catching Candy off guard, who had
stopped and then jumped at the last minute barely missing
the rope as it hit the asphalt.

Candy then decided to show off, showing Felicia she could
jump rope and give her the middle finger at the same time.

Then, spinning around to face Tiffany, she continued to
jump, with her hands on her hips, as sweat dripped down her
face, and her beads bounced up and down on her forehead.

The girls continued to turn the rope and call out names, none
of which included the letter M, then she heard it "Marcus!"

"Pe..." Candy threw her arms up in midair and let the rope
catch her wrist.

"You stopped on Pete", Tiffany said with a smirk.

"No I didn't I stopped on ..."

"Marcus!", the voice yelled again cutting Candy off before
she got the name out of her mouth, it was then she realized
she had heard his name but not from her playmates.

"Marcus, I know you hear me boy", a woman screamed,
standing on a porch a few houses up.

"Get up here right now", she said as the wind lifted her robe,
revealing her panty line, while she stood outside, in her
shower cap, with matching pink slippers on her feet.

"Ooh, you see that", Marcus heard one of the young boys
say as he ran off.

"Candy and Pete sittin in a tree", Felicia and Tiffany teased until Candy snatched the rope from both of their hands and screamed at Tiffany.

"You hit my arm wit the rope on purpose you high yella Bitch."

"Candy Brown, I know I ain't just hear you out there cursing", a voice came from the front porch of the big blue house across the street.

"No mama, I ain't curse."

"Yes she did Mrs. Brown; she called me the B word", Tiffany said while giving Candy the finger on the low.

"Candy you come in this house right now", her mother commanded with both hands on her shapely large hips.

Candy gave Tiffany an evil glance before doing as she was told.

Once Candy reached the porch, her mother, Terri Brown, raised her right hand, making Candy draw up and duck as she ran through the front door.

Terri followed behind her, but stopped at the door and turned to see Tiffany's mother, Denise across the street, at her screen door, waving for Tiffany to come inside, then looking up, Denise waved at Terri with a big smile on her face.

"Hey girl", Terri screamed while waving back, then under her breath she said, "ya high yella Bitch", turning around to make sure Candy didn't hear her.

"Felicia you come in here too", Terri yelled out.

"It's gettin dark and your momma ain't home yet", Felicia sprinted into the house before the words got out of her mouth good, because she knew just as well as Mrs. Brown there was no tellin when her mother would be home or if she would period.

Felicia walked into the well kept home, so much different from the one she lived in. She took a seat, right next to her friend, on the big, comfortable, blue and white, couch and smiled, only to get a frown in return, from Candy.

Rolling her eyes and twisting her neck to the opposite direction, Candy folded her arms and smacked her lips.

"So!", Felicia said, as she bugged her eyes out at Candy.

Terri walked back towards the kitchen and towards the aroma that had drifted into the living room, that familiar scent of fried chicken and sweet Jiffy cornbread.

"Mmm, Mrs. Brown that smells good", Felicia said as Terri walked past, only to hear Candy smack her lips again.

"Candy what's yo problem", Terri asked, coming to a stop by the doorway to the kitchen.

"Nothin mama I ..."

"Mrs. Brown she mad cause Marcus Flowers was lookin at Tiffany", Felicia interrupted.

"No I ain't", Candy said through clenched teeth.

"Who is Marcus Flowers? That lil four eyed thing who was out there? That's what got my baby all worked up?"

"No Mama, she lyin", Candy said with her lips poked out.

"I was bout to say, for one you too young to be worried bout some boy anyway, and for two that lil rough lookin boy ain't nothing to get worked up over."

"He ain't rough lookin", Candy mumbled.

"Ooh, look at her, my lil baby gettin mad bout some lil ole Marcus Flowers", Terri teased as she entered the kitchen, then poked her head back out the doorway and said, "now his daddy, that was a fine black man there. If he wasn't so crazy, I might've got wit him myself before you or Marcus was even thought about, but no, he got wit that sorry ass Irene down there and caught her doin him wrong in his own house and went and killed that ole ugly man she was sneaking around wit and tried to choke her halfway to death. Only thing stopped him was Marcus came out his room screamin and carryin on. I hear by the time he come home Marcus'll be a grown man, mmh hm, yes sir, Terrance Flowers! Big fine black man! Big strong crazy motha fu...", Terri caught herself as she realized she had got caught up in her own words and forgot she was talking to the two young girls in front of her who now looked at her with their mouths wide open as if in shock.

Terri, realizing she had been rambling, covered her mouth and regained her composure. Then, she went back into the kitchen, as she yelled back to the girls, not wanting to look them eye to eye, "ya'll go wash ya'll hands and get ready to eat."

Marcus stood by the kitchen table with his two sisters and brother, all younger than him, watching as his mother took out six plates and covered them each with one chicken leg, potatoes and macaroni, in equal portions. All except for one plate, which had three pieces of chicken on it, two breast and a leg, which she placed at the head of the table, and the others by the remaining seats.

"Ya'll sit down and eat", she said, then yelled into the living room, "dinners ready". As the others sat down to eat, Marcus reached into the refrigerator to grab the kool-aid pitcher.

"Pour me some of that boy, (sthh, sthh, sthh)", the big belly man in the doorway said as he stood over him, cup in hand, rubbing his large stomach with his free hand and sucking his teeth, "sthh, sthh, sthh", Marcus hated that sound his mothers boyfriend made constantly, like he was sucking spit through his teeth.

"Sthh, sthh, sthh, hurry up boy, you act like you deaf sometimes".... (Sthh, sthh, sthh) "that's enough! What you tryin do overflow the cup?"

Marcus hurried to the counter, got out cups for everybody else, filled them and placed them at the table, then joined the rest to eat.

"Sthh, sthh, sthh, well what we got here" (sthh, sthh, sthh) "fried chicken um-hmm, macaroni, potatoes" (sthh, sthh, sthh) "sho looks good Irene."

"It taste good too Lenny", Marcus said with a big greasy grin on his face and crumbs on his cheek.

Lenny looked at Marcus and took a bite out of his chicken

and gave his nod of approval as he dug into his plate.

Marcus continued to smile, thinking to hisself, "that's the only time he ain't makin that noise when he stuffin his fat ass stomach."

"You want some hot sauce baby", Irene said handing the bottle to Lenny, not waiting for an answer.

"I want some", Marcus' little brother Mario said.

"Ain't but a lil bit boy", Lenny said as he shook the half full bottle over all three pieces of chicken until there was none left. Then, picking up the chicken leg, he wrapped it in a piece of white bread and bit into it as the red sauce soaked through the bread onto his fingers.

"Umm, umm", he moaned while chewing the chicken with his mouth half open, revealing his ill manners to everyone at the table. He stopped to beam at Marcus, who stared at him with a big smile and what seemed to be a look of admiration.

"Pig", Marcus thought to hisself.

After dinner, Marcus took a bath, after his brother and two sisters were through. Then went into his room and put on his make shift pajamas, which were really no more than a T-shirt and old swim trunks, with the lining in them that looked like underwear, and hopped into his bed.

Hours had passed and Marcus lay there staring at the ceiling when he noticed Mario leave the bedroom and creep down the hallway.

Marcus ignored his brother, who he assumed was going to the bathroom and continued to stare at the ceiling.

He lay there thinking about the little girl up the street, who looked almost white, with her pretty, long hair, which she always wore in pigtails with bright bows holding them in place.

Then he thought of the other one, who always stared at him in a strange way as if she hated his guts for some reason, always rolling her eyes at him and curling her lips when he walked by as if he smelled bad or something.

What was it about him that Candy Brown seemed to hate so much? He wondered.

A loud crash came from the kitchen interrupting Marcus' thoughts. "What the hell", he heard Lenny say, then he heard the door to his mother's bedroom open and footsteps trampling down the hallway.

"Boy what the hell you doin", he heard Lenny yell, then he heard what sounded like a belt buckle rattling.

"Bring your ass here", Lenny yelled at the top of his lungs.

"I'm sorry" he heard Mario cry out, then Marcus flinched when he heard the loud sound of leather smacking against skin.

Whap! Whap! Whap! Each crack of the belt followed by continuous screams and broken English.

(Whap!), you lil motha (whap!) fucka (whap!) I (whap!) told you (whap!) whap! whap! whap!

Marcus grit his teeth and started to breath heavy as his little brother screamed in agony for what seemed like forever.

That same sound over and over, Whap! Whap! Mixed in with horrible screams and what sounded like chairs being knocked over in the kitchen, then the sounds got closer coming from the living room, then the hallway.

"Mamma, mamma!" He heard Mario scream; finally Marcus heard his mother's voice.

"All right Lenny, that's enough, damn! I gotta go to work in the morning you makin all this damn noise."

(Whap!) (Whap!) "Get yo ass in bed boy", Marcus heard Lenny scream as Mario ran down the hallway to his mother.

Marcus lay still in the bed looking at the shadows of his mother and little brother cast upon the wall in the hallway.

Mario continued to cry, Marcus didn't move but could see his mother's shadow hovering over Mario's, she appeared to be checking him for wounds, then he saw a third shadow appear, it was Lenny.

"Didn't I say get in that damn bed", Lenny yelled. Then Marcus saw a shadow raise up high into the air and cock back like a Cobra ready to strike, then snap downward on Mario's small shadow. Whap!

Mario ran into the room screaming and jumped into his bed, then went from screaming, to crying, to sniffling with an occasional moan.

Marcus heard his mother's voice, "Lenny that don't make no damn sense, did you see them whepps on that boy? You ain't have to whoop him like that!"

"What! I ain't have to do what!" Lenny barked.

"I fed that lil mufucka tonight and every night, don't tell me nothin bout what I ain't have to do! I'll whoop yo ass like that, then what!"

Marcus bit his bottom lip upon hearing those words, biting it so hard he could taste the metallic taste of blood on his tongue.

Then he reached under his mattress and pulled out a small throwing dagger he had bought at the Flea Market a few weeks back. He began to pace as Lenny continued to curse at his mother.

"I wish you would come out yo mouf again when I whoop any one of these mufuckers, I'll put whepps on yo ass." Marcus traced the sharp tip of the knife with his fingertip as he stood close to his bedroom door and peeped into the hallway towards his mother's room.

"If only I was older", the angry eleven year old thought to hisself, then he looked back at his brother, who lay in his bed shivering with large ashy whepps all over his legs, arms, chest, back, everywhere visible to the eye.

"Who the fuck you talkin to!" He heard Lenny continue to curse at his mother, "say somein else, I'll whoop yo ass!"

"And if you do", Marcus thought to hisself as he stood staring across the hall at his mother's bedroom door, chest heaving up and down, with the knife gripped tight in his hand. "I'm gone stick this knife straight through you!"

Marcus continued to stare at the door, until it opened all of a sudden and he saw his mother come out. She was looking back over her shoulder as Lenny continued to fuss. Then she turned to face Marcus, who held the knife against his leg, out of her sight, and stepped to the side as she entered the room.

She went towards the small bed and covered Mario up then kissed him on the forehead. "Go to bed Marcus", she said as she was leaving the room, then stopped and gave him an awkward look. "Go to bed", she repeated in a soft tone.

Marcus did as he was told but it was hours before he fell asleep. He laid there, knife still in his grip, long after Mario was sleep and the only sound throughout the house was Lenny's loud snoring.

As Marcus lay there in the bed listening to Lenny snore he thought to hisself, "it would be so easy", as he drifted off to sleep, "so easy, so easy."

CHAPTER 3

Marcus jumped up and out of bed, still half sleep, when he heard the sound of gunshots. Reaching frantically under his pillow, he then realized it was only the TV which he had left on when he fell asleep a few hours earlier.

He looked to his left only to see Candy, still sound asleep, facing away from him with her bright green panties bunched to one side, allowing one of her butter pecan brown cheeks to be fully exposed.

Marcus leaned towards her and kissed her softly on her bottom. Rolling out of the bed, he stretched, trying to shake off the sleep.

After turning the TV down he approached the sink in the small hotel room and washed his face and brushed his teeth until the gold, which covered his whole top row, glistened.

He moved back towards the bed and took another glimpse at Candy, laying there asleep, with her ass hanging out, thinking to hisself, "should I?" "Nah!"

After deciding not to wake her, he began to stretch then dropped to the floor and began to do pushups.

Candy, still laying on her side playing sleep, gave a heavy sigh and rolled her eyes, then thought to herself, "here I am ass hangin out and this nigga wanna do pushups."

Marcus, neither aware of the fact that Candy was awake or had turned up the volume on the TV purposely, continued with his early morning routine.

As he went down and up, he counted off his reps under his breath. Upon reaching number seventy-one, he began to rise up again and felt the weight of Candy's foot, on his back, smashing him face first into the floor.

"Oh excuse me baby, I didn't know you were down there, I'm still half sleep", Candy said with a smirk on her face.

"Damn Candy!", he replied as she proceeded to the bathroom and shut the door. Marcus shook his head and continued his workout.

Candy undressed as she carried on a conversation with herself, "nigga wanna do pushups, when he can be pushin up on all this", she said, patting herself on the ass, before stepping into the bathtub.

Candy turned the shower on and let the water run through her hair, each individual drop racing down her neck, towards the small of her back, and coming to a brief stop, upon reaching the hump that intersected between her lower back and her thick pecan brown thighs. It was at this spot that all the small droplets of water combined only to form larger drops of water, then each drop picked up speed as they made their way over the soft contoured hump and came crashing to the surface of the tub with a repetitious splashing sound as the water came cascading down through the center line separating her left cheek from the right, looking similar to a waterfall falling between two cliffs.

Candy let out a heavy sigh out of frustration. It had been weeks since Marcus had last touched her.

"If I catch that nigga cheatin on me I'm gone kill him", she said to herself under her breath.

The tension she was feeling soon came to a halt due to the hot water and the aroma of watermelon and kiwi that filled the bathroom as she lathered up with the scented body wash, Marcus' favorite.

The scent working it's way under the door and into the bed area of the hotel room rushed up into Marcus' nostril as he inhaled deeply while going down for another rep.

Marcus, overcome by the smell, decided to catch up on his exercise later.

Rising to his feet, he walked towards the bathroom, stopping long enough to check his physique in the mirror. After giving hisself a once over he gave a nod of approval, satisfied with his reflection, he reached for the door knob only to find that the bathroom door was locked.

"Candy open the door", he yelled out.

"Hold on", she answered back, Marcus began to remove his clothes and by the time Candy got to the door he was fully undressed.

Candy took a step back, looking him up and down, as he entered the steam filled bathroom. Candy snatched a towel off of the rack, brushing up against him as she bent over in front of him, and began to dry herself off from the ankles up.

Marcus couldn't resist; he walked up behind her and put his hands on her hips pullin her towards him.

"Oh no you don't", she said removing his hands as she turned to face him, "I think you better get in the shower, seeing how you just worked up a sweat", "Mr. Muscle Man!"

She said with a sarcastic tone before pushing him out of the way and walking out the door, looking back just long enough to see the confusion on his face and the hard on she had just left him with.

"You better put some cold water on that baby, it looks painful", she said right before blowing him a kiss and shutting the door in his face.

Marcus shook his head laughing to hisself as he jumped in the shower, which was still running due to Candy's quick exit.

"Fuckin brat", he mumbled.

Marcus was use to Candy's have it her way attitude, so all he could do was ignore her and proceed with his shower.

Candy pulled two bags out of the small closet, one

containing her clothes the other filled with the money they had taken from Leon less than twelve hours ago.

She decided she would dress comfortable for the day. Choosing a bright orange one piece jumpsuit, similar to those worn by mechanics, she stepped into the form fitting, velour outfit and pulled her arms through the sleeves. She zipped it up, just far enough to leave a little cleavage showing between the large blue letters that spread across the front, spelling out Rocawear.

She sat on the edge of the bed and popped the tags off of the blue and white cuffs of the sleeves.

Reaching underneath the bed she produced a shoebox with a fresh new pair of Timbs in them and slipped them on. Not even bothering to lace them, instead she just stuffed the laces down into the sides of the boots and walked over to the full-length mirror on the closet door to check herself.

"Sexy, sexy", she said to herself as she sprayed her neck, chest and wrist with a fragrance called Very Sexy by Victoria's Secret.

Giving herself one last spray by the crotch, "just in case Marcus gets hungry", she said.

Checking herself out one more time in the mirror admiring the way the velour outfit showed off her curves. She snapped her fingers "almost forgot", she said as she made her way to her purse and pulled out the Strawberry flavored lip gloss. Once applied, her lips looked wet and shiny. Afterwards, she used lip liner, tracing the edges of her beautiful lips. Looking in the mirror, she blew herself a kiss.

"Now we talkin", she said as she made her way back towards the bed, grabbing the other book bag, she dumped the large stacks of bills on the center of the mattress. Taking a seat she unwrapped a stack and began counting.

As far as Candy was concerned this was money well earned and well deserved after all Leon had put her through.

Leon was a local neighborhood player, so to speak, who ran the club for Peabo, who was actually the real owner.

Peabo, one of the cities biggest coke dealers, had been using Club Fantasy amongst many other businesses consisting of neighborhood stores, beauty salons and laundry mats as a front for his drug operations for many years.

Leon, no more than one of Peabo's flunkies, was in charge of the club; he was also in charge of Peabo's finances on the Eastside of town. Once a week Leon would gather up all money earned by each individual worker in the "organization" as Peabo called it. He was also responsible for getting the money to Peabo "every cent accounted for."

Candy had known Leon for a long time. Ever since she was younger, she had seen him on the corner, in her old neighborhood, serving the fiends.

As she got older, she began to notice Leon looking at her in a way that always made her uncomfortable.

She never liked Leon, mainly because she had seen him degrade Felicia's mother many times on the block when she was fiending.

Once she had even caught Felicia's mother crying to Leon, literally begging for a hit, when she was walking into the neighborhood corner store.

When Candy had come out of the store she caught a glimpse of Leon standing behind the dumpster as if he was taking a leak, but as she made her way up the street she looked back over her shoulder only to make eye contact with Leon who was also looking back over his shoulder staring at her with a big smile on his face.

It was then that she noticed Felicia's mother down on her knees behind the dumpster doing Leon "a favor", as he called it, for a hit.

It hurt Candy to see that and she was glad Felicia had stayed behind to watch TV instead of walking to the store with her on that day.

By the time Candy had reached the eighth grade she was already beginning to fill out "in all the right places."

She remembered how Leon would always pull up beside her

at the bus stop in his red Eldorado and offer her a ride to school.

"Nah, I'm alright", she would always say and he always replied with "one day lil mama you gone need to get somewhere and I'm gone be the only one who can get you there, then what you gone say? Just hope I don't turn you down when that day come."

Then he would pull off with a big grin on his face.

"Candy if I was you I would've took that ride", Tiffany would always say.

"I bet you would you high yella Bitch", Candy thought to herself.

Tiffany, who had filled out even more than Candy was "hot in the ass" as Candy's mother would say and was always trying to be the center of attention.

Especially when Marcus was around, by this time Marcus had also matured.

Two years older than Candy but only one grade ahead, Marcus now stood at 5'10" with thick curly hair, a rusty brown complexion and a sneaky smile that always made him look like he was up to something.

Even though he was a little rough around the edges, compared to alot of the other boys at school, he always caught Candy's attention and Tiffany's as well.

But everyone caught Tiffany's attention, or she was always trying to get their attention rather.

Marcus never could figure out what Candy had against him. As usual, she still had a habit of rolling her eyes or snurling up her nose when he came around.

This gesture use to make him wonder did he smell bad or something, but he was quick to cancel that thought due to the fact that no sooner than Candy would give him the "you stink" face Tiffany would say "hey Marcus" stretching his name out "you smell good, what's that you got on?"

"Humph", he would hear Candy say under her breath.

Marcus always sat in front of Tiffany, Felicia and Candy.

Who always insisted on sitting three to a seat on the school bus. Due to the fact Tiffany would always squeeze in between Candy and Felicia so she could play in Marcus' hair all the way to school.

"Tiffany why don't you just sit up there with him", Candy snapped with attitude as she sat on the edge of the seat hanging halfway in the aisle.

That's when Candy would lick her lips and bat her eye's at Marcus' best friend and say "yeah Rhameek, why don't you come sit wit me and Felicia and let Tiffany up there with Marcus."

"Cause I ain't tryna be smushed up between ya'll young hoes in training", Rhameek would say.

"Who you callin a hoe", they'd say in unison.

"Whatever hoes", he'd say stressing the word, "anyway ya'll need to lean back and quit breathing ya'll hot ass breath down me and my man neck."

Marcus would only laugh; he never was much for words unlike his best friend, who always had plenty to say.

Rhameek was a little foul mouth, slick talking prankster, always referring to girls as "hoes", a habit he picked up from his uncle who had raised him and played father figure in his life.

Rhameek's uncle was an old player who went by the name "Zone."

Candy had heard many stories about Zone, "the Pimp", when she was a little girl and all the neighborhood women would congregate at her mother's house on Friday's for their weekly spade games and gossip sessions.

But a foul mouth wasn't the only thing Rhameek inherited; he also picked up a hot temper that couldn't be cooled by anybody once the fuse was lit.

Rhameek was the total opposite of Marcus. He was about Marcus' height, but a little chubby, but unlike Marcus he never shut up and he stayed decked out in the latest Polo gear and kept a pair of crispy white sneakers on his feet.

Rhameek was also far from slow; he had always known why Candy acted the way she did, even though Marcus seemed to be blind to the fact.

He knew all her attitude was a big front. Thanks to his uncle, wasn't too much a woman or anybody else could hide from Rhameek.

"Candy that nigga Leon sho be on you, you betta watch his ass", Rhameek would always tell her.

"My uncle say that nigga ain't no good."

Candy had never told Felicia what she had seen her mother doing behind the dumpster that day; because she knew it would hurt her and embarrass her all at once.

So she kept it a secret and decided she would leave it at that, but that knowledge alone use to have her fuming on the inside when Leon would come around and Felicia would get all dreamy eyed and go on and on about how cute Leon was and how she wished she was older.

"If I was a lil older I'd be tryin to get wit him", she would say.

"You old enough now", Rhameek would say "he like em young and dumb", then he'd look at Candy and add "ain't that right Candy."

Rhameek always got under Candy's skin, but she also knew he only spoke the truth, most of the time and his analysis of Leon turned out to be on point.

CHAPTER 4

One day, Candy, Felicia and Tiffany had decided to walk to the store just to kill time. Just as they were about to leave the store, it was as if the bottom had fell out of the sky and it began to rain out of nowhere.

They had decided to stay in the store until the rain let up. That was when Leon had walked in with one of his associates following close behind him.

"Go get a case of Michelob", he told his partner before approaching Candy and her friends with a big smile on his face.

"How ya'll young ladies doin, looks to me like ya'll stuck", he said rolling a toothpick around in his mouth.

"Nah, we all right", Candy responded.

"You still in denial lil mama, come on it's pouring down rain, ya'll gone be waiting all day for it to calm down out there."

"Me and my man Ronnie here", he said pointing towards his friend, "we got a nice cozy room right up the street we just gone chill, smoke a lil bud and drink a lil beer, ya'll welcome to join us, I'll be glad to get you home before your curfew lil Miss Candy", he said with a sneaky grin. "What you gotta be home by five, right."

Candy spat with attitude "I'm not that young nigga."

"We'd be glad to ride", Tiffany interrupted, "come on ya'll it's raining and I'm not gonna stand in this store all day", Tiffany said as she followed Leon and Ronnie who had already started walking out the door towards the big red Cadillac parked out front.

Candy looked at Felicia who shrugged her shoulders and

darted out into the rain and hopped in the car with Candy right behind her.

"I knew you'ld see it my way", Leon said giving Candy the eye, by way of the rearview mirror.

"Ya'll ladies want a drink", Ronnie said offering each girl a beer.

"Yeah", Felicia and Tiffany said at the same time.

"How bout you lil girl, you ain't drinking?"

Candy snatched the beer from Ronnie's hand.

Neither girl had ever drank before with the exception of Tiffany who had already done many things Felicia and Candy hadn't, drinking being the least of her actions.

Felicia was just going with the flow and Candy had let the "lil girl" comments get the best of her, which is why she decided to take a drink.

The first sip almost made her gag. It was the worst thing Candy had ever tasted in her life, but she continued to sip it. After a few sips, the bad taste seemed to disappear and once the buzz kicked in Candy was caught up in the moment.

Once they got to their destination Leon rolled up a few joints in zigzag papers, and filled the room with smoke.

Candy passed up on the weed but still caught a buzz from the smoke that filled the air; it wasn't long before even she found Leon humorous.

"He's not so bad", she thought to herself.

Tiffany was trying to be the center of attention as usual, running her mouth constantly and edging Candy and Felicia to drink more and more.

It got to the point Candy didn't really know what was going on, all the voices in the room began to sound like chatter.

Candy began to get hot and dizzy and although Tiffany seemed to be used to this felling it was obvious it was taking a toll on Felicia as well.

"Take me home", Felicia blurted out of nowhere.

"What?", Leon said.

"I said take me home, I'm sick."

Before Leon could respond Felicia began to walk towards the bathroom and only made it halfway before throwing up all over herself.

"Damn girl, you can't handle a few beers", Leon yelled from across the room.

"Take me home", was all Felicia said.

"Okay, okay, lil mama I'm gone let Ronnie run you home", Leon said as he dug in his pocket and threw Ronnie his keys.

"It's still early, ya'll two can chill till Ronnie comes back and we can run and get us a bite to eat and I'll take ya'll home."

"I don't know", Candy said.

"Come on Candy", Tiffany pleaded "I'm not ready to go yet, stay with me."

Candy looked to Felicia who stood in the bathroom doorway wiping herself off the best she could.

"Go head, I'll be all right", Felicia said with a sickly smile.

Candy didn't put up much of an argument because she was so buzzed up and didn't feel like she had the energy to move anyway.

Once Ronnie and Felicia had left, the last thing Candy could remember was drinking another beer and listening to the music as Tiffany began to dance around the room in front of Leon.

Candy watched with her mouth wide open, in shock, when she saw Tiffany approach Leon and straddle his lap, then began to grind on him slowly.

Candy closed her eyes in disgust and the moment she closed her eyes, for what should have been a simple blink, something obviously went wrong.

Candy woke up in the room hours later and she was lying in the bed alone, with no pants on.

Candy jumped up, something wet and sticky was on her thighs and she was in pain like never before.

"Tiffany", she called out, "Felicia".

No answer. Candy took a minute to get her thoughts

together.

Once she figured out where she was and remembered how she got there, it was obvious what had happened to her while she was out.

Candy's eyes flooded with tears but she bit her bottom lip and tried to hold them back.

She looked towards the clock on the nightstand and she saw that it was way past time for her to be home. Luckily she had enough money on her for a cab; she called the cab and got dressed.

While waiting on the cab she called Tiffany, "hello" Tiffany answered.

"Tiffany why the fuck did you leave me here alone", Candy spat.

"What! I ain't leave you alone, I left you with Leon, I had Ronnie to drop me off. What's wrong?"

"I think he had sex with me", Candy said.

"You think", Tiffany laughed "well let me verify, your thoughts are correct, he had sex with you right after I finished with him", Tiffany continued. "And let me tell you, the way you was whining and carrying on you would think you was a virgin or something."

"I am a virgin", Candy said as she held her stomach and folded over in pain.

"Well somebody's been lyin bout their sex life", Tiffany said. "Well, anyway, you're not a virgin anymore", she added as she began to laugh.

"What the fuck is wrong with you Tiffany how could you let him do that to me", Candy cried.

"What do you mean Candy, I ain't see you fightin it, yeah you whined a lil bit but that was expected wit him all up in you like he was."

"Tiffany you knew I was out of it, you know I've never even drank before."

"Oh well", Tiffany said with a lack of concern "you know what they say, you can't hang wit the big dogs! Anyway, look Candy I gotta go we got school tomorrow and by the way, your mom has been looking for you."

That was the last thing Candy heard, right before the dialtone.

"Stupid yella Bitch", Candy cursed, throwing the phone against the wall.

By this time her cab had arrived and she walked out of the room without looking back. It hurt her to walk. She was in pain all over it seemed.

Once she got home she managed, by some miracle, to slip past her mother with some excuse she had made up on her way home. Luckily, Terri didn't press the issue too much, because Candy seemed to be in an ill mood.

She went straight to her room, grabbed a towel and pajamas and made her way to the bathroom, where she soaked in the tub for hours, trying to ease the pain she felt physically and mentally, as she thought to herself about how she had been deprived of her innocence against her will.

Candy had never had sex before, although she had lied many times about sexual experiences just because a lot of other girls were doing it, but in reality she had been saving herself for the right time. But Leon had taken that all away from her.

Although she was in pain there were no signs of blood, "thank God", she had heard so many stories about girls "getting their cherry popped", that she had expected it to be a bloody ordeal.

"Just rumors, I guess", she thought to herself but that didn't make things any better because her first experience was something she dreaded and would never share with anyone.

"You gone pay one day", she thought to herself as she lay in the tub and let the water ease her pain.

"I told you, you was gone pay mufucka", Candy said under her breath, as she sat on the edge of the bed counting the money they had taken from Leon with a smile on her face.

"What you say baby?", Marcus said as he stood in front of Candy, who was so busy counting money and daydreaming she didn't even notice him standing there.

When she looked up to respond, the first thing she made eye contact with was the tip of his manhood, which seemed to stand at attention and stare her in the face.

"Marcus", she screamed. Flinching, as if he had just pointed a gun at her.

"Baby back up a lil bit and put that turtle back in his shell", she said as she smacked "turtle" as she called it with a fresh wrapped stack of hundreds, causing it to go limp.

Marcus laughed as he walked to the other side of the room and put his boxers on.

Candy let out a deep sigh of frustration due to the fact she had just lost count. It didn't take much for her to lose focus around Marcus. It was as simple as giving her a quick peek.

"Marcus, you made me lose count."

"Keep yo eyes off the prize Candy", he said in response, "ain't my fault you hot in the ass!"

"Whatever nigga", she said throwing the money down, deciding to count it later. Instead, she decided to lay back and relax while Marcus got dressed.

Marcus decided to go with a pair of dark blue baggy jeans, a pair of orange Air Force Ones with a white check on the side, a orange Rocawear shirt with blue letters across the front and then he topped it off with an orange and blue fitted cap with a big "G" on the front of it.

Candy loved the way Marcus wore his hat, hanging off of his head, cocked to the side with the brim leaning forward, as if it was about to fall off his head at all times.

She never could figure out why the hat never fell off his head.

"I defy the laws of gravity", he would say to her.

"What does the "G" stand for?", she asked.

"What am I", he responded as he grabbed the brim of his hat and tilted it, "Deuce Trey" as he called it.

Candy sucked her teeth and rolled her eyes.

"By the way baby, you look real jazzy", he said with a big shiny gold smile and a wink of his eye, then he let his tongue trace the bottom of the grill that covered his top row.

"I hate when you do that with yo tongue", she lied, knowing Marcus knew better, and at the same time knowing Marcus wanted to snatch her Rocawear suit off of her right there on the spot.

It was a known fact that orange was Marcus' favorite color and he loved to see her in it.

"One glimpse of these orange thongs and he'll eat me alive", she thought to herself as she stood up and approached him, wrapping her arms around his neck.

"Come here sexy", she said as she pulled him close and wet his lips with the cherry flavored lip-gloss she wore.

She loved the way he always hugged her and held her tight as if he was trying to squeeze the life out of her.

Marcus was no longer the little boy she had a crush on, he was now a man, standing 5'10" with wide shoulder's and big arms that she loved to lay her head on. And their childhood crush had grown to be a love that was inseparable.

Marcus squeezed Candy tight up against him as he kissed her soft lips, then her nose, then her forehead before letting her go.

"Come on get your bow legged ass over there and let's count this money", he said as he stood waiting for her to walk off.

"Why you still standing there then, you better come on", she said, not about to count the money by herself.

"Come on baby, you know why I'm standing here" he said "you know I wanna see you do that walk."

"Boy you crazy", she laughed as she turned then strolled towards the bed real nice and slow.

It drove Marcus crazy to see her walk especially in heels, but Timbs would do for now. When she stopped and stood still he really lost it. Loving the way she stood with her right leg cocked back, with her toes pointed inward.

"Damn baby where that horse at you been riding?"

"Marcus shut up and help me count this money", she said throwing a stack in his direction.

After Marcus finished counting the stacks he had gathered on the dresser, he looked at Candy who had her stacks neatly spread across the bed.

"I got seventy-five", he said. "What you got?"

"I got fifty-five", she said.

"Not bad", Marcus commented. "Not what I expected but not bad at all."

Marcus looked at the ceiling, doin a quick calculation. "One hundred and thirty thousand", he said laughing.

"One hundred and fifty thousand mother fuckin' dollars", Peabo screamed as he picked the eight ball up off the pool table and threw it at Tiffany, barely missing her head by inches, shattering the large glass door that led to the balcony of his studio apartment.

The sound of Tiffany's scream was followed, simultaneously, by the sound of breaking glass, horns blowing, and a loud crashing noise. The eight ball flew out the window, and over the balcony, falling five stories.

It had landed on the windshield, of an unfortunate passerby's, brand new, CLK. Cracking the window, it had caused the car to swerve, which in turn caused other cars to swerve and collide, until the scene, down below, in the streets, was almost as chaotic as the scene that played out from up above.

"Bitch, you gone pay for that window too", Peabo yelled, as spit flew out of his mouth and clung to his long black beard, which had a streak of gray going down the center.

"But Peabo", Tiffany cried.

"But my ass", he continued as he snatched the pool stick up off the table and threw it across the room at her as if it was a spear and he was a descendant of the Zulu tribe.

Tiffany let out another scream as she ducked then ran to the opposite side of the room, leaving one of her shoes still standing in the spot she had just ran from.

She then began to hop on her bare foot while making an effort to snatch her other heel off. In case Peabo decided to chase her, she wanted to be able to run without wobbling from side to side as if she was a pirate with a peg leg.

Her instincts had served her right, because no sooner than Tiffany had got on level ground Peabo stormed across the room towards her.

"Explain to me why I'm a hundred and fifty grand short, you no good yella"...

"Peabo baby, it wasn't my fault", Tiffany pleaded as she ducked his attack dipping to the left as she hiked up her skirt to get a better stride and sprinted across the room not caring that all her business was showing.

Peabo, now almost out of breath, stopped and wiped the sweat from his forehead, with the sleeve of his shirt, as he contemplated the best way to get his hands on the much smaller and much faster Tiffany.

"Peabo what about Leon, he's dead", Tiffany said as she nervously paced back and forth on the opposite side of the large apartment.

"Fuck Leon" Peabo replied as he stopped by the bar and poured a glass of Remi and swallowed it in one gulp, gritting his diamond filled teeth together and frowning as the liquor set his chest on fire.

Peabo began to move away from the bar and Tiffany circled the opposite direction, matching every step he made with one of her own.

"Tiffany", Peabo growled as he paced side to side.

"Explain to me why you was so late making the pickup anyway?"

Tiffany continued to move to her left making sure she stayed within long range of Peabo and kept some type of furniture between them at all times.

"Peabo baby", she whined. "I had to go watch over the girls at the Bachelor party for your man Play Dough, you said you wanted to make sure he enjoyed hisself so I thought it would be best if I made sure everything went alright personally. I'm sorry baby", she continued "but that's why I was late getting to Leon."

"Bitch, how I know you ain't take my bread", Peabo barked.

"Come on daddy, you know I ain't got the heart to do nothing like that, me kill somebody?"

Peabo had caught his wind and Tiffany began to move farther away, sensing that he was about to charge at her once again.

But instead, he came to a standstill and stood, glaring at her. The whole room went quiet.

Peabo stood, 6'3", 260 pounds solid, looking across the room at the small, petite beauty who stared, wide eyed and nervous, back at him.

Peabo smiled as he thought to hisself how the whole scene reminded him of something he had seen in National Geographic. A big powerful Lion trying to catch a small, but quick, Gazelle.

Tiffany seeing him smile, relaxed but kept her distance.

"Come here Tiffany", he said speaking calm this time "don't make me chase you no more."

"No Peabo", she said realizing she was close to the door and she could exit before he was able to reach her. "I'll come back when you calm down."

"Don't make me ask you again", he barked raising his voice again.

Peabo turned and faced the wall behind him and Tiffany took advantage of the opportunity to make a break for the door.

But no sooner than she had got halfway across the room, Peabo reached up and grabbed a handful of darts off of the board he was facing and turned around just in time to catch her reaching for the door knob.

"OW", Tiffany screamed as one of the darts went deep into her thigh, causing her to forget about the door knob and reach for her leg.

But no sooner than she was pulling the dart out she felt another one hit her on the left side of her ass.

She let out another scream, but before the sound came out of her mouth good, she found herself gasping for air. Peabo had took advantage of the moment to close in on her, lifting her off of her feet by her neck.

"You wanna make me chase you", he yelled as he held her up so high their eyes were level.

Tiffany's eye's bulged out her head as she struggled, kicking her feet back and forth trying to break his grip.

Just as she was about to pass out, Peabo looked down and cursed. Blood came dripping down Tiffany's leg and trickled off of her foot, splattering all over him as she continued to kick her legs in a desperate attempt to break free.

Peabo released his grip, letting her drop to the floor as he continued to curse.

"Look at my motha fuckin pants", he screamed.

"Oh you gonna pay for this shit", he said.

"You gonna pay for this window, these pants; and you done bled on my Gators Bitch, and my carpet! Get your sorry ass up and go wash that shit off before you be paying for a whole new carpet up in this mutha fucka."

Tiffany, still gasping for air, managed to get to her feet. Covering the small holes the darts left in her flesh, she tried not to drip anymore blood on the carpet, as she ran to the bathroom.

She locked the door afraid Peabo wasn't through with her.

The small round holes the darts had made weren't that bad, just a little deep and painful as hell, and also seemed to bleed a lot.

"Lucky for me", she thought to herself, knowing the only reason Peabo wasn't still choking her at the moment was because she had started bleeding all over his snow white carpet.

She was also glad she only left a few spots of blood, because she knew he was serious about her paying to have it cleaned.

"At least I don't have to replace the whole thing", she thought to herself as she took a bottle of peroxide out of the medicine cabinet and dapped at the wound on her thigh with a cotton ball.

She removed her skirt and turned her perfectly round butt towards the full length mirror as she looked over her shoulder and applied peroxide to the small hole on her left cheek, which was now beginning to turn purple and red leaving a big bruise around the edge of the small hole.

"One of the drawbacks of being high yellow", she thought as she caught a glimpse of the bruises on her neck as well.

Tiffany turned to face the mirror, wondering how she had got in this situation, as she heard Peabo in the other room still throwing a tantrum.

She thought back to how she had found Leon laying on the stage with a puddle of blood underneath him, face down in heels and a G-string.

She didn't know how long he had been laying there, but it couldn't have been long, because the music was still playing when she entered the club.

One of the DJ'S pre-recorded mix CD's continued to bang out one of her favorite Project Pat songs as the strobe lights flickered above Leon's body.

She let out a scream then stopped herself, covering her mouth hoping no one would hear her and come running after her.

But she couldn't run, She was froze as she looked around the empty club and figured she must be alone or otherwise she would have given herself away already.

Pulling herself together, she was about to make a quick retreat, when she remembered why she had come in the first place.

"Peabo's money", she thought to herself.

She had just talked to Leon about four hours earlier and had told him she would be there within an hour.

She hadn't expected to be so long at Play Dough's bachelor party, but he had said he wanted to get with "the main attraction" and he would give her a little something extra to "do something strange" as he called it. She was always down for making something extra no matter what.

Tiffany ran to the main office and the first thing she saw was the door to the safe wide open.

She also found Leon's clothes on the floor. Tiffany dug through the back pockets of Leon's pants and removed his wallet and looked around as if someone were in the room with her. She removed the small wad of one hundred-dollar bills that were inside and shoved them in her bra.

She dug in his front pockets and found the keys to his desk drawer, where he kept his books.

She walked over to the desk and unlocked the drawer and found the small black book, right beside a very large chrome handgun. and two stacks of money tucked in the corner of the drawer.

Tiffany counted the money. Each stack amounted to ten thousand dollars a total of twenty grand.

Tiffany flipped to the last page that was written on in Leon's book and read the figures at the bottom of the page, right beside that days date the figures read one hundred and fifty thousand dollars.

Her eyes got wide when she saw the number.

"Peabo's gonna shit bricks", she thought out loud.

Tiffany assumed the twenty grand was Leon's last take for the night and he never had an opportunity to put it in the safe with the rest of the cash.

She stuffed the money in her purse and placed the black book inside as well, knowing Leon had already probably called in his take for the night but she didn't think it would be wise to leave the book laying around for the police to find.

"Might as well take this too", she said as she picked the gun up with her index finger and thumb, holding it at arms length away from her, as if it might bite her, and dropped it in her purse with the rest of the things she had collected.

"Damn, I need to call the police", she thought, as she was about to walk out of the office.

She decided against using the office phone knowing the police would more than likely check the phone records.

She decided she would use her cell phone. Digging through her purse, she realized she had left it in the car.

Leaving the office, she took another glimpse at Leon's dead body. She felt the hairs on the back of her neck raise up, at the sight of him laying in a puddle of blood.

The club was now silent. The mix CD had come to an end, but the lights still flickered and danced around the stage.

Just as she had turned to walk away from the stage she noticed something silver on the floor as the strobe lights flickered on and off.

She reached down and picked it up and read the name on the gray and blue candy wrapper "Zero bar."

"You no good Bitch", she said to no one in particular as she looked around the room noticing all ashtrays had been emptied and the club had been cleaned spotless other than the wrapper she had just found.

She shook her head in disbelief as things began to make sense to her.

Tiffany then stuffed the wrapper in her pocketbook with the rest of her junk and ran to the exit and to her car.

Once she reached her car she decided to leave the scene and call Peabo at once.

She could remember how Peabo shot through the roof once she had told him about Leon or better yet how all the money she was supposed to have picked up was gone.

She had stopped at a payphone and made an anonymous call reporting gunshots at the club as Peabo had instructed her to do.

Then she had got back in her car and made her way to one of his apartments in the center of the city.

"Good thing I left that money in the car", she thought to herself as she remembered how Peabo had reacted when she handed him the black book she had found. Which only confirmed his loss. "One hundred and fifty thousand dollars."

Tiffany took her time cleaning herself up. Not planning to leave the bathroom anytime soon at least not until she no longer heard Peabo in the other room cursing and throwing a fit.

"One hundred and fifty thousand dollars", she kept hearing him say.

Tiffany got into the shower. Although in pain, she found the strength to crack a smile as she thought about the one hundred and fifty thousand dollars that was missing.

Because minus the twenty thousand she had found, she knew that left one hundred and thirty thousand floating around out there somewhere.

She had a good idea where it was, now all she had to do was figure out how to get her hands on it...

"Get me a Zero bar baby", Candy said as Marcus got out of the car at the gas station.

"You ain't gone be satisfied till all yo teeth fall out, eating that junk all the time Candy", Marcus replied.

"The better to suck you with my dear", Candy shot back then stuck her tongue out of her mouth and licked her lips.

"Maybe I better get you ten of em then", he said with a smile on his face as he walked off.

Candy leaned back in her seat and smiled, admiring her man from afar.

Candy's moment of bliss was interrupted by a ring on her cell phone.

"What Felicia", Candy said already knowing who it was on the other end due to her caller I.D.

"What's up Bitch", Felicia responded "you can't get your nose out of Marcus ass long enough to call nobody?"

"Whatever", Candy said as she began to laugh. "At least I ain't running around with my nose up Rhameek's ass while he got his nose up half the girls in the city ass."

"Girl you know I don't do Rhameek", Felicia shot back.

"Whatever Felicia, I saw the nigga car over yo crib about three nights ago, when I was about to pop up on you. But changed my mind once I saw his ride, I figured ya'll was busy."

"Wrong again, Mrs. Brown", Felicia said.

"I was having problems with my new DVD player and I had Rhameek to come over and hook it up for me, thank you very much."

"Felicia, you kill me with your lies, you and Rhameek been doin it up for years, I don't know why ya'll think ain't nobody up on ya'll lil masquerade."

"Anyway like I was sayin Bitch", Felicia butted in "you can't call nobody."

"As a matter of fact, Bitch", Candy said putting emphasis on the word, "I'm less than ten minutes away from your crib. Marcus was about to bring me through there. I was gone hang wit you a while, have him to drop me off. He gotta go track Rhameek down. He ain't been able to catch him all day, and you know how he is bout his boy. Anyway, maybe we can go shopping?", Candy continued.

"That sounds good to me", Felicia said "also sounds like we got us some money."

"Don't worry bout all that, I'll see you in a few."

"Take your time girl", Felicia said before hanging up.

Candy put her phone down as Marcus jumped in the car, holding his own phone to his ear.

"Damn, Rah still ain't answering, hope that nigga all right", he said.

"That nigga probably somewhere laid up Marcus, don't worry", Candy said, as she ran her fingers across the back of his head, playing with the thick curls of baby hair on the back of his neck. The only visible curls left on his head, due to the fact, he had let his curly hair dread up over the years.

"Yeah you right", Marcus replied not looking convinced.

"Rhameek get yo ass up", Felicia screamed as she ran from her living room into the bedroom where Rhameek lay, in his boxers, snoring.

Felicia also half dressed with nothing on but Rhameek's football jersey and a pair of red thongs, slapped Rhameek across the back.

"Girl, what the fuck is you doin?" Rhameek cursed as he raised up with slob running down his cheek.

"Get up", Felicia said with panic in her voice.

"Candy and Marcus on they way over here, they only bout ten minutes away and he been tryin to call yo ass too."

Rhameek jumped up and hopped into his pants in one swift motion, as Felicia sat on the bed to pull her pants on.

Rhameek snatched his jersey over her head, leaving her topless as he put it on and ran for the door. With his boots in his hands, he jumped off the porch and hopped into his truck.

Felicia ran out the door behind him, "you forgettin your phone", she said as he crank up his Black

F-150, about to pull off.

Rhameek stuck his arm out the window and grabbed the phone, noticing it was off when he tried to check his missed calls.

By the time he looked up Felicia had ran back towards her front door.

"Felicia I told you bout cuttin my fuckin phone off", he yelled as he pulled off.

Felicia waved him off and ran into her house slamming the door behind her.

Rhameek sped off, deciding to take the back way out of Felicia's neighborhood knowing Marcus would come from the other direction.

Once he got to the end of her street he made a quick right turn, scraping one of his twenty-six inch rims on the curb in the process.

"Damn", he cursed knowing he had probably scratched the rim and hoping he hadn't cracked it.

No sooner than he had bent the corner, Marcus and Candy turned onto Felicia's street, coming from the opposite direction.

Marcus pulled into Felicia's driveway and threw the car in park.

"All right baby", he said as he began dialing Rhameek's number once again.

"What time ya'll think ya'll gone be done?", he asked Candy.

"Don't worry bout me Marcus. Me and Felicia gone be..."

"Just a minute", Marcus interrupted throwing a finger in the air as he began to speak on his phone.

"Rah, where you been, I been tryin to catch you since last night."

"What's up Playboy", Rhameek said. "You know these hoes be holdin ya boy hostage and shit, cuttin my phone off so they can have me all to they self."

"Oh yeah?" Marcus replied "who was it this time?"

"New money, playa", Rhameek lied. "You don't know her, just a lil somein I met at the club last week... what's the bizness" he said, changing the subject.

"Ain't nothin, I'm droppin Candy off at Felicia's crib as we speak. They bout to go shoppin and things of that nature, I came across a lil somein, I'm tryna get up wit you and do what we do."

"I got ya playboy, say no more, meet me at my crib I'm almost there."

"Give me fifteen minutes", Marcus said before hanging up.

Returning his attention to Candy, "what was you sayin baby."

"Oh you mean before you cut me off", Candy said with a

frown on her face, then continued "I was sayin take your time cause we gone do it up at the mall. Buy us some nice sexy outfits and we might even go play the town a little tonight."

"Oh yeah?' Marcus said with a smirk on his face.

"Don't make me have to come lookin for dat ass."

"Baby" Candy said as she leaned across the seat and put her lips to his ear, while grabbing his hand and pulling it around her waist. "You never had a problem finding this ass before", she purred as she put the palm of his hand on her bottom and squeezed it tight, causing him to cupp one of her shapely cheeks in a tight grip.

He pulled her towards him and kissed her on her soft, shiny lips, tasting the Strawberry flavored lip-gloss she wore.

Candy pulled away slowly, breaking Marcus' strong grip, and winked her eye at him before opening her door and sliding out of her seat, making sure he got an eyeful of her "eye candy" when she stepped out and bent over to , supposedly, tie her shoe.

Marcus sat in silence as she made her exit, taking time to admire her assets as she stepped out of the car.

"I'm takin her to the tattoo shop tomorrow and I'm gone put my name across dat ass in big letters", he thought to hisself.

Candy straightened up and caught Marcus smiling. "What you smilin like that for nigga?"

"A lil inside thang", Marcus said as he put the car in reverse.

"Inside thang my ass', Candy shot back. "You and that hoe ass Rhameek probably up to something, let me catch you slippin Marcus."

"Don't start Candy", Marcus said as he began to back out of the driveway.

"Don't you start wit yo sneaky ass", was all he heard before turning the radio up full blast and laughing to hisself as he pulled off. Candy continued to rant and rage, her mouth moving a hundred miles an hour as she made her way into Felicia's house.

"How did I end up wit this crazy mufucka" he said out loud; talking to hisself and laughing as he continued to drive, looking back at Candy in his rearview.

Marcus leaned back and mashed the gas, with the music blasting, as his mind began to drift back to the days of old.

CHAPTER 5

"Marcus, give that girl her hair back." Marcus' mother yelled as Candy stood on Marcus' front porch, embarrassed, while Felicia and Rhameek stood to the side laughing.

Marcus dangled the long ponytail in the air teasing Candy with it.

"This ain't her hair mama."

"She bought it, it's hers", his mother said with a grin on her face.

"Give it back to her."

"All right ma", Marcus said "want me to put it back in for you?"

"No", Candy snapped as she snatched the long weave out of his hand.

Marcus couldn't understand for the life of him why all the young girls wore fake hair to make their hair appear longer.

"Why you wear that mess?", he asked Candy.

"Cause I want to, that's why", she said as she let Felicia snap the long ponytail back in place with a few bobby pins.

"I can't stand that mess", he said.

"So", Candy snarled "I ain't wear it for you, everybody else like it" she said with attitude.

Candy was upset but tried not to show it.

Marcus' mother had moved so he and Candy no longer lived in the same neighborhood, but the move was convenient for him and Rhameek, who had moved months earlier, because now they were only a block away from each other.

Candy and Felicia had decided to take a stroll, more like a "hump" to see what Rhameek and Marcus were up to.

"And here he is playing childish games"; she thought to herself.

"Anyway Felicia let's go" she said as she turned away from Marcus, with a quick snap of her neck, making her ponytail slap him in the face before she stomped off.

"Where ya'll goin', Marcus said as the two girls began to walk off.

"I'm goin to see my friend Tyrone", Candy snapped as she made her way to the sidewalk with Felicia in tow.

"Bye Rhameek", Felicia said with a smile on her face.

"Bye hoe," Rhameek shot back.

Felicia rolled her eyes and caught up with Candy, who stood waiting, with her hands on her hips, as if she were in a rush.

"Ain't no Tyrone live over here", Marcus yelled as the girls walked off.

But Candy ignored him and continued to walk off, switching her hips back and forth.

"Look at her walkin like somein stuck up her butt." Marcus said to Rhameek as he let out a fake laugh.

Quiet as kept, Marcus had always liked the way Candy walked. She was short and bowlegged with thighs like a track runner, but other than that, he had no interest in her, at least that's what he kept telling hisself.

"Who is Tyrone?" He asked Rhameek who only shrugged his broad shoulders and said "beats me homeboy!"

"Come on " Marcus said as he hopped off the porch and began to follow the girls who were now half a block away but still in plain sight.

"Where we goin", Rhameek said.

"To your house", Marcus mumbled as he began to walk at a fast pace.

Rhameek shook his head and smiled to hisself as he tried to keep up with Marcus.

Once they were halfway up the block they noticed Candy

and Felicia had come to a halt by the bus stop, where a few neighborhood guys also stood, waiting on the bus Marcus assumed.

As he and Rhameek approached the bus stop he saw Felicia caught up in conversation with one of the guys. Candy stood to the side with her hands on her hips and her legs bent in an awkward position.

"Why ya'll standing here like ya'll tryin to sell ass?" Rhameek said as he and Marcus stepped up beside the girls.

"Shut up Rhameek", Felicia said taking her eyes off the guy she was talking to, only for a second, only to notice that he and his friend were walking off by the time she turned back to face him.

"That's Tyrone?" Marcus asked Candy, who now stood with her arms crossed and her nose in the air.

"No and why?" She snapped.

"I was just asking", Marcus said.

"Why ya'll at the bus stop? I thought you was goin to see your friend."

"He wasn't home", Candy said "so we decided to catch the bus home, its gettin late and it's a long walk back."

"Wasn't home?" Marcus thought to hisself, knowing Candy and Felicia hadn't made any stops on their way up the block.

"We could've walked ya'll home", Marcus said.

"Hell nah", Rhameek interrupted.

"That's bout a forty five-minute hump."

"We ain't say that when we came all the way over here to see ya'll" Felicia said.

"See us?", Rhameek replied "I thought ya'll was just stoppin through. On your way to see Tyrone." He said mocking Candy.

"And he ain't home after all that walking ya'll did" Marcus added; still wondering who the hell Tyrone was.

"He's probably at football practice", Candy replied.

"Anyway ya'll want us to walk ya'll home or not", Marcus said getting irritated.

"That's alright, here comes the bus", Candy said as she struggled to dig in the pockets of the tight shorts she wore and pulled out a few quarters.

The bus pulled up to the curb and came to a stop, with a loud squeak and hissing noise, as the doors flew open.

Marcus dug in his pockets and pulled out a few bawled up bills and some change, then looked up at Rhameek who only rolled his eyes and shrugged his shoulders.

Marcus then looked at Candy who also rolled her eyes before stepping on the bus.

Felicia trailed right behind her, watching Marcus the whole time, with a big smile on her face.

Felicia motioned for him to get on the bus with a discreet nod of her head.

Marcus in turn motioned for Rhameek who reluctantly made his way up the steps and boarded the bus last.

All four made their way to the back of the bus, where they sat side by side.

"It sure was nice of ya'll to ride with us" Felicia said breaking the silence.

"No problem", Marcus responded. "Just want to make sure ya'll safe."

"Safe", Candy blurted out then began laughing.

"What ya'll gone do if somein was to happen? Run and get help!"

"Whatever Candy" Marcus snapped back.

"Maybe we can take that horsehair out you head and whip em with it."

Felicia and Rhameek looked at each other and rolled their eyes as Candy and Marcus continued to go back and forth.

"You make me sick Candy."

"So Marcus" she responded. "Why ya'll get on the bus then? We don't need no protection" she hissed. "Ya'll can't protect nobody anyway."

"I was tryin to look out for your nappy headed ass. Plus I wanted to go see what Tiffany was up to anyway" Marcus continued. "By the way, do she still got that long, pretty hair?"

Marcus knew that would strike a nerve, he hadn't seen Tiffany in a while. For some reason she hadn't been with Candy and Felicia in a while.

As a matter of fact, he hadn't seen much of any of them lately due to the fact that he and Rhameek were a grade ahead and had moved on to high school leaving the girls behind.

But even though he didn't go to school with them anymore and had moved, he still would at least see Felicia and Candy at the mall on the weekends. Where most of the kid's hung out at, but no Tiffany.

"Humph", was Candy's only reply for the remainder of the ride.

Her and Marcus were quiet as Rhameek and Felicia sat back and picked at other people on the bus.

By the time they had reached their old neighborhood it was late, the girls were just barely making their curfew.

Rhameek and Marcus didn't have a curfew so it made no difference to them.

The four of them made their way up the block.

"I want a Zero bar", Candy said as they came upon the neighborhood store.

"I hate those things", Felicia replied; then laughed "besides, we got zero dollars."

"I'll get you one", Marcus said. The first words he had spoken since they were on the bus.

Candy stopped in mid stride and turned to face Marcus.

Felicia and Rhameek made eye contact with each other and shook their heads from side to side as Candy made a show of trying to decide if she wanted to take Marcus up on his offer.

"Alright", she said as she walked off, leaving the rest behind, looking back over her shoulder to make sure Marcus was following her lead.

"We'll be out here", Rhameek said as Marcus followed

Candy into the store.

Once inside the store Candy made her way to the isle where the Zero bars were located.

She had fell in love with the white chocolate covered candy bars the first time she tasted one.

She loved almost any kind of candy; "it was a wonder she still had teeth in her mouth", her mother would always say.

"Just tryin to live up to the name you gave me Ma!", Candy would always reply.

"You ever try these Marcus?", she said holding the candy bar up in his face.

"Nah", Marcus said.

"You should try it; you can taste mine if you want."

"Alright", Marcus said as Candy stepped by him, brushing up against him, her ponytail slapping him in the face.

Candy got halfway down the isle then stopped and bent over to reach for a pack of bubble gum on the bottom rack.

"We better hurry so you can catch Tiffany before it's too late", Candy said as she bent over.

"Who?" Marcus said as he stood staring at Candy from behind, her tight shorts riding up her thighs as she bent over.

"Tiffany", she said as she straightened up with two packs of Watermelon bubblegum in her hand.

"Oh, Tiffany" Marcus said "I'll see her another time it ain't that important anyway. I was just going to say hey to her that's all."

Candy gave Marcus a sly smile and proceeded to move up the isle.

"Can I get these too", she said, stopping by the potato chip rack; grabbing a bag of Doritos and walking off, chips in hand, before Marcus could reply.

Once they reached the register Candy placed her items on the counter and the heavyset lady behind the register began to ring them up.

"Oh yeah", Candy said snapping her fingers as if she'd just remembered something.

" Be right back", she said signaling the lady at the register to hold up as she made her way to the section where the sodas were and returned with two Strawberry Sodas.

"I got Felicia one too, you don't mind do you?"

"Nah, that's cool" Marcus answered with a fake smile on his face.

Once the lady behind the register finished ringing up the items she put them in a bag, which Candy grabbed and made her way to the door, as Marcus held his hand out to receive his change which was only a nickel and a few pennies.

Marcus made his way out of the store where the others stood waiting.

"Thank you Marcus", Candy said before taking a sip from her Strawberry soda.

"You welcome", Marcus answered, staring at Candy as she removed the bottle from her lips, which were now bright red.

Candy stuck out her tongue which was also red from the drink, "what!", she said.

"You want some", she offered as she held the bottle out to Marcus, who declined.

"Oh you can't drink after me"; Candy said "somein wrong wit my lips?"

"Nah", Marcus said as Candy got within inches of his face, her nose almost touching his.

"Then taste it", she said as she leaned forward and kissed Marcus on his lips.

"Ooh", Felicia yelled from the sidelines. Marcus flinched from the sound of her voice, he had forgotten that Felicia and Rhameek were even standing there.

"How does it taste?", Candy asked with a big smile on her face, not believing what she had just done herself.

Marcus was speechless he just nodded his head.

"I told you it was good", Candy said as she took another sip then held the bottle to his lips and tilted it up as if she were feeding a baby.

Marcus took a sip then wiped his chin off where a little bit of soda had dripped on him.

"Yeah it's good" was all he said as he looked at Rhameek who only shrugged his shoulders.

"Look, we can make it the rest of the way by ourselves", Candy said "it's almost time for the bus to come back through, that way ya'll want miss it."

"You sure?", Marcus said.

"Yeah I'm sure, thank you for the candy and stuff."

"No problem"

"Why don't you give me your number so I can call, make sure ya'll got back all right."

"I ain't got no phone" Marcus said looking at the ground. "But I can call you from the phone booth."

"I can't give out my number", Candy said "my mom is strict", both stood looking at the ground.

"Give him my number", Felicia said "you be there everyday anyway."

Felicia wrote her number on a piece of the brown paper bag from the store and handed it to Marcus.

"Just call when ya'll make it home and I'll relay the message', Felicia said.

Candy and Marcus said their goodbyes. Marcus was still trying to figure out what had just happened between him and Candy.

"But that soda did taste good" he thought to his self as Candy walked off grabbing Felicia, who was now in Rhameek's face, by the arm.

"You wanna taste my soda Rhameek?", Felicia said licking her lips.

'Sure" Rhameek said as he snatched the plastic bottle from her hand and turned it up, drinking the whole soda.

"Taste good" he said before handing her the empty bottle back and burping in her face.

Candy laughed as she pulled her angry friend away by both elbows.

"You better be glad she won't let me go", Felicia yelled as

Candy continued to pull her up the street by both arms.

"Later", Rhameek said laughing as he waved his hand at Felicia then winked his eye and blew a kiss at her, which made her even more furious.

Rhameek continued to laugh as Candy struggled to keep Felicia under control all the way up the street.

Rhameek then turned to face Marcus; "look at you" he said "all goo-goo eyed and shit."

Rhameek was about to say something else when Marcus saw him look up, "here come the bus" he said "let's get to the bus stop."

Marcus stood looking at the ground.

"Come on what you waitin for?" Rhameek asked, looking back at his friend.

"Oh man; say you didn't" Rhameek shouted.

"Marcus I know you didn't."

Marcus didn't open his mouth, instead he dug down into his pockets and turned them inside out. A nickel and a few pennies fell out and rolled across the ground as Marcus looked at his friend and shrugged his shoulders.

"Oh man, you spent our bus fare on her?" Rhameek screamed 'I don't believe this, I can't wait to tell my Uncle Zone bout this stunt you just pulled."

"Sorry dawg" was all Marcus could say.

"Whatever" Rhameek said "good thing I got on my traveling shoes" he smiled as he slapped Marcus on the back.

"Let's get to humping then."

Marcus smiled back at his friend and they made their way back home, talking the whole way about a little bit of everything from girls to school, to what they planned to do in the years to come.

"I'm gone be a major player like my uncle", Rhameek said then laughed.

"What you laughing at", Marcus asked.

"I was just thinking' Rhameek said "you'll probably still be walking and givin Candy all your damn money!"

Marcus laughed out loud to hisself as he sat at the red light.

The family in the lane next to him looked at him as if he was crazy.

Marcus, realizing he probably looked crazy, sitting in the car by hisself laughing, straightened up and threw a peace sign up to the young boy who sat in the back seat with the window rolled halfway down and his chin resting on the top edge of the window.

"Nice car", the boy said.

"Preciate it lil man", Marcus replied as he noticed the young lady driving the car smiling ear to ear in his direction.

Marcus flashed her a million-dollar smile in return, the sunlight bouncing off of his gold teeth as he tipped his fitted cap to the side.

The light turned green and Marcus waved goodbye to the nice looking young lady and caught a glimpse of her blushing.

"Ma I want a car like that" he heard the "lil man" say as he pulled off and made a left turn, the rims on his Cadillac reflecting light and causing heads to turn at the busy intersection.

Marcus thought about the way things had turned out. Rhameek was still his man and he was right about one thing he was still a sucker for Candy.

"But I ain't walkin"; he said out loud talking to hisself again.

But he had made that walk to and from his old neighborhood many times just as she had made that "hump" to see him on plenty of days.

He remembered how he had given her the number to the phone booth at the corner store in his neighborhood and how she would call the number every night at 7:00 on the dot.

He would be there with Rhameek waiting for the call, and how they would talk for hours or until Candy had to get off.

He frowned as he thought of the first time they had sex.

It was the first time ever for him and evidently her as well, considering the outcome.

It still made him cringe when he thought about the blood all over his hands and on his sheets.

He had heard stories about girls getting their "cherries popped" but he always thought the saying was just a figure of speech.

Well it was, but nobody had ever told him why they called it that, but once it happened he assumed they called it that because it looked as if he had been playing in a bowl full of mashed up cherries.

"Ugh", Marcus yelled looking at his hands as if it were blood still on them from that day.

Marcus turned the radio down as he made a right turn onto Rhameek's street.

"Oh shit", he said as he bent the corner and saw a red Mitsubishi Eclipse and a dark green Toyota Camry parked in the middle of the street, both blocking Rhameek's F-150 in the driveway.

He pulled up and came to a stop by the mailbox then threw his car in park and sat back with his window rolled down as he observed the three ring circus that was taking place in his boy's front yard.

Two girls stood in the bed of Rhameek's F-150 screaming as Champ, Rhameek's pit bull, ran back and forth alongside the truck barking and growling, trying to leap up into the back of the truck with the two girls. Rhameek stood on his front porch laughing, holding a mayonnaise jar full of red Kool-aid, with big ice cubes floating around in it, in one hand and Champ's leash in his right hand.

'Rah you ain't shit", the tall dark-skinned girl yelled as she swatted at Champ with her tennis shoe in her hand. Her long micro braids were pulled back in a ponytail, she had beads of sweat dripping so hard Marcus could almost see her breast through the pink tennis dress she wore.

"Damn, Serena Williams", Marcus mumbled to himself.

"Get him, get him, please get him!" Cried the short light skinned girl who stood in the center of the truck bed, crying and screaming frantically. Her long pretty hair frizzled all over her head as she continued to jump up and down screaming and crying, her black thongs showing as she made an attempt to climb on the roof of the truck with her mini skirt hiked up on her back and her red ass hanging out for all to see.

Marcus laughed as the light skinned girl tried to pull herself up on the roof of the truck, evidently not having enough sense to take her heels off to get a better grip, her feet kept slipping and she was unable to get to higher ground.

"Try again Red" Marcus yelled, hoping to get another peek at the short, but thick, girls nice shapely behind.

"Rah please call him off", the pretty red girl cried with tears streaming down her face.

"Would you shut the fuck up", the dark skinned girl yelled at her, then turned her attention back to Rhameek just as she caught Champ with a solid blow to the side of his head with her tennis shoe.

"How you like that Chump", she screamed. But Champ, not one to give up, continued to leap up and down, by the truck bed, trying his best to get to the two girls.

"When I'm through fuckin this dog up Rhameek" the dark skinned girl cursed "I'm gonna fuck you up, then I'm gonna fuck this cryin ass red ass Bitch up."

"Rhameek who is this girl" the light skinned girl screamed, still crying at the same time.

"I'm his woman Bitch!", the dark skinned girl yelled.

"Rhameek, what is she talkin about?" The light skinned girl cried "how could you do this to me? I mean, look at her!" She said as she gave the girl with the micros a look as if she was disgusted at the sight of her.

"Oh that's it!" The tall dark skinned girl said as she turned and smacked the shorter girl across the face with her tennis shoe.

The scene was chaotic, the two girls fighting on the truck bed, pulling hair, kicking and screaming, Champ barking and growling, jumping up and down beside the truck and Rhameek standing on the porch laughing.

Marcus shook his head and got out of the car.

"What's up Bra',", Rah said as he bawled his hand into a fist as Marcus did the same and they banged their knuckles together.

"Do somein bout dat shit Rah."

"Come on dawg I know you enjoyin this, I saw you lookin at my shawty ass."

"Whatever nigga", Marcus said with a smile.

"You gotta get yo nose out Candy's ass sometimes, explore the world homeboy" Rhameek said, then turned his attention to his dog.

"Champ, come here boy." Champ stopped barking almost instantly and ran to his master.

"That's my man", Rhameek said praising his pet as he gave him a hard pat on the back.

Rhameek passed the leash to Marcus as he made his way to break up the girls who were still wrestling on the back of his truck.

Marcus bent down and snapped the leash onto Champs collar, then the big brown dog stood on his hind legs and placed his big paws into Marcus' hands, exposing his wide white chest.

"Good to see you too big man", Marcus said as he released the dog from his grip and rubbed the top of his head. Rhameek broke the two girls up and after a few more minutes of arguing and a few threats from Rhameek to let Champ go again, both girls decided to leave.

"OK" the short light skinned girl said as she hopped into her Mitsubishi.

"Don't call me nigga, fuck you and that dumb ass red Bitch!" The dark skinned girl cursed before pulling off, her tires squealing in the process.

The red girl hesitated then pulled off slowly in the opposite direction.

"What was that all about", Marcus said.

"That was drama, my nigga!" Rhameek laughed.

"Talisha, the redbone pulled up behind me at the red light and followed me home." Rhameek said sounding like a narrator. "Anyway, she fussing and tryin to figure out where I been. Then, the other broad, Shanice, pulled up out of nowhere, also wantin to know where I been and 'who the red Bitch is' as she put it." Rhameek paused. "Long story short, I tell them hoes to kick rocks. So, I try to go inside the crib and these broads following me, playing twenty-one questions.

But, before they can make it up the porch good, I turn the knob and Champ bust out the door on they ass! You know how he get, you should've seen them broads climbing all over each other tryin to get up on the back of that truck. Anyway, while Champ kept em company, I went inside, poured me a cup of Kool-aid and that's bout the time you pulled up." Rhameek finished, taking a deep breath as if the brief narration took a lot out of him.

"Anyway, you want some Kool-aid dawg?"

"Nigga you crazy", Marcus said as he followed Rhameek inside.

"Tell me again about Leon in the thong and heels", Felicia said laughing as she admired herself in the dressing room mirror.

"Would you shut up" Candy whispered between clenched teeth as she also admired herself in the adjoining mirror.

"You so paranoid Candy", Felicia whispered back "ain't nobody in here but us, besides I'm glad he got his; after what he did to you back in the day, it was due time."

"I agree Felicia, but let's wait till we leave this mall to talk about it, you blowing my concentration. By the way, how do I look?"

"Almost as good as me" Felicia responded.

"Whatever girl, I know I'm sexy", Candy replied.

"Let's get the stuff to the counter and get up outta here, we need to catch the shoe store before we leave and our hair appointment in another hour."

"And you need to do something with that wig!", Felicia interjected then took one last look at herself in the form fitting satin dress.

"You one to talk", Candy said as she removed her dress and placed it back on its hanger before slipping back into her Rocawear jumper.

"Would you please get out that mirror and come on! You got all night to look at yo'self."

"Quit hatin girl", Felicia said as she slipped the dress over her head and turned her back to Candy.

"You gone be lookin at this all night", she said while patting herself on the butt. "Cause yo girl gone be up in the club fly, and showin her ass all night long."

Candy rolled her eyes and began to laugh as Felicia strutted to the opposite side of the dressing room and slipped back into her jeans.

"You happy? We can go now!" Felicia said after pulling her T-shirt over her head and slipping her shoes on, then she left the dressing room not waiting for a reply.

Candy followed close behind as they hurried to the register and placed a few outfits on the counter.

"What's up, how ya'll ladies doin today?" The guy behind the counter asked as he began to ring up the items.

"Oh, we alright", Felicia said, while leaning forward on the counter "we just lettin it do what it do baby."

Candy laughed to herself at the sight of the tall light skinned man behind the counter blushing like a school boy with a crush as Felicia commenced to lick her lips and flirt with him.

"She so hot in the ass", Candy thought to herself.

"Will this be separate?", the guy asked.

"No just do us both, together, at the same time." Felicia said in a seductive tone.

Candy was amused by the way Felicia was carrying on, as well as by the nervous movements the guy made as he rang up their total.

"That'll be two thousand two hundred twenty two dollars and thirty-seven cents", he said reading off the amount slowly.

Candy counted twenty three one hundred dollar bills and laid them on the counter, noticing that only after she began counting out the money did the clerk begin to remove the ink tabs from the clothing.

"What ya'll ladies gettin all dressed up for?" He asked as he folded the items and placed them in a bag.

"Oh, just gone play the town a lil bit tonight", Felicia said.

"Oh yeah?, maybe I'll see ya'll out somewhere." He stated as he slid the receipt and change from the purchase across the counter.

"Maybe!" Felicia said as she grabbed the change, letting her fingers brush his hand "and if you do see us."

She paused and took a fifty dollar bill that he had just given her and planted a big kiss on it leaving a sticky lip print across the surface before reaching over the counter and sticking the bill to his cheek, then she continued "maybe you'll buy us a drink."

Candy rolled her eyes and grabbed her bags off of the counter and walked off shaking her head. Felicia waved bye to the guy behind the counter, who just stood watching with the fifty-dollar bill still stuck to his face. Felicia made a show of switching her hips in an exaggerated manner as her and Candy left the store.

"You so full of it", Candy said. She and Felicia both began to laugh as they made their way to the shoe store.

Rrrratt-rrrrat, the large assault rifle rang out releasing a large burst of fire from the barrel as shells ejected from the side of the weapon. Rrrratt-rrrratt.

"Who else want it, wit ya boy!" Marcus screamed at the top of his lungs as the weapon continued to erupt with a thunderous sound that filled the room.

The sound of the gun seemed to excite Champ as well, because he began to bark and growl as if he was ready to attack at any moment.

"Get em boy", Marcus screamed at Champ while releasing another loud burst from the weapon.

"Would ya'll please cut dat shit out", Rhameek yelled from the kitchen "I can't concentrate."

Marcus pressed the pause button causing Champ to stop in his tracks and stare at the sixty four-inch screen, with his head tilted to the side, as if he was trying to figure out what went wrong.

He moved towards the screen and began to sniff at it and then turned to face Marcus. Looking from Marcus to the TV, then back at Marcus. He wagged his tail, with his head tilted to the side, once again, as if asking Marcus, "What's up?"

"Don't look at me dawg!" Marcus said "you heard yo master."

Champ let out a big puff of air through his nostrils and made his way to a corner in the room and sniffed around before plopping down, with his chin resting on a pair of Rhameek's old chewed up Timbalands.

Marcus dropped the joystick on the couch and went to join Rhameek in the kitchen.

"You and that damn dog bout to drive me crazy up in here." Rhameek said as he stood over the kitchen counter with a cake mixer in his hand and beads of sweat on his forehead.

"And you bout to drive me crazy takin all day, me and Champ bored dawg", Marcus slurred.

"Takin all day", Rhameek replied as he hit the switch and the tongs on the cake mixer began to spin.

"I'm tryin to whip this up like Candy got you whipped bra, that's all, I'm sure she took her time with you didn't she?"

"Kee-Kee, ha-ha" Marcus faked a laugh as he took a seat at the kitchen table, and examined Rhameek's handiwork.

"Put the fan on the table and cut it on low for me", Rhameek instructed him. "I'm bout to wrap this up and get dressed, everything should be nice and dry by then Playboy, then we can go do what we do."

"Sounds good to me", Marcus said as he put the fan on low speed and set it to rotate from side to side so it would cover the entire surface of the table.

"Don't take all day Rah, tryna get all fly and shit, save all that for tonight."

"I got ya bra, anyway where we goin tonight?"

"Wherever the wind blows us." Marcus replied as he turned the hot water on in the sink and filled it with dish detergent before dumping the Vision Ware pots and the tongs from the cake mixer in the water to soak.

CHAPTER 6

"Hello" "What's up Vette, this is Felicia, I'm calling to see if you ready for me and Candy yet."

"As a matter of fact I'm finishing my last head now.", Yvette said as she sprayed a little spritz on her customers hair and leaned back to examine it making sure everything was in order.

"Where ya'll at anyway?"

"We less than ten minutes away", Felicia answered "just makin sure you was ready for us."

"I'm ready and waitin girl, you and Candy come on. The seat'll still be warm when you get here", Yvette said before hanging up her cell.

"Who dat? Candy who?" The lady in the chair asked as she spun her chair around to face the mirror.

"Candy Brown girl", Yvette replied.

"Humph" the lady in the chair grunted while checking out her reflection. "She think she hot shit."

"Tammy you just mad cause Marcus want pay yo ass no attention", Yvette said as she made her way to the opposite side of the shop and tilted the hair dryer back, checking on another customer who sat under the hot dryer, halfway asleep, with a head full of rollers.

Yvette studied the girl's hair and said "fifteen more minutes" before pulling the dryer hood back over her head.

"Chile, Marcus been beggin for this forever", Tammy said.

"Marcus who?" The girl under the dryer asked, waking up all of a sudden, she tilted the dryer hood back off of her head.

"Angel you so damn nosey", Yvette said "and I told you, fifteen more minutes under the dryer."

"Marcus who?" Angel repeated, ignoring Yvette.

"Marcus Flowers girl", Tammy stated.

"You talkin bout the one who mess wit that raggedy as Candy", Angel said.

"Yeah girl", Tammy said, her voice rising knowing she had the floor now.

Yvette plopped down in the chair as soon as Tammy got out of it.

"I heard she got that nigga sprung." A girl said, who sat near the back of the salon, with one foot in bubbling water, and the other hanging off to the side, as one of Yvette's co-workers seemed to struggle with a callus on the side of her foot.

"I heard he got her sprung", a girl who sat in a chair by the door stated as she lowered the Ebony magazine she was reading and closed it, placing it on her lap, as if she were no longer interested in reading the article on Bobby and Whitney. "My home girl use to mess wit him back in the day, she say he a fool wit it."

"I don't know", Tammy said "but he definitely ain't sprung, cause he stay tryin to get some of this, but when I do decide to give him some I'll let you know if he a fool or yo home girl just fooled you."

"I know that's right girl", Angel said as she and Tammy began to laugh and gave each other a high five.

Yvette sat quietly in her chair, shaking her head, as the girls continued to gossip.

"Look there the bitch go now." Tammy said, looking out the large glass door.

"And there go that tired ass Felicia too", Angel added.

Yvette sat back and had to fight back the urge to laugh out loud when Candy and Felicia entered the shop. The only thing that could be heard was the sound of blow dryers blowing, magazines rattling and someone popping bubble gum towards the back.

"Hey girl", Tammy said as she grabbed her purse and met Felicia in the center of the salon with a hug. "It's been so long and look at you Candy, you and Marcus still together?"

"Yeah, we still together", Candy answered as she made her way towards Yvette's chair.

"You look like you takin care of yourself", she continued. "Ya'll ain't had no kid's yet?"

"No kid's" Candy answered.

"Awe that's too bad", Tammy replied.

"So what you tryin to do with this mess?", Yvette said to Candy, cutting Tammy off.

"I'm not sure; I'll just let you do your thing I guess", Candy answered.

"Ya'll goin out tonight?", Tammy said, butting in.

"Yeah we goin somewhere", Felicia stated.

"It's goin down at the Hilton tonight", Angel said, putting her two cents in, as the dryer came to a stop.

"Yeah that's where all the baller's gonna be, ya'll need to come out there, we can chill in the V.I.P or somein, find us some men", Tammy said winking at Candy and nudging Felicia with her elbow.

"Anyway I'm out!, hopefully I'll see ya'll out there tonight, bye Vette!" Tammy said, as she began to walk towards the door.

"Umm, speaking of bye", Yvette said, snapping her fingers to get Tammy's attention. "How bout you pay me, before you walk out that door, so I can Buy me a few drinks, wherever we end up tonight!"

"Oh girl I almost forgot", Tammy said as she began to dig through her purse.

"Umm hmm", Yvette said "that's what I'm here for girl to

keep yo head straight."

"See ya'll later", Tammy said, after paying Yvette for her services.

"Bye girl" everyone in the shop said in unison as the door closed and the shop fell silent, momentarily, except for the sound of the bell, hanging from the door, jingling, signaling that the door was closed.

"That bitch talk too much", Angel said breaking the silence.

"I know that's right", the girl with the magazine said.

"I heard she got that thang!" The girl towards the back of the shop said as she placed her other foot in the tub of bubbling water.

Candy looked at Felicia and Yvette who both rolled their eyes.

"Let me see what I can do with this mess", Yvette said to Candy with a smile on her face, as Felicia grabbed a seat beside the girl with the magazine and got an earful of the latest "word on the street."

"And did ya'll hear bout them finding Leon dead in the club last night", the girl beside Felicia blurted out.

"No!" Felicia said looking shocked and hurt "what happened girl?"

"All I know" the girl continued "is they found him dressed in thongs and heels."

"Thong and heels!" All the girls chanted at the same time.

"In thongs and heels!" Rhameek repeated for the tenth time as he continued to laugh while wiping tears from his eyes.

"Marcus you a sick individual for real bra."

Marcus sat in the passenger seat of Rhameek's truck, with a smirk on his face, as Rhameek continued to laugh, and swerve all over the road.

"Rah, watch the road dawg, you trippin."

"I got this playa, you just lean back and watch the hoes watch me when I pull up." Rhameek said as he pulled into the lower parking deck, causing the girl's who were leaving the mall to stop and stare, as well as those who were entering.

Rhameek circled the parking deck twice before finding a space to park at the packed mall.

"What you doin", Marcus said as Rhameek backed into a handicapped parking space.

"I got dis", Rhameek said as he pulled a handicap sign from the armrest compartment and placed it on the mirror before hopping out of the truck.

Marcus shook his head and opened his door just in time to see a mall security truck rolling up from his side. He jumped out of the truck and was about to suggest that Rhameek move, when he saw him come around the front of the truck, walking with an exaggerated limp. His left arm tucked tight against his chest, with his wrist and hand folded in an awkward position.

"Hey", Rhameek slurred as he raised a deformed looking hand and waved to the officers.

Marcus, worried about the guns they carried in the truck, struggled to keep a straight face as the officer on the passenger side waved back to Rhameek and the security truck continued to roll by.

"Nigga, you know we dirty and you doin dumb shit", Marcus whispered.

"I told you, I got dis. They gone yet?" Rhameek asked as he continued putting on an act, limping towards the mall entrance, not wanting to look over his shoulder and blow his cover.

"Nah, they stoppin dawg, they watching us." Marcus said as he looked back and saw the truck leaving the parking deck.

"What they doin now", Rhameek asked as they got closer to the entrance.

"They still right there don't look back", Marcus said as he continued to follow behind Rhameek.

'Damn" Rhameek cursed as they approached a gang of girl's who were leaving the mall.

Rhameek couldn't help but notice the girl's as they stepped to the side trying to avoid him.

"Damn", he said again as he made eye contact with one of the girl's, admiring her thick thighs, when she walked by in her short shorts. She looked back at him with a frown on her face.

"This broad think I'm a retard", Rhameek thought to hisself as he started to turn to get a good look at her from behind. Marcus stopped him. "Don't look back, keep goin!"

Rhameek kept limping, until he finally reached the door.

"Damn dawg, the police still watching?" Rhameek questioned. "Marcus, they still watching?" he repeated again, still not hearing an answer. But, instead, he heard the sound of girl's giggling from behind. "Marcus", he called out, once again, and got no answer.

Rhameek decided to sneak a peek, over his shoulder, when he heard one of the girls laughing out loud again.

He looked back only to see Marcus, way behind him, surrounded by the group of girl's who were all still giggling.

"Bye Marcus" the girl's said as a chorus as Marcus walked away from them grinning and caught up with Rhameek.

"That's fucked up", Rhameek said noticing the security truck was nowhere in sight and the girl's were climbing into a Black Suburban. The "thick one" Rhameek had his eye on climbed into the driver's side.

"Bye Marcus", they all screamed and giggled like schoolgirls as they pulled off.

"How you gone play me like that", Rhameek said "what them broads talkin bout?"

"Nothing", Marcus said "the usual, just being hot in da ass, tellin me I'm cute, askin what I was gettin into, shit like dat, I told em I just came out here to take my handicapped homeboy shoppin and they were just tellin me how sweet that was of me", Marcus laughed then continued.

"You should run dat game more often Rah, somein bout a man who look out for the disabled, turn a woman on."

"Fuck you", Rhameek said as he entered the mall. "You get her number", he asked "I got to get wit the driver."

"Nah" Marcus said "I told em I had a woman."

"You what!" Rhameek yelled causing people in the mall to turn and look at him as he no longer limped but pimped through the mall beside Marcus.

"You heard me, I told em I had a woman and that only seemed to turn em on even more, somein bout a faithful man turn a woman on", Marcus said sarcastically "especially a faithful man who look after the disabled."

"Ha, ha, ke-ke", Rhameek said as he and Marcus made their way into the black owned urban wear store.

The whole atmosphere changed as they stepped over the threshold into the store and the soft mall music was drowned out by the sound of Jay-Z booming out of the speakers, which were mounted high up on the walls, one in each corner of the store.

"How ya'll doin", a short brown skinned girl asked, approaching Rhameek and Marcus with a smile on her face.

"I got something for you in the back", she said pointing at Marcus "just came in today, your favorite color too, I knew you would come through today."

"What about me, you got somein for me in da back?" Rhameek said as he rubbed his palms together and took a conspicuous look at her backside, which he noticed, looked extra fat in the tight Baby Phat jeans she wore.

"I don't know? I just might have somein for you back here", she said blushing "what size you wear?"

"That look like a perfect fit; right there", he answered, looking at her butt "and if not, I'll make it fit", he continued, making the girl blush even more and smile from ear to ear.

"Umm! OK", the girl said, clearing her throat and fanning herself, "ya'll give me a minute I'll be right back" she said before walking off.

"She love me dawg!" Rhameek said as the girl walked towards the back.

"You gone catch somein one day", Marcus stated.

"Hata" Rhameek replied as he made his way towards the back of the store, making sure none of the other employees were watching, before slipping through the door marked "employees only."

Marcus laughed as Rhameek disappeared through the doorway.

Marcus bobbed his head to the music as he moved from rack to rack checking out the assortment of urban wear.

The store had everything from Sean John, to Rocawear, G-Unit, LRG, Coogi, Bathing Apes, you name it they had it.

As Marcus continued to browse around, he noticed a nice form fitting dress made by Baby Phat.

"That would look good on Candy", he thought to hisself as he got one of the worker's attention and had him to pull the dress down from the wall.

"You can just set it on the counter", he told him "I'm gone look around some more."

Marcus continued to look through the racks and found a pair of jeans that caught his eye.

"Yeah, those would look good on you"; he heard a voice say. Marcus turned towards the voice and saw a short, brown skinned girl. She wore glasses and had big dimples. "But I think these would look better on you", she said, pulling another pair of jeans off the rack and holding them up against his waist line as if she was sizing him up.

"I never seen her before", Marcus thought to hisself "must be a new worker."

"What size are those you got on", she said.

"Thirty-eights", Marcus answered.

"Oh, these are thirty-sixes, hold on", she instructed him as she turned her back towards him and began to look for his size.

She continued to ramble and search for the right size as she stood wide legged with her right leg bent back, showing off her petite, shapely, bow legged frame.

"Here we go, thirty-eights" she said, as she turned to face him. "Try these on."

"I think I like the ones I got better", Marcus responded.

"Well try them both on", she said "trust me. These will look better on you."

"How long you been working here?" Marcus asked, out of curiosity, as the girl snatched the jeans he was holding out of his hand and swapped them for the ones she had picked out.

"I don't work here, try them on first", she demanded.

"You don't work here", Marcus thought to hisself. "I think I'll try these on", he said taking the jeans he had picked out from her hands and giving her the other jeans back.
Before she could respond, Marcus stepped into the small dressing booth to try on the jeans.

After less than a minute had passed there was a knock on the door "let me see how they look" he heard the girl say from outside the door.

"I got to come out to use the mirror anyway" he stated.
"Who the fuck is this girl", he said under his breath before stepping out of the booth.

"They all right", she said as she closed the door and looked at his reflection in the mirror on the outside of the door.

"Now try these on", she said, handing him the jeans she had picked out once again.

Marcus looked at the jeans she held. Shrugging his shoulders, he took them from her, before stepping back into the booth.

"Let me see" she said, through the door, as soon as he began to slip the jeans on.

"Hold up", Marcus answered before stepping out of the booth again to check his reflection.

"See I told you", the girl said.

"They all right", Marcus responded.

"I'll put these back on the rack", she said heading towards the rack.

"Hold up", Marcus stopped her "I still want those, just

throw em on the counter right there."

"Well come on, let me find you a shirt to go with those jeans", she said grabbing him by the arm and pulling him towards the counter with her.

As she laid the jeans on the counter she noticed the dress Marcus had picked out earlier.

"This is nice", she said "how much is this?" She asked the guy at the register.

"Two hundred and fifty dollars", he answered "it's his though, it's the last one."

She turned her attention to Marcus "Oh you buying this for your girl or something?"

"It's definitely not for me", he said.

"How you know it's the right size?", she asked.

"I know her size."

"Yeah right", the girl said as if she didn't believe him "is she bigger than me?", she asked.

"No, bout the same size."

"What about her chest? Is her chest like mine?" She asked, showing off her cleavage. "Cause she gotta have a lil chest for this type of dress."

"She can fit it" was the only reply.

"Oh, well does she have hips like mine or smaller?" The girl continued to ask questions as she turned to the side "is her butt bigger than mine?"

"I don't know", Marcus answered, getting tired of the questions.

"Well anyway", she threw the dress down on the counter and walked to the rack closest to her. "I like this shirt; it'll look good with those jeans."

Marcus took the shirt from her and examined it.

"You sure you know your girl size?, I could try that dress on for you if you'd like, since we bout the same size."

"Nah, I'm straight", Marcus answered "I always buy her clothes, I know all her sizes."

"So you tellin me you know her shoe size, bra and panty

size."

"Absolutely", he answered.

"OK, well since we the same size, what you think my bra and panty size is?", she asked.

Marcus checked her out and ran down everything, from shoes to shirt size, and hit all on the nose.

"Not bad", she said "but I asked you what my bra and panty size were."

Marcus shook his head, realizing she wasn't gonna let it go, he blurted out an answer.

"Oh my God, you know your stuff", she said, blocking his path to the dressing room, as he tried to make his way back to the booth to put his own jeans back on.

"You gonna go get her some panties when you leave from here? She can't wear just any kind of panties with that dress."

"This I already know", Marcus said "and I just might have to go get her some now that you mention it."

"Victoria's Secret is upstairs'", she continued "maybe you can get me some panties too", she teased. Marcus laughed.

"You trippin", he said.

"For real, they got a sale on thongs", she said with a smile on her face. "That's all I wear, I got some on now." She continued as she turned her back to him and grabbed her low-rise jeans by the waist, folding them down. "See."

Marcus looked around to see if anybody else was looking as the girl pulled her pants down just far enough to reveal the thin straps connecting to the thong, which seemed to disappear down into the creavace of her backside.

She turned to the side. Running her thumbs across the strap, lifting it above the waist line of her jeans, she continued to show him the thin strap that ran from the back, to the front, of her thongs.

"You crazy", Marcus said as he stepped around the girl and opened the door to the dressing booth.

The girl grabbed the door as he entered. "Can I come in

there with you?"

"Nah, you trippin", Marcus answered, trying to pull the door shut as she held on.

"You scared of me?", she asked.

"Hell nah!"

"Well let me in." She said, not lettin go of the door.

Marcus grabbed his jeans out of the dressing room and stepped out, pushing past the girl, making his way to the counter with his own jeans and shoes in his hands.

He dug into his jean pockets and pulled out a knot of money, then told the guy at the register to ring him up. He tore the tag off of the new jeans he had tried on and handed it to the guy so he could scan the tag at the register.

"I'll just keep these on", he said before bending over to put his shoes on.

When he arose back to a standing position the girl was standing beside him, staring straight into his eyes.

"Oh, it's like that!" She said.

"Cute but crazy", Marcus thought to his self.

"That girl must got you sprung", she said.

"Whatever", Marcus replied as he paid the guy at the register for the few items he had picked up.

Once the guy slid him his bag and his change, Marcus snatched up his own jeans, that he had wore into the store, and began transferring his things into the pockets of his new jeans, when he realized, his cell phone was no longer clipped to the side of them.

He looked around and began to pat himself down in search of the phone as he walked toward the booth to see if he had dropped it, then back towards the counter.

"You lookin for this?" The girl said, holding the phone up.

"What is you doin wit my phone?", Marcus asked.

"I put my number in it, call me! The names Tamika", she said "I put it under Tony; so you won't get in trouble" she added, with a grin on her face, as she tossed him his phone and left the store.

"Crazy ass broad", he said under his breath as he watched her leave.

Now that the "stalker" was gone, Marcus decided to go back into the booth and put his own jeans back on. "I gotta erase that number", he thought to hisself as he stepped into the booth.

Once he finished changing he decided to look around some more to kill time, finally able to shop in peace he found a few more outfits to add to his collection.

"Here you go" he heard a voice say. He turned and saw the girl who had went to the back of the store holding the outfit she had put up for him.

Marcus had forgot about her, he noticed her eyes were a little glossy and her hair was a little ruffled up.

"Preciate It" Marcus said as he took the orange and brown, Velour, Sean John sweatsuit from her hands.

"What do you think?" she asked blushing.

"Yeah this tight, you know what I like."

"Yeah, I knew you'ld like it" she said.

"You find anything dawg?" Rhameek said, as he popped up out of nowhere.

"Yeah how bout you", Marcus responded.

"Yeah I found a lil somein", Rhameek said looking towards the girl, making her blush again as she walked off with a smile on her face.

"Boy it's hot in this mufucka" Rhameek announced, wiping beads of sweat from his forehead.

"Yeah I bet", Marcus replied, making his way to the counter to pay for the rest of the things he had picked up. Rhameek followed behind him, snatching a few items up himself, not really taking a lot of time to dwell on what he was picking up.

Once they were through paying for their gear they made their way out of the store. Rhameek stopped to whisper something in the girl's ear, making her giggle and blush once again, before they made their exit.

"Dawg you wouldn't believe what happened to me while you was back there doin whatever it is you was doin." Marcus said as he and Rhameek left the mall. He ran down the whole scenario, about the stalker, reminding himself once again "I gotta erase that number. Damn, what did she say she listed it under? I'll figure it out later." He told himself, as he continued to tell Rhameek what had happened.

"What, and you ain't let her in the booth wit you!" Rhameek yelled, as they got into his truck and pulled off. "Candy got you fucked up!"

"You crazy!" Marcus replied.

"Whatever!" Rhameek snapped "ain't no secret, everybody know."

"What you mean everybody know?"

"I mean everybody know girl", Yvette answered as she added the finishing touch to Candy's hair "ain't no secret; Marcus got you head over heels."

"Yeah right", Candy replied "I think you got it backwards."

"She in denial", Felicia blurted out from across the room.

"Felicia I know you ain't talkin bout no denial, let's not talk about you and Rhameek." Candy countered.

"Rhameek?" Yvette said.

"She lying. Don't listen to her." Felicia shot back.

"I was about to say!" Yvette continued "cause that nigga was over my house all day yesterday."

"What", Candy screamed, all this being news to her. "When you and him start kickin it?"

"Not me and him, but him and my sister." Yvette said, clearing things up. "I let her use my crib while I was here at the shop yesterday. But want do it no more girl, cause they ain't even have the decency to change my sheets."

"I knew that nigga smelled like sex when he came to my house", Felicia thought to herself, while trying not to show any signs of anger on her face.

"That nigga ain't no good" Yvette continued. "Candy I

don't see how you put up with Marcus being around his hoe ass so much; and Felicia let me find out you and Rah got a thing goin on."

"Vette, Candy just trying to get off the subject of her nose being crammed up Marcus ass, don't listen to her." Felicia stated.

"Whatever Felicia, like I said ya'll got it backwards ya'll not lookin at the big picture." Felicia and Vette gave a baffled look at each other wondering what the "big picture" was.

"And to answer your question Vette, Rah cool wit me, you know we all grew up together and Marcus got a mind of his own. Besides he know I'll bust his head wide open if he try me. And on top of that, I know Rah ain't gone let nothing bad happen to my baby either."

"You right about that" Felicia agreed.

"I heard he's been known to show his ass behind Marcus", Vette said.

"That's an understatement", Candy replied "and that's visa versa, they look out for each other." She said as she got out of the chair and checked her new do, in the mirror, from all angles.

"Candy get yo conceded ass out the way, so I can do Felicia's nappy ass head, ya'll forget I'm tryin to go out tonight too."

"Yeah Candy, get out da way", Felicia said bumping Candy to the side and plopping down in the chair, "and as for you Bitch", she said turning her attention to Yvette. "Just to let you know, my hair ain't nappy. Besides, I got a bag of the best at the mall today. So get yo needle and thread and make me look like Beyonce."

"Come on Felicia!" Yvette whined "I know you don't want no sew in, dats gone take all day, I gotta do my head too."

"Vette please! You ain't gotta do nothing but put some water on your head and it'll curl up, wit yo half breed ass. And you wastin time talkin", Felicia said, leaning back in the chair, making it clear she wasn't backing down.

"Beyonce Bitch!" She added, snapping her fingers at Yvette, as she began to sing Beyonce's "Crazy in Love" out loud.

"You make me sick Felicia, you could've at least had it braided already." Yvette said as she snatched up a comb and began to part Felicia's hair.

Candy couldn't help but laugh as Yvette proceeded to braid Felicia's hair, while both continued to argue back and forth.

Candy checked her watch and decided to call Marcus to see where he was at.

"What's up", Marcus answered on the third ring.

"Where you at?" She asked.

"I'm in the car with Rah. We just left the mall", he answered "where you at?"

"I'm in the shop, I just got my hair done. I'm waiting on Felicia now."

"Who you gettin fly for, one of those niggas?"

"Shut up Marcus" Candy said "Baby I'm hungry" she added.

"You hungry" Marcus repeated.

"No" Rhameek said, as he sat beside Marcus, shaking his head.

"What you want to eat?" Marcus continued.

"Hell no" Rhameek mumbled, still shaking his head.

"Just get me anything, me and Felicia both, and tell Rah quit hatin; Love you."

"Love you too baby" Marcus said before hanging up.

"Sucka' ass nigga", Rhameek said "you buying me somein to eat too nigga" he added "and puttin gas in here."

Marcus turned the volume up a notch on the radio.

"And we gone eat at my favorite spot, hope she like jerk chicken nigga." Rhameek continued as he headed towards his favorite restaurant, which was on the way to Yvette's shop.

CHAPTER 7

"Mufucka's probably out here spending up my paper right now, as we speak" Peabo said as he sat in the passenger seat, at the red light, rubbing his temples.

Tiffany sat behind the wheel and said nothing; afraid she would set Peabo off again.

She had been driving him around all day, listening to him complain non-stop for hours. Any other day she would've been glad to 'push the Benz'. But at the moment, she only wanted to return to her own car and get as far away from Peabo as possible.

She knew he was like a time bomb waiting to go off and she didn't want to be around when he flipped out again.

"I let one mufucka steal from me and get away wit it then everybody'll think I'm sweet. I got to make an example outta whoever did this." He spat, staring at Tiffany with blood shot eyes. "It ain't money, it's principle" he continued.

"Yeah right", Tiffany thought to herself. Peabo was one of the 'tightest' niggas she had ever met in her life; when it came to money.

Peabo was loaded, but wasn't the type to give away anything. And if he did, there was always a catch to it.

"Make this left and drop me off at Mike's shop", Peabo said.

"Thank God", Tiffany thought to herself as she did as told and turned onto the side street leading to the rim shop. Heads turned as she pulled into the parking lot. The females were breaking their necks and posting up, trying to be seen, as the wine red Benz pulled in and came to a stop; in front of the big display window that read "Shine Time Rims", in big graffiti type letters across the glass.

Male heads turned as well. But most looked in the opposite direction, once they realized Peabo was in the car, not wanting to become part of any unnecessary drama. They busied themselves by turning their attention to other things, such as bending over to tie their shoes. Looking at their watch, checking the time. Or scrolling through their cell phones, checking the call log to see who's call they had ignored hours ago, deciding now was a good time to call them back. Anything to avoid making eye contact with the hot tempered Peabo.

"You go ahead and do what you do, I got things to take care of, I'll catch up wit you later on." Peabo said before hopping out of the car. "Oh yeah, one more thing, don't spill shit in my car. Cause if you do, you'll be buying me a new one."

Tiffany rolled her eyes after he slammed the door shut and walked away.

"Hey Peabo" she heard two of the girls say; before she pulled off.

"Groupie Bitches" she spat, thinking out loud, as she left the parking lot.

"What's up P" Big Mike said as he came outside of the building to greet Peabo. Mike was the owner of Shine Time Rims and he was also Peabo's right hand man.

"Ain't nothing, same ole same", Peabo responded as he gave his man dap.

The two of them looked like linebackers colliding on a football field as they gave each other a brotherly hug and a pat on the back.

Mike was just as big as Peabo, if not bigger, they both disappointed their high school coach when they decided to drop out of school and pursue a life in the streets.

Both were powerful men with NFL potential. But instead,

they chose to use their muscle to ball in a different league. Besides, they were never really into sports. They only played football because it allowed them to injure others without consequence.

"I already know what's bad, but what's good wit ya today brah?" Mike said, making small talk. He was already aware of everything that had happened but Mike wasn't the type to dwell on problems. He already had his ear to the streets and when something came up he would be prepared to deal with it. But until then, it was business as usual.

"You look stressed out brah", Mike continued "why don't you go inside, I got some Cognac in back, fix you a drink and chill, I'm bout to throw these rims on this lil nigga truck right quick, I'll be wit you in a minute."

"Ain't that what you got hired help for." Peabo said.

Mike laughed; showing off a mouthful of diamonds. "Yeah but you know I like to get my hands dirty" he said as he pulled his shirt off and threw it to Peabo. He then snatched up one of the twenty-six inch rims that was leaning on the wall, ready to be mounted. And carried it in, through one of the bay doors, as if it was a brief case, rather than rolling it.

"Somebody bring me the lugs" he yelled as he approached the truck, that sat raised up on the hydraulic lift. And slapped the rim into place, without much effort.

"What the fuck you lookin at?" The owner of the truck said to his girlfriend, who stood to the side, staring at Mike's physique a little too hard.

"I was looking at his tattoo's" the girl said innocently, referring to the blood shot eye's that were tattooed on the back of Mike's bald head, and the I. C. U. tatted across his back, in large red letters, dripping with blood.

"I'll be inside in a minute", Mike shouted to Peabo.

Peabo took a look around, before entering the building. And caught a glimpse of one of the girls in the parking lot; eyeballing him.

He gestured for her to enter "ladies first" he said, speaking to the girl; who wasted no time taking him up on his invitation.

"Take yo time Mike" he shouted before following his new acquaintance into the building, admiring her thick thighs and curvaceous hips as she squeezed by, brushing up against him while making her way inside.

Mike put the last lug nut in place and stepped back to admire his handiwork. The bright sun bouncing off of the rim he had just mounted onto the right rear end of the truck made the diamonds in his mouth glisten as he smiled at his reflection in the large chrome rim.

"Looks nice", he said turning his attention to the owner of the truck. "Big man want you hand me one of them other rims so I can get you all set to go" Mike said.

The customer made no protest and struggled to lift one of the rims, deciding to roll it instead, towards the bay doors. Mike shot his girlfriend a smile and a wink, on the low, before snatching the rim up with one hand.

"Preciate it big dawg, I'll take it from here." He said as he hoisted the rim up and slapped it into place, once again without much effort.

"What you think baby?", the owner of the truck said to his girlfriend as he tried to catch his breath from wrestling with the huge tire.

"Sho is big." She said with a smile on her face. "And the rims are nice too." She thought to herself as she continued to admire Mike from afar.

"What's up ladies", Rhameek said as he burst through the door at Yvette's shop with a Styrofoam tray in one hand and a chicken leg in the other. Marcus followed close behind with two trays in his hand.

"What's up ya'll" Yvette responded as all of the other girls in the shop waved at Rhameek and snuck a peek at Marcus out the corners of their eyes.

Marcus gave both trays to Candy, who opened hers

immediately after setting Felicia's to the side.

"What's up babe?", Marcus said, giving Candy a kiss on the forehead, since her mouth was already full.

"Slow down Candy", Felicia yelled from across the room.

Rhameek took a seat under one of the empty dryers and began to flirt with a few of the girls who were under the other dryers, about to nod off, before he made his entrance.

"What's up Yvette?", Marcus said, as he left Candy alone with her food, and took a minute to observe Yvette's handiwork.

"Ain't nothing Marcus", Yvette answered "Trying to get these broads up outta here. So I can go get fly like them, and hang out for a lil bit tonight."

Marcus smiled and turned his attention to Felicia, who seemed to be in pain, as Yvette continued to whip her head into shape.

"I see you got a fresh bag of hair Felicia." Marcus joked.

Felicia responded with a flip of her middle finger as she cut her eyes towards Rhameek, who was, evidently, engaged in an entertaining conversation with the two girls under the dryer. Because, both were giggling and smiling ear to ear.

Marcus, noticing Felicia's attention was elsewhere, glanced back at Candy, who was still stuffing her mouth, before he made his way to another chair to observe Kenya, one of Yvette's co-workers.

"You gone be here for awhile" he commented to the girl who sat in the chair, with a look of frustration on her face, as Kenya took her time weaving tiny micro-braids into her hair.

Marcus continued to walk about the salon, checking out the other girls who were hard at work in "Yvette's house of Beauty."

"Hard curls, huh?" He said, touching the tiny curls on the back of a girl's head; with two fingers. "You need a lil more spritz", he said before moving down the line to the next booth.

"That's nice" he said, complementing the next girls hair

"everybody can't wear an updo. It suits your face though."
"Thank you, I was hoping it looked alright", the light
skinned girl said, with a big smile on her face, making her
already chinky eyes look even smaller.

"That's you all day" he responded before walking off.

Felicia bumped Yvette with her elbow drawing her attention
to Candy, who sat with a chicken leg halfway to her mouth,
as she glared at Marcus from a distance.

"I see you got a lil Doobie Wrap goin on." He said to the
girl in the next booth, making her blush. "And what we got
here?" He said approaching a girl at the nail station. "I see
you gettin a fill in, why you don't just cut that acrylic mess
off and go natural with French tips", he suggested.

The girl seemed to be contemplating his advice when
Candy's voice boomed across the room "Marcus" she said,
as if she were talking to a child.

Marcus turned only to see Candy staring him down. "Ain't
you and Rah got somewhere to be?" She said.

"Uh, No!" Marcus answered before turning his attention
back towards the nail station. "What's this color called?" He
asked the nail tech who was hard at work. Before Marcus got
an answer, he felt a thump, as the half-eaten chicken leg
Candy threw in his direction hit him on the side of the face.
Marcus turned towards Candy with a look of confusion on
his face.

"You doin too much!" she barked. "Don't make me show
out in here!", she said, pointing towards the door.

"What's wrong baby?"

"Bye Marcus, see you later on", she stated flatly, still
pointing towards the exit. Marcus looked around,
embarrassed, as all the other women in the shop gave him
that "DAMN!", "she got you in check" look. Marcus turned
towards Yvette and Felicia.

"Go on. Git nigga!", Felicia said imitating Candy and
pointing at the door. "And take your mutt with you." She
added, pointing towards Rhameek.

Rhameek gave Marcus a look of disbelief and shook his head "couldn't be me" was the look he gave Marcus.

Marcus looked towards Candy one last time. She stood, stiff as a statue, still pointing towards the exit. And he decided it was time for him to leave; before she got completely out of hand.

"Come on Rah" he said as he headed for the door with Candy on his heels.

Rhameek stood, giving the girls one last slick line before walking off, stopping only long enough to snatch up Felicia's tray full of food.

"What you doin Rah?" Felicia whined.

"What it look like", he responded before heading towards the door, following Candy as she escorted Marcus all the way out.

"And you give that back" Candy demanded, pointing at the box in Rhameek's hand. She held her hand out, waiting for him to hand the food over.

Rhameek smiled before opening the box. Candy watched as he, nonchalantly, pulled out a chicken leg and bit a chunk off of it, then slapped the half naked bone into her extended palm.

"I ain't Marcus" he said as he made his way out the door and left Candy standing, with a chicken bone in her hand, and a look of anger on her face.

Peabo sat with his head laid back, staring at the ceiling. He felt all his muscles began to relax as all the tension from the day's events seemed to disappear almost instantly.

He exhaled deeply and turned his attention from the ceiling to the girl kneeling in front of him. The girl began to rise slowly, removing the glass of Hennessey from Peabo's grip. Maintaining eye contact with him, she raised the glass to her lips and let the thick creamy substance drip slowly from her lower lip into the glass.

Peabo watched with a look of amazement on his face as she

stirred the drink with her finger, mixing the new ingredients into the Hennessey. Then parted her lips again, allowing three big ice cubes to roll out of her mouth, one by one, into the glass.

The girl flashed him a big Colgate smile, then winked her eye at him, before turning the glass up and downing the drink with one gulp.

"Taste like Kailua with Cream" she said, setting the glass down on the table. "Plus a girl need her protein" she added.

"It does the body good" Peabo replied; admiring her thick thighs and other assets, as she walked towards the makeshift bar in the back of Mike's rim shop and poured Peabo another drink in a fresh glass.

"Fat ass and hospitable, what more can a man ask for", Peabo thought to himself.

Peabo was glad he decided to stop by Mike's shop, this girl was just what the doctor ordered, the perfect remedy for his frustrations.

She didn't waste no time for small talk, no sooner than they had entered the small room in back and he had fixed his drink and took one sip, she had pushed him down onto the couch and asked him, "Do you like magic?"

Before he could respond, she stuck her fingers in his glass and fished out three big ice cubes, one by one. Swallowing them whole, she opened her mouth; showing him they were gone.

"That's a hell of a trick", he said "and you didn't even get a brain freeze."

She smiled and responded, "I haven't done the trick yet baby, this is the part where I need your assistance."

"What you need from me?" He asked.

"Come on baby, everybody knows a magician can't perform without a magic wand." She said as she unzipped his pants.

The last thing he remembered hearing was the words "Abra Kadabra", then he felt a warmth like never before engulf him. Then he began to feel a cold chill run through his body, and a tingling sensation flow through his spine, causing his fingers and toes to go numb. His mind seemed to drift and his eyes rolled into the back of his head, causing a kaleidoscope of colors to explode behind his eyelids. Then he had come back out of the Blackness, as if returning from an outer body experience. And that was when he had found hisself staring at the ceiling.

She walked towards Peabo seductively, then leaned forward, handing him his drink; showing him a little cleavage in the process.

"So you liked my trick?" She asked with a devilish grin.

"Absolutely baby" Peabo said, stroking his long beard, before taking a sip of his drink. He watched as she grabbed his old glass from the table. She poured more Hennessey over the same three ice cubes that she had swallowed earlier; minus the milky substance that she had gulped down along with the Hennessey.

"How did she do that?" He thought to hisself.

"A magician never reveals her tricks" she said, holding her drink up to the light, swirling the ice cubes around in the glass as if she knew what he was thinking.

"You read minds too?" He asked. She only smiled in response, showing off her full, wet lips. "You ain't even tell me yo name" he continued.

"You don't strike me as the type who would care."

"Well let's just say, I'll definitely be calling you soon. And when I do, I need to know what to call you by."

The girl smiled again " You can call me Rhonda" she said "and you might as well get use to callin that name big boy."

"It's like that?" Peabo questioned, not looking convinced.

Rhonda pulled an ice cube from her drink and put it in her mouth. Peabo watched as she began to chew on the ice, making a muffled crunching noise as she approached him.

Rhonda continued to crush the ice up in her mouth as she grabbed Peabo's hand and placed it between her legs, underneath her skirt.

She felt like wet silk as she stood over him guiding his hand
back and forth. She swallowed the ice then spoke "is it like
that?" she said as she continued to rub his hand between her
legs.

Peabo was aroused as he felt her pulsate. She let out a slight
moan and he felt her warm juices turn cold, as she tensed up,
squeezing his hand, tight, between her thighs.

Rhonda laughed, when she saw Peabo's face twist up in
confusion, as she removed his hand and took a few steps
back.

"You tell me if it's like that" she said as Peabo sat, looking
dumb founded, looking from her to the solid ice cube he held
in his hand.

"What the fu..."

"Abra Kadabra" she interrupted with a sly grin.

"Call me" she said as she walked towards the door, stopping
long enough to write her number on a napkin that lay on the
small bar.

Peabo still sat motionless as she left the room. He shook his
head, as if coming out of a trance. Looking around the room,
making sure nobody was around, he leaned forward to sniff
the ice cube he held in his palm.

With a shrug of his shoulders, he put the ice cube in his
mouth and crunched it up. Then, he raised his glass of
Hennessey to his lips and threw his head back, consuming it
in one gulp, before making his way to the bar to snatch up
the napkin with her number on it.

"While you right there pour me a shot" Mike said as he
entered the room, wiping sweat from his forehead. Peabo
filled a glass and turned to face Mike, who reached for the
glass with grease covered hands.

"Look at you" Peabo grimaced, looking at the grease marks
that were scattered all over Mike's chest and arms. "What
you do, lay on the tires nigga?"

Mike waved Peabo off before plopping down on the couch.

"How long you had that new parking lot groupie hangin

around here, Mike?"

Parking lot groupie's were what Mike and Peabo called the numerous girls who seemed to hang at Mike's place of business on a daily basis trying to 'snag a baller', which didn't bother Mike too much, because it was convenient for him and his boys when they wanted to get their rocks off.

They didn't have to go any further than his parking lot, where the girls gathered everyday and hung around gossiping about everybody that stopped through the shop, including each other.

"Which one?" Mike asked.

"The one who just left", Peabo answered.

"You mean that thick ass broad who just left outta here and peeled out in that blue Lexus?"

"Lexus" Peabo repeated "you been tricking a lil too hard these days Mike, you lettin these groupie's make a come up off you like that?"

"Picture me paying a Bitch" Mike said "besides I never seen her, but two times, and that was when she followed you in the door and when she left out. As a matter of fact, I don't even remember seeing her pull up."

"Me either" Peabo said "but I'm glad I came when I did Playboy. Cause while you was out there getting greasy, I was back here gettin shined up." He said as he poured himself another drink, then took a seat beside Mike and began to tell him about Rhonda and her "bag of tricks."

Rhameek sat on the porch, laughing, while Marcus flipped him the bird.

"Unk the nigga sprung I'm telling you and he scared to death of her", Rhameek said as he continued to laugh after giving his Uncle Zone the rundown on the incident at the mall as well as the scene at Yvette's salon.

"Let me tell you somein Marcus, this old money talkin, I been doin this since presidents had small faces and before ya'll young niggas was even thought about, so pay attention to what I'm bout to tell you." Zone said, pausing long enough to take a sip of the Gin he held in his hand and making sure he had their undivided attention.

"Here we go again, he done got this nigga started 'drunk Pimpin' 101", Marcus thought to hisself as Zone continued. "Love is a beautiful thing, love can make you laugh, make you cry, make you do right or make you do wrong."

"Ain't that an Al Green song", Marcus interrupted.

"Love will even make you kill", Zone continued as if he didn't even hear the comment.

The last words rang in Marcus' ear as Zone spoke them. Visions of the night before flashed through his mind, as well as past events in his life; how many times had his love for Candy caused him to act violently?

"Love will also sometimes make you deaf, dumb and blind to the fact that, maybe, you the only one in love" Zone paused, taking another sip of Gin before moving along. "There's a difference between sayin you love someone, and really being in love with them. Its rare that you find two people who are really in love with each other. And its usually the one that's really and truly in love who gets hurt in the end."

Marcus frowned and was about to protest when Zone threw up a finger.

"Hold up young money, let me finish. I know you and Candy got 'somein special' goin on" he said, making quotation marks with his fingers. "And its something that's been going on for as long as I can remember, but the question is, to whose benefit? I also know, the girl done had yo nose open since you was yay high" Zone said, as he stood and raised his hand, palm down, to a height just below his waist. "And she keep you running around, flipping out on niggas, risking yo life and shit, cause you head over heels in love. But when shit hit the fan and yo ass get caught up, what then, where she gone be? You think love gone keep her in yo corner? I hate to say it young blood, but truth is, they only care bout one thing, and love don't pay the bills!"

"Ya'll act like she don't be out here flippin out over me" Marcus said, sounding defensive "as a matter of fact, ain't that what started this conversation? The fact that she just showed her ass over me!"

"Yeah, you right" Zone said "to an extent, because we did start this conversation because of her showing out. But, don't get it twisted, don't get me wrong Marcus, Candy a good girl, but she a woman first, never forget that. Truth be told, it sounds to me like she flipped out to show ownership over yo black ass. That wasn't bout you, or her love for you. That was bout her, it was bout showin them other hoes that she got you in check. She know you a good man, and she know all them other broads lookin for a good man. I mean, you got her out here spoiled to death, having everything her way, and them other hoes see that. It's 'Candy's World', that's the attitude you got her runnin around wit. Truth is, you just another piece of property for her to flash in their face, something everybody else want, but can't get cause its hers, no different from that big ass rock she runnin round here flaunting on her finger. You an object nigga. And just like all the shit you give her, its only valuable to her if she feels like its something that the others want. But like I said, wait till you find yo' self in a predicament where you no longer the 'Grand Prize' then see how far she willing to go to keep you, or if she even want you period; or any of the shit that comes with you. I hate to tell you Marcus, but that Bonnie and Clyde shit died with Bonnie and Clyde. They don't make women like that no more." Zone said, as a matter of factly, concluding his speech.

"No offense Zone" Marcus said "I know you a Playa from the Himalayas and all. But you don't know what you talkin bout."

Zone only responded with a slick grin as he gazed out towards the front yard, where Champ lay, stretched out in the grass, enjoyin the sun. Zone walked to the edge of the porch and picked up a big rawhide bone, which belonged to his own pit "Zeus."

"Champ here you go boy" Zone called out as he threw the big bone out into the yard. The bone landed beside Champ with a thud as it hit the ground. Champ stood and approached the bone. Sniffing at it, momentarily, he decided he wasn't interested, and returned back to his previous spot to lay back down in the sun.

Marcus sat in silence, thinking about everything Zone had said "he don't know shit" Marcus thought to hisself.

"I'm bout to fix me another drink" Zone said breaking the silence, as he opened the front door to enter the house. As soon as he opened the door, his dog, Zeus, burst out of the house and ran to Rhameek, then to Marcus, just long enough to sniff and greet them both with a lick on the palm, before jumping off of the porch. Zeus ran across the yard where Champ still lay, sprawled out in the grass, minding his business, until Zeus approached the big rawhide bone that lay in the yard.

Almost immediately, Champ jumped to his feet and began to growl, challenging Zeus to touch the bone.

Zeus refused to back down, especially since the bone belonged to him anyway. And within seconds, the two huge dogs were locked up with their massive jaws entangled in a death grip.

Marcus watched as Rhameek jumped off of the porch and ran to break the dogs up. While Rhameek struggled with the dogs, Marcus turned to look at Zone. Standing in the doorway with a fresh drink in his hand, he glared at the dogs with a smirk on his face.

Zone took a sip of his drink. Turning his attention to Marcus, he let out a slight chuckle before walking off, shaking his head from side to side.

"Wise ass", Marcus mumbled before hopping off the porch and running to help Rhameek break the two dogs up.

CHAPTER 8

The atmosphere was similar to that of a block party, when they pulled into the crowded parking lot of Club Oxygen. The line was wrapped around the building and growing longer and longer as more and more girls crossed the parking lot, looking their "best". Some with every intention of "snagging a baller", some hoping to catch their man in the act of "balling too hard" and some who probably wouldn't even make it to the line, thanks to the 'parking lot pimps' that simply played the hoods of their cars, hoping to detour some of the well dressed ladies to the hotel.

"I told you it was gonna be packed tonight" Felicia screamed over the music as she entered the parking lot.

"Felicia turn that shit down" Yvette yelled from the backseat.

"Vette you complain too much, you and Candy both" Felicia countered.

"The music too loud, the smoke choking me, blah, blah, blah" Felicia continued mocking Candy and Yvette. "Ya'll hoes should've rode with yo sister Yvette. Cause ya'll gettin on my nerves."

"Whatever" Candy interrupted from the passenger seat " would you please just park so we can get up outta this car."

"I know that's right", Kenya, Yvette's co-worker chimed in from the back seat, "cause I'm tryin to get up in here and find me a baby daddy."

"Say it again girl" Felicia said, reaching back to give Kenya a high five.

"There go two spots right there" Candy said, pointing Felicia in the right direction. Felicia headed for one of the spaces as Yvette waved her arm out the window for her sister to follow their lead. Heads turned as both cars parked and all the doors flew open on each one.

The eight girls stepped out, after giving themselves one last look in the rearview mirror; making sure their hair was tight and their lips were nice and wet looking.

The catcalls began immediately, coming from all directions as the girls strolled across the parking lot. Candy, Felicia, Yvette and Kenya took lead as Yvette's sister, Crystana, and three of her friends followed close behind.

"Damn, that line is long." Erica, one of Crystana's friends, stated.

"Don't worry about that" Felicia said "just stay in step." The girls eased up towards the front of the line, not even bothering to look around to see where all the "psst","psst" and "hey sexy" or any other creative remarks were coming from.

"What's up ladies?" One of the bouncers said waving them to the door "where's my man" the bouncer asked turning his attention to Candy.

"He's probably in there" she answered.

"Nah not yet, but I'm sure he'll be here soon, ya'll go ahead up in there." He said as he held the line, allowing them to pass.

"Thank you" the girls said in unison. The bouncer waved them off with a smile before turning his attention back to the long line "alright ya'll back it up! Let's get some order out this mothafucka!" he yelled.

"Damn!, yo man got it like that?" Erica said as they walked through the door.

Candy only responded with a half smile; not liking the twinkle in Erica's eye, or her sudden interest in her man.

The music began to get louder and louder as they passed the front counter, not bothering to pay because it was ladies night. Felicia immediately began to gyrate her hips on rhythm to the music as she continued to walk, heading straight for the bar. "Apple Martini's on you" she yelled, pointing to a guy in a button down shirt; who she didn't even know. "What ya'll want?" she said, looking at the other girls. The girls began to scream out orders at the bartender. While Felicia stood, with her hands on her hips, eyeballing the guy in the button down, until he, reluctantly, dug in his pockets; producing enough cash to cover the tab.

"Thank you sexy", Felicia said as she got close up on him, caressing his cheek, causing him to smile from ear to ear. Candy and Yvette stood off to the side, observing Felicia as she went through the motions only long enough for the others to get their drinks.

Then, she whispered something in his ear, making his smile grow even bigger, before she walked off, giving him an eyeful of her backside, rolling her eyes as she walked towards Candy and Yvette.

"You ain't no good" Yvette said, laughing at Felicia as she approached.

"No good?" Felicia said "six drinks for free, I think I did better than good. And if ya'll two hoes wasn't tryin to be all suditty, it would've been eight" she continued.

"No thank you, somebody got to drive ya'll drunk asses home tonight " Candy said.

"I know that's right" Felicia and the others chanted, holding their cups in the air.

"But anyway" Felicia said "we ain't spend all this money on these fly ass outfits to stand still and pose. If that's the case, we could've left them on the mannequins in the mall. And lord knows, I ain't seen a mannequin, yet, that make a dress look like this." She said as she poked her ass out and began to walk back and forth, in front of the other girls, as if she were a model on a runway.

"Felicia you happy you finally grew a lil ass" Yvette said.

"And you mad cause my hair is as long as yours tonight;

Miss America" Felicia shot back as she flipped her hair at Yvette and made her way into the crowd with Crystana, Kenya, Erica, Neese and Shanice following close behind.

All six of them moved to the music as they blended into the thick crowd, with Candy and Yvette taking up the rear; following their lead.

"Where you been all my life?" Rhameek said to the bartender as she poured him another shot.

Marcus leaned on the bar, beside him, drinking a double shot of gin; with grapefruit juice. Checking out his surroundings, as a girl approached and leaned on the bar next to him.

"What's up?" she said.

"Chillin" Marcus replied.

"What ya'll gettin into tonight?" She pressed on.

Marcus sipped his drink then responded "just having a few drinks that's all."

"You don't talk much, do you?" The girl said, smiling, showing off her big dimples.

Marcus shrugged his shoulders and smiled back. The girl moved in closer "so what's up, you wanna go to the V.I.P. wit me?"

"Nah, I'm good; we bout to bail in a few minutes" he answered.

The girl poked her lips out, exaggerating her disappointment. Then, she took her index finger and traced it down the center of his chest, all the way down to his crotch. "Too bad. Maybe next time?" She said, before walking off.

Marcus continued to sip his drink as she moved across the room, her calf muscles flexing in the high heel shoes. She walked gracefully across the floor. Looking back over her shoulder, she winked at him before she made her way to a table full of guys. Bending over, she whispered something to one of them, showing Marcus a view of what he was missing out on.

"Nigga you kill me" Rhameek said, turning his attention from the bartender to Marcus.

Marcus stood in a daze, sipping his drink, while admiring the girl from behind and thinking how her ass was shaped like one of those heart shaped boxes of chocolate that they sale on Valentines Day.

"You said somein?" Marcus said snapping out of his trance.

"You heard me nigga, I said you kill me, always tryin to be Mr. Goody two shoes." Rhameek said, making quotation marks with his fingers.

"Why? Cause I ain't want a lap dance?" Marcus questioned.

"I'm just sayin dawg; loosen up." Rhameek responded "I mean, I know you in love and shit. I love Candy to death too. But you best believe, she at the club right now wit a gang of niggas in her face. Kee-Kee'in and Ha-Ha'in, having a good time, while you sittin here lookin crazy, scared to get a dance and even more scared you actually might like the shit."

"What!" Marcus snapped "You act like I never got a dance before."

"Yeah, when the moon blue" Rhameek waved his hand "you'll be all right Playboy."

"I'm alright now dawg", Marcus gave a weak smile "besides, same way Candy don't like me in no broads face, Kee-Keein," He made quotation marks with his fingers. "She know not to have no niggas all in her face wit all that kee-kee, ha ha shit."

"Yeah right."

"Anyway. Lets get one more drink, then we got to get to the club before the bar closes" Marcus said, changing the subject.

"Hold up Playa. We gone make it. I already told the fellas to meet us out here, then we all gone ride out together. Just give em a few more minutes and we out." Rhameek said slapping Marcus on the back.

Marcus only nodded as Rhameek turned his attention back to the bartender.

Marcus glanced across the room, only to catch the girl with the big dimples staring him directly in the face as she danced for the guys at the table. She moved slow and sensuous, never breaking eye contact with Marcus, as she continued to entertain the group.

She smiled and Marcus averted his eyes to his cell phone; as if he was about to use it. Then he looked back up, only to see her still staring at him.

He took another sip of his Gin, emptying the glass. Then turned to face the bartender to avoid her gaze. "Give me another double" he said. He looked up at his reflection in the mirror behind the bar and caught a glimpse of "Dimples" reflection, and then he saw Rhameek's reflection and realized Rhameek was watching him.

Rhameek shook his head from side to side.

"What?" Marcus asked. Rhameek didn't respond.

"I wish these niggas would hurry up." Marcus continued as he checked the time on his cell phone. The bartender slid him another drink then got back into her conversation with Rhameek. Marcus sipped from his glass, while focusing his attention on anything but the mirror in front of him, as he sat in deep thought; thinking about what Rhameek had just said.

"Don't worry Playa, I was just fuckin wit you" Rhameek said as if he was reading his homeboys mind.

Marcus looked up to see that Rhameek had ended his conversation with the bartender and had slid close to him. "I'm just sayin, enjoy yo'self. Cause I'm sure she doin her right now."

"I'm enjoyin myself dawg, this what I do for fun" Marcus said, holding his glass up. "I lay back and chill, that's what I do and I'm sure she doin the same."

"And I'm sho you absolutely right Playa." Rhameek said, raising his own glass up in the air; toasting his partner.

"What's up Candy, it's all right if I speak to you ain't it?"

"Boy you crazy" Candy said breaking out into a fit of

laughter as the guy in front of her continued to look around, pretending to be paranoid, with a mock expression of fear on his face.

"I mean it's all right if I say hello to you ain't it? That nigga ain't hiding in the corner nowhere, waitin to jump out on a nigga, is he?"

Candy continued to laugh.

"I'm serious baby girl you got that nigga fucked up, he ain't got to never worry bout me tryin you if that thang make a nigga lose his mind like that."

"Sonny you stupid boy" Candy said, still laughing, while Yvette stood beside her, rolling her eyes, as one of Sonny's partners whispered weak lines in her ear.

"I mean damn Candy, what is it bout you make a nigga act like that?" Sonny asked looking her up and down.

Yvette cleared her throat and pushed the "game whisperer" away from her, then turned her attention to Sonny.

"Nigga you bein a lil too nosey." Yvette said "and if you know what I know, you'll go find you somein else to do, before dat nigga fall up in here for real."

Sonny bawled his face up at Yvette "what the fuck is you talkin bout Vette? Candy know I'm just trippin wit her, me and her go way back." He said glancing at Candy with a slick grin on his face.

"Whatever! How bout you trip yo lil ass on over there somewhere" Yvette said pointing out towards the dance floor "and take yo smelly breath friend wit you."

Sonny's boy gave her a hurt look "why you got to act like that MA?" He said.

Yvette waved him off, "Miss me wit that MA shit nigga, cause I never have and never will feed or clothe yo ass. And I be damn if I'm gone be the one to teach you to aim yo lil ass wee-wee at the toilet."

"Come on MA you trippin!"

"Nigga can't you comprehend? I ain't yo mammy!" Yvette snapped raising her voice "come on Candy."

Sonny and his boy stood looking dumb founded as Yvette pulled Candy away.

"Vette why you do that, what's wrong wit you?"

"What's wrong wit me!" Vette said raising her voice another octave "Bitch if Marcus would've walked up in here and seen that nigga all in yo face, skinnin and grinnin, it would've been some action up in here."

"He was just trippin Vette. He didn't mean no harm."

"Candy you can't be that naive, the nigga was gettin a lil too personal, lookin you up and down and asking you "what make that nigga act that way." Yvette said imitating Sonny "we go way back" she continued mocking him.

"Chile please" Yvette spat "only reason he know either one of us is cause his cousin use to mess wit my sister, bout four years ago, and he talkin dat way back bullshit."

"I'm sure he ain't mean it like that" Candy said. Yvette rolled her eyes.

"You been round Marcus too much Vette. You think everybody up to something."

"Whatever Candy. And you been round Marcus far longer than me, so if I know the nigga will go blank, like this", she said snapping her finger. "Then you damn well should know better."

"So what you sayin Vette, I ain't suppose to conversate wit nobody?"

"No Candy, I'm just sayin when you conversate be aware of what you conversating about."

"Whatever Vette, he ain't mean no harm, let's go find Felicia and the others." Candy said as she began to walk off then stopped and opened her purse. "You sure you don't need one of these?" She said to Yvette, producing a small tampon from her purse.

Yvette rolled her eyes and flipped her middle finger up at her. "No thank you Candy. But I'm glad you came prepared, cause if Marcus fall up in here and catch you 'kee-keein' and carryin on, somebody might need a few of those to plug the holes he gone put through they ass." Yvette countered, killing Candy's attempt at a joke.

"It ain't that serious; he was just joking Vette." Candy repeated again before walking off.

Sonny stood at the bar watching as Yvette and Candy continued to move along. "Look at that ass on her." He said motioning for his partner to look.

"Yeah, red thick."

"Fuck Vette red ass nigga, I'm talkin bout Candy."

"Yeah, she is thick to death dawg" his boy replied "I heard that nigga of hers is a fool."

"Yeah, he a fool alright" Sonny said "he a fool if he think ain't nobody else out here hittin that, you see how that Bitch was gigglin all in my face. Fuck that punk ass nigga, cause I'm gone dig up in that. And when I'm through, he can have the Bitch back."

"I know that's right dawg" his man said, giving him dap as they watched Candy and Yvette fade away into the crowd.

CHAPTER 9

Marcus rolled through the parking lot, at a slow pace, taking in the scene that surrounded him.

"Look at these killas" Rhameek said as he sat in the passenger seat, looking at a group of guys who were 'mean muggin' them as they passed by.

Marcus continued to roll at a slow pace. Then came to a sudden stop, when he looked in the rearview mirror and noticed that the car that was following him had come to a halt.

"What these niggas doin" Marcus said.

Rhameek turned in his seat. Looking back just in time to see the passenger door on the Delta 88, that was following them, fly open. And the group of guys they had just passed, throwing their hands up in the air.

"Look at this mufucka" Marcus said, turning the radio down only to hear the 'killas' that were giving them the eye copping pleas.

"It ain't like that dawg" one of them said.

"Shut the fuck up, I ain't talking to you" the short stocky guy who hopped out of the Delta 88 barked at the guy who was talking.

"I'm talkin to this one right here, why you screw facin my folk when they rode by?"

"My bad, I'm just drunk dawg, that's all. I ain't mean no harm." The guy responded; sounding like he was about to break down crying, as he looked wide eyed at the man in front of him, who only stood about 5 feet tall. He was holding a gun that was almost as big as he was.

Rhameek hopped out of the car, catching his mans attention. "Shawt Change, leave them niggas alone dawg."

"Rah these niggas lookin like they wanna try ya'll or somein", Shawt Change said, speaking to Rhameek without breaking eye contact with the group of guy's in front of him.

"Light em up!" the driver of the Delta 88 yelled as the guy's in the back of the car began to laugh and yell out the window as well.

"Yeah Shawt Change make it crack one time!"

"Ya'll cut dat shit out" Rhameek yelled "Shawt Change put dat shit up, look around you dawg you scaring all the women off."

Shawt Change looked around and realized he had the flow of traffic backed up and noticed a few girls scurrying across the parking lot, some ducking behind cars; out of fear that something was about to jump off.

"And Ron, you need to quit boostin that nigga up." Rhameek continued, this time speaking to the driver of the Delta 88.

Rhameek jumped back in the car with Marcus and observed Shawt Change in the rearview as he said a few more words to the group of guy's before hopping back in the big Blue Delta 88 and slamming the door, allowing the flow of traffic to take it's course once again.

Marcus turned the music back up, as if nothing ever happened, and proceeded to roll through the parking lot; looking around as the atmosphere returned back to normal. The girls who were trying to get away from the area, just seconds ago, began to make their way back to their spots; where they were posted up before. And the parking lot pimps got back on their job; glad nothing had transpired before they had a chance to snag a bed partner for the night.

"Can't take them fools nowhere" Rhameek said before he burst out laughing.

Marcus laughed as well; "yeah he had em shook back there." Marcus replied.

"Anyway lets park and get inside where the real action at." Rhameek said. Marcus made one last pass through the parking lot before backing into a V.I.P. slot close to the entrance. He and Rhameek sat in the car, with the windows down, watching the girl's stroll by, making their way towards the line.

Marcus laughed as a small group of girls stopped right in front of his car and began to move their hips to the rhythm of the sounds blasting from his stereo.

"That's my shit" he heard one of the girls say as the "Zap's Greatest Hits" CD commenced to play and Roger Troutman's voice echoed across the parking lot.

"Hey lady... let me tell you why... I can't live my life... without you... ohh baby..." Marcus continued to laugh as the girls continued to dance as if they were at a neighborhood fish fry instead of a club parking lot.

"Drunk ass broads" Rhameek said, laughing as Roger Troutman continued to hold the girls in a trance with his computer digitized voice. "I... wanna be your man... I wanna be your man..."

Marcus looked to his left and saw Ron, Shawt Change, G-Lo and Fly moving towards the line. "There they go" Marcus said as he rolled the windows up and cut the music off; earning himself a look of disappointment from the females who were dancing.

Ron had parked in a secluded spot, like he always did, making sure he chose a spot that he could get to quick and make a swift exit if necessary.

Rhameek and Marcus got out of the car and made their way towards the entrance, where Ron and the others stood engaged in conversation with the girls who were just dancing in front of his car.

"What's up dawg" the bouncer said as Marcus and Rhameek approached.

"Ain't nothing" Marcus replied as he slapped hands with the huge bouncer, greeting him with a semi-bear hug and slap on the back.

"What's up Playa" Rhameek said, greeting him in the same manner.

"Yo girl already up in there dawg" the bouncer said as he half patted Marcus and Rhameek down. "I see ya'll got the squad wit ya" he said, pointing towards Shawt Change and the others, who were still occupied with the group of girls. "Do me a favor and tell em to be good tonight" the bouncer continued.

"Don't worry. We got em big dawg" Marcus said before turning his attention towards the others. "What ya'll gone do? We bout to fall up in here!"

"Ya'll go ahead" Ron said, waving them off with a big smile on his face, while cutting his eyes towards the 'fish fry dancers', "I'll be in, in a few."

"Yeah me too" G-Lo added.

Marcus gave a nod and proceeded through the door as Rhameek and the others followed close behind. He knew Ron and G-Lo probably wouldn't even make it inside, they preferred the parking lot over the club, and he also knew Ron always parked in a secluded spot for two reasons. For one, in case something jumped off, he kept an arsenal in the car and wanted to be in a strategic position if the need arose to use them. And for two, he always managed to convince a female to "sit in the car and chat with him." And he didn't want to take any chances of his car being spotted by his "crazy ass baby mama" Charlene, while he and a girl were in the midst of "chatting."

They entered the club, stopping only long enough to pay at the front counter and greet a few of the other bouncers they knew.

Marcus and Rhameek headed for the front bar. Shawt Change and Fly went in the opposite direction, choosing to go to the bar that sat directly in the middle of the crowded dance floor instead.

Marcus approached the crowded bar, and made eye contact with one of the bartenders, before throwing four fingers in the air. She gave him a big smile and a nod before laying fours cups out on the bar.

He and Rhameek watched as she went to work, mixing the alcohol from several different bottles, all containing white liquor, then added something to it; giving it color.

"Four Red Devils", she said as she slid the cups, filled with what looked like Hawaiian Punch, towards Marcus. He passed two of the cups to Rhameek and took two for hisself, after sliding her a few bills across the bar. "Thank you baby" the bartender said, knowing the extra bill was her tip.

Marcus took a sip of the drink and frowned up, due to the potency of it. "Thank you" he said after fighting back the burning sensation in his chest.

"You know I got to make it strong for you baby", she replied. "But do me a favor and be good tonight, because if you get in any trouble I'm gonna feel like I made those drinks a lil too strong and I know you don't want me to start watering you down like I do these other niggas."

"I definitely don't want you watering me down" he responded. "You got my word, I'll be good." He said flashing her a smile before walking off.

He and Rhameek took up a spot on the wall in the hallway that led from one section of the club to the other. This was Rhameek's favorite spot, because he could catch girls going in and out of the bathroom, as opposed to walking around, breaking a sweat, and bumping shoulders with others all night in the crowded club.

Marcus leaned back against the wall, staring at hisself in the full-length mirror that covered the wall in front of him, from floor to ceiling, and extended the full length of the hallway.

He wore a pair of white Air Force one's with a Khaki material covering the heel and toe of the shoes. The Nike check on the side was covered in a Khaki material as well.

The shoes went well with the Khaki pants and shirt he donned. The outfit was similar to a Dickies suit, the only difference being the Sean John signature written on the back pocket of the pants, and the small pocket on the shirt. The shirt was unbuttoned, showing off a bright white tee shirt underneath; setting a nice backdrop for the modest chain he wore, which only came to the center of his chest.

The light bounced off of the charm that dangled from the chain. Between that and the light reflecting off of his grill, as well as his hand, he was easy to spot. He adjusted his fitted cap, also covered in a Khaki material with white lettering on the front, giving it that trademark tilt and lean, before removing the Fendi frames from his face; just long enough to clear a few smudges from the dark lenses.

"You bout pretty as me" Rhameek said after watching Marcus go through the motions. Marcus placed his frames back in position and responded with a light shimmering smile.

Rhameek began to imitate Marcus, taking advantage of the moment to check hisself out. The big diamond studs he wore in both ears glistened as he brushed his hand over his Caesar, letting the light bounce off of his pinky ring while admiring the waves that covered his head. His chain was far from modest; he wore a heavy link, which hung to his belly, with a large, diamond flooded cross hanging from it. He also wore a flashy wristwatch on each arm, the face on both covered in ice. "I'm a two timing nigga" he would say; when girls asked why he wore two watches. Rhameek had no shame about his doggish ways with women, he was actually proud of the reputation he had and loved to hear the ladies say "Rhameek you ain't shit."

His sneakers were blinding white, with money green Nike checks on the sides; matching perfectly with the green and white Polo shirt he was wearing.

"Excuse me Miss" Rhameek said, stopping a girl who was leaving the bathroom "would you mind doin me a favor?"

"What kind of favor?" she said, looking at him suspiciously.

"I was just wondering if you could tell me how I look." He said as he took a few steps back and began to rotate in a full circle.

The girl only shook her head and blushed, trying to hold back her smile as she waved Rhameek off and continued to move along down the hallway. "She's speechless" Rhameek said.

"Probably don't wanna open her mouth cause she scared she gone choke on all that cologne you wearin." Marcus replied.

"Hata" Rhameek said as he began to make a display of wiping hisself down from head to toe.

"You missed a spot Playa", a female voice spoke. Marcus and Rhameek both turned their attention to the source. A thick, voluptuous stallion stood in front of them both, in her revealing attire, with a sensual smile on her face. She reached out with her manicured hand, and grabbed Rhameek's shirt collar, giving it a slight pop, "there you go Playa." She said as she brushed his shoulder off for him.

"What would I do without you Rah Rah baby?" Rhameek said with a smile on his face.

"Settle for less." She said, returning his smile with one of her own.

Rhameek threw his hands up in submission "you absolutely right" he stated. "How things goin?"

"I do what I do and I get it done" she said with a wink of her eye. Rah Rah licked her lips and turned her attention towards Marcus, "what's up sexy. You ain't speakin today?"

Marcus cleared his throat "What's up Rah Rah."

She laughed at his nervousness "I'll see ya'll later, alright? I got things to do." She said.

"Get it done then" Rhameek said, slapping her on the ass as she turned to walk away.

She stopped and looked back, "Rhameek you know not to make this thing jiggle like that in front of Marcus", she said, rubbing her hands across her firm, shapely bottom "look at him. He already can't keep his eyes off of it."

Marcus turned his attention towards his drink, and instead of using the straw, turned the whole cup up, gulping down the liquor.

Rah Rah laughed and walked away slowly, showing off her goods.

"That's my girl!" Rhameek exclaimed as she walked away, then he turned to face Marcus who stood staring at her with an empty cup in his hand.

"Look at you; wipe yo mouth Playa you droolin."

Marcus took a napkin and wiped the excess liquor from his chin. "Shut up dawg. Ain't nobody droolin" he argued, not sounding convincing.

"Yeah, whatever, I see how you get all choked up and shit every time she come around. That's why she my number one Bitch, one hit of dat and you'll be like Candy what! Candy who!" Rhameek joked.

Marcus didn't respond, but instead turned his attention towards a familiar face that approached.

Candy and the others were on the dance floor doing their thing. The eight girls were huddled in a tight circle, dancing amongst each other. They stepped away from every man that tried to ease up on them from behind. They continued to dance while ignoring the remarks the men made upon being rejected.

"Gay ass Bitches!" a few of them barked, not taking rejection so well. Occasionally Felicia would grab a passerby and work him over, throwing it on them until she got a rise out of them then sent them on their way.

The DJ switched up the whole vibe and the girls decided to exit the dance floor, not wanting to get caught in the midst of a brawl that was sure to be induced by the heavy bass driven crunk music.

"Let's go to the bathroom and freshen up" Candy suggested. All agreed and they started working their way through the masses, hoping to make it through the crowd without someone spilling something on them and ruining their outfits.

"What's up sexy?" The girl said with a smile on her face, as she approached Marcus and Rhameek.

"What's up, and how did you know my name?" Rhameek replied.

The girl laughed and responded "well actually I was talking to this one" she said pointing at Marcus "but it's nice to meet you too, sexy!" She continued as she extended her hand towards Rhameek. "I'm Tamika. And, you are?"

"Rhameek, but sexy'll do sweetheart, nice to meet you Tamika."

"And how are you?" Tamika said turning towards Marcus.

Marcus smiled as she faced him and she smiled in return, not aware of the fact that Rhameek was standing directly behind her mouthing the words "damn dawg!" As he began to admire her backside and made humping gestures behind her.

"You seem to be in a good mood" she said, not realizing Marcus was trippin off of Rhameek.

"I'm chillin" Marcus replied, not really wanting to engage in conversation with the girl who had hounded him at the mall earlier.

"So does the mystery lady always let you come out alone like this?" the girl asked.

"Nah, she out here somewhere." he answered.

Tamika frowned up "couldn't be me, leaving a man like you to roam around by himself." She said, moving closer as Marcus leaned away from her until his back hit the wall.

Marcus raised a hand to stop her as she moved in a lil too close, "look I think you need to..."

"Oh shit!" Rhameek blurted out, cutting Marcus off in midsentence. Before Marcus was able to look up, he felt something wet splash across his face, followed by a plastic cup that hit him in the chest. And the cup was followed by a solid slap to the side of his face, all in one swift motion.

"What the fuck is this!" Candy screamed, pinning him to the wall and nudging his forehead with her index finger. "Nigga you in here tryin me!"

"Candy go head wit dat bullshit" Marcus countered "it ain't like dat."

Candy mugged him, palming his entire face in her hand. She continued to give him the fifth degree as Yvette, Felicia and the others stood back watching the scene unfold.

"Candy chill out" Felicia said, while she and Yvette shot Tamika nasty looks.

Tamika only smiled, making eye contact with them all as she spoke up. "I'm sorry it's my fault, I was only asking him a question, he made no advances towards me."

Candy stopped and faced Tamika "well that's nice to know, but I got this, thank you." She snapped "this nigga knows the do's and don'ts" she continued as she turned back towards Marcus and bawled her fist up as if she was bout to swing on him again.

"Candy you wrong for this shit" Rhameek said as he grabbed her hand, preventing her from swinging.

Tamika shook her head from side to side then turned and walked off, squeezing between Felicia and the others, smiling the whole time. "Excuse me ladies" she said as she weaved through the girls and went about her business.

"Who this Bitch think she is?" Felicia said, kicking her heels off.

"No Felicia, it ain't her fault, it's this sorry ass nigga" Candy said, trying to break free from Rhameek, and get to Marcus.

Tamika stopped long enough to look Felicia up and down, from head to toe, and let out a slight giggle, before proceeding down the hallway.

Marcus stood to the side, wiping hisself off as Rhameek held Candy, while Yvette and the others held a barefoot

Felicia, not allowing her to pursue Tamika.

"Let's go dawg" Marcus spat "ya'll get ya'll girl" he said before walking off.

Rhameek handed the task, of holding Candy back, off to Yvette; before following Marcus towards the exit.

Candy continued to kick and scream as Marcus headed for the door.

"I see you found yo girl" the bouncer out in front of the club said as he observed the stains on Marcus' shirt.

"How'd you guess?" Marcus replied.

The bouncer laughed, dapping Marcus and Rhameek before they left.

"I ain't been in this mufucka a hour yet and look at me" Marcus complained as he unlocked his car doors.

"Don't worry bout it Playboy" Rhameek replied "It's only soda."

"That ain't the point Rah" Marcus continued as he sped off leaving the club parking lot. "That's twice today she done shined on me on some dumb shit, I mean less than twenty four hours ago we was on some Bonnie and Clyde shit, I just murdered a mufucka right in front of her and here she is tryin me like I'm a scrub."

"That's only cause she know you not gone hurt her dawg." Rhameek assured him. "But on some real shit, you need to quit gettin yo ass whooped over some ass you ain't touched" he continued "speaking of which, who was Shawty?"

Marcus laughed "that was the girl I told you about at the mall today and second of all ain't nobody whooped my ass."

"First of all, you done got chumped, and got yo ass kicked today" Rhameek said "and second of all, you a betta man than me. And third, I oughta kick yo ass fo turning that down." Rhameek said as he gave Marcus a friendly tap on the jaw.

Marcus cracked a smile as he turned the music up and continued to drive; trying to clear his mind of all that had transpired.

"Candy, you know you was wrong" Yvette said as they all gathered in the mirror; inside the ladies bathroom.

"Yeah Candy you should've whooped that broad's ass" Felicia said.

Yvette continued "it was obvious he was ignoring her, whoever she is, Candy."

Erica butted in " I don't blame you Candy. If I had a cutie like that I'd keep him in line too."

Candy cut her eyes at Erica, then turned her attention back towards the mirror "Whatever Yvette. You and Felicia both always take up for dat nigga, Marcus ain't no saint."

"Candy I've known him just as long as you have" Felicia interrupted "and no, he ain't no saint. But you know just as well as me, he ain't exactly the devil either, unless."

"You piss him off!" Felicia and Yvette said as a chorus, giving each other dap.

"Who was his friend?" Erica asked, butting in again.

" Oh, that was hoe ass, disease infested Rhameek." Felicia replied.

"Yeah girl, stay away from that one. He ain't no good." Yvette's sister added.

Candy and Yvette looked at each other and rolled their eyes before heading towards the door; with Felicia and the others following close behind.

As they filed out of the bathroom, one behind the other, Felicia began to tug at Candy's arm "look at what the cat done drug in" Felicia whispered.

"What's up Fee, long time no see" Tiffany rhymed as she approached Felicia, giving her a fake hug. "And look at you Candy" she continued as she walked a circle around Candy, checking her out.

"You look like a million dollars" Tiffany said, loud enough for everyone to hear, before leaning in close to Candy's ear and whispering "or should I say, you look like a lil over a hundred thousand dollars."

Candy made an attempt not to look shocked as she gave Tiffany a big fake smile in return "thank you, and you look nice yourself, Tiffany.." Candy stated dryly.

Tiffany produced a business card, from out of nowhere, handing it to Candy "call me sometimes girl. We can go on a shopping spree or somein, just me and you." Tiffany said, nudging Candy with her elbow and winking her eye "you be sure to call me Ms. Brown, we have so much to talk about." She added before walking off.

"Oh yeah!" She said, coming to a halt and turning around as if she had just remembered something "did you hear about Leon?" Candy nodded her head "isn't that such a terrible thing? Probably over money, the things people do for money." Tiffany added before turning and walking off into the crowd.

Candy and Felicia gave each other an awkward look.

"What was all that about?" Yvette questioned "I thought ya'll ain't do her."

Candy waved her off "ya'll hungry?" She said, changing the subject as she headed for the exit; not waiting for a response.

Marcus dropped Rhameek off and decided to head home, he and Candy hadn't been home since the incident with Leon. It was like second nature for Marcus to spend a night or two at a hotel, after doing any type of dirt; just in case things traced back to him some way or another. Considering the "nosey ass lady next door" as he often called her, hadn't phoned him with any news of police knocking on his door, or even worse, angry gunmen on his doorstep, he assumed the coast was clear.

Besides, he knew Candy would probably stay with Felicia the remainder of the night. And the last thing he wanted to do was lay up in a hotel room alone.

"Stupid ass!" He cursed out loud, speaking to no one, as he rode alone through the still of the night, thinking about the performance Candy had put on at the club, drawing unwanted attention; Marcus loved attention, but not the kind she had brought upon him.

"Stupid!" He repeated, out loud again. He inhaled deeply, making his chest rise to capacity. Exhaling slowly, with his jaws puffed up as if he were blowing a trumpet, he released the air through pursed lips.

The sight of the house was the only thing bringing a little relief to him at the moment. Marcus pulled into the driveway and put the car in park.

Picking up his phone, he began dialing Candy's number. Then he reconsidered, and threw the phone down in the passenger seat.

"Ole stupid ass" he said once again, leaning back and allowing his mind to drift as he viewed the stars through the moon roof of his Cadillac "why do I even put up wit this shit" he mumbled to hisself, still staring up into the night sky.

CHAPTER 10

A familiar tune began to play on the radio. "From the first time... I saw your face...girl I knew I had to have you..."

Guy played out of the stereo as Aaron Halls voice filled the small bedroom.

"All my love is for you... whatever you want I will do... you're the only one I want in my life... for you I'll make this sacrifice..."

"How do I open this?" Candy said "you do it."

"Just tear it open Candy" Marcus replied as Candy held the condom in her hand; looking confused "give it here" he said, taking it from her and opening it before handing it back to her.

"It want go on" she said, attempting to put the condom on for Marcus.

"Let me do it" he said as he tried to help her roll it down. "It's too little" he said, not realizing the real problem was the fact that they were trying to put it on inside out, making it difficult to pull down. They both pulled on it at the same time tearing it in the process.

Marcus cursed, then got up and opened another one. This time, he got it on with no fuss. He looked at Candy and smiled. Proud of his erection, he stood long enough for her to get a good look.

"I want you to ride it" Marcus said as he laid down and leaned back on a pillow. Candy sat naked except for her socks and a T-shirt.

"I don't know how too, I never got on top before" Candy replied.

"It's easy just get on top and roll around" Marcus instructed, not admitting that he'd never done it before either. This was their second experience with each other and he refused to admit that it was really his second experience period.

Candy reluctantly straddled Marcus and frowned as he clumsily inserted himself inside of her, and pushed in hastily, while pulling her hips downward. Candy grunted and there was a loud farting noise. They gave each other an awkward look and laughed. Both were inexperienced and didn't realize there was a lot of air trapped inside of the condom when he put it on, this gave off a whoopee cushion effect as the air was forced out of the rubber.

"Now just move" Marcus said. Candy began to move her hips back and forth, she winced in pain as Marcus lowered his hips and thrust upwards.

The "Guy" CD continued to play in the background as Candy and Marcus both frowned up, Marcus was in as much pain as Candy due to the fact that his manhood was getting bent backwards as she rolled and wiggled awkwardly on top of him.

"Ooh!" Felicia screeched, bursting through the bedroom door and approaching the bed.

"Felicia get out!" Candy yelled while pulling the covers over her shoulder's, covering her and Marcus.

"Candy what you doin on top of him" Felicia continued "I know his thang ain't in you?" She said, raising the covers from the foot of the bed, and looking underneath them.

"Ooh, Candy his thang is inside you; I see it!" Felicia screamed.

"Get out Felicia!" Candy yelled again.

"Shut up Candy, don't nobody wanna see Marcus lil thang!"

Marcus laughed as Candy threw a pillow in Felicia's direction.

"Yo hot ass, I'm gone tell yo mama!" Felicia said before running down the hallway screaming Rhameek's name, ready to tell Marcus And Candy's business.

Candy turned her attention back to Marcus and they both burst out laughing, then the laughter turned to smiles as both stared at each other, saying nothing. Marcus, caught up in his own world of thoughts, continued to smile and stare her directly in the eyes looking at his own reflection in her pupils, wondering if what he was feeling, right at this very minute, was what so many people called 'love'. Or were they just two kid's caught up in the moment. Most importantly, he wondered if she was feeling the same thing he was feeling.

"Marcus what's wrong wit you?" Candy said.

"Marcus what's wrong wit you boy, what you thinking about!" Marcus jumped at the sound of Candy's voice.

"It's just me" she said as she reached through the window; touching his shoulder.

"What was you thinking, sittin out here asleep, with the car running?" she questioned. "You could've knocked the car out of gear and drove right through the living room." She said before shaking her head and giving him a slight smile.

Marcus, still half-asleep, returned her smile "what you doing home?" he asked.

Candy shrugged " I called your phone and you ain't answer so I called Rah and he told me you came home" she said as she opened the driver's door and began pulling him from the car. "Come on lets get you in bed wit yo stupid, drunk ass."

Marcus didn't protest. He shut the engine off and followed her lead as she guided him into the house, down the hallway and into the bedroom, where he fell into a heap on the bed.

Candy pulled his shoes off and began to undress him, after he seemed to slip into a coma almost instantly. Candy shook her head and smiled to herself as she admired her man, sleeping like a big baby, then she let out a puff of air as she thought about the girl at the club. "You make me sick" she said, thumping him on the head as hard as she could. Marcus only responded by rubbing his forehead and rolling over.

Candy rolled her eyes as he began to snore loudly "you make me sick" she repeated again before undressing herself and laying down beside him. With her chest against his back, she closed her eyes and let the rhythm of his loud snores serenade her to sleep.

Candy's eyes bulged out when she felt the huge hand cover her mouth and nostrils, cutting off her air supply. She tried to scream and this only seemed to make her eyes bulge out even more and the veins in her neck rise to the surface as she tried to force out a cry for help, but the grip on her was too strong and no air escaped through her mouth or nose. This caused her ears to pop as she continued to struggle at an attempt to get Marcus' attention. She felt herself being snatched up off of the bed and all she could see was the pillow that she had been sleeping face down on. She couldn't spot Marcus or her attacker through her peripherals as her body was lifted up off of the mattress.

She began to kick, while suspended in mid-air. Reaching down, she tried to pry herself free from the arm that was wrapped around her waist.

She could see no face but could feel her captors hot breath on her neck. She continued to kick and struggle but couldn't get the arm that held her by the waist to loosen its grip. Tears began to fall down her cheek, only to be stopped by the large hand that covered her face, as she continued to try to break the Boa Constrictor like grip from her waist, while at the same time, using her other hand in an attempt to pry the attackers hand from her mouth. She began to dig her nails into his hand but it was no use.

"Marcus" she screamed, but the words couldn't make it past her muffled lips. Where was he? She wondered and why hadn't he felt her struggling when she was snatched from the bed, why couldn't he hear her muffled cries? She thought, as she felt herself fading off into a state of euphoria; due to the lack of oxygen to her brain.

The attacker turned her to face the foot of the bed, where she saw another figure standing in the darkness. If she could speak she would've unloaded with a flurry of all the worst words she could've thought of when the face at the foot of the bed came into focus.

It was Tiffany, standing there with a smile on her face, and a straight razor in her hand. The light from the moon beamed in through the bedroom window, reflecting off of the razor's sharp edge.

It was at that moment that Candy looked into the vanity mirror positioned behind Tiffany and caught a glimpse of Marcus' reflection. He seemed to be still sound asleep, oblivious to the drama that was going on. And it was then that Candy realized, she no longer heard him snoring.

She turned her attention back to Tiffany who still stood there smiling, but this time Candy noticed that the razor she held was dripping with blood.

"No!" Candy screamed as loud as she could, not realizing her screams actually sounded like a low whimper, as she jumped up from her sleep, kicking and flailing her arms wildly. She put her hands on her chest and could feel her heart beating as if it were about to explode. The room was silent, except for the sound of Marcus snoring.

Realizing she had been dreaming, she cursed under her breath and lay back down. Thinking to herself, this was one time she was actually glad to hear Marcus snoring beside her in bed.

Then her thoughts went back to Tiffany as she lay staring at the ceiling, wondering how much Tiffany knew or if she knew anything at all.

"She couldn't know" Candy said, speaking under her breath as she closed her eyes and struggled to lose herself back into a dream state. This time, praying for a good dream as she slowly drifted back to sleep.

BIRD IS DA WORD

It had been weeks since Leon's death and the world hadn't missed a beat. The earth still turned in the same direction, at the same speed and Leon had been mourned in the usual fashion. A funeral filled with cries of "we love him and miss him" and a chicken dinner afterwards, filled with friends and family who all watched as Leon's 'baby mama' got into a knockdown, drag out brawl with another girl claiming to be Leon's 'baby mama.' In the end, the fight was broken up by two of Leon's friends, who walked both baby mama's off in opposite directions and coincidently both ended up in bed with one of his friends by the end of the night. And days later all of the tears were dried up for good, just as sure as Leon's corpse lay in the ground dried up and decaying. He was now no more than a memory, a name that would only be mentioned on occasion by family members and drunken friends, standing on a corner pouring cheap liquor onto the concrete in his honor.

"For my niggas who ain't here" Peabo said, holding a glass of Hennessey up in the air as if he were toasting to the heavens.

Tiffany rolled her eyes as Peabo put the glass to his lips and threw his head back, downing the Hennessey in one gulp.

Peabo glared at Tiffany "I'm sure if they was here they wouldn't want me wastin this good Cognac all over the floor" he said with a menacing grin on his face "especially since their departure already cost me."

"Baby that's mean!"

Tiffany rolled her eye's again as she turned her attention towards Rhonda, who sat on the opposite side of the room, curled up on the couch with her feet all over the cushions. Rhonda continued to talk as Tiffany thought about how Peabo would flip out if she were to put her feet on the couch like that.

"You shouldn't say things like that P-Baby" Rhonda continued.

Peabo turned his attention to Rhonda and began to move towards her.

"Beat her ass" Tiffany thought to herself, with a smile on her face, as Peabo came to a stop and hovered over Rhonda as she lay on the couch.

"Who you talkin to?" Peabo said.

Rhonda raised up and stood barefoot on the sofa, making herself just a little taller than Peabo.

"I'm talkin to you "Lil Daddy" she said, poking him on the forehead playfully with her index finger. Peabo let out a loud laugh and wrapped his arm around her waist as she leaned forward and gave him a wet kiss.

"I'm bout to make a few calls" he said as he moved away from Rhonda slowly, winking his eye at her before leaving the room.

Tiffany was furious as Rhonda, still standing on the couch, blew a kiss at Peabo then plopped down on the couch as if it were a trampoline.

Rhonda looked at Tiffany and smiled, Tiffany did not do likewise.

For the past few weeks Peabo had been spending a lot of time with Rhonda and less time with her. Actually, both were in his presence most of the time. But Rhonda seemed to get all of his attention. Unlike Tiffany, Rhonda had no problem with sharing Peabo. But Tiffany didn't feel the same. In fact, Rhonda had even stated clearly she had no problem sharing Peabo with Tiffany and Peabo was happy to hear this.

He was even happier when she told him that she also wouldn't mind if he wanted to share Tiffany with her.

Tiffany barely knew Rhonda and despised her already. She had been around for only a few weeks and was already doing things Tiffany would never be able to get away with. Tiffany wanted to question Peabo, about where she came from, but knew better.

She was already treading on water, due to the money that was lost when Leon was killed. Peabo still blamed her for being late for the pickup. And to make things worse, about four days ago, Rhonda had pulled some "psychic friends, Ms. Cleo bullshit", As Tiffany referred to it, that had Peabo spooked.

They were all in Peabo's loft apartment having drinks when Rhonda had pulled out a stack of Tarot cards and began to shuffle them, "P-Baby you want me to tell you your future?"

Tiffany hated when Rhonda called him "P-Baby" as if she had known him for years.

Peabo grinned then gestured for her to proceed. Tiffany had removed herself from the table and moved towards the couch. She remembered how Peabo had commented about her "plopping down on the couch too hard", when she had sat on it.

She had watched from across the room as Rhonda began to flip the cards one by one and Peabo gave her his full attention as Rhonda filled his head with a bunch of mumbo jumbo about "someone in his midst being untrustworthy" and that someone being a female.

Peabo had constantly cut his eye's at Tiffany as Rhonda spoke. Then to top it off, she flipped some card and spoke of "thieves amongst him."

That really seemed to get Peabo's attention, considering Rhonda knew nothing about the money he had been robbed for previously. And as if that wasn't enough, she had told him about some "angel" who would enter his life and save him from all this evil. That was the icing on the cake and to Tiffany's surprise for some reason Peabo seemed to take all of Rhonda's mystical, magical bullshit serious. Even worst, Tiffany was beginning to think that Peabo was convinced that she was the untrustworthy one and Rhonda was the so-called "Angel" who was gonna end all of his grief.

"Bullshit" Tiffany said under her breath as she now sat staring at Rhonda, who had assumed her previous position, stretched out with her feet on the couch.

"You say something Sweetie?" Rhonda said with a smile on her face.

Tiffany replied with a fake smile of her own "just thinking out loud."

"You shouldn't do that Sweetie" Rhonda replied " cause then people will always know what you're thinking."

"Well I guess it doesn't matter when there's a mind reader in the room now does it." Tiffany responded before getting up and going to the bar for a drink.

Tiffany didn't trust Rhonda and knew she was far from an "Angel" but she had to admit, since Rhonda appeared, Peabo didn't seem to be to concerned about the money he had lost anymore. But, then again, she also knew he still had other things to handle. He was too busy making money to dwell on money that was lost. But she also knew that he was a man of principle and the incident was far from forgotten.

It was just a matter of time before the word started to circulate and he found out who was behind the whole thing.

Tiffany could feel it in her gut; that she knew who was behind it. And if they didn't pay up, and pay up soon, she would make sure word got out, and all fingers would point towards Candy Brown.

CHAPTER 11

"What's up" Candy said, speaking into her cell phone. "I'm pullin up now. Where are you?"

"I'm right down the street, at the light baby girl. I'll be there in a minute." Was all she heard before the phone hung up. Candy sat in the grocery store parking lot, listening to the radio, checking out her surroundings as a black Chevy Caprice pulled up beside her with the music blasting.

The dark tinted window on the driver's side rolled down and Sonny sat behind the wheel, grinning from ear to ear.

"What's up girl?" Sonny said after turning his music down.

"Nothing much" Candy replied as she began scanning the parking lot.

"There you go peepin around and shit" Sonny stated.

Candy sighed "you know how people are Sonny, the wrong person see us talkin and might get the wrong idea and I don't need them problems."

"What they gonna say? They saw you talkin to a friend, so what!" Sonny said nonchalantly. "Ain't like you doin nothing wrong, right!"

"Yeah we know that" Candy answered "but they don't know that."

"Anyway" Sonny interrupted "I had you to meet me so I could give you this." Sonny handed her a flyer. "I'm havin a party at the Reggae Club tonight, the directions are on the flyer. Stop through if you ain't got no plans. I know you and yo man might be doin the quality time thing, so if you don't show up I'll understand."

"Chile please" Candy remarked "I told you he be too busy to spend time with me lately, I'll be there."

"Good." Sonny said "and don't worry, you won't know nobody there. I guarantee it. So you ain't got to worry bout nobody gettin the wrong idea, should you decide to say hello to me or wave at me or somein, it'll be safe."

"Sonny you crazy" Candy laughed as she stepped out of her car. "I'll be there boy, I'm bout to go up in here and get a few things out of the grocery store." She said as she began to walk off.

"Yeah go home and cook that man a good steak dinner or somethin." Sonny said as she walked away.

"Yeah right" Candy replied as Sonny pulled away. She began looking around, hoping nobody had seen her and got the wrong idea.

She knew how people were quick to twist things around, and the grapevine could take a friendly conversation and blow it all out of proportion.

Yvette had already tried to blow things out of proportion once, but Candy knew Sonny wasn't interested in her, nor was she interested in him. She had spoke to him on numerous occasions since that night at the club.

She had run into him at the store two days after her "big performance" and Sonny had approached her laughing and joking about her actions at the club that night.

"What's up Tyson" he had joked. And after a few minutes conversation they had exchanged numbers, due to the fact that Sonny had told her he could get her a discount at her favorite shoe store, in which his cousin was the manager.

Every since then, they had made friendly chit chat from time to time.

Candy hadn't really said much to Marcus since the incident at the club. And Marcus still seemed to hold a grudge, and still wouldn't admit that he was up in the "mystery girl's" face.

Marcus had been spending alot of time with Rhameek

'Handlin Business' as he called it. And Candy found her self stressing alot about the situation with Leon and worrying about the fact that Tiffany seemed to know something.

Although weeks had passed, she still hadn't said a word to Marcus, about Tiffany. In fact, she hadn't said much to him at all, about anything, not even about the terrifying dream she had, which still had her spooked.

"Why should I worry about him? Besides, he still ain't apologized for being in that broad's face." She reasoned. Meanwhile, she spent alot of time alone, only speaking to Felicia on a day to day basis and Sonny when she felt like she needed a laugh.

"Nothing wrong with having a friend guy" these words echoed in her head, but the voice she heard wasn't hers. it was Sonny's. "It's harmless."

Marcus sat in a trance, staring at the wall, his eyes moving around the living room scanning numerous pictures of him and Candy that were spread everywhere. Some on the end tables, some mounted high on the wall above the fireplace and others scattered to and fro, so that no matter where he looked he had to see a picture of him and Candy hugged up with big smiles on their faces.

Images forever frozen in time, surrounded by a wooden frame and covered by glass to preserve and protect them from wear and tear over the years. Moments captured in mili-seconds with a mere press of a button, creating memories that would outlast life itself.

Even after there is no more Candy Brown and Marcus Flowers, there would forever be these photographs. Symbols of love and happiness to any and everyone who may lay eyes upon them. Marcus sat staring at the pictures, wishing that what the pictures depicted was real life, wishing the pictures were more than a pose designed to create illusions of everlasting happiness to the eye of the observer. Because, in realty, it had been weeks since he and Candy had shared such a moment.

He sat wondering how in the midst of so much chaos could Candy even find time to make an issue out of something so stupid. How could she even bring herself to question his love for her; after all the times he had literally laid down his life upon the line for her.

And now here she was walking around as if he owed her an apology or something. As if her grudge was more important than the fact that a man was just buried; and they were the ones responsible for his death.

"Women" Marcus mumbled as he dug down in between the cushions of the couch he sat on and pulled out an all black 9mm he kept hidden there at all times. He began to point the gun at different objects around the room, pressing the button on the side, making a red dot appear on every object he pointed at.

After ten minutes, he grew bored and stuffed the gun back in it's hiding spot. Then lay back, staring at the ceiling as the frustration continued to build up and eat away at his brain, until his thoughts began to come in flashes; like highlights from a championship game on sports center, showing only the key moments that had led him to where he was today.

Marcus came out of his trance when he heard the doorknob turning; he was so deep in thought he hadn't even heard Candy pull up. Once she entered the house she only glanced in his direction, rolling her eyes, as she proceeded to the kitchen with a single grocery bag.

"Marcus you could've took the trash out" she complained.

"Here we go" Marcus thought to hisself, knowing this moment was long over due. Candy had been walking around with an attitude for the longest and it was a known fact that when she wanted to get something off of her chest she would start nit picking and bitching about small things until an argument was incited.

And Marcus also knew what the arguments always led to in

the end. Sometimes he felt like Candy started drama just to get to the part that came after the argument. And since Marcus was in no mood for Candy's nonsense, he decided there was only one way to avoid the whole confrontation; and that was to skip all the loud talking and get straight to the point.

Candy continued to ramble on and on as Marcus rose from the couch and approached the kitchen, where she stood with her back to him. She was still complaining about anything she could think of, from the kitchen light being on, to the fact that Marcus had left a single dirty cup in the sink. Candy pulled something from the grocery bag and bent to place it in the cabinet under the sink as she still continued to mouth off. And that's when Marcus made his move.

Snatching his belt off, he approached her from behind while looping the end of the belt through the buckle, creating a small noose. By the time Candy began to raise up, and realize Marcus was standing right behind her, it was too late.

"Marcus, what you..." Candy never completed the sentence, Marcus over powered her and somehow managed to bind both her wrists inside the loop he had made with the belt. Candy tried to pull away from him but was unsuccessful. Marcus ignored her as she struggled in an attempt to break free and began to curse at him.

"Let me go" she screamed as he spun her around till she faced the sink and began to wrap the belt around the faucet, tying her to it, so that she stood slumped over the sink, with her back turned to him.

"Let me go you sorry mutha..." she screamed as she kicked her leg back at him, hoping to hit him in the groin.

Marcus said nothing as she wiggled and cursed, unable to free herself from the faucet, which swiveled from left to right, only allowing her limited motion.

"Don't touch me!" She screamed as he reached underneath her skirt and ripped her panties off of her. Candy began to kick at him again.

"I said don't touch me, go touch that Bitch that was in your face" she screamed again.

Marcus didn't respond, instead he grabbed her from behind and forced hisself deep inside of her, causing her to let out what sounded like a combination of a moan, a grunt and the words "I hate you" all at the same time.

Marcus continued to mash himself deep inside her as she began to wiggle frantically, like a fish caught on a hook.

"I hate you" she screamed. "I hate you"... "I hate"... "you"... "I hate"... "I"... "I" her words began to fade as he continued to enter her with deep strokes from behind, causing her to raise up on her toes, and bite her bottom lip, as her words faded and turned to moans. Her eyes rolled up in her head as Marcus dug so deep she could feel her feet leaving the floor, a few centimeters, every time he thrust himself inside her.

"Marcus, oh Marcus" she began to scream as he continued to pound her, making the veins in her neck pulsate as she began to pull on the faucet.

"Marcus" she screamed as chill bumps began to pop up all over her body and the muscles in her arms tensed up as she began to pull harder and harder on the faucet.

"Marcus...Marcus...Marcus... Oh my God!" She chanted as she began to shake violently reaching her climax. "Oh shit!" was the last thing Marcus heard her scream before he heard a loud cracking noise as Candy exploded. And at that same moment, water exploded from the sink, from the spot where Candy had ripped the whole faucet out of place, causing water to gush all over the counter as well as spraying Candy in the face as she in turn began to gush all over Marcus' manhood and her knees buckled, causing her to collapse to the floor.

Without a word, Marcus reached down to loosen his belt, which was still wrapped around her wrists, with the faucet still dangling from it.

After retrieving the belt, he pulled Candy to her feet and left the kitchen. Leaving her leaning against the sink, panting, with her hair all over her head as she began to make an effort to get the water spraying from the broken sink under control.

"Mufucka think that make shit alright, like he King Ding a Ling or somein" she mumbled under her breath as a chill began to creep up her spine, causing her to shiver and her knees to buckle slightly, as if effected by an aftershock after a big earthquake.

She had to bite her lip to muffle the slight moan that escaped as she exhaled and let out a sigh of relief before cracking a smile. Then she looked over her shoulder to make sure the private moment she had just experienced was, in fact, a private moment.

"Still don't make shit better" she replied stubbornly under her breath as she bent down, turning the knob under the sink to cut the flow of water off completely. Then, raising up, she began to fan herself with her hands as she stared out through the kitchen window at two young boys who stood in the street arguing.

A young girl stood on the sidewalk watching as the words escalated into a fistfight. "Duck nigga" Candy said to herself as if she were a ringside trainer, "Damn!" She said, imitating Chris Tucker, as the guy took a blow to the chin, sending him crashing to the asphalt.

"I told you to duck" she said as if she could really be heard. She continued to watch as the guy who remained standing approached the girl on the sidewalk and took her into his arms.

"Oh that's so sweet" Candy said right before she noticed the girl pushing the guy away, obviously giving him a piece of her mind from the way her head, neck and arms became animated as her mouth seemed to move continuously.

Candy's nose was practically touching the window as she watched the girl move from the victor and crouch down beside the guy who was lying in the street, obviously punch drunk.

The winner of the battle stood to the side, with a look of disbelief on his face, as the girl helped the other guy up off of the ground and tediously checked his face for scars before leading him away, helping him stagger down the street.

"Young love" Candy heard Marcus say from behind her. She turned to see him standing a few feet away from her, looking out the window as well.

"Lil man just learned a valuable lesson" Marcus continued. "See, the thing wit women is, you can fight wit all yo heart to prove yo love, go to extremes for em, go all out, blood sweat and tears trying to be the champion in their life and after all that...in the end...she only gone end up pickin some loser."

Candy opened her mouth to say something, but no words came out, as Marcus locked eyes with her and seemed to be gazing through her.

Then he flashed a big smile and approached her "look, I got somein to handle, so I'm bout to step out for a while" he said as he leaned forward to kiss her. Candy, still holding a grudge, almost feigned away from him but thought better of it, as he kissed her on her lips which still seemed to be stuck in midsentence.

"I take it you'll be goin out tonight" he said, taking a few steps back while holding her hands in his.

Candy wondered if he could feel her palms sweating as he held her hands. Then she finally opened her mouth and formed the words "I don't know, I ain't really made no plans."

He only replied with another smile before kissing her again. Then he released her hands from his grip and walked away. Candy leaned against the counter and began to stare at the floor as she heard the front door open and close, then she heard the door open again.

"Candy I love you" she heard him say before the door closed again.

"I love you too" she said, not getting the words out fast

enough.

She stood in the quiet kitchen alone, pondering for a few seconds before finally moving towards her purse which lay on the kitchen table. Digging through it, she pulled out the flyer Sonny had given her. After a few minutes of studying the flyer and contemplating, she reached into her purse again, producing her cell phone; and began dialing. The phone rang three times before there was an answer, "What's up babe?" Sonny answered enthusiastically.

"Oh nothing, I was just calling to make sure... you did say I was on the V.I.P. list didn't you?"

"For sho" he replied "won't be no waitin in line for you baby girl, so I guess that means I can definitely expect you tonight then?" He added.

"Yeah" Candy replied as she turned to face the window and looked towards the sidewalk, where the guy with the knockout punch still stood. "I'll be there."

"That's what I'm talkin about" Sonny said, sounding pleased "so I'll see you later then!"

"Yeah later" Candy replied before hanging up. Her attention still focused on the guy on the corner, who stood with his fist still clenched and a look that could kill on his face.

"Blood, sweat and tears" she heard Marcus' voice echoing in her head. "In the end they always pick the losers"...

Marcus drove along the highway at a slow pace. He had managed to get hisself tied up in heavy traffic. Wishing he had taken another route to his destination, he let the car creep along, with his foot riding the brake, as he leaned back in the seat, with the A.C. on full blast, trying to fight the heat as he let his mind ponder over the way Candy had been acting lately.

"What's really goin on?" He thought to himself. It wasn't unusual for Candy to act out the way she did at the club. She was always a little on the jealous side, but she was carrying this incident to the extreme.

He knew that a girl being in his face at the club wasn't the true source of her peculiar actions lately. He knew there had to be something else playing a part in all this. And he was beginning to wonder if she was cheating on him.

"Hell no!" He thought, or at least he hoped "besides, we done did too much real shit together" he thought out loud. "She'd never cross me for another nigga, after all we been through, especially now!"

He let his mind wonder for a second as he continued to roll on the crowded highway "nah" he said out loud, looking at hisself in the rearview mirror and smiling "we too tight for that, we come too far"...

"Pay attention girl, I'm tryin to keep you from shootin yo damn self!" Marcus snapped as Candy stared at the small handgun he held "this is the safety" he said flipping the switch on the side.

"Red means fire, always remember that, it's easy, red means you finna burn somein up." Marcus cocked the gun back slowly; so she could see the shell being fed from the clip into the chamber, or 'one in the head.'

"So that's the chamber?" Candy asked, as if she were a student in class.

"Yeah, dats da chamber baby", Marcus smiled as he let the copper colored shell slide into the chamber, and out of sight. "Now it's ready. As I said before, it's on red, so that means fire."

Marcus flipped the switch on the side again making the red dot disappear "this is safe" he continued as he began to pull the trigger and it moved back and forth with no effort at all.

"As you see it won't fire like this" Marcus pushed the button on the side. "This is the clip release" the clip fell out and he caught it in midair, then placed it in his pocket before racking the gun back once again, this time making the bullet eject out of the chamber and catching it in his hand.

"Now what I just showed you is how to take a live round out

of the head" he smiled, then added "on one of them slow nights when you ain't get to pop nobody."

"You stupid" Candy said with a smile on her face.

Marcus held the gun up "as you see the weapon is still racked back, this is what happens after the last round is fired. And when this happens, you simply hit this switch." He said as he flicked another switch with his thumb and the top part of the gun slammed forward.

Candy jumped at the sound of metal slapping metal...

Marcus sat in his car, laughing, as he continued to reminisce about the day he had taught Candy how to operate her first gun...

"Now I'm gonna show you a trick" he said, racking the gun back once again, letting it stay at a locked position. "This is in case you empty a clip and need to reload quickly" he said as he pulled the clip from his pocket.

"Pretend I just emptied a clip and it's racked back, I simply pop in a fresh one" he said inserting the clip in the butt of the gun "and hit the switch." The gun slammed forward again, making Candy flinch. "And we ready to fire again."

"So you're sayin theirs one in the head right now." Candy asked.

"Absolutely" Marcus smiled "there's one in the head." He paused then continued "but of course, that tricks for us veterans who carry extra clips, you'll probably never empty a clip outside of a shootin range, but it never hurts to know a thing or two."

He smiled as he handed the gun to her. She began to examine it; before pressing the button to release the clip. Then she racked it back, causing the shell to pop out and hit the floor, pinching her skin in the process.

"Dammit" she cursed.

Marcus laughed as he took the gun from her "alright Charlie's Angel, you just learned yo first lesson."

"What's that?" She said with a frown on her face.
"Watch yo fingers."

"I said, watch yo fingers nigga" big Mike repeated to the guy who stood beside him, holding the rim in place. "I wish you'ld get the fuck out the way. Do I look like I need some help?" Mike snapped as the guy flinched and moved to the side. "You can tell yo ass ain't neva had nothin befo" Mike continued as he stepped back to look at the twenty four inch rim he had just mounted on the older model Expedition.

"You in the game now youngen" Mike said, slapping the young boy on the back, damn near knocking him over. "You gone have the whole hood on yo dick now." He said as he lowered the truck until it touched the ground.

"Yeah I'll get a lil attention" the young boy said as he rubbed his hands together and admired his trucks new look. "But I'm still sittin low wit that nigga Darryl ridin around the hood on them twenty eight inch wood grain spinners, them mufuckas look like ceiling fans when that nigga pull up and stop."

Mike raised an eyebrow "Oh yeah, what he got em on?"

"Dawg dat nigga got a big ass Escalade ESV; out here swervin on these hoes."

"Darryl who?" Mike pressed.

"Darryl Wallace from 36th Street" the boy answered.

"You talkin bout lil ass Darryl who be ridin round in that beat up ass Impala?" Mike questioned.

"That's him! Nigga just bust out of nowhere, shining on niggas, got the hoes in the hood goin crazy. Shit, I even heard he in the process of trickin that Impala out as we speak."

"Oh yeah?" Mike replied for the second time.

"Yeah, must've hit the lottery or somein, I don't know, I don't care. All I know is, I'm bout to get in where I fit in, and see how these hoes get when I ride through today." The young boy said with a big grin on his face as he extended his hand to give Mike dap.

Mike waved him off "give me my money and get yo lame ass up outta here" Mike said, without so much as a smirk on his face, making the boys grin disappear. There was an awkward moment of silence after he handed Mike a few bills and stood waiting for his change.

"Thanks for the tip" Mike said as he turned his back to the guy and began to walk off, leaving the garage and heading towards his office. The young hustler would've stuck up his finger or mean mugged him from behind or maybe even mouthed the words "fuck you" or something if not for the set of eyes that were tatted on the back of Mike's bald head looking at him like "I dare you."

Instead, he simply hopped in his truck and drove off, as Mike went through the door separating his office from the garage.

Mike picked up the phone at the desk and began to dial. Peabo answered on the second ring "Big Mike, what's up baby!"

"Ain't nothin Playa" Mike answered "just got word from a lil bird; thought we might wanna check it out or somein tonight."

"Say no more" Peabo said before hanging up the phone.

Mike hung up the phone and began to hum a tune to himself as he pulled the blinds down in the shop and flipped the open sign to the side that read closed, before making his way to the back to prepare hisself for the night.

CHAPTER 12

Marcus and Rhameek sat at the table, comparing stacks.
"Notice how my stack is always bigger than yours"
Rhameek replied " one of the benefits of being a bachelor."
"Here we go again" Marcus responded as he picked up one
of the thick rubber bands off of the table, and stretched it
between his index finger and thumb, and began to point it at
Rhameek as if his hand were a gun.
"Say one more word" Marcus threatened.
Rhameek threw his hands in the air "you got me dawg."
"That's four words" Marcus replied before lowering his
thumb, allowing the rubber band to snap off of the tip of his
index finger and fly towards Rhameek, who felt a stinging
sensation across his forehead, before he was able to react.
Marcus burst out laughing as Rhameek cursed at him and
began to rub his forehead in the spot where the rubber band
had made contact.
"Get him Champ!" Rhameek yelled, causing Champ's ears
to perk up, as he stood at attention, as if he were ready to
attack. Champ looked around, with his tail straight, but after
a few second's passed and he realized no one was in the
room except for Rhameek and Marcus, his tail dropped and
began to wag as he tilted his head and gave his master a
confused look.
"Never mind" Rhameek said waving the dog off "some
guard dog you are." Champ huffed at the remark and
plopped back down on the floor.

Marcus laughed again and Rhameek did likewise.
Rhameek's phone rang cutting their laughter short.

"What's up" Rhameek said, putting the phone to his ear.
After a few words, he hung up, with a smile on his face.

"Who was that?" Marcus asked.

"That was Rah Rah, she was puttin me up on game."

"Oh yeah?" Marcus replied.

"And she also told me to tell you, she saw you lookin at her
ass, at the club. She said all you got to do is say the word and
you can get a taste."

Marcus laughed "I ain't fuckin wit Rah Rah ass, she'll never
have me runnin round here all crazy and shit."

Rhameek nodded in agreement "yeah cause she one devious
Bitch, I'm glad she on my team."

"For sho" Marcus exclaimed as he busied himself counting
another stack and wrapping a rubber band around it.

Darryl sat in his apartment, watching the big screen
television he had just purchased a few days ago. He had it set
on picture in picture mode, watching Scarface and Belly at
the same time.

The walls in his apartment vibrated as Mary J. Blige sang at
the top of her lungs about "No more tears."

"That's my shit!" Alicia said, sitting on the couch across
from Darryl, with her feet propped up on the coffee table and
her legs open just enough for Darryl to get a glimpse of the
red panties she wore underneath her tennis skirt.

"Yeah Mary J. alright" Darryl said picking up the stereo
remote "but I gotta get my Gangsta' on" he said as he hit the
button, and the CD changer rotated, and Trick Daddy began
to blast out of the speakers. Darryl jumped out of his seat and
began to bounce around the room; singing along with Trick
Daddy.

"Anybody wanna mufuckin die...come see... I... who me...T
Double D Nigga.."

"Ooh, I love that thug shit" Alicia said rubbing her knees

together.

"That's why you here wit me!" Darryl barked, beating his chest. "I'm the realest nigga doin it out here baby."

Alicia gave him a sexy smile as he continued to brag to her about how "real" he was.

Darryl was feeling good about hisself. He'd had a "thing" for Alicia for years, but she never seemed to notice him. Now, here she was sitting on his couch with an overnight bag on the floor right beside her. Who said "money couldn't buy happiness." The past few weeks had been like a dream for Darryl, women were practically falling out of the sky.

"Amazing what something as simple as a car can do for a nigga in the hood" he thought to himself as he looked out the living room window at the big truck parked outside. The Cadillac ESV was almost longer than his whole apartment, and sat almost as high.

Darryl's cousin, Travis, had to go do about eighteen months Fed time; for a probation violation. Before he left, he had decided to leave his ride with Darryl, as well as a little product and cash.

And since Travis lived out of town, nobody knew the difference when Darryl popped up in the new wheel's; throwing money around like he was out of his mind.

"I run this shit round here" Darryl screamed as Alicia sat staring at him, grinning from ear to ear, with her legs open a little wider than before.

"You like thugs baby" Darryl said, stickin his chest out for emphasis. "Come here, I got somein for yo..."

The door seemed to explode, cutting him off in midsentence. Everything happened so quick, the only thing Darryl saw was Alicia's eyes grow large. Before he could turn all the way around, he felt hisself being lifted up into the air, then slammed face first into the wooden coffee table; making it collapse into pieces.

Alicia let out a scream. Then, her scream became muffled. Darryl was in a daze as he tried to rise up off the floor.

"What the fu..." he uttered as blood seemed to pour out of his mouth and nose.

Darryl put his hands to his lips, it felt as if some of his teeth were missing but he really couldn't tell because his entire face felt numb. He struggled to get to his feet, unaware of his surroundings. The ringing in his ear dissipated as his blurred vision began to come back into focus and that's when he saw three huge men, with mask on, in his living room. One of them towered over Alicia, holding her from behind, with one hand over her mouth and the other one in a vice grip around her throat. Another guy stood by the front door. Darryl could see where the doorframe had been torn off. The third guy stood facing Darryl, hovering over him, with a menacing smile. The light bounced off of the man's teeth, the black ski mask providing the perfect backdrop, magnifying the glare as he spoke.

"Nice truck outside" the man said "nice jewelry" he added as he palmed the two large chains in his hands and examined them.

Darryl was frozen. "Take it dawg, you can have it" Darryl stammered " the keys to the truck on the table" he said pointing to what use to be the table, forgetting he had just broken it into splinters.

The big man laughed, causing the other two masked men to laugh as well. For some odd reason the song "Mo money Mo problems" began to play in the back of Darryl's mind. No, it wasn't in his mind, the CD changer had switched disk again. He could hear Alicia's muffled cries from the other side of the room. And when he turned to face her, she seemed to be even more horrified by the sight of Darryl's face; or was this horror simply induced by the big man who held her in his grips. The masked man began to grope her, causing tears to well up in her eyes.

"Let her go dawg" Darryl half demanded, half pleaded, with his hands bawled into tight fist.

This only made the "groper" lift up her shirt, revealing one of her breast. Then, he smiled, through his mask, as he began to squeeze it in one of his massive hands.

Darryl could hear Alicia screaming through the man's latex covered palms as she began to wiggle around in an unsuccessful attempt to break free.

"You gone tell us where the money at?" The man standing closest to Darryl asked, causing him to turn his attention back to him " or, are you gone make us do this the hard way?" He said, with a big diamond studded grin, as if he would prefer it the hard way.

"What money?"

The big man let out a slight chuckle as he began to wrap Darryl's chain around his fist, causing it to tighten up on his neck like a noose. "I see we gone do this the hard way." He said as he began to lift Darryl into the air, letting his feet dangle as the chain cut off his air supply.

The big man spoke to both of his accomplices. "Now this is what you call top quality jewelry", he explained "nothing like that hollow shit that'll pop when you yank it."

The other masked men began to nod in agreement as Darryl began to claw at the big man's forearm trying to break free.

"No sir, you can't just yank this off a nigga neck," the big man continued "this here cost some change, speaking of which" he said as he lowered Darryl to the floor and loosened his grip "where the money at?"

Darryl began to gasp for air as blood continued to trickle from his mouth and nose.

"I don't know what you talkin bout", Darryl said after catching his breath "here take this shit, just let her go." He pleaded as he slid the long chains from around his neck; leaving them bunched up in the big mans fist.

"Do we look like we came here for some jewelry " he barked as he wrapped the rest of the necklace around his fist and punched Darryl square in the face, causing blood to splatter on his sleeve.

This only intensified the pain Darryl was already feeling.

His whole face felt like it was on fire, and things seemed to move in slow motion. The big man spoke again but Darryl couldn't understand his words, he felt like he was on the verge of losing consciousness as he staggered, struggling to stay on his feet.

"Wrap her ass up", the big man yelled. The man by the door gave a nod and walked towards Alicia, holding a roll of duct tape in his hand. He pulled a short piece and tore it with his teeth, then placed the small strip over her mouth, while the other intruder held her still. Then, spinning her around, he taped her hands behind her back. Taking time to lift up her skirt to check out her goods, he looked back over his shoulder. Sneering at Darryl, he began to rub on her behind.

"Last time I'm gone ask, you don't produce somein real quick like and we gone run the train on this fine young specimen while you watch." The big man said as he grabbed Darryl by the collar and placed him in a chair, facing Alicia. He slumped in the chair, feeling helpless. The man with the duct tape stopped groping Alicia, long enough to come wrap his wrist up behind his back, and his ankles to the chair.

Darryl tried not to face Alicia, who looked at him with pleading eyes "look, it's somein right there, under the couch, just let her go, please!"

The big man cracked a smile before walking towards the couch and flipping it over.

"What the fuck is this!" Big Mike barked as he pulled the ski mask off of his face. "Do I look like I came here to catch a buzz, you lil stupid motha fucka!" He said holding up one of many large freezer bags full of weed.

Darryl's heart dropped, his knees would have buckled had he been standing. He didn't know Mike personally, but he knew enough about him to know that this wasn't a simple B and E or robbery. And he also knew that if Mike was in his crib, somehow he had stepped in some deep shit. "It's in the bedroom closet dawg, it's all there, you can have it, just please don't kill us." He blurted out; knowing that he had already pushed his luck.

Mike motioned for one of the guys to check the bedroom closet.

"I'm sorry Alicia" a bloody face Darryl apologized, facing Alicia, who stood across the room, terrified and shaking as she sobbed, causing the duct tape over her mouth to bubble up every time she exhaled.

Minutes passed, but seemed to Darryl like hours, before the guy came back with a large Timberland box.

"That's it, its all there" Darryl said. Mike looked at the small box, then at the man carrying it, who only shook his head before opening it and showing Mike the contents.

"What's this, you think this shit is a game nigga?" Mike barked "fuck it, kill em!"

"Hold up, that's all I got dawg, I swear."

Mike pulled two small stacks from the box, no more than fifteen grand, and a set of digital scales.

"Nigga you mean to tell me yo lil cornball ass done blew over a hundred grand in a few fuckin weeks!" Mike yelled as he threw the box at Darryl, hitting him in his, already bloody, face with it.

"One hundred grand, no dawg I don't know what you takin bout! Travis only left me like twenty grand and his jewelry and his truck and ..."

"Who the fuck is Travis?" Mike said, cutting him off.

Even under the circumstances, Darryl looked towards Alicia with a look of embarrassment on his face. "Look there's a letter he wrote me from the pen; it was in the box."

Mike glanced at the floor and spotted the letter on the floor beside the Timberland box.

Mike shook his head in disbelief and began to laugh as he read the letter out loud:

" P.S. Darryl do not, I repeat, do not fuck my truck up. And remember, the cash I left is for me to fall back on, not for you to trick off with. I'm puttin my trust in you lil cuz. Don't let me down.

Holla back,
Travis

"Damn Darryl looks like I was wrong dawg, what can I say except your cousin Travis would be real disappointed in you right about now Darryl." Mike let out another loud chuckle, then his whole facial expression changed up instantly "thing is, the damage is done. You understand, nothing personal right?" Mike stated before turning his attention to the big man holding Alicia "she seen my face, bag her up."

Alicia's eyes grew large as the man produced a large plastic bag from his pocket.

"Hold up!" Darryl pleaded "we ain't seen shit, I swear we ain't gone call no police."

"Come on Darryl my man, you know hoes can't keep they mouth shut." Mike said "it's a pity, she such a fine young lady." He stated flatly before giving his man the go ahead with a simple nod.

Alicia stood, trembling, with her hands still behind her back. Darryl tried to speak one last plea but his words seemed to form a knot in his throat and he was unable to produce a sound as he saw the man pull the tape from Alicia's mouth. No sooner than she made an attempt to scream, he dropped the clear plastic bag over her head. And the other masked assailant approached with the duct tape, and swiftly taped the bag shut around her neck.

Darryl's eyes welled up as the bag began to fog up and seemed to tighten up on Alicia's face, as if being vacuum-sealed, as she made a desperate attempt to get air.

The man in the mask released her, allowing her to run and stumble around the room frantically, like a headless chicken. Knocking over the C.D. case as her knees buckled, she fell to the floor, convulsing, as if she were suffering from a seizure.

"No!" Darryl sobbed at the sight of the beautiful young girls life literally being sucked away as she fought to hold on, while flopping around on the floor like a fish out of water, until her movements became no more than a slight tremble and she finally ceased to move at all.

Mike looked at his wrist watch and hit the timer "three minutes forty five seconds, that's a new record Darryl my man, you should be proud of Shawty." He said as he reset the timer on his watch to zero "you ain't gone let a girl beat you though, right!"

"Hold up!" Darryl yelled out, at the top of his lungs, as the other masked man pulled a bag from his pocket and threw it over Darryl's head, holding it in place, while his accomplice wrapped the tape around his neck.

Darryl began to jerk violently, almost immediately. Having used most of his air to scream out in a last minute cry for help, it didn't take him long to succumb to the same fate as Alicia. He continued to struggle until, finally, his chair tilted to the side and came crashing to the floor as Mike and the others quietly made their way out the front door.

"Candy what's wrong, you not enjoying yo'self?" Sonny asked with a look of concern on his face.

"Yeah I'm straight Sonny, my mind just elsewhere. That's all." She said as she and Sonny sat in the VIP section, on the plush couch that was positioned at the back of the club.

"Don't let that nigga stress you like that baby girl" he said, wrapping his arm around her shoulder. "Smile a lil bit, enjoy the party!"

"Alright" Candy said with a slight smile on her face.

"That's my girl" Sonny stated as he pulled Candy closer in a "friendly" embrace and began to lean towards her.

"What's up Sonny" a female voice chanted, causing Candy and Sonny, both, to look up.

"Just what I needed" Candy thought as she looked up, only to see Tiffany standing in front of her; with a big shit-eating grin on her face.

"I didn't know you two..."

"We just friends" Candy stated, cutting Tiffany off as she

slid out of the crook of Sonny's arm.

"Mmm hmm" Tiffany said, seeming to be preoccupied with her cell phone, ignoring Candy's comment.

"Anyway" she said, snapping her phone shut and placing it in her purse. "This is a nice party Sonny." She stated as she slid on the couch in between Sonny and Candy.

"And I ain't know you knew my girl, Mrs. Flowers, right here. Oops! I mean, Ms. Brown. My fault girl, you and Marcus been together so long I get yall's last name mixed up."

The mention of Marcus' name made Candy feel guilty for some reason.

"He's just a friend" she thought to herself "why should I feel guilty?"

"Glad you enjoying the party Tiffany", Sonny said "and yeah, me and Ms. Brown" he said putting emphasis on the last name "go back a long way, we road dawgs."

"What a coincidence" Tiffany chimed "cause see I've known Candy since we was like yay high, ain't that right Candy?"

Candy shook her head, confirming the statement.

"Anyway, after all this time, I never knew you two were friends", Tiffany continued "and if ya'll have known each other that long, then I'm sure you must know Marcus."

"I've heard a lot about him" Sonny stated dryly.

"Where is he anyway?" Tiffany asked, facing Candy.

Candy shrugged her shoulders, "him and Rhameek out somewhere I guess."

"Now that's a name I hear a lot nowadays" Tiffany blabbed on. "Rhameek's became quite the ladies man from what I hear."

"That's Rhameek alright" Candy replied. Sonny cleared his throat "will ya'll two ladies excuse me for a minute while I run to the ..."

"Go ahead" Tiffany cut him off "we'll be right here."

Sonny got up and strolled towards the men's bathroom,

leaving Candy and Tiffany behind.

Candy leaned back and crossed her arms. Tiffany's grin became bigger, revealing every single pearly white in her mouth.

"Girl good thing I walked up when I did", Tiffany said "it looked like that nigga was breathing down your neck, who he think he foolin with that friend shit" she remarked "niggas is so sneaky nowadays Candy, that's why us girls got to look out for each other." She continued "I mean just think, it's a good thing it was me who spotted you and not one of these two faced, trouble makers ready to start a rumor at the drop of a dime."

Candy gave Tiffany a grave look. She was about to speak, when Tiffany cut her off. "I mean, cause Lord knows what Marcus might do if he even suspected you was cheatin on him."

Candy started to comment, when Sonny approached.

"Ya'll girls enjoying yo'self?"

"Definitely" Tiffany answered "we just discussing the usual girl things, men and money" she smiled and Sonny shook his head.

"But you know the only thing us girls love more than men and money is the mall" Tiffany said nudging Candy with her elbow "ain't that right girl!"

"That's right" Candy said with a fake smile on her face.

"Then again" Tiffany stated "I said that backwards. What I meant to say is, the only thing we love more than men and the mall is money!" She said stressing the last word.

"Anyway it was good seein you two, Candy you tell Marcus I said hello, I'm about to mingle a little bit, bye Sonny!"

Tiffany scooped up her cell phone, from the couch, and strolled off.

"Bye Tiffany" Sonny replied.

"So, I guess you did run into somebody you knew" he said, facing Candy.

Yeah" she replied, looking down at her hands.

"What's wrong Baby girl?"

"Nothing Sonny I ... I just."

"Oh you wouldn't believe what I did" Tiffany said, popping up out of nowhere, interrupting them again. "I picked up your phone by accident girl" she continued as she handed Candy her phone "it looks just like mine, we always did have the same taste." She blabbed.

"Thank you" Candy said, taking her phone from Tiffany's hand, with a hint of suspicion in her eyes.

"No problem, girl" Tiffany smiled "anyway, talk to you later" she said as she walked off once again, this time with a look of triumph on her face.

"You alright baby girl?" Sonny asked again as he brushed a strand of hair from Candy's face.

"Yeah I'm good" she said, forcing a smile as she tried to block Tiffany out of her mind and enjoy the party.

CHAPTER 13

Felicia sat alone, staring at the cell phone she was holding in her right hand.

Her finger had been resting on the call button for the last thirty minutes. She had been trying to find the strength to push it, but was unable. It was as if it would require two thousand megatons of pressure to suppress the small button which would send a signal to a satellite, which in turn would send a signal to the caller at the other end, summoning their attention with some melodic ring tone. In this case, that particular ring tone would be, "Don't save her" by Project Pat, which was the tune Rhameek had set his phone to play whenever she called.

Felicia let out a heavy sigh as she sat, frozen, with the phone in her hand, alternating her attention to the object she held in her left. That object was identical to six other objects that lay spread out on the couch beside her.

She let out a muffled groan as the little blue "plus" sign appeared on the home pregnancy test. This was the seventh one she had tried today and it was obvious, no matter how many different stores she had purchased them from, or how many different brands she had tried, the results were not going to change.

"Why me God!" She screamed, looking up at the ceiling. Then, turning her attention back to the phone, she began staring at the letters on the screen, "DAWG" with Rhameek's phone number printed underneath.

Letting out another loud groan, she threw the EPT test across the room.

"I gotta call Candy" she thought out loud, deciding against calling Rhameek as she scrolled through her list of contacts until she found Candy's name.

Pressing the send button and placing the phone to her ear, she slumped back on the couch; letting her body slide all the way down; until she was seated on the floor.

Candy finally answered after several rings "What's up!" Her voice boomed through the receiver, accompanied by a barrage of loud music.

Felicia, caught off guard by the background noise, pulled the phone away from her ear momentarily. "Candy where you at? Sound like you at the Club or somein."

Felicia heard the loud music began to fade gradually as Candy made her way into the bathroom.

"Probably cause I am at the Club." Candy replied. "What's up!"

Felicia looked at the pregnancy test sprawled out on the couch and figured this was not the right time for this discussion.

"What's up?" I need to be asking you that, considering you at the club and ain't call yo girl to see if she wanted to hang out tonight!" Felicia snapped.

"I'm sorry girl, it was a last minute decision, I was out ridin and Sonny called me and ..."

"Hold up!" Felicia interrupted. "Rewind that real quick, cause I almost thought I heard you say Sonny."

"Probably cause I did" Candy replied smugly.

"Candy have you lost yo... where is Mar... I know you ain't at the club wit Sonn... you know what, I don't even want to know Candy" Felicia stated, finally getting her words together. "Don't even tell me, cause I know you ain't that stupid, so I'm not even gonna ask, cause I don't want no parts of that drama you bout to bring on yourself."

"Felicia, it ain't like that. We just out here..."

"I don't wanna know Candy, cause when Marcus kill yo ass I don't want him thinkin I had nothing to do with nothing, so don't say another word, I ain't seen nothin, don't know nothing! Good bye!" Felicia said, hanging up the phone before Candy could respond.

"Oh God why does thou foresake me!" Felicia screamed, holding her hands to the ceiling. "Lord please forgive her, cause she knows not what she's doing!"

Felicia stood up, grabbed her car keys and raked all of the pregnancy test into her purse, stopping only long enough to tie a scarf over her head, which was covered in rollers, she made her way outside, wearing nothing but pajamas and bedroom shoes.

Slamming the door behind her, she began cursing out loud as she walked to her car.

"What I do to deserve this God? My best friend gonna end up dead, and not only that, I'm pregnant by a real life Dawg." She screamed as she got in the car. Leaning her head on the steering wheel, she began to cry. "God, please let these test be wrong, please God! Please! I don't wanna give birth to puppies."

She pleaded as she finally pulled herself together; long enough to crank up the car and pull out of the driveway.

The tires made a chirping sound as she sped off down the quiet street, on her way to another twenty-four hour pharmacy to buy another pregnancy test, hoping this time her prayers would be answered.

Candy looked at her phone, "I know she ain't just hang up on me!" She said as the words "call disconnected" flashed on the screen.

Frustrated, she rolled her eyes and stomped out of the bathroom, swinging the door open. When all of a sudden, the door came to an abrupt stop with a loud thud.

"This is payback ..., knew these Bitch niggas ..., from way back ..., witnessed me strapped wit Mac's ..., knew I wouldn't play that ..."

Marcus and Rhameek stood on the porch at the old style home on the deserted looking back street, where all was quiet except for the sound of music blasting from inside of the house.

Rhameek shook his head as he began to knock on the door once again.

"This the shit I be talkin bout!" He spat, looking at Marcus, who only shrugged his shoulders and turned his attention to an unlikely looking couple who strolled up the sidewalk.

The short, Asian lady blushed and waved at Marcus and Rhameek as she and the tall Black guy who accompanied her moved towards the house. By- passing the front porch, they cut through the yard and headed towards the back.

No sooner than they had disappeared around the corner, a heavy set lady came from the direction they were headed.

"Crazy ass niggas" she cursed as she walked past Marcus and Rhameek, not paying either any attention as she made her way down the sidewalk, with her hand bawled into a fist, as if she were clutching a piece of gold.

Rhameek began beating on the door again, still receiving no answer, as the music continued to blare out and laughter filled the house.

"This some bullshit" Rhameek cursed as he jumped off of the high porch and headed towards the back.

When he and Marcus bent the corner, they could hear the voices inside getting louder. The back door flew open as they approached, and a middle aged Black man exited, shaking his head as he passed them.

"Crazy ass niggas!" He spat.

Marcus and Rhameek looked at each other then entered the house.

"People all over the world!" Ron screamed at the top of his lungs, over the music, singing the theme to Soul Train. "Let's get it on... its time to get down!"

Marcus took in his surroundings and was amused by the scene before him. Rhameek continued to curse, to no avail, because he couldn't be heard over the loud music and ruckus that was unfolding.

Marcus couldn't help but laugh at the sight of the two long lines of people that stretched from the kitchen to the living room.

"No wonder the streets empty" he thought as Ron began to chant the Soul Train theme again and the music continued to blast out of the large stereo system.

"People all over the world!" Ron screamed over the music as he stood on the coffee table, in the middle of the living room, with his khaki's sagging; showing off his boxers.

"Who next?" He yelled out as one of the ladies in the kitchen threw her hand in the air waving a Fifty-dollar bill.

"Come on then wit yo bad ass, let me see what you got!" he shouted.

The two rows of people that extended from the back door to the living room parted, making room for the "Fifty dollar lady" as she made her way down the isle towards Ron, who stood on the table dancing and bobbing his half braided head, while holding a piece of crack, the size of a soft ball, in his palm.

"Ain't no party like a crack house party, cause a crack house party don't stop" he chanted as the lady began to gyrate her hips and drop to the floor, doing her best impression of a Luke dancer.

"Dats what I'm talkin bout baby", Ron screamed "shake dat ass, I'm a give you a big one for dat baby girl" he stated before taking the fifty dollar bill from her hand and breaking off a chunk of the rock the size of his thumbnail.

"Who loves you baby!" He yelled as the lady smiled from ear to ear, obviously happy with what she had received for fifty dollars.

"I said who loves you baby, huh? You see dat! You tell J-Lo, Puffy ain't got shit on me! Dats bigger than that rock Colby bought his old lady when his ass got caught cheatin! Know what I'm Talkin bout! Holla at ya boy!" Ron ranted as he hopped off the table and smacked the lady on the ass.

"Damn you got a soft ass! Girl you go to rehab and put some teeth in yo mouth you'ld be a keeper." He joked as she danced her way back down the line towards the back door.

Ron followed close behind her, bobbing to the music as he approached Rhameek and Marcus, who still stood in the crowded kitchen taking in the atmosphere.

"What's up dawg!" Ron yelled, giving Marcus dap.

"Why you ain't answer the front door nigga?" Rhameek interrogated.

"What's wrong nigga, you get some grass stains on yo sneakers?" Ron countered as he turned and began to dance his way back down the line.

"People all over the world" He sang as he began to crip walk towards the living room; with Rhameek and Marcus following close behind.

Rhameek walked towards the stereo and turned the volume down.

"Look at this nigga" he said, pointing towards G-Lo, who lay on the couch asleep.

"How the fuck he sleepin through all this?"

"He on dat purple dawg, nigga been blazin all day" Ron stated as he punched G-Lo in the chest.

"Get yo ass up and take care of the rest of these people for me." He said, passing the "softball" to G-lo, who jumped up; wiping slob from his chin.

"Alright people!" He yelled, getting everyone's attention.

"G-Lo gone take care of ya'll, lets make it quick, party over, until next time, Love... peace... and..."

"Soul!" The customers chanted in unison as Ron did his Don Cornelius impersonation.

Rhameek shook his head "ya'll up in here trippin! Music all loud, G-Lo sleep, ya'll niggas slippin. A mufucka could've just ran up in here and took all ya'll shit!"

"Hell nah!" A voice boomed from down the hallway. Rhameek turned around at the sound of the voice and noticed

Shawt Change, for the first time, sitting in the bathroom; on the toilet, with his shirt off and the door wide open; so he could see down the short hallway into the living room.

"Ain't shit goin down in here!" Shawt Change barked as he reached back and flushed the toilet. "No pun intended." He added as he pulled a length of tissue from the roll of Charmin that was hanging from the long barrel of the AR-15 that rested on his lap, pointing towards the living room.

Rhameek turned his head deciding he'd seen enough, if not too much, already.

"Dawg why is you shittin with the door open?" Rhameek questioned.

"How else I'm gone see the Soul Train line" Shawt responded.

"People all over the world!" Ron added, then began snapping his fingers and dancing again.

Marcus laughed as he plopped down on the couch.

"Crazy ass niggas" Rhameek mumbled, joining Marcus on the couch.

Shawt Change came down the hallway with a can of potpourri spray in one hand and the rifle in his other hand, with the barrel throwed over his shoulder, minus the tissue roll.

"What's poppin daddy" Shawt Change said, placing the gun on the table before giving Marcus and Rhameek dap.

"Damn Dawg!" Ron, still full of adrenaline, blurted out, "I was lookin forward to seein dat China doll come down the line. Hey Shawt Change, you eva seen dat nigga, Fast Eddie, do the Runnin Man? Hey G-Lo, roll up da purple, nigga. And give me my damn rock!" He continued ranting as he turned the stereo back up a notch and began bouncing.

G-Lo entered the room, dropping what remained of the small boulder on the stereo case, along with some crumpled up bills, before falling back on the recliner that sat adjacent to Rhameek and Marcus.

"Where ya'll niggas coming from?" G-Lo questioned "Rah

what happened to yo shoes?"

"The backyard what happened to my shoes nigga!"

"What ya'll niggas doin comin to the back door?" G-Lo asked.

Rhameek waved him off "take yo ass back to sleep or somein."

G-Lo shrugged and dug down in his pocket producing a small blunt, obviously from earlier, and lit it up before taking a deep toke.

"Where dat nigga Fly at?" Marcus asked.

"Dat nigga in back" Ron blurted out "you know dat nigga thank he Magic Don Wand and shit."

"Its Don Juan nigga" G-Lo interjected.

"Nigga its Magic Don Wand" Ron argued.

"You don't know shit!" G-Lo countered.

Ron began to rub his head aggressively, causing his half corn rowed head to frizzle up. "Nigga I done seen 'Pimps up, Hoes down' fifty leven times, how you gone tell me ..."

"Fifty leven! What the hell is that?" G-Lo laughed "Nigga that ain't no damn number. And its Don Juan, like I said... and matter of fact nigga, that's 'American Pimp' you be in there watchin every day."

"Nigga how you gone tell me what's in my VCR" Ron barked.

"That's a DVD player nigga", G-Lo laughed.

"Nigga you gone make me..."

"Make you what?" G-Lo interrupted as he raised up out of the recliner and poised himself for combat.

"Oh, you buckin nigga?" Ron blurted as Rhameek sat on the couch, rubbing his temples and shaking his head.

"Shawt, please do somein bout them niggas" Rhameek pleaded.

"Alright" Shawt Change laughed, then jumped up on the coffee table. "Ya'll sucka ass niggas bluffin, ya'll ain't gone do nothing!" He instigated.

Within seconds, Ron and G-Lo locked up and began

throwing each other all over the room, as Shawt Change jumped up and down on the table.

"Three count rule nigga, First man who tap lose!" He chanted as Ron and G-Lo tumbled around on the floor.

"Nigga quit pullin my dreads!" G-Lo barked.

"Anything goes" Ron replied right before he let out a loud yelp. "Oh you bitin' now nigga?" Ron growled.

"Anything goes" G-Lo shot back.

"Lawd please help these niggas" Rhameek prayed as he slumped back on the couch and watched them continue to tear the living room up, while Marcus sat beside him, bawled up in a fit of laughter, and Shawt Change continued to jump up and down on the table, cheering both combatants on.

"Man what the hell is ya'll doin up in here" Fly screamed over the music and ruckus.

Everyone looked up. And even Ron and G-Lo froze at the sight of Fly, standing in the hallway; with nothing on but his boxers, with his skin glistening from head to toe.

"Ya'll interrupting my menagetoir up in here, got my hoes all scared and ready to leave and shit."

There was a brief moment of silence; nothing could be heard, but the music playing in the background, as everyone in the room focused their attention on Fly. Then they all looked at each other and burst out laughing.

"Nigga what type of shit you on?" Ron blurted out as he and G-Lo got to their feet and both began pointing at Fly's feet, while laughing.

The others joined in at the sight of the cotton balls stuffed in between each individual toe on his right foot.

"Ya'll don't know nothin bout that" Fly protested "you know them hoe's say I got pretty feet."

"Look. The nigga got clear polish on the other foot" Rhameek chuckled.

"And red polish on the pinky toe" Marcus added.

"Fuck ya'll!" Fly cursed "nigga this here is what you call foreplay. See, these two particular young ladies like to give me, what they call, a head to toe treatment", he boasted.

"Look like they done rolled yo lil ass in baby oil!" G-Lo joked.

Fly gave him an irritated look. "That's called lubrication you dumb, nappy headed, degenerate, product of irreconcilable differences." Fly remarked, causing G-Lo to hesitate for a moment.

"What?" G-Lo scratched his head, then responded "nigga fuck you!, that's why yo draws on backwards; runnin round here wit the pee hole in back! Mufucka lookin like a Snoop Dog stunt double on crack." He chuckled.

Fly waved him off and left the room, with both hands covering the back of his boxer shorts, as everyone in the room resumed laughing.

"Hold on ladies! Where ya'll goin?" They heard Fly's voice echo from the back. "I told ya'll I got it under control."

"Fuck dat Fly; we out" They heard the girls say as the bedroom door creaked open.

Marcus stifled a laugh as the two girls crossed the threshold into the living room. Both were three times Fly's weight and had at least two inches on him, height wise; without heels on. Everyone in the room held back their laughter at the sight of their slender framed friend trailing behind the two Amazonian women, as he copped pleas all the way out the front door and to the driveway, until they got in their car and pulled off.

Everyone burst out laughing at the sight of Fly standing alone at the end of the driveway; the excess oil causing him to glisten under the moonlight as he turned and slowly made his way back into the house.

"What the fuck ya'll laughin at!" He demanded.

"Nigga what yo lil ass was gonna do wit all dat?" Rhameek asked, still laughing.

"Man ya'll mufuckas don't understand my pimpin" Fly stated as he stomped down the hallway.

"O.K. Pimpin" Rhameek replied "while you back there, can

you go head and bring us what we came for so we can get up
out this madhouse."

Rhameek wasn't usually the nervous type. But for some
reason, every time he entered this house, he felt as if the
Swat team was due to swoop in at any moment.

It was a known fact that the house was the subject matter of
many "Neighborhood Watch" meetings. But it was also a
known fact, to everyone who attended these meetings, that
the inhabitants of this particular house had absolutely no
respect, whatsoever, for the law or anything to do with it;
and they wouldn't hesitate to enforce the laws that they
themselves had created within the sheltered neighborhood.

"Besides", one of the older ladies at the meetings often
reasoned, "before them, this whole neighborhood was
terrible. Yeah they loud and obnoxious but one things for
sure, as long as they around here we won't ever have to
worry bout seeing a dealer in every cut and corner like it
used to be before they moved in! At least now I can walk my
dogs when I feel like it; so I have no problem giving up a
little peace and quiet as long as we gettin safety and security
in return."

"I agree" one of the other old ladies would say "it's rare we
even hear gunshots round here anymore, and when we do, its
just them running off trouble, a little trouble is better than a
lot of trouble, I always say. Besides, they sho do spend a lot
of money when we throw our big black pot fish fry's on the
weekend's."

Everything that was said at these meetings was far from
secret, because of the fact Marcus paid the "fish fry lady" to
keep him posted on everything that went on at the meetings.
But this fact wasn't enough to ease Rhameek's mind,
because he always feared his homeboy's wild streaks would
one day attract attention from the wrong people.

Rhameek's phone rang, cutting off his thoughts.
Recognizing the ring, he stood up and headed for the porch

as he answered.

"Yeah" he said, placing the phone to his ear as he opened the screen door. At that instance, the phone made a beeping noise and went dead on him.

"DAMN", he cursed. "Marcus, let me hold yo phone for a second."

Marcus tossed him the phone. "I'll be back" he said as he caught the phone and stepped outside to call Felicia back.

Marcus looked out the window as Rhameek walked all the way to the end of the driveway.

"Here you go Dawg!" Fly, now fully dressed, said as he entered the room and tossed Marcus a black leather-shaving bag.

Marcus unzipped the bag and smiled at the sight of the rubber band wrapped bundles of cash inside.

"You know we keep it live round..."

"What the fuck!" Rhameek cursed, his voice booming from outside, causing everyone to raise up and look out the window, only to see him standing with the phone in his hand; looking at it as if he was about to throw it on the pavement and shatter it in a million pieces.

"I don't believe this shit!" He barked as he fumbled with the phone a little longer, then snapped it shut as he stalked back towards the house.

"What's up Dawg?" Marcus inquired as Rhameek entered the house.

"Ain't nothing Dawg" Rhameek replied, brushing the question off, as he glanced at the bag in Marcus' hand.

"Look fellas we bout to be out, I'll call you lunatics tomorrow." He stated, giving each one dap, while unsuccessfully trying to conceal the look that covered his face, a combination of disappointment and anger.

"All right Dawg" Shawt Change replied "everything all right ain't it?"

"Yeah everything cool" Rhameek replied before marching out the door, with Marcus following close behind.

"Rah, what's up Dawg?" Marcus questioned as they pulled away from the curb, in the black F-150, with Rhameek behind the wheel.

"Ain't nothing Dawg, you know how them hoes be hounding yo boy, that's all," he laughed tossing Marcus his phone back; before plugging the battery charger into his own.

"Ain't them niggas some of the craziest mufuckas on the planet?" Rhameek said laughing and changing the subject.

"Hell yeah" Marcus agreed as they rode off into the night; while recounting some of the more interesting moments during their short stop at the "mad house" as they often called it.

"Sonny I'm so sorry!" Candy apologized once again as she and Sonny stood outside of the club beside her car. "I didn't know you were by the door, I didn't mean to..."

"It's o.k. quit apologizing", Sonny said as Candy continued to dab at his nose with a piece of tissue. "Chill out lil mama, it ain't even bleedin no more." Sonny added with a smile.

Tiffany sat only a few spaces away, on the opposite side of the parking lot, with a big grin on her face as she watched Candy and Sonny carry on.

"Shame, shame, shame" Tiffany said, under her breath, as Candy moved in closer to Sonny.

"See, no blood!" Sonny said, taking the tissue from Candy and showing her there was no traces of blood on the fresh Kleenex she had just pulled out of her car.

"I'm sor..." Candy started as Sonny placed an index finger to her lips, interrupting her attempt at another apology.

"Shhhh... no more sorry's, please, its o.k., I promise you!" He paused "but, if you really wanna make me feel better", he stated while removing his finger from her lips and tapping hisself on the cheek, with a grin on his face.

Candy smiled and leaned forward, planting a kiss on his cheek; around the same spot he had just pointed at.

"Now I'm all better!" He said, making her laugh.

"Look baby girl, I'm not gonna hold you up; its gettin late and all good girls need to be home. Besides, I'm sure your man's worried about you, and I don't wanna be the cause of nobody's sorrow. So I'm gonna talk to you later." He said as he spread his arms for a "friendly" hug.

Candy accommodated the gesture. But when she leaned forward and hugged him, a chill ran through her body as the air flowed from his nostril; down the nape of her neck, causing her to pull away swiftly.

"Thank you Sonny" she smiled, pulling away from him and opening her car door. "I enjoyed myself tonight!"

"I'm glad" he said with a smile, before walking off with a final wave goodbye.

Candy sat in her car, gripping the steering wheel, as she watched Sonny cross the street and make his way back inside the club, where his party was still going on. She closed her eyes and took a deep breath.

Upon opening her eyes; she almost jumped at the sight of Tiffany, pulling up beside her, in a Crimson colored Jaguar.

Candy let out a sigh and rolled her window down, as she locked eyes with Tiffany.

"He is so... not your type, Candy" Tiffany stated while shaking her head in a disappointed fashion, "have you ever heard the saying "a good man is hard to find?"

"Lord knows I've been looking for ages, I mean if I ever get so lucky to stumble across the right one; you know the type" she winked "the type that'll go out his way to please you under any circumstances", she hesitated "the type who'll kill for you!" She said with a menacing grin. "If I had that type of man I'd be at home with him right now...", she paused then placed her index finger in her mouth, to the base. She began rolling her eyes back with a look of ecstasy on her face, covering her finger with saliva as it slid slowly across her lips and tongue.

Letting out a low moan, Tiffany studied her finger as if she had just pulled a strand of her hair from her mouth. Then making a flicking motion towards Candy, causing her nails to click, she finished her sentence. "I'd be at home doing whatever's necessary to please him." She stated as she let out a little school girl giggle, then stretched her tongue out of her mouth, and made it curl at the tip, as it touched her nose.

Candy watched as Tiffany slid her tongue out of her mouth dramatically. "All that snake Bitch missing is a fork on the tip of her tongue." She thought to herself.

"I know what's up Candy!" Tiffany said, her smile fading and her face turning to stone, "so we can do this the hard way, or the easy way. Think about it, and give me a call. I'm trying to be a lady about this." She hissed, before pulling off, leaving Candy to ponder on her ultimatum.

Candy let out a loud scream and banged her fist on the steering wheel as her mind raced one hundred miles an hour.

"Too much goin on!" She cried as she cranked up her car and headed home.

Rhameek pulled into his driveway, right next to Marcus' car. "Alright Playboy, I'll catch you tomorrow" he stated, slapping Marcus on the back.

Marcus looked at his watch. "I guess dat mean you ain't takin it in, huh?"

"Nah", Rhameek answered "you know me, booty call!"

Marcus cracked a smile. Giving his man dap, he hopped out of the truck and went directly to his car, where he stood for a moment; wondering about Rhameek's peculiar mood as he watched the big truck back out of the driveway.

Marcus shrugged it off, figuring it must be 'nothing' as he pulled out right behind Rhameek. Both made their way down the main street, then turned in two different directions, one heading home and the other heading wherever the wind blew him.

CHAPTER 14

"You had to know, Felicia!" Rhameek barked.

"I swear I didn't know, Rhameek" Felicia said with tears welling up in her eyes. "Rah why you mad at me? You act like it's my fault or somein!" She cried out, no longer able to hold the tears back; hurt by the way Rhameek was carrying on.

Rhameek was a dog, but he had never actually flipped on Felicia or showed any signs of anger like he had displayed tonight; when he burst into her room, raving like a mad man.

"Look, don't cry Felicia", Rhameek said, showing another emotion he had never shown before; compassion. "It's o.k. I believe you, I'm sorry, I know it's not your fault" he said as he took her into his arms and began to comfort her. "I'm just upset that's all, this shit just caught me off guard. But it wasn't right to point the finger at you."

Felicia lost control when she laid her head upon his chest and felt something she had never felt before in the midst of their lust filled escapades in the past.

She was sure that what she felt this time was a natural feeling. Burying her face into his chest, she let the tears flow as she listened to the rhythm of his heart; skipping a beat.

She cried as she thought to herself how this man she had grown up with; and known for so long, was soon to be the father of her child.

"DAMN Felicia!" He cursed, pushing her back, just a little, but not forcefully. "You gettin snot and shit all over my shirt, it ain't that serious."

"That's the Rhameek I know!" Felicia thought to herself as he wiped her tears away.

"Stop crying. I told you, I'm sorry. I had no right placing any blame on you. But don't worry, it's nothing I can't handle. You just gotta promise me you not gonna say a word to Candy about it just yet, cause I'm definitely not gonna tell Marcus nothin. Just let me sort this out!"

"But when will that be Rah? It's gonna come out sooner or later."

"Just let me handle that Felicia, just promise not to say nothing to Candy, that's all I ask! O.K.?"

"O.K." Felicia mumbled as Rhameek grasped her face and kissed her gently on the lips.

"I'm gonna take care of everything." He said, as he backed away and headed out the door, leaving her to contemplate about what his intentions might be.

Placing her hand over her stomach, she thought of the life she held within her womb as she hoped and prayed he didn't have his mind on taking a life; because at this moment, her mind was set on just the opposite.

"Lord please let us see eye to eye on this situation", she prayed.

Marcus slept uncomfortably that night, with Candy by his side.

When he had come home earlier, she lay in the bed as if in a comatose state, but in fact, unbeknownst to him, she had only beaten him home by minutes and pretended to be in a state of slumber when he entered the house.

Marcus tossed and turned as his subconscious tumbled in a frenzy of dreams.

"Where's yo daddy at boy!" His mother's boyfriend teased, letting out a barrage of laughter through rotted teeth, as Marcus' mother stood silently in the corner; with black eyes and a neck brace.

Then he saw his father's shadow standing over him, nodding approvingly, as he drove a large butcher knife into Lenny's chest. Then his mother's voice cried in the background, pleading for Marcus to return home, as his father grasped his hand. His mother's voice became more distant as he and his father entered a small cell, allowing the cold, steel bars to slam shut behind them.

Marcus looked at his reflection in the mirror that was mounted on the wall in the small cell, and saw that he had grown older.

He heard a child giggle from behind and turned to see a younger version of himself, standing outside of the bars, holding a small Nerf football.

Breaking out into a sweat, he backed away from the bars and began to look around the small cell, noticing his father was no longer with him. He was alone.

He turned to face the bars again. And this time he saw, not only a younger version of himself, but saw a younger version of Candy; wearing pigtails and hair bows.

The young Candy and Marcus were holding hands and waving at him, with big smiles on their faces, as a form emerged from the shadows behind them.

"Candy" Marcus whispered as the silhouette came into the light. It was a full-grown Candy, she didn't respond. Instead she ignored Marcus as he extended his hands through the bars in an attempt to touch her.

"What did I tell ya'll kid's bout talking to strangers." The adult Candy spoke, scolding the young Candy and Marcus as she took them both by the hand and lead them away into the shadows.

"WAIT!" Marcus cried out as he continued to reach through the bars.

The young Candy and Marcus turned and waved good-bye, one last time, before fading off into shadows, lead by the older Candy, who never looked back or acknowledged Marcus' cries.

"WAIT!" He screamed once again, only to hear his voice echo in the darkness as he slid to the floor; in tears as he placed his face in his palms.

"Just like your daddy" he heard a voice say, causing him to look up.

His mother stood over him, shaking her head, as he realized he was no longer in a cell, but was in his mother's living room. And he was no longer an adult, or young child; he was a teenager.

"What have you done this time Marcus? What am I gonna do with you?" She said, shaking her head with a look of pity on her face. "Get up off the floor and go clean yourself up, I'll get rid of this," she said "I'm tired of cleaning up behind you." She added, holding a large handgun up, as Marcus stood and noticed his shirt was covered in blood.

Marcus looked from his shirt to his mother, who was now gazing out the window; crying.

He made his way to the window and pulled the curtain to the side, and saw sirens whirling around outside as a crowd stood out in the street; looking at a body that was sprawled out on the pavement.

Marcus felt hisself growing dizzy, upon realizing, the body on the pavement was an adult version of himself.

He felt an unusual feeling of vertigo overcome him as he began to fall backwards slowly.

He could feel hisself drifting away from reality as he witnessed bright lights flickering, accompanied by loud popping noises. Marcus continued to fall backwards. He grasped his stomach and felt his blood leaking between his fingers as he hit the asphalt, and the gun continued to pop and throw flames in his direction.

He groaned in agony as the unknown gunman stood over him and laughed out loud, as he pointed the gun at Marcus' face; and the bright light flashed from the barrel once again.

Marcus felt numb as the flash turned into yet another flash and another and another. The flashes continued. And it was then that Marcus noticed the flash was not from a barrel, but instead, it came from a camera.

He tried to speak but could not speak, or move, as the crime lab technician continued to hover over him, taking pictures.

"I'm not dead" Marcus screamed, but no one heard him. "Wait", he pleaded as the technician instructed the others to "bag him up." "But I'm not dead" Marcus tried to scream, once again, as the bag was zipped up; all the way over his head, sending him into a state of blackness.

"I'm not dead" he screamed, once again as he tore his way out of the body bag, only to find himself inside what appeared to be a casket.

"I said I'm not dead!" He yelled, bursting out of the casket, only to find himself in a church filled with people.

The people looked at him, with a look of disgust on their faces, and began shushing him. "Shhh"

"Would you be quiet" an usher scolded Marcus, as he sat upright in the casket, looking around at all the people in the crowded church.

"Have you no respect" an older lady spat "can't you see the Reverends talking?" It was at this moment that the Reverends voice rang loud and clear through Marcus' ear.

"Do you Candy Brown take this man to have and hold, for richer or for poorer, through sickness and in health, till death do you part?."

"I do" Candy said as she turned and raised her veil and began to kiss the man in front of her, a man who Marcus had never seen before.

"Who the fuck is that?" Marcus barked as he jumped from the casket and felt himself falling, for an eternity, before hitting the floor.

"Marcus, what's wrong?" Candy said as Marcus lay on the floor, beside the bed, fighting to untangle himself from the bed sheets.

"Candy, who is he?" Marcus barked, causing Candy's heart

to beat at an accelerated pace as she stepped away from him.

"Who is who? Marcus I don't know what you talkin a..."
Candy started as Marcus finally untangled his face.

He sat on the floor, looking at Candy with a confused look
on his face, as she stood by the doorway with a look of terror
in her eyes.

"What the fu..., how I get on the floor?" He said looking
around disoriented. "Candy why you standing over there
looking crazy?" He asked as he stood and began looking
around as if he were still confused.

"Oh..., I..., you... was having a nightmare baby" she
stuttered "you scared me, you fell out of the bed and was
kickin and screamin and stuff, I..., are you o.k.?" She said,
easing away from the door as she headed back towards the
bed and began wiping sweat from his brow.

"Yeah I'm o.k.", he said catching his breath "must've been a
hell of a dream", he laughed.

"Must have" Candy replied, smiling back at him faintly.

"Come on baby, lets go back to sleep," she said as she lay
back down, her heart beat finally returning to normal upon
realizing that Marcus' question to her was, in fact, no more
than subconscious rantings.

But Marcus found sleep again, much faster than her, as she
lay wondering what he had been dreaming about.

"What are you doin Candy?" She thought to herself as she
slid against Marcus and coiled herself around him, tight, as
she kissed him on the forehead and finally joined him in a
now peaceful sleep.

Rhameek sat in his living room in a trance. He had been up
all night, trying to figure out the best solution to the problem
at hand. Looking down, he turned his attention, once again,
to the photo album in his lap and gazed at the childhood
photograph.

It was an old picture of Felicia, Marcus, Candy and himself
all bunched up together in a small photo booth, an attraction

at the local carnival they had often attended when they were younger.

Rhameek laughed at the sight of the picture. Even then, at the age of seventeen, he and Felicia were sneaking around. And to this day, neither had confessed to the matter.

"Things were so innocent back then." He thought as he gazed at Candy and Marcus, hugged up with big smiles on their faces. While he sat beside Felicia; making rabbit ears behind her head.

Frustrated, he threw the photo album to the floor with a loud thud, causing Champ to stir from his sleep.

Rhameek stood and paced the floor as he began to contemplate on a way to deal with his situation.

He had been weighing his options all night and only saw one reasonable way to solve it. Actually his mind was set the very moment he had spoke to Felicia, but he had chose not to elaborate on it at the moment. Because he knew in his heart, she wouldn't agree with his decision. Therefore, he knew he would have to handle it on his own, and in a way that Felicia nor anybody else would know he was responsible.

But there was no time to waste. And all he could do was hope that Felicia would keep her word, and not bring it up to Candy, because, he definitely wasn't going to bring it up to Marcus.

But he also knew Felicia couldn't "hold water" and it was only a matter of time before she blabbed off to Candy. So he knew he had to deal with it sometime soon and get it over with; before anyone found out anything.

Marcus and Candy both stirred from their sleep, at the sound of the doorbell, and the sound of someone banging on the door simultaneously.

Rolling over, Marcus looked at the clock, which read twelve fifteen in the afternoon.

"I'll get it", Candy murmured as she got up and snatched up her robe, before heading out of the bedroom.

Marcus, shocked that he had slept so long, got out of bed

and made his way to the bathroom; where he turned the shower on.

"I'm coming" Candy said as she approached the door and looked out the peephole, before opening it to a distraught looking Felicia.

"Girl why is you banging on the door like you crazy!" She said as Felicia pushed past her.

"Where's Marcus?" Felicia whispered.

"He's in back, what's wrong?"

"Is he sleep?"

"No, why?"

"Go get dressed", Felicia whispered again "we got to talk girl!"

"Hold on" Candy said, without hesitation, knowing that it was evident Felicia had some "for her ears only" conversation that she didn't want Marcus to hear.

"Marcus, that's Felicia" Candy said, entering the bathroom, as she slipped on a pair of sweat pants and a big t-shirt and began brushing her teeth.

"I'm bout to ride with her somewhere real quick; we'll be back in a few minutes..."

Marcus gave her a suspicious look and nodded, knowing it was no use in trying to figure out what Candy and Felicia were up to.

"You hear me baby?" Candy questioned, now facing him, with a mouthful of toothpaste.

"Yeah I hear you" Marcus replied while thinking to himself "baby? She being awful nice today."

He looked at her wearily as she rinsed her mouth and sped out of the bathroom, in a hurry to meet Felicia, who still stood by the door waiting anxiously.

"Girl I got something to tell you!" Felicia screamed, through clenched teeth, as they eased out the door.

CHAPTER 15

"Sounds like a hell of a situation you got here Rah; and you already know how I feel; my sayin is "if you play in it, you lay in it", but if you choose to handle it this way I got no choice but to back you one hundred percent." Zone said, looking Rhameek directly in the eye, then shook his head as he began to scribble on a piece of paper.

"One day you gone learn though Rah, all things can't be kept in the dark forever and sometimes we got to let nature take it's course and except responsibilities for our actions", he said as he raised an eyebrow and slid the piece of paper across the table.

"But since you choose to handle it this way, I suggest you call this number, he's a friend of mine and he's real discreet, he's been around awhile; good at what he does and he owes me a favor."

Zone hesitated "Tell him I sent you and tell him he no longer owes me after he handles this, cause now it's you who'll be in my debt", Zone said as he slapped Rhameek on the shoulder and stood up to leave the small restaurant.

"And you can start by payin that tab and don't forget to tip; Uncle Zone's a big tipper." He added with a wink before leaving out the door.

Rhameek shook his head and laughed as he dug in his pocket to pay the bill.

"Crazy old man" he mumbled as he looked out the window and saw a shapely older lady hop out of the passenger side of the big Cadillac Deville and open the driver's door for Zone.

Rhameek observed the lady's body and noted that she looked better than most girls in their mid twenty's.

Meeting Rhameek's gaze, she smiled and waved, before jumping back in the passenger side.

Rhameek let out another laugh as the Cadillac pulled out of the parking lot at a slow pace.

Making his way out of the restaurant, he studied the piece of paper Zone had given him. Then he flipped his phone open and began dialing the number that was written upon it.

"You what? Oh my God!" Candy shrieked, almost jumping out of her seat, as her and Felicia sat in the crowded McDonald's, sharing a large box of fries while drinking milkshakes.

"Wait till I tell Marcus" Candy beamed.

"You can't tell Marcus" Felicia said looking serious.

"Why not?" Candy asked.

"Cause he gone tell Rhameek!"

"So what!" Candy stated "come on Felicia, I know Rah loves to clown on you bout a lot of things; but he'll be happy for you, just like I'm sure Marcus will too."

"Candy can't you hear? I said you can't tell Marcus!"

"But Felicia."

"But nothing!" Felicia interrupted "besides you ain't even asked me who the daddy is yet."

"Well I was gonna get to that", Candy said "but I thought maybe since you didn't say it off gate, then maybe you didn't know who it is; you know you get around young lady!" Candy stated sarcastically.

"Ha... Ha...Ha...!" Felicia faked a laugh "I know you ain't talking bout nobody getting around; after last night." Felicia shot back, watching the smug look on Candy's face disappear, as she obviously caught the reference to her being out with Sonny.

"But we'll get to that later" Felicia continued "like I said, you ain't ask who the daddy is!"

"Alright! Who?" Candy asked, taking a sip from her milkshake as Felicia leaned over the table to whisper in her ear.

Candy's eyes grew big suddenly and she began to gag and choke as the milkshake she was sipping shot out of her nostrils, causing Felicia to jump back and knock her own cup off the table.

Everyone in the restaurant looked in their direction as Candy, still choking, managed to let out a loud scream.

"You Bitch! Oh my God! Stop lying!" She screamed as she grabbed a napkin and began to wipe herself off and fell into a fit of laughter.

Felicia leaned back in her seat, with her arms crossed, glaring at Candy, as Candy pointed at her accusingly.

"I knew it, I knew it, I knew it!"

"You ain't know nothing." Felicia said "would you please stop makin a scene Candy!" She snapped as Candy continued to rant and rave.

"Oh my God, I don't believe this" Candy said.

"Believe it!" Felicia stated as she got up out of her seat "come on, I'm taking yo silly ass home. And don't say nothin to Marcus."

Felicia turned and began to walk away as Candy followed close behind, asking a million questions, all of which Felicia ignored, from the time they left the restaurant till the time she dropped Candy off, refusing to say anything else about the situation; except for her parting words.

"DO NOT! I repeat DO NOT tell Marcus!" She said before Candy opened the door to exit the car.

"Okay Felicia! I won't, I promise." Candy replied still beaming "give me a hug! I'm so happy for you girl!"

"Candy get the hell out of my car! I don't even know why I told yo silly ass." Felicia said as she pushed Candy out of the car and drove off.

Candy entered the house and found Marcus in the bedroom, walking around in his boxers.

"What you grinnin from ear to ear for?" He inquired; noticing how her face seemed to glow, "must've been some good gossip!"

Candy rolled her eyes then decided to change the subject before Marcus began prying for information.

"Just girl talk" she said, looking him from head to toe, shaking her head once her eyes reached his feet.

"Aaagh!" She groaned "why do you do that?" She questioned, pointing to his feet.

"Do what?" Marcus asked with an unknowing look on his face.

"That!" She exclaimed, pointing to his feet again " why is it every time you get out of the shower you can't do like normal people and at least put on bedroom shoes, since you insist on having something on your feet... but nooo, not you, you just gotta walk around in boxers and Timbs!"

Marcus shrugged the comment off and proceeded to dig through his closet, looking for something to wear.

"That urks me so much!" She continued as Marcus simply ignored her.

It had baffled Candy for years, trying to figure out why Marcus never seemed to just kick back and relax around the house; it was common for him to walk around with nothing on but boxers and Timbs, or sneakers, even when he had the urge to wear pajamas.

And it irritated her even more when he would leave the house with nothing on, except for his pajamas, to go to the convenience store, which was around the corner.

"You must want me to kick yo ass!" She would snap, claiming that the thin pajamas did nothing to cover his "goods."

"You ain't finna leave up out this house wit yo shit swingin for all to see!" She would tell him; but Marcus always ignored her remarks and proceeded out the door.

Candy didn't even like for him to wear sweat suits, claiming "his print was a little too visible"; demanding that if he wore sweat pants he had to take off his loose fitting boxers and replace them with "tighty whitey's" to hide "his bizness" or "her bizness" as she called it.

"That ain't for everybody's eyes", she would say.

Marcus always responded "just cause you a dick watcher don't mean these other females walkin round dick watchin!"

Marcus came up out of the walk-in closet, scratching his head, still undecided about what to wear, and found Candy still staring at him with her eyes focused on his boots. He never could figure out why she constantly complained about his "weird habit", a habit which he personally found to be normal.

"Why you frowning up?" He asked as she continued to shake her head, then left the room.

Marcus smiled as she made her way down the hallway. "Deep down inside I know it turn you on!" He called out to her.

"Yeah right!" She screamed back with a thin smile spread across her face as she stopped at the laundry closet and began to sort out a load of laundry, deciding which items would go to the cleaners. The pile going to the cleaners usually consisted of the majority of her clothes.

Candy stood in the hallway, caught up in her work, when Marcus squeezed by her with a pair of jeans in his hand, which he threw in the dryer, setting the knob on 'permanent press' before starting it up.

"Haven't you heard of using an iron?" She questioned.

"Takes too long." He responded as he leaned against the dryer and folded his arms. "So what's the good news?"

"What you talkin bout now Marcus?"

"I'm talkin bout how you and Felicia leave up outta here all swift and incognito, then you come back, face glowin, and grinnin ear to ear;" Marcus gave her a knowing look "must've been good news!"

Candy waved him off. "You nosey!"

"So I guess dat means it's a secret?"

"Good guess!" Candy shot back as she continued to separate the clothes.

Marcus laughed and then changed the subject, "so, what you do last night?"

Candy cleared her throat, then said "nothing. I rode around a little, then came home and went to sleep."

Marcus studied her with a raised eyebrow; he had been with Candy long enough to notice the fact that Candy always cleared her throat before telling a lie, nor would she make direct eye contact with him.

Deciding not to press the matter, he stopped the dryer and grabbed his jeans before heading back towards the bedroom; singing an old song made by a group called 'Code Red' under his breath. "Don't get caught slippin."

Minutes later, Marcus emerged from the bedroom wearing a two piece blue Khaki set.

The shirt was unbuttoned, exposing a crispy white Tee. The white and blue Adidas Shell toes, he wore on his feet, complimented the outfit. He also wore a blue fitted cap on his head, with 1000 Grams embroidered across the front in white stitching.

"Marcus why did you put those jeans in the dryer if you wasn't gonna wear em?" She asked as she sat Indian style, beside a bundle of clothes, looking up at him.

"Why ask why!" Reaching down, he pulled her to her feet, then continued "I'm bout to go lolli-gag around a lil bit, while you doin this. Who knows, I might come back wit a lil surprise for you" he winked "call me when you get dressed and situated, and I'll be back to get you. That is, if you got time to hang out wit me for a while." He said as he leaned forward and gave her a peck on the lips.

"Where we going?"

"Anywhere!" He stated, speaking over his shoulder as he made his way towards the door, "so tell yo boyfriend you gone be tied up for a while."

"What you...", Candy began before hearing the front door shut, "talking about?"

Candy heaved in a deep breath and blew out a gust of anxiety through puffed jaws when, almost as if on cue, her cell phone began to ring. "Hello."

"What's up Sunshine?"

"W-what's up Sonny" Candy responded as she peeped around.

"Ain't nothin, just making sure you made it home safe and sound last night."

"Yeah, I got here o.k."

"What's wrong? You sound down; you ain't get in trouble last night did you?"

"In trouble for what?" Candy snapped "I ain't got no curfew."

"My bad lil mama! You just don't sound like yourself."

Candy sighed "nah Sonny; I'm just tired, I ain't get much sleep last night."

"Oh! One of those nights!" Sonny stated slyly.

"Ha-ha-ha Sonny!" Candy retorted.

"Just jokin' wit you Candy; but maybe if it would've been one of those nights you wouldn't be so uptight right now."

"What's that suppose to mean Sonny?"

"Nothing! I'm just sayin."

"Just sayin what?"

Sonny laughed "I ain't mean nothing by it Candy; I'm just sayin you need to loosen up. You my home girl and I hate to see you running round here all tensed up and stressed out all the time, like last night for instance, you could barely enjoy yourself without looking over your shoulder!"

"Boy Please! Looking over my shoulder for what?"

"I don't know, I guess you was scared Maaarcus was gonna see you!" He stated, saying Marcus' name in a sing song manner.

"Whatever Sonny, I'm grown and I don't need no

permission to hang out, ain't like I was doing nothing wrong, so Marcus don't mind."

"Oh! So you sayin he knew where you was at?"

Candy became quite.

"I thought so!" Sonny laughed.

"Whatever Sonny. I ain't gotta tell, or ask Marcus nothing bout where I wanna hang out at, or who I wanna hang out with; ain't like I know his every move."

"Oh! Big talk from a lil woman" Sonny chuckled.

Candy laughed "anyway silly, what's up?"

"Ain't nothing; I was just seeing if you wanted to hang out again tonight?"

"Mmm, I don't know Sonny; me and Marcus suppose to hang out a little today; I don't even know where we goin."

"Well it's bout time he made time for you!" Sonny exclaimed.

"I know that's right!" Candy agreed.

"Well look, I was talking bout later on anyway, so if he cuts your night short or leaves you hanging, which you've told me he's known to do, give me a call." He continued " I got a suite booked for the rest of the weekend, and me and a few friends gonna check out the fight tonight; you know have a couple drinks, nothing major, just a lil social gathering; so if you feelin sociable you welcome to stop through."

"Yeah, that's all I need, someone seein me walk into a hotel, Sonny!"

"Yeah that probably would be a bad thing 'if' you were doin somethin you had no bizness doin, but that ain't the case; but I understand that Marcus might not understand; and we don't wanna get him upset now do we!" Sonny mocked.

"Don't nobody care about Marcus getting upset!" Candy lied.

"Well, if I was you I'd be concerned, especially if he act anything like how you acted at the club that night ole girl was all in his face."

Candy bit her lip and gritted at the mention of the incident at the club; she was just beginning to get over the whole thing but Sonny had brought the whole situation back to the forefront of her mind.

"Don't get me started on that tired ass hoe!" Candy snapped.

"Well I see you're already familiar with her nickname, because she's definitely usually referred to as ' hoe' in many circles."

"Oh, so you know her?" Candy asked.

"What! Are you playin; who don't know her!" Sonny lied. "Baby girl is well known in the streets, although, more people would probably recognize the top of her head before anything else."

"So you've had dealings with her?" Candy asked.

"Hell no! Ya boy ain't into spreading hisself thin like that; I don't lay up wit any and everybody, its too much shit out her to catch! But I can't say the same for everybody else. And, unfortunately, when women carry theyself like she does, its nobody's secret."

"And how does she carry herself?"

"Come on! What I gotta do spell it out? She's a hoe and that's that, but if I was you, I wouldn't worry too much bout yo man fuckin wit her; cause ain't like he gone leave you for her or nothing. If anything, he probably done got his rocks off a time or two; cause that's all she's good for."

Candy bawled her face up at the comment. "Sonny you talk like you done heard somethin or know more than what you sayin!"

"Look Candy, lets not go there. Cause sprinklin salt ain't my thing. And you and ya boys bizness is ya'll bizness, so it ain't my place to go there. In fact, let's change the subject. Like I said, if you can come through and kick it wit me and my folk for a minute, I'll be there all night." Sonny stated, while Candy sat holding the phone; not saying a word. The wheels in her head seemed to be turning at a rapid pace.

"Candy! Can you hear me?"

"Yeah I heard you" Candy said snapping out of her trance.

"You know what Sonny; I just might stop through there later on if I get a chance."

"Alright Candy, sounds like a plan, just hit me up like I said, I'll be there all night." Sonny said before hanging up.

Candy snapped her phone shut and began to throw all of Marcus' clothes in the washing machine, not bothering to sort or separate the colors from the whites as she mumbled under her breath to herself.

"Nigga wanna run round here fuckin wit stray hoes and want me to be his 'lil angel'," Candy stated making quotation marks in the air with her fingers. "Who the fuck he think he is! What goes around comes around nigga, remember that!" She spat out loud, as if Marcus were in the room with her.

"Nigga got one more fuckin time!" She cursed as she got up and stomped off toward the bedroom.

CHAPTER 16

Tiffany stood, staring out of the large picture window, overlooking the lake; pretending to be preoccupied by the sight of the ducks that covered the grounds where Peabo's Lake Norman home was located.

She frowned; watching as some of the ducks bobbed their little heads in and out of the water while the others waddled around the edge of the lake pecking at the grass. But it wasn't the ducks that caused her to frown nor was it anything she saw outside of the window; in fact it was what she saw in the window that caused her nose to flare up and the corners of her mouth to drop to the bottom of her chin.

Tiffany rolled her eyes as she continued to stare into the window, urked by the sight of Rhonda's reflection in it.

Her blood boiled as Mike and Peabo sat at the bar, behind her, laughing while Rhonda played bartender and hostess.

Tiffany turned around to face the trio, long enough to make eye contact with Rhonda.

Rhonda gave her a sly grin as she mixed another round of Hennessey and Coke for Mike and Peabo, who both sat facing her, caught up in a fit of laughter as she entertained them.

Tiffany took advantage of the moment and flipped Rhonda a bird; Rhonda continued to joke with Mike and Peabo as she nonchalantly scratched her nose with her middle finger, inconspicuously replying to Tiffany's gesture.

Tiffany turned her attention back towards the window,

thinking to herself how the reflection in it had so much meaning.

She, could see a silhouette of her own reflection, looking like a ghostly image that was slowly fading out of the picture. She could see Mike and Peabo both with their backs turned to her and she could see Rhonda's reflection a little more clearer than her own, but the reflection was still transparent.

"I see right through you!" Tiffany mumbled to herself, as the three of them continued to laugh and make conversation at the bar.

"You know what the problem is wit these niggas out here today?" Peabo said before taking a sip from his drink.

"Yeah I know exactly what's wrong wit these niggas" Mike replied "they too busy worrying bout what the next man got to go get they own."

"Exactly!" Peabo slurred as he slammed his glass down on the bar and slid it towards Rhonda for a refill. "I mean, we out here doin us; we ain't bothered nobody, feel me?" Peabo continued as Mike gave a nod in agreement "mufuckas come barkin up our tree!"

"Shakin our bush!" Mike added "and that's like shakin an apple tree in the Garden of Eden."

Peabo leaned back on his barstool, raising his hands to the ceiling as if he were in church and Mike had just read an enlightening verse from the bible.

"See! You feel me; you always feel me, that's why I fucks wit you!" Peabo slurred as he patted Mike on the shoulder, then leaned towards him; until their faces were only inches apart "So what you sayin is, those apples might look sweet, they might be easy pickin but they poison!"

Mike raised his glass and replied "you said it, I didn't!" Before throwing his head back and engulfing the strong drink in one gulp.

Peabo let out a loud laugh as Mike and Rhonda joined in.

"Yeah that was a cute analogy Mike" Tiffany stated dryly

from across the room "especially the part about the forbidden fruit." She added while glaring Rhonda's direction.

The room became quiet until Rhonda let out a giggle and stated, " somebody got they panties on backwards again!" Which only triggered another boom of laughter from Mike and Peabo.

Tired of the fiasco, Tiffany stomped out of the room heading towards the front door.

"Where you goin?" Peabo barked as Tiffany turned the doorknob.

"Oh, I was just going to see if I can find somebody to turn my panties in the right direction for me!" She stated before walking out and slamming the door behind her.

But even the huge door wasn't enough to block out the outburst of laughter that followed her to the carport. Tiffany found herself outraged at the fact that her comment had only brought more laughter out of Peabo; she could remember a time when a statement like that would've earned her a backhand across the mouth, but Peabo seemed to be so preoccupied with Rhonda lately that he acted as if she was non-existent and everything she said went in one ear and out the other.

It wasn't unusual for Peabo to bring other women around Tiffany, but never before, had any other woman had the privilege of coming to this particular house which Peabo called "home" and it infuriated Tiffany to see him bringing in " strays from the streets."

The fact that he trusted another woman enough to show her where he lived is what worried her the most. Tiffany could reflect back to the day she herself had gained that trust and it was on that very same day, that she had taken her first step towards gaining full access to Peabo and all that belonged to him; access that had been denied to everyone except for her and Mike up until this point.

Tiffany snatched a set of keys from the wall and almost exploded when she opened the door of the crimson colored

Jaguar and was greeted by the sight of Rhonda's possessions sprawled all over the car. But it wasn't the purse that lay in the passenger side nor was it the shopping bags that lay in the backseat that struck a nerve, although they contributed to her anger, what really got under her skin was the sight of Rhonda's stiletto's laying on the floor board, on the driver's side.

"I know he ain't been letting this Bitch drive this car" she uttered to herself as she scanned the headrest and observed strands of hair, which only confirmed her suspicions.

"Oh this Bitch doin way too much!" Tiffany barked as she picked a strand of hair from the seat and held it at a distance as if it carried the plague.

Shaking the hair from her fingers, she turned her attention back to the stiletto's that lay on the floorboard. "What this triflin hoe been doin! Driving barefoot!" Her voice echoed throughout the carport as she leaned over the seat and opened the compartment on the armrest. Spotting a small pack of Kleenex; she removed one of the small towelette's then, meticulously, grasped the straps connected to the heels, using the Kleenex as a barrier between her fingers and the shoes.

Tiffany held the shoes up high as she walked towards the small wastebasket that sat in the corner, all the while, keeping her free hand over her mouth and nose as if the shoes carried an airborne disease.

She didn't remove her hand from her face nor did she take a breath until after she had stomped the small pedal on the wastebasket. She dropped the shoes and the contaminated Kleenex inside. When the lid slammed shut, sealing the shoes fate, she smiled then strolled back towards the Jag.

Once inside, she crank up the car and adjusted the seat to suit her stature. She was about to place the small pack of Kleenex back in the armrest, when she spotted the small Platinum colored credit card that lay at the bottom of the compartment along with some receipts.

Tiffany gritted her teeth as she began to ramble through the receipts.

"Oh hell no!" She cursed as she looked back and forth from the receipts to the bags in the backseat, only to find there was a bag, from each store, matching the receipts she held in her hand.

Her eyes got as big as fifty-cent pieces as she checked the part of each receipt that read "total" accompanied by a large number on each purchase.

"I know he ain't gave this Bitch no card!" Tiffany cursed as she jumped out of the car and began pacing the floor, letting her mind go back to the day Peabo had given her an identical card and told her "use it at will!"

Tiffany was already bothered by the fact that Peabo seemed to be slipping; by bringing this stranger into his home. Now, she began to feel as if she was being replaced; a thought she couldn't bare to think.

"Ain't nobody takin my place!" She vowed out loud as she walked towards the rear of the car and placed the card, face up, behind the rear wheel.

"You bout to get cancelled Bitch!" She declared as she jumped back into the driver's seat. Hitting the button on the garage remote, she backed out slowly, allowing the rear tire to roll over the card. Hanging her head out the window, she kept the already scuffed card in sight as she continued to inch back, slowly, making sure the front wheel rolled over the card as well.

Once she hit her target, she stopped and began to turn the steering wheel from left to right, repeatedly, grinding the card between the wheel and the concrete slab.

Tiffany smiled, pleased with herself, as she pulled out of the driveway and peeled off down the secluded street that led from Peabo's home to the highway.

Tiffany laughed out loud upon completing her task, "so you think you can afford to have two Bitches runnin round out here wit these" she stated to herself with a sly grin on her face as she dug through her purse and produced her very own Platinum card.

"We'll see about that!"

Mike and Peabo were finishing off their glasses when Rhonda offered to make them another.

"Nah, I'm good", Mike stated as Rhonda began to refill Peabo's glass, not waiting for an answer nor bothering to add any Coke this time around.

"You tryna turn my man into an alchy ain't ya!" Mike commented as Rhonda filled Peabo's glass to the brim.

"He a big boy, he can handle it." Rhonda commented as she leaned over the counter and gave Peabo a wet kiss. "Ain't that right daddy?"

Peabo was about to respond when he was interrupted by the sound of Rhonda's cell phone ringing.

"Hold that thought" she said before answering the phone, "hello... hey daddy! How are you doin?" Rhonda stated, speaking into the receiver.

"It's my biological daddy" she said to Peabo, in a low whisper, with her hand covering the receiver. "Yeah, I'm doin fine, everything's o.k." she continued as she stepped from behind the bar and made her way across the room.

Peabo admired her voluptuous frame from behind; Mike also stole a glance or two as she sashayed into the adjoining bedroom to talk to her father in private.

"That girl somein else" Peabo remarked, turning his attention back to Mike.

Mike responded with a nod while focusing more attention towards the glass in Peabo's hand. Peabo seemed to be drinking heavy on a day to day basis, he pondered. It wasn't unusual for him to drink daily. But lately, Mike had noticed Peabo was consuming three times more than usual.

"P-Man don't you think you've had enough." Mike commented, as Peabo was about to take another gulp.

"What is you my daddy nigga? You sounding like Tiffany

right about now!" Peabo stated while looking at Mike with bloodshot eyes.

"Easy Cowboy! I'm just sayin, you been goin heavy on the bottle lately, that's all nigga. And hell nah, I ain't yo daddy...you think you would've came out lookin like that if a handsome brother such as myself made you?" Mike joked, slapping Peabo on the back, bringing an icy grin to his face.

Peabo laughed then changed the subject, he was about to bring up the events from the previous night but his words were cut short when he heard Rhonda's footsteps as she re-entered the room.

Rhonda approached with a big smile on her face as she leaned over Peabo's broad shoulders, wrapping her arms around him, from behind, and began planting kisses on his neck.

Peabo grinned "what got you all rowled up?"

Rhonda giggled " nothin baby, I just haven't spoke to my daddy in a few weeks."

"When you gone invite him over? I'd like to meet him" Peabo replied.

Rhonda gave him a surprised look, shocked that he wanted to meet her father.

"I think we can arrange that!" She exclaimed as she picked up Peabo's glass and drank the remainder of the Hennessey.

"Damn!" Mike blurted out loud, unintentionally, as he witnessed the two ice cubes in the glass disappear as Rhonda gulped the last of the liquor, then slammed the glass on the table.

Peabo, also mesmerized by the feat, didn't even hear Mike's comment.

"Oops!" Rhonda quipped "daddy, I'm sorry. I ate your ice!"

"More like swallowed it." Mike thought as he admired Rhonda's juicy lips.

"That's o.k. baby. I'll get it back later." Peabo grinned and pulled her closer to him, kissing her, while palming her ass. Mike took advantage of the moment to get a nice close up of the "goods" which Peabo held in his hands.

Mike cleared his throat and rose from the barstool, "dawg I'm out, I got somein to handle." He stated as he turned and walked away, swiftly, so no one would notice the bulge in his pants, as he made his way to the front door.

"Call me if you hear somein." Peabo yelled as Mike closed the door behind him.

"Come on baby; let's go see if we can find those ice cubes!" Peabo said, pulling Rhonda towards the bedroom.

"But daddy, you sure you got enuff room for any more ice in that mouth of yours." Rhonda said, making Peabo smile, a broad smile, showing every diamond in his mouth.

"I'm sho we'll find some room for it, don't worry bout that!" He exclaimed, slapping Rhonda on the ass as she pranced towards the bedroom, leaving a trail of clothing behind her.

CHAPTER 17

Detonate

"Marcus, I have something to tell you" Candy said as she lay in the bed, with her head resting on his chest.

Marcus noticed something wet trickling upon his bare chest, causing him to raise up. Palming Candy's chin, he looked her in her tear stained eye's and asked "baby what's wrong?"

"If she tell me she cheatin on me I'm bout to flip the fuck out" he thought to hisself as he gave her a concerned look.

Candy inhaled deeply and began pouring her heart out to Marcus, explaining to him that he was in fact the second man to ever have sex with her. She could see Marcus' jaw clench, causing a large vein to rise across his temple as she continued to give him all the details of the events that had taken place long ago; this was the very first time she had ever spoken to Marcus about the time Leon had violated her.

Marcus sat quietly, with a furious look on his face, leaving Candy in a state of confusion as she brought her story to a close and was met with total silence.

Candy wasn't sure how to interpret the look on his face, nor his lack of words. The silence seemed to engulf the room and Candy could feel her heart crumble as she began to regret she had even told Marcus the secret she had held in the confines of her mind for so long. Not able to stand it anymore, Candy began to sob uncontrollably, and was about to get out of the bed, when Marcus grabbed her by the wrist and pulled her close to him, holding her in a strong embrace.

"I'm so sorry Marcus... I didn't know... I was drunk and I passed out... I didn't know... I didn't... please don't hate me!" Candy babbled, while crying like a scolded child, with snot dripping from her nostrils.

Finally, Marcus broke his silence; once the knot that had formed in his throat gave way, allowing him to speak.

"Candy listen" he began, trying not to choke on his words. "I'm not mad at you; Candy it ain't yo fault baby what makes you think I'd hate you? Baby I love you. And you know I'd never let nobody hurt you and get away with it; past or present!" Marcus said through clenched teeth.

"That nigga gone pay for what he did to you. And he gone pay for every time you had to think about what he did to you... I promise you that!"

Marcus sat in the tattoo parlor, numb to the needle gliding across his flesh, as his mind time traveled to the past. His thoughts drifted as the tattoo artist continued to carve away at what seemed to be an empty shell; showing no signs of life.

After numerous unanswered questions and comments, the artist came to the conclusion that Marcus' mind was elsewhere. "Oh well". He adjusted his finger on the gun, making sure he stayed within the lines as his right hand tediously shaded in the area along the edges of his latest masterpiece.

Marcus' mind continued to drift as the artist dabbed at his piece of work with a damp washcloth, that he held in his left hand, removing the excess ink and blood that seemed to emerge from Marcus' flesh like sweat.

"You know I never did like that slick grinnin ass nigga, no way!" Rhameek hissed, after Marcus' account of Candy's past encounter with Leon.

"So what you wanna do dawg? Rhameek questioned then added " I say we hit that nigga pockets for old time sakes, kill two birds with one stone so to speak!"

The last remark caught Marcus' attention " what you mean, kill two birds with one stone?"

"You know that nigga Peabo right?" Rhameek questioned.

Marcus gave a nod, then answered "I don't really know the nigga, just know of him... you know I don't socialize much, what about him?"

"Put it this way; my Uncle Zone got old beef wit the nigga, he pulled some grimy shit on Zone way back in the days... you should see how the lil bit of hair Zone got left on his head bristles up when he hear his name."

"Nigga what that got to do wit Leon and "throwing rocks at a bird" as you say?"

"It got plenty to do wit Leon, cause that club Leon's runnin ain't his shit! It's Peabo's, and so is the money that flows through it; both legal and illegal. So hittin Leon's pockets and Peabo's pockets is one in the same. And to set the record straight, it ain't 'throwing rocks at birds nigga...its killin two birds with one stone!"

Marcus shrugged "whatever, it don't make me no difference. Rocks, stones, birds...it don't matter how you put it, besides I'd like to rock that nigga Leon wit two eagles; I don't care bout all that other shit!" Marcus stated coldly.

"I feel you" Rhameek stated then paused as he thought about the story Zone had told him, numerous times, about a young, up and coming, Peabo.

Zoned Out

Zone was far from a sucker. And in his prime, if he had any problems with anybody, he'd address that problem with two large, Hawk Bill, blades that he kept strapped to the vest he donned underneath the flashy double breasted suits he was known for wearing. In fact, Zone was so attached to the two blades he had nicknamed "Rip and Run" that he had instructed his tailor to stitch two special made pockets into every vest, for every suit, he ever had made.

"No reason I can't be lethal and pretty at the same time" Zone reasoned; but neither Zones reputation nor two razor sharp blades, with gold engravings, and pearl handles, was enough to detour a young and determined Peabo from running up on one of Zone's 'designated hoe stroll's'; located on West Trade Street, and announcing.

"This block is being closed for reconstruction and when I leave and come back, any Bitch still standing out here, when I arrive, will be left laying here when I depart!"

No sooner than Peabo had left the scene all of Zone's girls began to disperse; choosing to deal with Zone's wrath over the young aggressive hustler who's name was gaining momentum due to numerous acts of violence, some urban legend, some true, that had been accredited to his reputation as of late.

The girls moved along, hips shimmying and heels clicking at a fast pace, scattering in different directions like roaches when the lights are turned on; trying to avoid being stepped on. But like always, there were two who chose to hang around, trying to grab that last morsel, that last crumb of bread that the others had left behind. But these two were far from roaches, and if one wanted to use any form of metaphoric phrase to describe them, it would be nothing in the insect or rodent family. if anything, they would have to be described as a well groomed Arabian race horse and her young foal.

"Zone gone break all ya'll hoes down a whole shoe size and make ya'll pull a seventy-two hour shift, in the poorest section of town he can think of, and still expect ya'll to meet your quota; when he find out how ya'll done high-tailed it up outta here!" Janice exclaimed as she stood her ground, refusing to leave on the account of some idle threats.

"That's right, scared money don't make money!" The young foal yelled.

Janice or just 'Jah Jah', as Zone called her, couldn't contain her laughter. Her full lips parted in a broad smile, showing off her pearly white teeth. Gingerly, she brushed her long silky hair to the side with her thumb and tucked the strands behind her ear, exposing her high cheekbones and beautiful green eyes.

"That was a lil old, but I'll give you credit for saying it wit spunk" Jah Jah stated, making her young protege' blush as she looked up at Jah Jah admiring her beauty.

Ranita was like the daughter Jah Jah never had, and she had kept her close to her every since she and Zone had stumbled across the young girl, sitting alone in the rain, under a small bus shelter, with no money and nowhere to go.

Jah Jah had insisted that Zone take the young girl in. Trusting her judgment and foreseeing the potential in the young beautiful girl, Zone had agreed. But what Zone didn't know, nor did the other girls, was the fact that for the last two years; since Ranita had been taken into the fold, she had never turned one single trick. Instead, Jah Jah had only allowed Ranita to play lookout as she put in enough work to cover her, and the young girls, expected take for the night.

Ranita, insisting that she would, one day, follow in Jah Jah's path, took advantage of this time to learn every in and out of the game her brain could muster.

She knew that Jah Jah was only trying to save her from the streets, and the things that come with it. But she, on the other hand, was ready to embrace the game and "break every niggas pockets she came across. This, she thought, was the perfect way to gain retribution against the abusive step father she'd left behind, when she ran away. And at the same time, repay Zone for the way he had taken her in and given her more love than she'd ever received in her life. The fact that she'd been recruited to 'play the streets' had no bearing on her affection for Zone, because in her mind, Zone had only put her in a position to do what she wanted to do most "break niggas and take them for everything they possessed."

The duo was standing on the corner, caught up in a fit of giggles. When, all of a sudden, a beat up van bent the corner. Jah Jah's warning bells went off, but too late. For no sooner than she had grabbed Ranita's arm and kicked her heels off, in an attempt to break out in a sprint, pulling an inattentive Ranita along with her, the van was right beside them.

"Don't run now!" A voice barked, as Jah Jah's feet seemed to catapult from under her. Her head snapped back as her pursuer grabbed a handful of her silky hair, causing her feet to fly skyward, bringing her down to the concrete with a thud, knocking the wind out of her.

"Jah Jah!" Ranita cried out, as she stumbled, due to the tight grip Jah Jah had on her. At that same moment, Ranita felt a tug on her hair. But, unlike Jah Jah, her hair simply slid off of her head, unveiling her corn rowed hair, which was covered by a stocking cap.

"Run!" Jah Jah ordered. Ranita hesitated before breaking out in a quick sprint.

"CATCH that Bitch!" Peabo barked as he maintained his grip on Jah Jah's hair, dragging her back towards the van, while still holding Ranita's wig in his other hand.

No sooner than Jah Jah was thrown in the van, her kicking

and screaming was brought to a halt, by a swift kick to the jaw. And her urge to fight back left her, at the sight of Ranita being drug back towards the van as well.

"SAY one more word; and we gone snap this lil Bitch neck!" Peabo threatened through clenched teeth, as Mike threw Ranita on the floor of the van; right beside Jah Jah.

Ranita let out a low moan as Jah Jah cradled her in her arms.

"What did you do to my baby, motha fucka?" Jah Jah hissed, turning her attention to Mike.

Mike only grinned as Peabo answered for him "that's the least of your worries Bitch! I warned ya'll hoes, now I'm gonna show you I'm a man of my word."

"That nigga stayed true to his word" Rhameek stated, with a glint in his eye, as he continued to run down Zone's past history with Peabo. "He dumped Jah Jah off, on the same corner he had snatched her from. And, if you see her now, you wouldn't recognize her. Cause, that nigga beat the shit outta her; making sure she'd never turn another trick in her life, ruined her face. They tortured and raped her for hours, nigga let his whole squad run through her and made Ranita watch. From then on out, the only time you'ld spot Jah Jah on that strip was if she was trying to cop a hit. Cause those sorry mufuckas shot her up wit heroin, then forced her to smoke crack, while they had they way wit her. It wasn't long before Jah Jah was just another one of his customers. And Ranita ain't been the same since she witnessed all of that. But even as young as she was at the time, Ranita had managed to escape. The way she tells it, that nigga Peabo wanted to have his way with her, after he got tired of working Jah Jah over; said he 'wanted her to hisself'; took her in a separate room. The sick mufucka stripped her down like he was bout to make love to her or somein.
She ain't put up a fight, cause she was in shock, or so it seemed. But no sooner than the nigga stripped her down and laid her on the bed, she caught a glimpse of a half empty

beer bottle on the nightstand. And as soon as the nigga had penetrated her, she grabbed the bottle and cracked it over his head, then sliced him up good when he stumbled off of her. Then, somehow, she managed to escape out of the window, while everyone else was in the other room busy having their way with Jah Jah... She always felt guilty bout leaving Jah Jah behind. Zone ain't been right since either; truth be told, Jah Jah was more than one of his hoes, and personally I think he was in love with her." Rhameek let out a big sigh as Marcus listened attentively.

"Zone ain't neva been a coward. But after that... after Ranita got word to him bout what had happened and he found Jah Jah all fucked up... it's like it took all the fight out of him. Zone'll get down for his, but he ain't no fool. Peabo was younger back then, but he rolled deep, and his whole crew was strapped to a T... Zone a loner, he ain't have no army, wasn't shit he could do but let the block go... And that's why its important, to me, that I touch this nigga, Peabo's, pocket. I know that's not what you after Marcus, but like I said 'two birds with one stone', and everybody's happy. Zone's done a lot for me; taught me alot, and I'd like to do something major in return. Now tell me you can't feel that dawg!"

Marcus sat in a trance, as Rhameek's words seemed to echo through his head.

"You don't feel that shit dawg?" Marcus frowned up as the tattoo artist waved his hand in front of his face, breaking his train of thought.

"What?" Marcus snapped.

"I said, you can't feel this needle or somein? You impervious to pain? You ain't flinched since I started this" the artist remarked "I mean, I know you human, cause you bleed like one. But you damn sho don't seem to have no feeling in your body."

Marcus smiled then replied "dawg, if you only knew! It's so many feelings bottled up in me, I feel like I'm bout to explode at any moment."

"Well good thing I'm finished, so you can go-head and pay me and get your crazy ass the hell out of here. Cause my insurance don't cover spontaneous combustion!"

Marcus laughed as he began to dig through his pockets to pay the artist. He couldn't believe a few hours had passed, since he had entered the tattoo parlor. He was so caught up in his thoughts, dwelling on the events from the past that had turned his plans for a 187 into a 211 as well; but the broad smile on Zone's face, when Rhameek had dropped the news on him about their plan, was enough to make Marcus feel good that his plan for simple vengeance had been remodeled a little just to suit Zone.

The tattoo artist accepted the large bills with glee, then pointed Marcus towards the large mirror on the wall. "Go check it out!"

Marcus made his way towards the mirror and admired his latest addition. The new tattoo held more meaning than any of the others that adorned his skin; so much meaning that it seemed more like it had risen from the depth's of his soul, as if his inner feelings had emerged from within and revealed themselves on his flesh, rather than ink applied by human hands.

"You like that?" The artist questioned.

"Absolutely!" Marcus responded, giving the artist dap before looking at his watch and realizing exactly how much time had passed since his arrival.

"Bandage me up. I gotta get up outta here." He instructed, knowing Candy was waiting on him to return home.

Rhonda lay in bed, beside an exhausted Peabo, running her fingers up the middle of his chest till they found their way to a large scar that ran in a snake like pattern from the right side of his upper chest. The long, ugly scar zigzagged across his collar bone and traveled in a diagonal line that ended just below his left earlobe.

"Looks like somebody cut you good right here baby" she

said, licking the wound. "You never told me how you got it."

"You never asked", he replied. Then continued "it's something that happened a long time ago, when I was just a young nigga stakin my claim to the game; just one small obstacle on my way up the ladder." He stated dryly.

"Well evidently baby, it wasn't an obstacle you couldn't overcome" Rhonda purred while grabbing his crotch.

"Small thing to a giant!" Peabo said with a smirk as he thought back to the young girl who had tried to cut his head off in the days of old.

"Small thing to a giant, huh?" Rhonda mocked as she stroked his manhood and licked her way down his abdomen in small circles. "You know what they say bout big things in small packages." She added before going down on him, numbing his train of thought as she sent him into a state of ecstasy.

Candy sucked her teeth after looking at her watch for the hundredth time. "I'm gonna have a surprise for you when I get back!" She mumbled to herself, mocking Marcus' comment. Her chest swelled as she took in a deep breath and began to count to ten, trying to make herself less angry at the fact that she had been waiting on Marcus to return for hours. And the fact that she had made haste in preparing herself for whatever venture he had planned, only made her angrier.

She had showered, dressed herself and applied make-up in record time; only to be put on hold.

"One hundred one... one hundred two... one hundred three," realizing that a count to ten was nowhere near enough to calm her down, she had thought that extending her count would help, so she continued, to no avail "one hundred and... to hell wit this!"

She cursed before kicking off her heels aggressively; sending one flying across the living room as she let out a loud scream and snatched up a small plaid blanket that lay neatly folded on the arm of the couch. Throwing the blanket over herself, she lay back on the couch, not caring if she messed her hair or clothes up.

The small, green, and white, throw blanket had been given to her by Marcus, early in their relationship, and she'd always found solace in wrapping the blanket around herself. And it always reminded her of times when Marcus was more attentive of her. Settling into her comfort zone, she grabbed the remote and switched on the television; just in time to catch a breaking news report on Channel 9.

The sight of the crime scene tape and Coroners Van caught her attention as the petite newscaster smiled broadly at the camera and began to speak.

"Breaking news today; as you can see were right here on the scene where two people were found dead in this small apartment on the Eastside of Charlotte.

The police haven't given many details on the situation but we do know it appears to be a possible robbery turned murder and sources say that the male and female were both found bound with duct tape and plastic bags over their heads.

We're not yet quite clear if this bit of information holds any truth and the Police are not ready to release any comments at this time, but as more details are given we will be giving a more elaborate account of the scene at hand. This is Felicia McNeil reporting live from Channel 9."

"Sounds like somebody pissed somebody off!" Candy stated to herself as she began flipping through the channels. All the while, thinking to herself, how violent the streets could be.

Finally, deciding to leave the television on B.E.T. she settled back into her comfort zone, allowing herself to be engulfed by the sounds and scenes of Robin Thicke's new video "Lost without you."

"I'm one to talk about violence." She thought to herself as

her mind lapsed back to the night of Leon's murder.

Candy had never been a big fan of violence, or so she thought, but she couldn't help but recall the fact that she seemed to have been possessed by an evil entity on the night of Leon's demise. She couldn't believe she was able to break Marcus down and convince him to let her go with him; initially his intentions, as far as she knew, were to simply rob Leon and give him a good beat down. But once things came into play, she realized that Marcus wasn't going to let Leon make it out the easy way. And she was so engulfed in the moment that she didn't want to see him left behind breathing.

She knew her hatred for Leon ran deep but what she didn't expect was the euphoric feeling that overcame her when she witnessed Marcus beating and kicking Leon, before forcing him to strip. In fact, it was actually she that had insisted that he dress in heels and thongs and dance on the pole. It was she who had wanted to see him humiliated; just as he had humiliated her in the past.

Candy's sense of euphoria had not only heightened when Marcus had finally decided it was time for the 'coupe de gra' but unbeknownst to Marcus, Candy had not once looked away when he had placed the Desert Eagle to Leon's gut, but instead, she had looked on in awe as the anticipation of the bang from the large handgun caused her to pulsate between her thighs. And once the gun rang out and echoed through the club, she flinched, not due to shock, but due to the fact that she had actually had an orgasm at the same moment the gun went off.

Candy couldn't explain her feelings, or her mood on that night. But she had felt like an alter ego had manifested itself to the surface. And she couldn't help but wonder to herself, if there was actually someone evil who existed, hidden deep down inside of her.

Candy's thoughts were interrupted as thoughts of the newscasters words echoed through her head "Male and

Female found dead in their home" and it was then that she thought, maybe she didn't like violence after all. The words "Male and Female found dead" seemed to hit a little too close to home. But just as quickly as she decided she didn't like violence, her alter ego surfaced again as she thought about Marcus' whereabouts.

"Stupid ass nigga probably out fuckin right now!" She blurted out loud as she snatched the blanket off of her and threw it to the floor, before grabbing her phone and scrolling through the call log until she reached Sonny's number. Just as she had began to contemplate calling him back, she heard the door knob turn and a smiling Marcus was met by a frown.

"What's up babe?" Marcus spoke out loud as his mind spoke words of another nature "what's wrong this time?"

"What's up!" Candy mocked "I been waiting on yo ass for about five hours" Candy exaggerated.

"Come on Can..."

"Don't come on Candy me nigga", Candy interrupted. "Nigga I'm tired of yo bullshit! Is this the big surprise you was talkin bout?" She hissed "well guess what? I ain't surprised ... I'm use to yo preoccupied ass runnin round fuckin wit those dirty ass hoes, while I sit around twiddlin my thumbs!"

"What is you talkin bout?" Marcus started.

"You know what I'm talkin bout nigga! I'm talkin bout you leavin me here lookin stupid, waitin on your ass, while you out somewhere probably wit yo nasty dick up in some nasty hoe! I ain't stupid nigga!"

Marcus shook his head in disbelief as she continued to rant.

"Where my surprise at Marcus? Cause I don't see shit in yo hands."

"I got yo ..."; he started as Candy threw her hand up in his face.

"Nigga I ain't tryna hear yo bullshit... you ain't got shit for me but a hard time and a headache!"

"Oh, I'm a headache?" Marcus responded, his anger rising.

"Damn right you a headache!" She started before noticing a small spot of blood on Marcus' shirttail. "Oh hell no! Nigga I know you ain't come walkin up in here wit no blood on the front of your shirt. What? You fuckin nasty hoes on they period now?"

Marcus had had enough, and was beyond explaining himself "you know what Candy? I ain't even bout to explain shit to you, bout no blood or nothin else, cause you got me this far from snappin on yo ignorant ass!" He gestured, holding his index and thumb less than an inch apart. "And furthermore, that shows how much you don't give a fuck bout nobody but yo'self. Cause otherwise, when you saw this blood on me, you should've been concerned wit my well being before you jumped to any conclusions bout some Bitches!"

Marcus' last statement toned Candy down a notch as she thought to herself that maybe Marcus could've been in an altercation, or anything. And in the midst of her hell raising, she hadn't, once, thought about every other possible way he could've got blood on his shirt.

"Marcus you right I ... are you alright? ... did something happen?" She questioned, her expression changing from anger to concern.

"Hell no ain't nothin happen" he barked.

Candy frowned up then spoke " so you ain't been in no fight or nothing?"

"No Candy" Marcus replied as he began to walk off. And just as quick as Candy's temper had calmed, it began to shoot back through the roof.

"Well tell me how it happened?"

"You know what Candy ... I ain't tellin yo silly ass shit! ... Do what you been doin ... assume the worst!"

"Oh nigga, it's like that? ... I was right. You have been wit some trifling, ragged out hoe ... I knew it!"

Marcus walked off, ignoring Candy as she raved on. "I'm sick of yo shit nigga! I want you to leave this house... pack yo shit and get out!"

"I wish I would pack my shit and leave" he remarked, waving her off, as he went into the bathroom with Candy following close behind.

"That's cool nigga; stay here then. Cause I'm gonna leave!" She screamed as she approached him from behind, only to be met with the sound of the bathroom door slamming in her face; creating a barrier between her and Marcus.

Candy reached for the knob and turned it, only to find that the door was locked.

Marcus stood in the bathroom, ignoring Candy, as he took off his shirt and removed one of the bandages that had came loose, allowing small drops of blood from his fresh tattoo to soak through his shirt.

"That's all right nigga, two can play... it's over between us."

"Whatever Candy" Marcus replied and proceeded to change the bandage, as she kicked and banged on the door like a mad woman.

"Oh you think I'm playin nigga? ... it's O.V.E.R.... you hear me?"

"Heard it all before, Candy" he replied calmly, as he unzipped his pants and began to relieve his bladder.

"I mean it this time Marcus ... I'm gone ... its over", she continued as she walked away from the bathroom and made her way down the hallway, towards the front door.

Candy grabbed her purse and opened the door. But before making an exit, she screamed down the hallway, making sure Marcus heard her loud and clear. "Remember; ain't no more 'us' nigga ... so when you hear anything bout me and another nigga, don't sweat it ... cause I'm not your woman no more. And if you see me wit a nigga, keep it moving!"

Marcus burst from the bathroom so quick that he hadn't had a chance to fasten his jeans or zip them up. Candy slammed the door and made haste to her car. And before Marcus got halfway down the hallway, his unfastened jeans fell to his ankles, tripping him. And in the short time it took for him to pull them up, Candy was already in her car, bending the corner, once he had reached the front door.

Marcus was fuming. Candy's last words had driven him overboard. And if she hadn't left as fast as she did, he'd had every intention of "burying his foot up her ass", knowing it was useless to try to catch up with her, he slammed the door shut and walked towards the couch. And it wasn't until he sat down, that he realized his jeans were wet; all across the front.

He had been so determined to get his hands on Candy that, when he burst out of the bathroom, he hadn't realized that he had pissed all over the front of his jeans.

"Ain't this a Bitch!' he grumbled as he lay back on the couch, frustrated and too pissed to worry bout some pissy pants.

CHAPTER 18

Tiffany stormed through the mall, cursing under her breath, her heels clicking and echoing through the corridor as she made her way towards the ladies bathroom.

The anger and frustration she had held inside, finally, surfaced and came to a head, once she had entered the empty bathroom.

"Motha fu... aghh! ... I swear to God I'm gon... I don't believe this nigga!" She cursed, letting out a flurry of incomplete sentences, as she snatched her purse off of her shoulder and threw it across the bathroom; sending it slamming into the mirror.

Caught up in her fit of rage, she didn't seem to notice the fact that her Gucci handbag had cracked the large mirror, from top to bottom, nor was she concerned with the miscellaneous items that fell from the purse.

"I ... know ... this ... nigga ... ain't ... played ... me ... like ... this!" She raved as she jumped up and down like a mad woman in church, engulfed by the Holy Ghost. Her feet levitating every mili second, only to meet the floor with a boom that would've made any college step team proud, as she continued to curse and emphasize every single word she spoke with a loud stomp.

Tiffany so caught up in the moment of rage, didn't notice the small tube shaped eyeliner, that had fallen from her purse, rolling in her direction.

"Mother fucka ... wanna ... play wit me!" She continued to curse as she leapt in the air once again, while with almost perfect timing, the eyeliner rolled right beneath her foot.

"I'm gon ..." her words were cut short as she came down and her right heel made contact with the small eyeliner tube, causing her to lose balance and come crashing to the floor.

Like an angel fallen from grace, she was overcome with a feeling of shame, as she sat on the floor and wept, not due to any pain she felt from the fall, but rather the pain inflicted upon her pride; that left wounds of embarrassment upon her ego.

She had entered the mall with every intention of pushing Peabo's Platinum card to the max, but her plan had backfired after she had spent about an hour in Cache', one of the more expensive stores in South Park Mall, carelessly throwing items on the counter. Everything from shoe's, shirts, pants, purses and belts lay piled beside the register as she arrogantly pulled out her card and was met by a smug look and a demanding smirk when the cashier politely handed her card back to her and a pair of scissors, then kindly stated "I'm sorry mam, but this card has been cancelled."

Tiffany sat on the floor, fuming, as she had recalled the way everyone in the store had seemed to be staring at her, and snickering, as she tried to exit the store with a look of indifference on her face. And just when she thought she had endured all of the embarrassment and humiliation she could take for the day; insult was added to injury, when two men entered the bathroom, laughing and reminiscing about the game they had watched the night before.

Tiffany looked up at the two men. They both stopped in their tracks, and looked at each other, with confused looks on their faces. It was then that Tiffany had noticed, for the first time, the urinals mounted on the walls of the bathroom.

"Are you alright miss?" One of them stated, extending a hand to help her up from the floor.

Tiffany tugged her skirt down, noticing that the helpful man's friend was helping himself to an eyeful of her pink-laced panties.

"I'm alright." She stated dryly as she brushed his hand away and stood up on her own, then left the bathroom with haste, after grabbing her purse, not even taking time to recover any of the small cosmetic items that lay scattered on the floor; choosing to let the items remain where they were, just as she had left the two men standing with baffled looks on their faces.

Regaining her composure, she strolled through the mall with her head held high as she reached into her half empty purse and pulled out her cell phone, which luckily remained in place and in tact.

The wheels in her head began to turn as she decided it was due time she put her foot down and make her presence known to any and everybody who seemed to be taking her for a joke lately.

"This is a good place to start" she chuckled as she sashayed across the mall parking lot and found a point of interest in her list of phone contacts, and began to dial.

Candy wasn't surprised by the brief moment of silence that seemed to consume the beauty salon as she entered. And like always, the moment of silence was followed by a barrage of smiling faces and greetings of "Hey Girl"... "where you been?"... "How you doing?"

Candy glanced across the room at Yvette, who gave her that "girl you know they was just talkin bout you" look. And Candy gave her that "girl I know" look, before greeting everyone in the room with fake smiles and hugs of her own, while making her way to Yvette whom she greeted with a sincere smile and embrace.

"How you doin girl? You ain't called me in awhile, where you been?" Yvette questioned.

"I been chillin." Candy answered, bluntly, as she made her way towards the display counter that held beauty supplies and began picking up a few items.

"Let me find out you bout to do your own hair" Yvette

stated as she noticed Candy picking up a blow dryer and curling irons.

"Nah girl, I just need these." Candy replied as she added a scarf and bottle of spritz to the items she held in her hands. Yvette gave her a curios look, then stated "what about the new curlers and dryer I just bought you, a month ago, for yo birthday?"

"Oh, I still got those at home girl." Candy responded as she began to think to herself that maybe it had been a mistake coming to the shop.

"So if you got those at home, why do you need these?" Yvette proceeded to question, only to receive a defensive look from Candy.

Yvette noticed that the shop had become quiet, a sign that everybody's ears were focused on her and Candy's conversation.

"Anyway girl" Candy began; changing the subject. "I gotta get back home. I got a million things to do around the house today."

"Hold up Candy; I'll ring you up." Yvette stated; stepping from behind her chair, leaving an irritated customer with her hair half done as she grabbed Candy by the elbow and lead her towards her office in the rear.

"Okay, spill it!" Yvette demanded, after closing her door to her office.

Yvette crossed her arms and leaned back on the door, making it clear Candy wouldn't exit the room without giving her an answer.

"Spill what Vette?" Candy replied, playing dumb.

"Candy you know what the hell I'm talking about!" Yvette stated, pointing at the items in Candy's hands, "don't play crazy wit me Candy, you don't need that stuff if you already got it at home. And you just said you was on yo way home to clean up or whatever... so what you need that for? Curlers... scarf... look like a travel pack to me, or an overnight kit. So which is it? You traveling somewhere, or you planning a slumber party somewhere? Look Candy, I'm your friend and I'm just sayin... I been hearing a lot of talk, I hear everything; and people been spottin you wit that low life at the club, at the store, all types of shit. And it don't take a genius to figure out, yo ass didn't plan on goin home tonight; I'm just sayin, I hope you ain't bout to do nothin stupid!"

"First of all, I don't know what you talkin bout," Candy retorted as she nudged Yvette to the side "and second, I got to get going." She continued as she made her way out the door, stopping only long enough to drop a fifty dollar bill at the unattended register. Not bothering to wait for anyone to ring her up, nor acknowledging the onlookers or her friend, following behind her, calling her name, she proceeded to exit the shop.

Yvette stopped short, deciding not to involve herself in the matter any further.

"What ya'll nosey Bitches looking at?" Yvette snapped, causing everyone in the shop to direct their attention elsewhere and resume their usual conversation of "who done what, when and where."

Candy pulled her phone from her purse, after slamming her car door, and began to dial. After a few rings, she finally heard someone answer.

"What's up Sunshine?" The voice spoke.

"What's up Sonny?"

Nightfall began to set in, as Felicia made her way down 85, headed for Sugar Creek Road. She drove down the highway at a steady pace; until she ran into what appeared to be a traffic jam.

"Ain't this a Bitch... must be a wreck." She spoke out loud to herself as she slowed the car down and fell in line with the rest of the cars that were being directed to one lane, causing everyone to move at a very slow crawl. Checking her watch, she cursed out loud and leaned her seat back in a more comfortable position. Then turned the volume up on her stereo, letting the sounds of Young Lloyd fill her eardrums, while her mind pondered on the phone call she had received earlier, requesting that she make her way to the Brookwood Inn at a designated time.

"Why a hotel?" She had thought to herself, but chose not to question the request, due to the fact that it sounded as if it was urgent that she be there. Brushing off her curiosity, Felicia had agreed to be there at the agreed upon time.

"Better late than never." She thought as she continued to creep down the highway, at a slow pace, while singing along with Young Lloyd. Then, all of a sudden, she began snapping her fingers as the mix C.D. changed pace, and T-Payne began to croon through her speakers. "Snap yo fingers... do yo step... you can do it all by yo'self."

"That's my shit!" She screamed as she began to lean from side to side in her car, gyrating her neck and snapping her head back, on beat, bringing a smile to the face of one of the Officers, who stood by his cruiser with his lights flashing, while directing traffic; stopping his task only long enough to do his best imitation of the popular hood dance as Felicia crept by him; with her system blaring.

"Get it baby! ... you off rhythm, but at least you tried!" She screamed, then broke out into a fit of laughter at the Officers unrhytmic attempt at the dance.

The Officer replied with a smile and a tip of his hat as Felicia proceeded to follow the flow of traffic down the backed up highway.

CHAPTER 19

Marcus swung vigorously; following each right hand blow with a left as he continued to alternate punches in rapid successions, connecting the large gloves on his hands to the heavy punching bag, creating a rhythmic tune as the chain holding the bag rattled with each blow; like tambourines blended with the sounds of war drums.

Marcus continued to swing, aggressively, with his eyes focused on the bag, while his mind traveled elsewhere, blocking out everyone else who inhabited the crowded gym; all caught up in their routines of weightlifting and basketball.

Marcus' mind was in a trance as his body continued to perform its task. Sweating profusely, he bit down, hard, on his mouthpiece, as thoughts of his past raced through his mind. His fist never missed a beat, as he thought of the way he had felt when he had drawn another mans blood for the first time. He thought of the rush he had felt when his blade had penetrated Lenny's flesh. He thought about the sense of power he had felt when Lenny, his mother's boyfriend, lay at his feet groveling. It was then, at the age of twelve, he learned the true nature of his capabilities. It was then that he also learned of his other half; that part of him that could surface at any moment, reacting in the most hostile manner when pushed too far. But just as quick as those memories invaded his mind, they faded, like a television changing channels, and thoughts of Candy entered his mind. Instead of calming him down, these thoughts seemed to be driving his other half closer to the surface. And it was at that same moment, his train of thought was interrupted by loud voices that seemed to disrupt the pictures in his mind.

"Damn he rockin that bag!" Was the first voice, like a whisper in his ear. And then came the second voice, that seemed to boom through his eardrum like a P.A. system.

"Yeah, looks good from over here, but that bag don't punch back!"

Marcus continued to swing, ignoring the voices thinking they were a figment of his imagination, until the loud voice invaded his eardrums again, with a statement that snapped him back to reality.

"I bet that nigga would fold like a broad if he felt one blow!" The loud voice spoke, bringing forth a chorus of laughter.

Marcus stopped swinging, and turned his attention towards the direction of the laughter. He made eye contact with the man who stood by the weight bench, in the midst of the hecklers. He was staring at Marcus, like a hunter would stare at his prey.

Marcus smiled at the sight of the big man who stood, at about 6'2", with his foot propped up on the weight bench. Breaking eye contact with the big man, Marcus glanced at the weights mounted on the bar. A quick calculation and Marcus figured that it was somewhere in the area of 405 lbs.

Marcus let out a loud, hysterical laugh. And then his laughter stopped, abruptly, as he pulled his gloves off and threw them to the floor, while approaching the big man.

"That's a lot of weight you pushin partner", Marcus sneered as he nodded towards the weight's, then faced the big man "but those weights don't push back" he stated, sarcastically, as the big man's friend's began to step out of the way, leaving the two of them face to face, glaring at each other.

"Nigga what the fuck you gone do I'll ..." Before the threat was able to roll off of the big man's tongue, Marcus had made his move.

The cracking sound echoed through the gym, causing all motion to come to a halt, as everyone stopped what they were doing and stared in awe at the sight of the large man dropping to his knees.

"You bout to say somein?" Marcus sneered; but all he got in response was a groan as the big man attempted, unsuccessfully, to form words with his broken jaw, which was twisted to one side.

"I ain't think so." Marcus stated calmly before snatching up his bag and exiting the crowded gym quietly. Once outside, he inhaled deeply, allowing the fresh air to flow through his nostrils as he looked towards the sky and noticed that the sun was beginning to fade.

Marcus made his way towards his car while his mind pondered on Candy's whereabouts; tired of wondering, he pulled his phone from his bag and made another attempt to reach her, only to be forwarded to her voice mail for the twentieth time.

Marcus' blood began to boil; as he thought of all the things Candy could possibly be doing. Then, just as quick as the thought entered his mind, it left. He let out a loud chuckle and crank up his car.

"She know better!" He stated out loud as he drove off and began dialing Rhameek's number.

Rhameek let out a deep breath, his chest heaving as frustration overcame him. He knew Marcus was probably wondering why he had cut the phone call so short.

He could hear the frustration in his friends voice as he made an attempt to tell him about what had went on with Candy earlier and he could almost imagine the look on Marcus' face when he had cut him off midsentence and stated "look dawg, I got somein to take care of I'll call you back!" And disconnected the call before Marcus could respond; but it was the caller whom Rhameek had on hold, on the other line, that had him preoccupied.

"Looks like she's headed towards the motel as we speak." The caller had stated right before Marcus had called, causing Rhameek to put the caller on hold just long enough to brush Marcus off and click back over.

"Alright Mo, I'm back", Rhameek stated once Marcus was clear from his phone line, "and this is what I want you to do; stay there and keep your eyes on her best you can until I get there. And if she leaves before I get on that side, call and let me know!"

"No problem Rah my man, I got it covered", Mo said in a laid back tone "you know, for a few dollars extra, I can go head and take care of this lil problem for you." He added.

"Nah bruh, I got this" Rhameek replied. "This is personal. I gotta clean this lil mess up, myself."

"Suit yo'self!" Mo replied as he parked and put his seat back in a comfortable position "but you know I'm the type who like to play seek and destroy; not hide and seek." He added dryly before hanging up the phone.

Those last words still echoed through Rhameek's head after almost thirty minutes had passed.

"What kind of nigga Zone done hooked me up wit?" He wondered "Nigga act like he want to kill the broad or somein." And as much as Rhameek hated the situation he saw no need to pull a 'Ray Caruth' move and kill the girl; all he wanted to do was clean up the mess that had been brought to his attention less than twenty-four hours ago. And he knew that all the talking in the world wouldn't be enough to solve the problem. So he had decided it would be best to take things in his own hands and deal with it; in his own way.

Rhameek could only hope that Felicia hadn't broken her promise and mentioned anything that the two of them had discussed to Candy; other than that, the only thing he was worried about was being recognized. But if things went well, the whole scenario would look like a robbery attempt. And other than a few bumps and bruises, no one would be seriously hurt. The problem would be solved in a flash, then things could hopefully go back to normal; once the third party was taken out of the equation.

Rhameek got within spitting distance of the hotel, and as he glanced at Shawt Change, sitting in the passenger seat, he couldn't help but wonder if he had made a mistake by involving someone else in all of this.

"Why you eyeballing me Dawg? ... I told you, I got yo back! ... this here gone be kept between me and you!" Shawt Change stated as if he was reading Rhameek's mind.

"I know you ain't gone say nothin to nobody Dawg!" Rhameek assured him "I just hope she don't recognize yo short ass!" He replied with a smile, trying to cover up his feelings of doubt.

"Listen Dawg, she'll neva see me, I promise ... stop worrying, I got this!" Shawt Change stated as he pulled a set of leather gloves over his hands and placed a rolled up ski mask on top of his head like a toboggan.

Candy paced around the room nervously, stopping only long enough to peek out of the window for the fiftieth time.

"Candy would you chill out!" Sonny stated as he sat slouched back on the couch in the large suite.

"I'm sorry Sonny, I just ..."

"Don't worry bout it!" Sonny cut her off, and began patting the cushion next to him on the couch "come sit down, you makin me nervous; peeking out windows like we in the dope house or somein." He said, bringing a smile and slight chuckle from Candy.

"Boy you crazy!" She giggled as she sat beside him on the couch.

Candy had spent the last few hours pouring her heart out to Sonny while pacing the floor and sipping glass after glass of Champagne. It had been years since Candy drank, and to her surprise, the light, bubbly Champagne wasn't so bad tasting. And on top of that, it made her feel at peace.

"Sonny you so nice to me", she stated as she kicked off her shoes and lay her head on his shoulder. "I'm sorry I spoiled your get-together." She added, reminding herself that Sonny had cancelled the night's festivities in order to comfort her in her time of need.

"You ain't spoiled nothing Candy", Sonny responded as he raised her chin up with his forefinger and made eye contact with her. "Believe it or not, I'm enjoying this time alone with you." He said before kissing her on her forehead.

Candy didn't know if it was the feel of his lips above her brow that made her tingle inside, or if it was the Champagne she'd been drinking.

"What am I doing here?" She thought to herself as she

glanced at the "overnight bag", as Yvette had called it, lying on the floor by the couch.

Yvette's words echoed through her head. "You either goin on a trip, or you don't plan on going home!"

Was it true that her intentions had been to stay out all night? And if so, had she planned on staying with Sonny all along? "No!" She told herself "I was just going to get a room somewhere 'alone' and go home after I cooled off." But if this was the case, she asked herself, "why did I call Sonny ... and why did I bring a bag with everything necessary for a nightcap up to this room with me?" She pondered as she was snapped out of her trance by the sound of Sonny's voice.

"What you thinkin about?" He asked, still holding her face in his hands, as he placed another kiss on her forehead.

"Nothing." She said, in an inaudible tone, as her eyes closed and she felt herself sink further into Sonny's arm, until her head was resting on his shoulder, once again. Then she felt the tingling sensation return, this time, starting at her forehead, slowly making its way to her eyelid, then her nose. It felt almost like a feather was being traced over her face, and it wasn't until the sensation reached her lips, when she opened her eyes and realized that the tingling sensation she was experiencing was not alcohol induced but was, in fact, Sonny's soft kisses making their way to her lips.

"No!" Her mind screamed as her body defied her, and she felt herself kissing him back "I can't!" Her mind continued to scream; but her mouth was unable to form the words. Her body seemed to have a mind of its own as her tongue tumbled around in Sonny's mouth, causing her to pulsate between her thighs. Her breast seemed to swell and her lips became hot as she felt her hands tearing away at the buttons on Sonny's shirt.

Sonny reached under her skirt and placed his hand between her thighs.

"No!" Her mind screamed again as he pulled her panties to the side and inserted his fingers "Tell him to stop!" Her mind said as she removed her lips from his to form the words, her mind had commanded her to speak "Tell him!" Her mind shouted as his fingers began sinking deep inside of her, until she opened her mouth and screamed.

"Oh Sonny!"

Felicia sat in the hotel parking lot, rummaging through her purse, until she found the small piece of paper she was looking for with the room number scribbled on it.

"I still don't understand why we couldn't have talked on the phone." She thought out loud as she got out of her car and began walking towards the hotel, in search of the room she had been told to come to.

Rhameek and Shawt Change sat in the car quietly, parked out of sight, making sure the hotel security was nowhere around.

The parking lot was clear, other than the car that was parked beside them; which was occupied by Zone's cohort, Mo.

"That nigga strange" Shawt Change stated, nodding his head towards Mo's car.

"Yeah, I know. But my Uncle say he good people, and I trust my Uncle" Rhameek stated "besides, he did what he was paid to do and that's all that counts. Now I gotta do what I gotta do; take care of this problem before it becomes a full grown problem; I just gotta stop this before it goes too ..."

"Look!" Shawt Change stated, cutting Rhameek's words short, as he tapped him on the side, getting his attention.

Rhameek glanced across the parking lot and spotted Felicia, walking with a small piece of paper in her hand. His chest heaved, as mixed feelings overcame him, at the sight of Felicia strolling across the hotel parking lot.

"I wonder did she tell Candy anything about this situation?" He wondered as he looked at Shawt Change and gave him a nod of the head.

"I hate to do it like this, but it gotta be done ... this ain't no way for a playa to act!" He stated as he opened his door and exited the vehicle, with Shawt Change in tow.

"Look, I might still need you after all!" Rhameek said, speaking to Mo, who still sat, slouched back, in the driver's seat of his car.

"What you want me to do?" Mo said with a grin on his face.

"Just come wit us" Rhameek answered dryly, " you don't need no mask, she want recognize you anyway" he stated as Mo got out of his car and they made their way across the parking lot while making sure they stayed out of Felicia's line of sight.

Candy's heart began to pound as Sonny pulled her shirt over her head and lifted her up onto the table that sat in the middle of the large suite. Then he began sucking on her protruding nipples, while his hands slipped her panties off.

"Bout damn time!" Felicia cursed as she finally found the room she had been looking for, and realized she had parked on the wrong side of the building to begin with. "Room 316. This is it." She said to herself, checking the paper in her hand for the fiftieth time, before knocking.

"Ain't this a Bitch!" She cursed again as she checked her watch and wondered if the backed up traffic had caused her to miss her engagement.

Knocking once again, she received no answer then stepped to the side and tried to peek in through the curtains. Unable to see inside, she sucked her teeth and became frustrated as she pulled out her cell phone and began to dial.

Placing the phone to her ear, she turned to her left and her eyes got big at the sight of a familiar car that was parked by the hotel swimming pool.

"Now what are you doing up here?" She mumbled to herself as she turned her attention back towards the door to knock, one last time, and was caught by surprise when she turned and saw two men in ski mask.

Felicia's heart dropped as her attempt to scream was cut short by the masked man's palm, which covered her mouth, as he spun her around and wrapped his other arm around her waist, lifting her off the ground.

"Don't even think about looking at me Bitch!" He hissed in her ear.

Felicia couldn't scream, due to the massive hand that covered her mouth. Her attempts to break free were useless. Her feet simply kicked frantically in mid-air as she tried to bite through the thick leather glove that covered her mouth.

Tears welled up in Felicia's eyes as one of her attacker's grabbed her leg's, while the other kept a tight grip on her mouth, and held her under her armpit with his free hand.

Felicia, determined to shake loose, used all of her strength to try to break free. In her attempt to shake loose, she had managed to free her mouth; only long enough to scream two words.

"My baby!" Then her mouth was covered once again. Her attempts to scream were useless. Her pleas were no more than muffled vibrations that could not be interpreted by her captors or anyone else within earshot. Only she could interpret the words that she tried to scream, repeatedly, until she blacked out. "I'm pregnant, don't hurt my baby."

CHAPTER 20

Chill bumps formed on Candy's flesh, when she felt her panties slide down her thighs, and over her ankles. She trembled as Sonny continued to suck on one of her breast, while squeezing the other one with his left hand.

Candy moaned as Sonny's mouth moved from her breast to the nape of her neck. While his right hand, no longer occupied with the task of removing her panties, was busy unloosening his belt.

The voices in Candy's head became mere whispers "what are you doing?" The voices grew more distant and all she could hear was the rattle of Sonny's belt buckle and the sound of his zipper unzipping.

Candy wanted to listen to the faint voices in her head that whispered "what are you doing? ... What about Marcus? ..." But her body wasn't in sync with her mind. Maybe it was the alcohol. Maybe it was the fact that she knew Marcus had been sleeping around that caused the voices to fade out, completely, as Sonny grabbed her hand and guided it to his manhood, which she unconsciously began to stroke causing it to throb, until Sonny took control and grabbed the pulsating rod in his hand and began to rub it, gently, against her outer walls.

Candy moaned. Then in one swift motion, Sonny penetrated her, hard and deep, causing her to rock back; and almost topple off of the table, as he spat out

"I knew you wanted this!"

Candy let out an agonizing groan. She grabbed the edge of

the table, trying to prevent herself from falling off, as Sonny rocked his hips back and thrust deep inside of her, bringing her out of her 'romantic mood' as he commented, "I know dat nigga wouldn't hittin it right!... you like this shit don't you!"

Candy held the edge of the table, with one hand, and stopped Sonny, in mid stroke, with her free hand.

"Hold Up!" She cried out.

"What!" Sonny snapped.

"Sonny just ease up a lil ... you talkin like I'm some kind of ..."

Sonny sucked his teeth and interrupted "quit trippin" he said, in an irritated tone, as he slid her hand to the side and began to push hisself inside of her, a little slower this time. But it was too late, because the voices had returned in Candy's head, except they weren't saying "don't do it" they were saying " I told you not to do it." As she began to regret she had even gotten herself into this situation.

And even the fact that Sonny was easing his way inside of her, slowly now, wasn't enough to bring back the feeling of euphoria she had experienced prior to him entering her the first time.

Candy knew it was too late to turn back now, the mistake had been made, so she closed her eyes as Sonny inched his way inside of her nice and slow, and that was when the whole world seemed to explode around her.

She felt her whole body began to float and tumble as if she were at Carowind's on her favorite roller coaster ride.

And that's when she heard Sonny let out a loud, gut wrenching moan.

Everything had happened so fast that it took Candy a brief second to realize that the crashing sounds in her head weren't due to feelings of ecstasy, nor was the floating and tumbling sensation she felt.

These were actually the sounds of the hotel door crashing in, and the impact of her half naked body hitting the floor made her realize that she had, in fact, been thrown from the table.

Candy groaned as she tried to shake off the blow her head had taken upon impact.

She felt disoriented as she raised up on her elbows and rolled herself over to a seated position, only to find Sonny lying beside her, groaning, as he held his crotch and rolled around on the floor, with his pants wrapped around his ankles.

Candy became fully aware of her surroundings then realized she had made a bigger mistake than she had thought. Regret filled her as she looked up and saw a man in a ski mask, hovering above her, with bloodshot eyes.

"Face the Goddamn floor and don't even think about lookin up at me again!" The man barked.

Candy began to shake as fear took control of her entire body. She did as she was told and rolled over, face down on the floor, while cupping her bare breast in her palms. She was too scared to look up, or move her hands in order to pull her skirt down, which remained hiked up to her waist, revealing her bare naked bottom to the intruders.

Her mind raced and she began to feel shame along with her feelings of fear. She feared what the masked man might do to her while she lay there half-naked. She also felt ashamed of the fact that she was in a room with a man, other than Marcus, half-naked in the first place.

She was also ashamed of the fact that she had allowed Sonny to enter her, even if it was just for a few seconds. And now she feared that by opening her doors of intimacy and laying out the welcome mat to a man she barely knew she had, at the same time, opened those doors to trespassers as well; vandals who would have no respect for her home, or her body in this case. People who would show no compassion and have their way with her; against her will.

Candy's eyes welled up as she whimpered, "please don't rape me."

"Shut the fuck up!" She heard a voice bark.

Not daring to look up, she wasn't able to see anything more than a pair of boots, which stood within inches of her face. But looking out of her peripheral, she could see Sonny, still holding his groin, as he rolled around on the floor like a wounded animal. It was at that same instance that she noticed two more pair of boots were standing next to Sonny, and she fought off every temptation she had to scream as the boots began to stomp him mercilessly.

"Bitch ass nigga!" She heard another voice bark, from Sonny's direction, as they continued to kick him in the face, drawing blood with every blow.

"Oh my God" Candy murmured as she saw the boots, near her face, walk away; then return with haste. She made no effort to look up. But she followed the boots, with her eyes, as she lay on the floor, stiff as a board, clutching her bare breast.

The sounds of the intruders stomping and Sonny's groaning invaded her ears as she kept her eyes on the pair of boots closest to her. She became nervous when she realized the man hovering over her was moving behind her.

Candy flinched when she felt the man's hands grab her skirt. "Please don't; please!" She begged.

"Shut up!" He barked.

Her heartbeat accelerated when she felt him tug on her skirt, pulling it down, until it covered the exposed portion of her body. She flinched, once again, as she felt something drop on top of her. All types of thoughts ran through her mind as she felt the blanket being dropped over her body.

She had already feared that the intruder might attempt to have his way with her. But now that she realized that there were three people in the room, her heart pounded out of fear of not only being raped; but gang raped.

"Say one word and we gone kill you" the man warned.

Candy chose to remain quiet. She could feel the floor beneath her getting wet as she lost control of her bladder and began to piss all over herself and shake profusely. While the man closest to her, made his way across the room, and began assisting the others in kicking Sonny all over the place.

Candy felt bad for Sonny. But more than anything, she thought of Marcus and wished he were there to protect her. She knew that Marcus would never let anyone bring harm to her; she knew that he would take on an army of men before he would let that happen.

"I'm sorry baby" she began to ramble in a low whisper as she cried and witnessed the beating Sonny was taking.

"Marcus I'm sorry!" She cried out loud this time, as she began to fear for the worst.

"Man shut her the fuck up!" The voice hissed as she saw two sets of boots heading in her direction.

Candy reacted off of instinct as she jumped to her feet in an attempt to run; only to get tangled in the blanket, which tripped her, and caused her to fall into one of the intruders arms.

She began to swing frantically until she was grabbed from behind, and gagged, before a pillowcase was thrown over her head, making it impossible for her to see or scream for help.

Realizing she had only succeeded in pissing her assailants off, she began to fear that they would now show no mercy upon her. Beyond desperation, she reached back and dug her nails into the man who held her from behind, bringing a loud groan from him, as she clawed his neck; deep enough to draw blood.

"Agghh!... my neck! ... my fuckin neck! ... you stupid ass B..." he started to curse before grabbing her arm and twisting it behind her back.

"Take this stupid mother... just take her outside and throw her ass in the trunk! We'll deal wit her later." She heard him command.

"The trunk?" Candy couldn't believe her ears. She hoped she had heard wrong, but once she felt her wrist and ankles being binded with duct tape, she knew she had heard right. Fighting was useless, and all she could do was think of

Marcus as two of the men wrapped her body in a blanket, and hauled her outside.

"You think you a real slick nigga, don't you!" The remaining attacker hissed "Look at you now Bitch!" He hocked then spit on Sonny, who lay on the floor, half conscious and unable to speak; due to the pain in his side, and the blood that filled his mouth.

"Get yo Bitch ass up!" He hissed. Lifting Sonny to his feet, he scanned the room and smiled upon sighting Candy's overnight bag; containing all of her beauty supplies and other miscellaneous items.

"You think you hot shit, huh?" The man spat, his mouth touching Sonny's earlobe.

"Oh you can't answer me nigga?... that's cool cause I'm gone give you the answer to that question!" All Sonny could do was remain limp as the man held him up. "Nah, you ain't hot shit.. But by the time I leave this room I guarantee you, you will be!"

Minutes later the man, now unmasked, joined the others at the car.

"Where she at?"

"She in the trunk."

"You know what to do wit her"; he spoke while his hand rubbed the deep scars she had left on his neck.

"Where you goin?"

"I got somein to tend to", he remarked with a grimace on his face.

"She clawed you pretty good!" All he could do was nod in agreement, before jumping in his car and pulling off.

Sonny regained consciousness only to find himself laying flat on his stomach with his wrist and ankles tied, to the bed frame, spread eagle.

"What the fuck?" He muffled through a sock-filled mouth. Turning his head to the side, he noticed a jar of hair grease, lying on the bed, beside his face.

He felt like he had been in a train wreck. He was in pain from head to toe. He had a confused look on his face when he glanced from the open jar of grease towards the large mirror, which had been removed from the dresser and placed against the wall beside the bed. His eyes grew big as golf balls once he saw his reflection. It was then that he realized, the pain he felt in his ass wasn't due to the ass kicking that he had received.

The masked man's last words replayed in his head "you think you hot shit don't you!"

Sonny began to jerk around frantically upon seeing the curling iron, that Candy had brought with her, protruding from his rectum. His eyes welled up when he saw the cord leading from the curling iron to the socket in the wall.

The light on the curling iron was glowing bright orange, indicating that they were on; but Sonny didn't need any light to tell him that. He could already feel the curlers heating up; he wiggled around desperately trying to break free. It was useless, he couldn't scream due to the sock lodged in his mouth.

The curlers were becoming hotter and he began to push, as if he were trying to defecate, hoping he could free himself from what was to come. But no matter how hard he tried, it was useless. The heat set in and he began to grunt and wiggle around in agony. He could feel his flesh melting and the smell of singed hair and "hot shit" filled the room.

Candy's heart pounded when the car finally came to a halt. It felt like she hadn't been riding in the trunk no more than ten minutes, but ten minutes was more than too long.

Trunks were for speakers, amps, Gucci bags and suitcases; but at the moment, she feared that maybe she was better off in the trunk, than facing what awaited her on the outside.

Candy grunted as she felt herself being lifted from the trunk.

"Don't try to run!" She heard a voice say as the tape was being cut from her ankles and wrist.

Candy's heart beat rapidly as she thought about all of the things these men were about to do to her.

"I hope they just kill me." She prayed to herself as she stood there, with a pillowcase over her head, and a blanket draped over the upper portion of her half naked body.

Candy braced herself and began to think of everything beautiful; flowers, trees, the beach. She tried to put her mind somewhere else, like she had heard numerous rape victims on talk shows say they had done when victimized.

No sooner than she had placed her mind in that beautiful place, she felt a hand grip her shoulder firmly; then the hand disappeared and she heard the sound of a car pulling off.

What seemed like an eternity, but was actually minutes, passed until Candy found the courage to remove the pillowcase from her head.

She had expected to find herself stranded in the woods or in a dark alley. She was surprised when she found that she was standing in the middle of a playground.

There was no sight of an angry gang of rapist or killers; instead, she was only confronted by the sounds of crickets chirping and a large owl that sat, gazing at her from a distance.

The owl blinked then turned his head from side to side, as it seemed to be asking her the same question that she, herself, wanted an answer to.

"Whooo, whooo, whooo"

"Who?" Her curiosity was overtaken by a feeling of relief when she glanced to her left and saw her car parked within walking distance.

She struck out running towards her car, where she found her keys hanging out of the ignition. Wasting no time, she jumped in, crank up the car, and sped away as fast as she could.

All of the doors at the hotel were wide open, as nosey spectators snuck a peek at the man being wheeled out of a room, face down, on a stretcher.

"I'm gonna kill that Bitch!" He growled, continuously, as the paramedics wheeled him towards the ambulance.

"I know she set me up...I'm gonna kill her" he groaned, incoherently, while the spectators giggled and gossiped amongst each other.

Sonny had awakened the entire hotel with his cries. He didn't know how he had managed to get the sock out of his mouth; maybe it was the pain alone that had built up enough pressure in his lungs to make the gag shoot out of his mouth; like a cork from a bottle of Moet. Maybe it was just adrenaline, either way, he was glad that his cries were heard and help had come.

Nonetheless, it was too late; the curling irons had hurt just as bad coming out, taking seared flesh with it. The damage was done, and as far as he was concerned, his first and only priority, after leaving the hospital, would be to "find Candy Brown!"

Felicia whimpered as she sat on the floor binded and blindfolded. She had no idea where she was at or whom her captors were. Only an hour had passed since she had been snatched, but that hour seemed like days as she sat in silence, contemplating her whereabouts.

As far as she could tell, she hadn't been taken far at all. She had only been carried a short distance, after being gagged and blindfolded in the hotel breezeway.

She had struggled until she had no strength left. The masked men were too strong. She had also stopped resisting, out of fear that the child she was carrying would be hurt in an attempt to tussle with the men.

She couldn't help but wonder what fate awaited her and her unborn child.

"And to think, I haven't even told Rhameek yet." She thought to herself.

At the same moment, even in the midst of everything, she

couldn't help but wonder why she had spotted Candy's car outside of the hotel, right before she was attacked.

"What was she doing here?" She asked herself. Her thoughts were interrupted by the sound of a door opening.

Felicia sat up and became alert, when she heard a group of men, laughing amongst each other, as they entered the room.

"Did you see how they wheeled that nigga up outta here on his stomach?" One man spoke as the others laughed.

"It looked like the nigga had a diaper on or somein", he continued "must be one of those 'in the closet' ass niggas; up here gettin his ass ripped up!" The laughter commenced as another man joined in.

"Yeah, well he out the closet now. Cause whoever he is, and whatever happened, its gonna be hard explaining to his lady; why he coming home wit a gauze on his ass at checkout time!"

The comment brought an outburst of laughter as Felicia sat in silence. Their conversation had confirmed that she was still somewhere in the hotel.

A knock at the door broke her train of thought. She heard the laughter die down when the door opened. It was then, when she heard a familiar voice speaking to her captors, that she remembered what had brought her to the hotel in the first place.

It had been the phone call that she had received from the very same person she heard speaking in the background.

"Tiffany!" She thought to herself "but why?"

CHAPTER 21

Rhameek had an aggravated look on his face, when he arrived at Felicia's house and noticed her car was nowhere to be seen.

"Hoe!" He spat under his breath, all the while, recalling the unusual feeling he had got in his gut, when he had spotted her in the hotel parking lot, earlier.

"Bitch probably got her legs throwed up in the air right about now!" He thought out loud as he snatched the gearshift in reverse and backed out of Felicia's driveway.

Deciding he would talk to her later, he picked up his phone and began to dial Marcus' number as he sped off, leaving Felicia's neighborhood in his rearview.

"You ain't gonna answer that?" Tamika remarked, with a broad smile on her face, showing Marcus her pearly whites.

"She's got a nice smile" Marcus thought to himself as he sat in the cozy love seat directly across from Tamika, who was stretched out on her couch.

The phone continued to ring. Tamika propped herself up on her elbow.

"Go ahead and answer your phone boy. I know it's your girlfriend. Don't worry, I want say a word." She stated, before licking her index finger, and crossing her heart.

The gesture made Marcus smile. It felt good to smile after being stressed all day, wondering about Candy's whereabouts.

He had spent the entire day calling Candy's phone, only to be greeted by her answering service each time. Frustrated, after the incident at the gym, he had found himself driving all over town, pissed off, until he had received an unexpected call from the "mystery girl from the mall."

He wasn't sure how he had let her convince him to come to her house, but after a little coaxing, he finally made his way to her home on Idlewild Road.

Marcus was impressed when he pulled up to the Tri-level house, but he became uneasy upon entering the plush home.

The sight of the large pool table that sat in the middle of the room made him think "this has to be some niggas crib!"

Tamika had assured him that this was, in fact, her home, and hers alone. Grabbing him by the arm, when he had made an attempt to turn and leave, she had stated.

" Oh, you think cause its a pool table in here, that means I got you up in some niggas crib?"

Not convinced, Marcus had once again, made an attempt to exit the house, only to have Tamika place herself between him and the door.

"Look baby; I promise you this is my crib. I live alone. And I promise you, ain't no niggas hidin in the ceiling or in the closet, waiting to jump out on your paranoid ass."

That had been the first time Marcus had smiled all day.

"Look, I'll prove it to you", Tamika added as she pulled him towards the pool table and grabbed one of the sticks that lay on it. "Lets play one game, and trust me, once I beat you, you'll know this table, and this crib, belongs to me." She boasted as she picked up the chalk and rubbed it across the tip of the pool stick.

Then placing her shapely lips centimeters away from the tip, she blew on it softly, getting rid of the excess chalk.

"You game, playboy?" she had said with a smirk.

Marcus had taken her up on her challenge. By the time it was over, he was convinced as well as impressed. He never got a chance to take a shot. He only got to sit back and watch Tamika, methodically, sink ball after ball into the pockets, all the while, making comments that made Marcus laugh.

And now, here he was, hours later, sitting across from her; smiling once again.

"You a funny girl", he stated before glancing at his phone, checking the missed call. "And that's not my girl calling."

"Umm hmm ... whatever nigga, why you ain't answer then? Ain't like you busy or nothing!" Tamika quipped as she began to rub her feet together.

"I mean all you doin is sittin here smiling at me." She lay back and slid her right leg up, slowly tracing her left foot with the well-pedicured toes on her right foot.

Marcus cleared his throat and became jittery as he watched her toes glide slowly up her ankle, making their way to her calf.

He admired the orange sherbet colored nail polish that covered Tamika's toes. His eyes were glued to her petite, unblemished feet. He, unconsciously, turned his head to the left; following her toes like an onlooker at a tennis match would follow the ball.

By the time Tamika had stopped, the heel of her right foot was all the way up to her crotch, causing her shorts to bunch up and reveal a slight hint of a panty line.

Tamika began to giggle, snapping Marcus out of his trance. Feeling embarrassed, he turned his attention to a photo that sat on the end table, next to the couch that Tamika was laying on.

"What is that?" Marcus inquired, pointing at the photo.

Tamika rolled her eyes, then sucked her teeth, before rising to her feet.

"That's just a picture of me, back home in Austin, Texas."

"That explains the horse" Marcus commented, observing the large white horse that Tamika seemed to be grooming in the picture.

"Yeah, I like to ride"; Tamika began, with a reminiscent look in her eyes "my family owns a ranch in Texas. I guess you could say they're a little wealthy."

"Is this how you got this big crib, way up here in

Charlotte?" Marcus questioned.

"Yeah, I'm the only child, and I got tired of Texas, my father didn't want me to leave; but since I insisted, he refused to let me leave, unless, he made sure I was living comfortable... so he found me this big house, furnished it, the whole nine... guess you could say I'm a lil spoiled."

"Why Charlotte though?"

Tamika shrugged, "Why not? I went to college with a few girls from North Carolina, and they use to speak highly of this city, so ... here I am!"

She smiled, with a devilish look on her face, as she sat on the arm of the loveseat and began to caress Marcus' eyebrows with her thumbs.

Becoming fidgety, Marcus asked "How long you been here?"

"Only a month and a half, Mr. twenty-one questions." She stated as she leaned in closer, causing Marcus to flinch.

"Umm ... that's a big horse in that picture. You never fell off it before?"

Tamika sucked her teeth again, and exhaled loudly, then palmed Marcus' face in both hands.

"Would you relax!" She demanded, as she slid off of the arm of the chair. "Let me ask you a question" she continued, while easing her way towards his lap. "If you was a horse and I was on top of you ... like this ... would you let me fall off?" Before Marcus could respond, Tamika was straddling him in the chair, with a tight grip on both sides of his collar.

Marcus felt his manhood swelling as Tamika began to gyrate slowly, while pulling on his shirt, like the reigns on a horse.

"I mean, if you was a horse, would you try to hurt me, or would you take me for a nice slow ride?"

Marcus' mind seemed to be everywhere at once. He wondered what was he even doing in this girl's house in the first place. Then he thought of Candy and what she probably was doing at the moment. He thought of the threats she had made, and all of a sudden, he found hisself caressing Tamika's back, tracing his hands up and down her spine as she reached down into his Girbeaud sweat pants.

Without losing rhythm, she continued to gyrate on top of him, as she pulled her shorts to the side.

She rolled her hips backwards, then forward, sliding Marcus' swollen flesh inside of her.

Marcus closed his eyes as Tamika pulled his face to her chest, and let out a low moan, as she engulfed him in her satin like walls, while whispering in his ear. "Don't let me fall ... mmff ... go slow ... ssss ... promise you won't hurt me."

WHEN THE LIGHTS COME ON

Champ raised up on his haunches. Alerted by the sound of a car pulling into the driveway, his ears perked up as he turned his full attention towards the noise outside.

His eyes remained locked on the door while his ears rotated to the left, like a radar dish, towards the sound of Rhameek snoring in his bedroom. Noting that his master was in the room, sleeping, Champ tilted his head to the side, allowing his ears to readjust towards the direction of the door.

He could hear the sound of the car door opening and closing. Crouching low, the huge dog tip-toed towards the front door, poised for combat, as he listened to the footsteps approaching from outside. Tilting his head towards the small crack between the door and the frame, Champ began to sniff vigorously, until, he picked up a familiar scent.

Champ backed away from the door and plopped down on his hind legs. He sat with his chest out and his head high, like a soldier saluting his Commanding Officer, as Marcus turned the knob and entered Rhameek's home.

Marcus smiled at the sight of the massive dog.

"What's up big man" Marcus whispered. Champ stood up, tail wagging, as he gave Marcus his front paw.

"I see Rhameek got you working third shift while he sleep on the job; again!"

Champ responded with a heavy puff of air through both

nostrils, then made his way back to the corner and laid down; resting his chin on Rhameek's old Timbs.

Marcus shook his head "crazy ass dog." He stated before he, himself, laid down on Rhameek's couch and stretched out.

Kicking his shoes off, he decided not to wake Rhameek up. Instead, he chose to lay back and think about the episode he had just encountered with Tamika.

He couldn't help but feel a little guilty, but he kept replaying Candy's parting words, from earlier that day, in hopes of justifying what had just happened. But, even the knowledge of her threats to be with someone else and that lurking thought that she was in fact, probably with someone the whole time she was avoiding his calls, wasn't enough to make him feel better about what he had done.

The last thing he remembered was Tamika's body interlocking with his, as she continued to whisper soft, comforting words in his ear, sending him into a hypnotic trance, as he bit down on his lower lip and closed his eyes, allowing her to take his mind away from everything bad.

Next thing he knew, he was waking up with Tamika straddling him as she snored lightly in his ear. It was then that he realized they both had fallen asleep, with their bodies still connected, like a plug to a socket.

Tamika was comatose; her eyes barely fluttered when he lifted her up and carried her to the couch, where he lay her down. He could still remember the serene look on her face when he had covered her with a small blanket that lay on the arm of the couch before, quietly, making his exit.

Marcus lay on Rhameek's couch, staring at the ceiling. His intentions had been to kill a few hours, kickin it with his boy, because he knew, nine times out of ten, Candy wasn't home. Even after what he had just done, he couldn't help but be filled with jealousy at the thought of where Candy was or what she might be doing. But still, the thought of her doing wrong wasn't enough to ease the guilt he felt for what he had just done.

Marcus realized that he had let hisself get caught up in the moment. The time he'd spent with Tamika had done nothing to help the problem. At the time, he was acting off of the assumption that Candy was doing something she had no business doing, so he followed suit.

"Tit for Tat." But as he lay on the couch, he realized it was a mistake, and the only thing he had achieved was making Candy's jealous fantasies a reality.

Candy paced the floor in her empty house. Her nerves were still rattled from the night's events.

When she arrived at her home she was relieved that Marcus wasn't there, due to the fact, that she looked roughed up, wearing an old T-shirt she had found in her car with her hair in a frenzy. In her haste to make it home to safety, she had forgot about the fact that she had come home smelling of sex and alcohol, and on top of that, she was also missing her underwear.

She had wasted no time cleaning herself up; knowing if Marcus would've caught her coming home like that, he would've killed her; three times.

Candy didn't know what she had been thinking, doing something so stupid. And in the process, not only had she let another man enter her, but she had also found herself caught up in the midst of Sonny's drama.

Now that Candy had cleaned herself up and calmed her nerves a little, she was no longer glad that Marcus was gone. Instead, she became uneasy, due to the fact, it was so late and he still wasn't home.

"Are the threats I made earlier the reason for his absence?" She pondered.

Candy began to wonder where he was and what he was doing. But, her guilty conscience wouldn't even allow her to get angry.

"Serves me right" she thought out loud, feeling bad for what she had done.

Instead of being filled with anger and jealousy, all she wanted was for Marcus to come home so she could feel safe in his arms. The incident earlier had made her realize the fact that no one could protect her like Marcus could. He'd put his life on the line, many times in the past, for her. And for that reason, she felt guilty and humiliated for crossing him in such a way.

"Stupid Bitch!" Candy cursed at herself as she leaned against the wall and slid to the floor. She sat, bawled up, with her knees to her chest, and began to sob uncontrollably.

She wished that Marcus was there to comfort her. At the same time, she knew that even if he was there, she could never tell him what had happened that night without the whole truth coming out. Regardless, all she wanted, right at this moment, was to be in his strong, loving arms; the same arms that engulfed her and always made her feel like she was wrapped in body Armour. Those arms that made her feel like no one and no thing could ever bring harm to her.

Candy jumped at the sound of her phone ringing. Wiping her eyes, she got to her feet and ran to the bedroom, where she had left her cell.

Picking up the phone, without looking at the caller I.D., she answered "Marcus!"

But it wasn't Marcus' voice that responded on the other end.

"Hey stranger" The voice chimed, causing Candy to frown up.

"Who is this?" Candy questioned.

"Now Miss Brown, I'm appalled that you don't recognize my voice; after all these years you've known me." Tiffany said, confirming Candy's suspicions.

"Look Tiffany, I ain't in the mood for your games." Candy snapped "and how did you get my number?"

"Aren't we rude", Tiffany said with a chuckle "what's wrong Miss Brown, P.M.S. got the best of you?"

"Listen Bitch; I ain't got time for ..."

"No Bitch! You listen!" Tiffany interrupted; cutting

Candy's words short.

Candy was about to respond, when the next voice she heard made her heart drop.

"Candy!" Felicia cried out "my baby, Candy don't let em hurt my baby!"

"Did you hear that Miss Brown? Isn't that wonderful!" Tiffany said with glee. "Who would've thought that our dear friend, Felicia, would ever have a baby?"

Candy was speechless as Tiffany continued.

"I mean we all know, Felicia's liver is whiter than those Zero bars you love so much. Who would've thought she could even produce a child!"

Anger filled Candy from head to toe as she began to blurt out obscenities.

"Tiffany I swear to God if you hurt her I'm gon ..."

"You ain't gonna do shit!" Tiffany cut in. "you ain't in no position to make threats Miss Brown, so my suggestion to you is that you shut the fuck up and listen good, Bitch!"

Candy bit her lip, fighting off the urge to respond, as Tiffany continued.

"First of all Bitch! ... let's clear one thing up, right now ... I don't give a fuck bout you, this nappy head Bitch or her baby! ... do you hear me Bitch?" Tiffany spat. "Bitch, I said, do you hear me?"

Candy was enraged but she knew Tiffany had the upper hand, so she simply responded, "yeah, I hear you."

Tiffany chuckled, as if she were enjoying the moment.

"Good girl!" She said cheerfully, "you know Candy, you can be so polite when you wanna be. You should try being well mannered a lil more often."

"What do you want me to do, Tiffany?" Candy asked, already knowing the answer, she became worried and frustrated all at once.

"Hmmm ... let's see" Tiffany said as she paced around Felicia.

Felicia sat on the floor, blindfolded and unable to speak,

now that her mouth was stuffed with the panties that Tiffany had, so crudely, removed in front of everybody in the room before, nonchalantly, forcing them into her mouth.

The men in the room had caught hard-on's, instantly, at the sight of Tiffany lifting her skirt and removing her panties. But, they were no longer aroused once they saw the thin maxi pad attached to the panties, with tiny red dots smeared all over it. The men frowned; realizing it was obvious that Tiffany was spotting.

Candy sat on the phone, patiently, as Tiffany continued to contemplate.

"Let's see, what do I want ... hmmm ... ", she feigned indecisiveness. "Oh, I know!" She said, snapping her fingers. "I want you to ... I want you to come over here, right now, cause I got three strong, handsome young men here wit me ..."

Tiffany paused and approached one of the men, and began rubbing his biceps, then continued "and I done got em all excited and can't even do nothing to help them ease all this pressure they got built up. Maybe you can bring your tired ass over here and suck em all off and let em bust off all over that ugly lil face of yours." Tiffany, amused with her own words, began to cackle like a witch. "And this one, standing in front of me, he's so cute Candy. I think you'ld like him." Tiffany stated as she palmed the man's crotch, while giving him a peck on the lips.

Candy sat on the phone, biting her tongue.

"Oh Candy! You no fun!" Tiffany giggled. "Seriously though!" Her tone became aggressive "Bitch you know what I want, you wanna see this Bitch again you'll gather up that money you stole, plus, you'll get up whatever extra money you and Marcus got layin around, I know that nigga be gettin it out here, so don't hold back; then you'll bring every penny to me."

Candy frowned up.

"Do you understand me, Bitch?" Tiffany barked.

"I understand" Candy replied, with a tear running down her cheek, as her body shook with anger.

"Good girl" Tiffany replied, with a yawn "girl I'm so tired, I been up all night. Being an evil Bitch is such hard work. Wouldn't you agree?"

"You would know" Candy replied.

Tiffany giggled "anyway, evil Bitches need they beauty rest too, so I think its time I go take a lil nap. Meanwhile, you go get that money together and I'll call you later with instructions, o.k.?"

"Yeah, I got you" Candy replied. She was already making her way out the door.

"Good, I'll call you later then ... toodles!" Tiffany chimed before hanging up in Candy's ear.

"Bitch!" Candy screamed as she jumped in her car and sped off.

CHAPTER 22

Marcus lay on the couch, tossing and turning as he mumbled under his breath.

"I don't wanna do it." He said, in a monotone voice.

Then his voice became aggressive "so you just gone sit back and watch him hurt her!"

"No I ... I ..." the monotone voice returned.

"Do it!" The aggressive voice interrupted.

"But I ... what if ..." the monotone voice began.

"What if he hurts her!" The aggressive voice interjected "what if he kills her!"

"No ... he want kill her." The monotone voice responded, calmly, as Marcus began to shake, violently, on the couch.

"How do you know he won't kill her?" The aggressive voice questioned.

Marcus' body stiffened, and his eyelids flicked open. He lay there, staring at the ceiling, with a hollow look in his eyes as the monotone voice returned. This time, with a trace of aggression, the voice answered with a hint of coldness.

"He won't hurt her, cause I'm not gonna let him!"

Marcus lay on the couch, stiff as a board, with his fist bawled up so tight, his knuckles were beginning to turn white.

"What's wrong with him? Is he still sleeping?" Marcus' mother asked, with a concerned look on her face, as she looked at the doctor for an explanation.

"Yes, Mrs. Flowers, your son is still very much asleep."

"Are you sure? His eyes are wide open and his lips are still moving."

"I assure you Mrs. Flowers, Marcus appears to be awake, but he is still under hypnosis, and will not come back to a conscious state unless I bring him back."

The doctor continued to speak as Marcus lay, perfectly still, with his fist clenched. His grip was tightening, so much now, that his nails were beginning to dig into his palms.

"Mrs. Flowers, I'm sure you're familiar with the term; sleep walking" the doctor inquired.

She looked at her son then scanned the walls in the doctors office, observing the numerous psychology degrees and plaques mounted on them. But the plaques weren't enough to keep her from wondering, had she made a mistake by bringing her son to this place.

"What does this have to do with sleep walking?" She asked, pointing at her son, who still lay on the couch, with his eyes wide open.

"Well, he's not sleep walking of course" the doctor chuckled as he received a serious look from Marcus' mother.

Clearing his throat, the doctor proceeded. "I'm trying to explain this in a simple, understandable manner Mrs. Flower's."

She crossed her arms and nodded.

"You see, when one sleep walks, the body continues to function while that person remains in a state of slumber. And as you know, this will cause a person to appear to be conscious when, in fact, they are completely unaware of their surroundings."

"But he's not sleep walking" She pointed out, again. She was growing impatient and frustrated.

"That is correct, Mrs. Flower's. He is not sleep walking, but as you see, his eyes are wide open and he appears to be awake. Although, we both know that is impossible, considering, he's under a hypnotic induced state of rest at this moment."

"I think we've already figured that out doctor!"

"Mmm ... yes of course" the doctor replied as he removed

his glasses. "What I'm trying to say Mrs. Flower's is Marcus is, indeed, asleep, but "he." The doctor said, stressing the word 'he', while waving his light over Marcus' eyes.

"He", the doctor stressed the word again "is wide-awake!"

Marcus' mother looked confused. She noticed Marcus' eyes followed the light from left to right.

"What do you mean when you say 'he'?" She questioned "I mean 'he' is my son! What are you talking about doctor?"

"Let me put it to you in a way that's more understandable; are you familiar with the story of Dr. Jeckyll and Mr. Hyde?"

Marcus' mother looked at the doctor as if he were crazy.

"I knew this was a waste of time and not to mention money; neither of which I have to waste!"

The doctor let out a sigh "Mrs. Flower's I'm just trying to explain ..."

"No! You just wastin my damn time ... I come all the way down here just so you could tell me my son is like some schizophrenic, mad scientist, who you read about in a book!" She spat, as she rose to her feet.

"I think you've said all I need to hear doctor, wake my son up, so I can go!"

"Mrs. Flower's, I assure you, I was only speaking figuratively; all I'm trying to tell you is, your son has an alternate persona which, in fact, of course, he is still himself, but for some reason this persona, which exist in us all, seems to surface and overcome Marcus to the point that rational thought is almost impossible ... and from what I've observed today, this process occurs when Marcus feels as if someone he's close to is in danger ... and the need he feels to protect this person, whomever it may be, seems to be a trigger for this irrational behavior."

Marcus' mother had stood with her arms crossed until the doctor was finished. Then, giving him a look of dismay, she simply stated.

"Wake my son up; I don't have time for this!"

"Mrs. Flower's, I'd like to refer you to a specialist."

"Wake my God Damn son up, right now!" She spat.

"But, Mrs. Flower's, it is detrimental that you get this treated ..."

"Wake my son up right now!" She repeated as she made her way towards Marcus and began to shake him "Wake up baby! We bout to get out of here!"

"Mrs. Flower's" the doctor continued to speak as she ignored him and began to shake Marcus vigorously.

"Wake up!" She screamed, slapping him on the face, as he lay still; with his eyes wide open, and fist clenched. "Wake up!"

"Mrs. Flower's! That isn't the proper way to ..."

"Wake up" she continued, ignoring the doctor's voice, as he tried to over talk her.

"Marcus, when I count to three, you'll wake up."

"One" ..."wake up baby" ... "two" ... "Marcus wake yo ass up!"

Marcus' eyes fluttered as he heard his mother's, and the doctor's voice, crowding his mind, like echo's in a cave, as he began to mumble "I want let him hurt you"

"Wake yo ass up boy!" ... "Marcus" ... "Three"

"Marcus wake up!"

Marcus jumped from the couch and rose to his feet. "Mama!"

"Nigga yo Mama ain't here!" Rhameek laughed as Marcus looked around in a daze.

"Nigga what you doin over here this time of night?" Rhameek asked while looking at his watch.

"Oh, I ... I just stopped by to holla at you, but you was sleep ... guess I must've dozed off."

"Yeah, I 'was' sleep nigga!", Rhameek replied "until I heard yo ass in here, kickin and hollerin and shit!"

"Yeah ... just had a bad dream I guess." Marcus replied.

Rhameek let out a slight chuckle "I figured that out when I heard you cryin out for your Mama, nigga let me find out you still a Mama's boy!"

Marcus waved Rhameek off.

"Anyway, what you doin over here? I called yo ass earlier, and you wasn't answering!"

"Yeah ... I was tied up" Marcus began " you remember that chick at the mall?"

"The dressing room chick?" Rhameek questioned.

"Yeah, her ... I was wit her when you called."

Rhameek raised an eyebrow at the statement. "Oh yeah? ... and what happened nigga?"

Marcus leaned back and dropped his head "what you think happened?"

Rhameek gave him a questioning look, then stated. "What? ... nigga you actually got you some!" He said, slapping Marcus on the back. "Must've been a bad experience ... cause you sittin here, wit yo head down, like you ashamed playboy, what's up wit dat?"

"I feel bad dawg" Marcus stated.

"Here we go wit dat 'holier than thou' bullshit!" Rhameek spat "what you feel bad for?"

Marcus hesitated; knowing a person like Rhameek wouldn't understand the concept of feeling guilty for sleeping with another woman.

"Look dawg" Marcus began "Me and Candy had an argument and she said a few things; made some threats, like she was gonna be wit somebody else, and I let that shit cloud my judgment. Next thing I know, I'm at this chick's house, and shit just happened."

"So what!" Rhameek said, throwing his hands in the air. "If she made a threat like that, you should've went out and got you ... lord knows I would've!"

Marcus gave Rhameek a frustrated look.

"It was just a threat dawg. For all I know, she been sittin at one of her friends house all day, watching TV."

Rhameek frowned "or, she could've been doin what you was doin!"

Marcus could feel the hairs on his neck curl up upon hearing those words.

"I doubt it dawg. You know she just tryna piss a nigga off, you know Candy ain't nothing but a drama queen, a spoiled brat. She just pushin my buttons, that's all." Marcus stated, matter of factly.

Rhameek let out a heavy sigh then began walking away. He headed for his bedroom as he spoke over his shoulder.

"Look playa; she wrote the check, you just cashed it. You ain't did shit wrong. It's just business, nothing perso ..."

Rhameek's words were cut off by a knock at the door.

"Get that for me", he yelled.

Champ sniffed the doorframe and began wagging his tail, while prancing around in excitement. Marcus knew there was only one person who Champ acted like this around.

"It's me!" Candy said from the other side of the door, confirming Marcus' suspicions.

"Hold on!" Marcus said, with a slight hint of anger in his voice.

He opened the door, and just as Candy entered with a distressed look on her face, Rhameek came from the bedroom, with nothing but his jeans and Timbs on.

Candy froze up when she looked at the familiar Timberland boots, with the bright, green, bubble gum sole's. Her mouth dropped to the floor when she spotted the bloodstains that covered the boots. It was then, when she looked Rhameek in the face and saw the long, deep, claw mark's that were stretched, all the way, down the side of his neck.

Her reaction caused Rhameek to freeze up as well. Stopping in mid-stride, his eyes followed hers. He looked down at the incriminating boots he wore, then placed his hand over his neck in an attempt to cover the large scars, as he thought.

"Damn, she know!"

At the same moment, Candy's thoughts were. "It was him. But, how did he know?"

All Rhameek could do was drop his head, as his mind

spiraled back to the night that had set off this unusual chain of events.

Rhameek and the others held in their urge to laugh at the sight of their slender framed friend, trailing behind the two big women, begging them to stay, as they made their way out the front door.

Fly continued to plead, to no avail, as the two girls jumped in their car and sped off.

Rhameek was the first to burst out in a fit of laughter, causing the others to follow suit.

"Look at that nigga!" Ron screamed.

"He look pathetic!" G-lo added as they all watched Fly, standing at the edge of the driveway, with a sickly expression on his face, and what looked like a bottle of baby oil rubbed all over him.

They all continued to laugh as Fly made his way back towards the house. The excessive oil on his body caused him to sparkle as the streetlight shined on him.

"What the fuck ya'll laughing at?" He demanded, only to receive a sly comment from Rhameek.

After a brief exchange of words, Fly stomped off, down the hallway.

"While you back there, can you go head and bring us what we came for, so we can get out this madhouse!" Rhameek yelled, while the others continued to laugh.

But Rhameek's last comment wasn't a joke. He was becoming uneasy, fearing it was just a matter of time before his homeboy's wild streaks attracted attention from the police, and he didn't want to be there when that day came.

Just as Rhameek was about to yell down the hallway for Fly to hurry, his phone rang. Recognizing Felicia's number on the screen, he stood up and headed for the door, not wanting anyone in his conversation.

"Yeah!" He said, placing the phone to his ear as he opened

the screened door.

At that same instance, his phone made a beeping noise and went dead on him.

"Damn!" He cursed, knowing Felicia would swear he'd hung up on her intentionally.

"Marcus, let me hold your phone for a second" he said, stepping back into the house long enough to grab Marcus' phone, before making his way back out the door.

He began to dial Felicia's number as he walked towards the end of the driveway. Just as he was about to dial the last three digits, Marcus' phone began to ring.

Rhameek put the phone to his ear, in an attempt to answer. Then, he realized that it wasn't a call coming through; it was an alert for a text or e-mail.

"Who is this?" Rhameek wondered as he looked over his shoulder. Deciding to be nosey, he pushed the button to view the text. It was then he saw something that blew his mind.

"What the fuck?" He cursed, causing everyone inside the house to raise up and look out the window.

"I don't believe this shit!" He spat, as he looked at the picture of Sonny and Candy on the screen.

He shook his head, in disbelief, at what he was seeing. He looked again to make sure his eyes weren't deceiving him, and to his disappointment, they weren't. It was, in fact, Candy on the photo. And, she was leaning forward, kissing another man on the cheek.

Rhameek noticed his loud reaction had drawn attention from the others inside. He continued to curse under his breath as he fumbled with the phone. He erased the picture, but it wasn't until after he erased it, he realized he had forgot to check to see who had sent the text.

"I'll worry about all that later" he told himself as he walked back towards the porch; deciding he would get to the bottom of things himself and not mention the photo to Marcus.

Rhameek wasn't sure what had provoked Candy to do something so dumb; but he knew what Marcus would do to her if he found out. He wasn't about to let his boy get into any trouble over a female, but he also wasn't about to let the situation go unattended.

"What's up dawg?" Marcus inquired as Rhameek entered the house.

"Ain't nothing dawg" Rhameek replied, brushing the question off, as he glanced at the black bag in Marcus' hand.

"Look fellas, we bout to be out. I'll call ya'll lunatics tomorrow." He stated; giving each one of them dap as he, unsuccessfully, tried to conceal the look that covered his face; a look that was a combination of dread, disappointment and anger.

"What's up?" Marcus asked in a scornful tone, breaking the silence. He gave Candy an aggravated look, as if he didn't notice the look of distress on her face.

Candy broke eye contact with Rhameek and turned to face Marcus. Tears welled up in her, already puffy, eyes.

"It's Felicia, Marcus they got Felicia!"

Marcus' whole demeanor changed as he and Rhameek spoke at once.

"Who got her?"

Candy began to sob, "Tiffany!" She blurted out.

"Tiffany?" Rhameek said with a confused look on his face.

Candy looked at the floor, too ashamed to look at Marcus, out of fear that Rhameek had already told him what she had done.

"Tiffany! ... she called me ... said if I don't bring her the money we took ... they were gonna hurt Felicia."

"Tiffany?" Marcus repeated "but how does she know about the money?"

"I don't know ... but she's been making accusations and threats since day one ... I guess she figured it out. And now, she's had someone to snatch Felicia up!" Candy said through sobs.

Anger filled Marcus "why you ain't tell me she been coming at you like dat, Candy?"

"I don't know I was ..." Candy began.

"You was being stupid is what you was" Marcus barked "let me guess ... you ain't mention it because you been too busy playin mad at me, behind some broad I didn't even know at the time."

Candy raised her head and looked Marcus in the eyes.

"I'm sorry. I was just jealous and mad." She cried. But, Marcus' last statement hadn't gone unnoticed.

"Some broad I didn't know (at the time)"

"I'm sorry Marcus, I should've said something ... but, right now, we got to get Felicia back, I ..."

Candy flinched, cutting herself off midsentence, when she saw Marcus reach under his shirt and produce a chrome .45, with gold engraving on the barrel.

The sound of the gun racking back echoed through the house.

"Let's go get her then!" Marcus said, looking at Rhameek, who simply nodded and headed towards his bedroom.

"Rhameek!" Candy screamed, causing him to stop and face her. "Listen, ya'll can't just go running up on them like that. Felicia might get hurt in the process. Let's just get the money, take it to em and get Felicia back!"

"Rah, go get yo tool!" Marcus stated, ignoring Candy, "we ain't givin em shit!" He spat.

Rhameek turned to walk away again.

"No, Rhameek wait!" Candy yelled as she reached out grabbing his arm. "Ya'll don't understand. Rhameek, Felicia's pregnant." Candy hesitated before dropping another bomb. "By you!"

Rhameek could feel his knees buckle. Grabbing the wall for support, he spoke in a cracked tone. "She's what?"

Rhameek leaned on the wall as he looked at Marcus, who he realized, was just as surprised as he was about the news.

Marcus closed his eyes and tilted his head back. He inhaled

deeply, allowing his mind to soak in everything he'd just heard. Then, leaning his head forward, he opened his eyes, and tucked his gun back in his waistband.

"Don't sweat it dawg" Marcus said, in a calm tone. He gave Rhameek an icy grin. "Don't worry ... I won't let em hurt her." Were the last words he spoke as he headed for the door.

The news of Felicia's pregnancy had left Rhameek in a state of shock. He still stood, frozen, on the wall, as Candy pursued Marcus.

"Where you goin?" She questioned, while running behind him.

"Just call me when you hear from that sheisty Bitch!" Marcus spat "I'm gonna gather up the money, you just go back in there with Rah; make sho by the time I get thing's together, he done snapped back to reality."

Candy looked her man in the eyes. She wanted so bad to tell him she was sorry for everything. She wanted to tell him about the mistake she had made. She wanted to ask for his forgiveness; but her lips trembled as she reached out and caressed his face. She tried to spit the words out.

"Go make sho Rah alright" he repeated, pulling his face away from her touch, as he jumped in his car and sped off.

Felicia sat on the floor, with pursed lips. Relieved to have the makeshift gag removed from her mouth, she was keeping her promise to, 'not so much as whimper out loud.'

Tiffany had also decided to remove the blindfold, since it was no longer a secret that she was behind the whole ordeal.

The tape that binded Felicia's ankles and wrist had become extremely uncomfortable.

"I'm thirsty" Felicia whispered to the huge man who sat at the table, flipping through channels on the TV.

Felicia cleared her throat to get his attention "I said, I'm thirsty." She repeated, in a low whisper.

"I heard you the first time." The man responded, but made no effort to move.

Felicia, beyond frustration, exhaled deeply and gave the man a menacing stare. She began to wonder where the other men had went. She also wondered, how much longer she would have to wait until Tiffany decided to make the exchange.

As if on cue, Felicia heard the door to the bedroom open, and looked up to see Tiffany heading in her direction.

"Ooh girl, I needed that nap" Tiffany said, while stretching her arms towards the ceiling.

"Has she been a good girl?" She questioned. The big man nodded. "That's good!" Tiffany said, patting Felicia on the head; like a puppy.

Felicia wanted to call her everything but the Mother of God. Holding her tongue, she decided the last thing she wanted was Tiffany's panties stuffed in her mouth again.

"You know all of this could've been avoided", Tiffany began pacing back and forth in front of Felicia "but nooo! Candy had to be a lil smart-ass. All she had to do was give me a lil piece of the money she got from Leon, but Candy was never the type to share."

Tiffany chuckled, slapping Felicia on her shoulder.

"Just down right stingy. I never knew what Marcus saw in her" Tiffany stated, as if she were expecting an answer from Felicia.

Felicia didn't open her mouth, out of fear that she would tell Tiffany what was really on her mind.

Tiffany ignored Felicia's refusal to respond and continued.

"And check this out girl! Don't you know I saw that Bitch all up on that tired ass nigga Sonny at the club." Tiffany hesitated and giggled.

"And you know my sheisty ass girl, I kind of 'accidentally' picked up Candy's phone while I was talking to her and Sonny. Then I just happened to 'stumble' across Marcus' number, matter of fact that's how I got your number too girl. Anyway, I go outside and sit in the car, how about the Bitch come outside, her and Sonny all in each other face. So, I decided to give Marcus a heads up. I took a picture of them with my cell phone" Tiffany stated, holding her phone up for visual effect. "And I emailed the picture to Marcus. You know, tryin to break up they lil unhappy home. But, it ain't work."

Tiffany continued to ramble. But, her last words had made things clear to Felicia as her mind drifted back to the confrontation she and Rhameek had at her home.

It was then, the same night Felicia had found out she was pregnant, Rhameek had dropped by unexpectedly. When Felicia saw him pull up, she built up her nerve, and decided she would tell him about the baby. But, she never got a chance to tell him. He had entered her home, going ballistic; talking about some picture he had seen on Marcus' phone.

"You had to know Felicia!"

"I swear I didn't know Rhameek."

She had lied. Even though, she had just spoke to Candy hours earlier and knew her whereabouts. It was in that same conversation that she had clearly told Candy she wanted no knowledge of her whereabouts.

"Rah why you mad at me? You act like it's my fault or somein." She had said as she began to cry, unable to deal with so much in one night.

"Look; don't cry Felicia. It's okay, I believe you. I'm sorry, I know it's not your fault." He had said, giving her a strong hug.

Felicia wasn't use to Rhameek showing her any compassion. It was on that night, she decided she would keep her child. But, she had chose to wait, until he wasn't upset, to tell him about it.

She had wanted to tell Candy about the email, but Rhameek had made her promise to keep her mouth shut.

"Don't worry its nothing I can't handle. You just gotta promise you not gonna say a word to Candy about it. Cause, I definitely ain't gonna tell Marcus nothin, not until I sort this out."

Felicia had wondered what he meant by "sort this out."

Hellooo!" Tiffany screamed while clapping her hands in Felicia's face. "Earth to Felicia!"

Felicia gave Tiffany an aggravated look.

"Have I been talking to myself?" Tiffany questioned, with her hands on her hips.

"You know what? You no fun. Let's go-head and get this Bitch traded for that bag of cash!"

Tiffany winked at the big man, sitting at the table, bringing a smile to his face.

"Call the others. Tell em to get a few extra hands, just in case somebody wanna play Captain Save A Hoe! I'm gonna call this Bitch back and tell her where to meet us."

Candy got up from the couch and walked towards Rhameek's bedroom. She found him pacing back and forth, with Champ following his lead.

"You gonna walk that dog to death." Candy stated, causing Rhameek and Champ, both, to stop pacing and look in her direction.

Rhameek had found no humor in her comment. He only responded with a cold glare.

His cold stare didn't go unnoticed. Candy decided it would be best to change tactics and get straight to the point.

"I'm sorry bout your neck" she stated, referring to the large claw marks.

Rhameek didn't respond.

"Look Rah, I know you pissed at me. But, right now, we gotta worry about Felicia. I just wanted to tell you, I know what I did was stupid. I made a mistake ... and I just wanted to say, thank you."

Rhameek finally spoke "what the fuck you mean, thank you?"

"I mean, for not telling Marcus." Candy responded. "I know you don't believe me Rah, but I really do love him, I just ..."

"You just what Candy?" Rhameek snapped "don't nobody wanna hear no bullshit excuses. And just for the record, ain't no need in thankin me. I ain't keep that shit from Marcus fo yo benefit!"

Tears began to cloud Candy's vision as Rhameek's words cut her like a knife.

"Marcus is my man and I ain't tryna see him hurt by 'nobody'. That nigga love you more than life itself!" He barked as he began pacing again "I ain't tell him, cause it would kill him, and not to mention, if he found out, he would probably kill you."

Candy dropped her head, unable to look Rhameek in his eyes.

"That's why I handled it myself; cause I ain't wanna see my boy hurt like that. And I damn sho ain't wanna see him gettin locked up behind killing yo ass ... you ain't worth it!"

Rhameek's last statement hit her hard. She had no response, and before she had an opportunity to reply, her phone rang.

"Its Tiffany" Candy said. Rhameek motioned for her to answer. He moved in closer, so he could listen in on the conversation.

"Hello!"

"You ready to do this, Miss Brown?"

CHAPTER 23

THE SLEEP WALKER

"You ready to do this dawg?" Marcus said, as he and
Rhameek sat side by side at the red light.

Rhameek responded with a nod.

"What about the others, are they where they spose to be?"
Marcus questioned; making sure everything was in order.

"As far as I know" Rhameek replied "I told them when and
where." He added, as he began to squirm around in his seat.

Marcus studied his friend for a moment, then looked up,
noticing the traffic light was now green.

"All right, let's do this" Marcus replied as he reached his fist
up towards Rhameek's window.

Rhameek leaned out of the truck and met Marcus' fist with
his own. The two friends locked eyes.

"I ain't gone let her get hurt dawg."

"I know" Rhameek replied, meeting his friend's gaze, as he
made an attempt to crack a smile.

"You ain't gettin outta payin child support, that easy,
nigga!' Marcus joked, as he revved the engine on his bike.

Rhameek let out a slight laugh as Marcus slammed the

shield down on his helmet and sped off on the powerful street bike.

"What you lookin at?" Rhameek said as he reached over and patted Champ on the head. The huge dog tilted his head and let out a puff of air, as Rhameek accelerated down the empty street, in a straight path.

Rhameek gripped the steering wheel, intently, as Marcus dropped behind him and turned off on a side street, taking another route to their destination.

"Who the fuck is this?" Peabo said, looking aggravated. "Answer that Rhonda; it's probably Mike."

"Oh I got it like that?" Rhonda smiled " I get to answer your phone now? I feel special!" She said as she got up from the couch.

She tightened up the straps on her pink, sheer, robe, while making her way towards the phone.

"You got it like that and then some!" Peabo replied, admiring the silhouette of Rhonda's voluptuous frame, underneath the thin robe.

Rhonda couldn't believe how comfortable Peabo was becoming around her. The thought of his trust in her made her smile, a broad smile, as she answered the phone.

"Hello."

"Bitch; let me speak to my man!" Tiffany snapped.

"Who you callin a Bitch?" Rhonda countered, getting Peabo's attention.

Peabo picked up the remote and pressed the pause button, so he wouldn't miss his favorite scene on the movie, "Carlito's Way."

"Who is that?" He questioned.

Rhonda ignored him and continued to bicker on the phone.

"Bitch you ain't got no man over here. But, you welcome to come join in anytime you feelin friendly" Rhonda said, with a chuckle, pissing Tiffany off.

"Bitch, just put him on the phone!"

"You call me Bitch one more time and I'm gonna put my foot so far up yo high yella ass they gon ..."

"Give me the phone!" Peabo demanded before snatching the phone from Rhonda's hand, causing her to stomp off and plop down on the couch.

Peabo smiled at the gesture, as he put the phone to his ear.

"What you want, Tiffany?"

Tiffany rolled her eyes, then stuck her middle finger up at the receiver, as she put on her sexiest voice.

"Damn, daddy its like that?" She whined.

Peabo, growing impatient, began to stroke his beard.

"What you want?" He repeated.

"I just wanted to tell you, I found out who got yo money, daddy. But, if you don't wanna talk to me right now, I can call back."

"Don't play wit me Tiffany! If you know where my money is you better tell me!"

A broad smile covered Peabo's face as he listened intently.

"P-Baby" Rhonda whined from across the room.

"Shut up Rhonda, I'm busy" he stated dryly, cutting her short as he continued to stroke his beard, while showing every diamond in his mouth.

"Good girl" Peabo stated, looking at his watch. "You should've called me earlier and let me setup the exchange.

"I just wanted to make you proud, daddy."

"Well, mission accomplished baby girl" Peabo responded, noticing the big frown on Rhonda's face as she began to poke her lip out and pout.

"I'm bout to call Mike. I want you to tell whatever flunkies you got wit you to snag these mufuckas and hold them till we get there." He said, before hanging up.

Peabo smiled, as he dialed Mike's number. "What's up! ... We got action ... meet me at the shop ... I'm on my way out, right now."

Peabo hung up the phone and headed towards his bedroom.

"Where you goin baby?" Rhonda questioned, as he began to

get dressed. "I know you ain't bout to leave me, and go to dat Bitch!" She spat, as she approached him from behind.

Peabo turned around, with a devilish look on his face, causing Rhonda to back up a few steps.

"First of all, this is buziness, and second, you don't question me ... no! Matter of fact, first of all, you don't question me!" He corrected himself. "You just be here when I get back. Matter of fact, don't be surprised if I bring Tiffany back wit me. Its due time ya'll squash whatever beef ya'll got ... so be naked when we get here, cause ya'll gon kiss and make up!" He demanded as he made his way out the door, leaving Rhonda standing with her arms crossed and her face frowned up.

"Improper pimpin promotes piss poor performance!" Zone answered his phone, with his usual greeting, as he rolled down I-85.

The call brought a smile to his face. He turned Al Green down a notch, so he could hear better.

"Okay ... I got you ... I'm on my way!" He said, coolly, after getting directions to his destination.

Hanging up the phone, he pulled the big blue Cadillac to the shoulder of the busy highway.

"Get out. I got somein to handle!"

"But daddy ... we on the highway I ..."

Zone gave the petite, Puerto Rican girl in the passenger side, a cold stare. She cut her own words short and opened the door.

"As small as those pretty lil feet is, I know, you got room for a pair of tennis pumps in that big ass pocketbook." He stated, dryly, as she got out of the car and closed the door, being careful not to slam it.

"Preparation!" He yelled out the window before pulling off, leaving the girl standing on the side of the highway.

"I'll be glad when yo old ass retire!" The girl cursed, under her breath, as the taillights on Zone's Cadillac faded off into the distance.

"Alright, everybody get ready. They should be here in a minute." Tiffany said, with a wicked grin on her face.

Everything was going as planned. She knew that she could get back in Peabo's good graces by informing him of the 'thieves' whereabouts. But, she wanted to make sure she got her hands on the money before he arrived, which is why she had stalled on calling him.

She had promised the flunkie's, she had gathered up, a lump sum of money; which is why she had insisted that Candy turn over any extra money she and Marcus had, as well as Peabo's money.

She figured she'd let the goons get a split off of whatever extra money was in the kitty, and she would take a lump sum of Peabo's money, and stash it before he arrived.

She figured he would be happy to get any amount back. Besides, she knew that Peabo was more bent on proving a point. "Don't nobody fuck wit Peabo", than he was on getting the cash. She knew he wanted to take care of the thieves personally.

Rhameek pulled into the old construction site. Scanning his surroundings, he wondered how long it had taken Tiffany to figure out such a desolate location to meet at. It was obvious that she wasn't half as dumb as he had thought.

Coming to a brief stop, he looked around for any signs that someone was present.

All he saw was a bulldozer and a few dump trucks, which were all used to haul gravel in and out of the old rock quarry.

Just as Rhameek began to grow weary of the situation, he saw a Burgundy Expedition emerge from behind one of the large rock piles.

Rhameek looked at his watch, then up at the sky. He noticed that day break wasn't far away.

"Alright, I hope ya'll niggas ready" he spoke to himself, out loud, causing Champs ears to rise up at the sound of his voice.

Rhameek exited his truck. Gripping his keys in his hand, he approached the Expedition on foot. Before Rhameek got too close to the vehicle, the passenger door flew open and a tall, slim, guy hopped out, holding a 40 caliber in his right hand.

Rhameek stopped walking upon seeing the gun. His palms began to sweat as he raised his hands in the air, making it clear he was holding nothing but some keys in his grip.

"Turn around!" The slim guy demanded.

"Yeah right!" Rhameek replied. The man gave him an irritated look then began to pat him down. Rhameek was testing the waters, trying to see what type of people Tiffany had bought with her.

"Dumb ass nigga" he thought to himself, knowing a veteran would've pistol-whipped him just for getting fly at the mouth.

So far, things were looking good. It was clear that Tiffany had bought, at least, one amateur with her. He wondered how many more people she had with her, and he hoped that they were all as naive as the one patting him down.

After checking Rhameek, thoroughly, the tall man gave an o.k. signal, and all of the doors on the Expedition opened.

Rhameek gritted his teeth as Tiffany exited the vehicle, accompanied by two huge dark skinned men. They had to be brothers. The similarities were obvious. They both walked with a slouch, with their huge, ape like, arms dangling by their sides.

The men could've passed as twins. The only discrepancy between the two was the fact that one held a large, chrome 357 revolver in his grip, while the other held what appeared to be a 9 mm.

"Rah, it's been so long!" Tiffany chimed, in a cheerful voice. She approached, with the two huge men walking on each side of her. "You still a cutie, I see why your name ringin all over the streets!"

"You don't look so bad yo'self" he replied, nonchalantly.

"And you still cool as a fan!" Tiffany chuckled as she continued to sashay in his direction, her black cat suit showing off her curvaceous frame as she approached.

Tiffany stopped, within a few feet of Rhameek.

"Where's Felicia?" He demanded.

"Where's Candy? And why did she send you instead of Marcus?"

Rhameek smiled "what, you ain't happy to see me? I'm hurt!"

"Don't bullshit me Rhameek!" Tiffany became serious "I'm tellin you right now, I got niggas all over this place!" She said, waving her arms in an arc.

"So I suggest ya'll don't try no slick shit. Let's keep this nice and clean."

"Listen" Rhameek said, getting frustrated "Candy couldn't find Marcus, so she came to me when you called."

"Now, I wonder why she couldn't get in touch with Marcus?" Tiffany said, scratching her head before, dramatically, snapping her fingers, as if a light bulb had cut on in her head. "Oh! I know! ... Don't tell me my lil Email broke up they lil 'happy home." She stated, making quotation marks with her fingers.

Rhameek raised an eyebrow, upon hearing her last comment. It was clear to him now; Tiffany had sent the picture to Marcus' phone.

"Listen, all that's irrelevant. You want the money. I got it. Besides, Felicia's my problem. So, where is she?"

Tiffany began to laugh, bringing a smile to the gorilla twins, and the tall man.

"Oh, that's right, you'ze the pappy!" She said, holding her stomach, as if her ribs were cracking. "I gotta tell you, I'm a lil disappointed in you playa! I mean ... tired ass Felicia?"

Rhameek looked at the three men, as if he wanted to pull his dick out and piss at their feet.

"Fuck ya'll laughing at?"

The laughter stopped then, all of a sudden, the two big men raised their weapons and planted them on his temples.

"We laughing at you nigga ... what!"

Rhameek bit his lower lip, as the barrel's forced his head to lean at a slight angle. It was clear to him that the 'ape brothers' were of no relation to 'tall man' when it came to the pushover department.

"Be easy playa; let's keep this clean" he said, mocking Tiffany.

"Exactly" Tiffany stated, nodding for the brothers to lower their weapons.

"This is how its goin down", she began "you gonna hand over the money and I'm gonna let you know where Felicia is; I go my way, and you go get yo baby mama, simple as that!"

Rhameek frowned, then decided enough time had been wasted. "The money's in the back of my truck."

Tiffany smiled, then sent one of the gorilla twins to the truck. The big Man reached the F-150 and spotted the large duffle bag. He signaled Tiffany, with a nod of the head, as he reached into the truck and lifted the heavy bag over the tailgate.

"Damn, this is what a mil feels like?" The big man said, in a deep, guttural tone.

Rhameek looked at Tiffany "lyin Bitch" he thought to himself.

Tiffany smiled and shrugged "yeah, give or take a few hundred thousand" she continued, as the big man dropped the heavy bag to the ground and reached for the zipper.

"Oh no you don't!" Tiffany screamed "you just pick that bag up, baby, and bring it to mommy!"

The big man blushed, then lifted the heavy bag. Throwing the strap over his shoulder, he wondered, exactly how much money was in it. The weight of the bag bought a feeling of excitement to him. He took guesses at how much it contained, and pondered on how he would spend his cut.

"Good boy!" Tiffany said, giving the monkey man a kiss on the cheek. "O.K. Rah ... it's been nice!" Tiffany stated, before walking off. The two big men followed her lead, leaving the tall man behind with Rhameek.

"What the fuck is this?" Rhameek spat "where's Felicia?" He yelled, realizing Tiffany had no intentions of letting him leave.

"Keep him right here, Slim. Peabo will be here soon", she said "and call the others, tell em it looks like this niggas alone, so they can come out of they lil hiding spots or whatever."

She winked at Rhameek, then said "Toodles!" Before sashaying off, towards the Expedition.

"You double-crossing Bitch!" Rhameek spat.

The tall man, feeling cocky all of a sudden, reached out and pistol-whipped Rhameek across the bridge of his nose.

Tiffany turned around, at the sound of the gun cracking against Rhameek's face. And just when she was about to reach for the door handle, she began to hear someone whistling a familiar tune.

Whistle While You Work

♪♪ ♪♪♪ ♪   ♪♪ ♪♪♪ ♪   ♪♪ ♪♪♪ ♪   ♪♪ ♪♪♪ ♪

"What the hell is that?" Tiffany questioned. She began to look around, frantically. "Slim!" She called out, causing him to cease the beating he was giving Rhameek.

"Yeah!" Slim answered, turning to face Tiffany.

"Call the others tell em to get ..." before Tiffany finished her statement, Rhameek took advantage of the distraction. Reaching up from the ground, he grabbed the tall mans wrist.

At that same moment, there was a loud cracking noise, right beside Tiffany. She began to panic. The ape twin, holding the duffle bag, grunted as his whole side seemed to explode. Tiffany screamed at the top of her lungs as the big man fell over dead, dropping the bag beside him.

The remaining gorilla twin began to point aimlessly, looking for where the shot came from.

Rhameek lay on the ground, tussling with Slim. Champ, still in the truck, went into a frenzy. The huge dog foamed at the mouth as he pawed at the window, while butting his head against it, trying to get to his master.

The slim man would've been no match for Rhameek, under normal circumstances, but he was still disoriented from the pistol whipping he had just received. Rhameek could hear Champ, in the background, barking frantically. It was then, as he lay on the ground, feeling like he was about to lose the fight, he remembered that his key ring was still dangling from his finger.

Rhameek fumbled with the key chain until his thumb found

the button that controlled the automatic windows on the truck.

No sooner than the windows had opened, Champ leapt out of the truck and ran, full speed, to his masters aid.

Tiffany ducked behind the Expedition. She watched the big man fire his gun frantically as he tried to figure out where the whistling was coming from.

♪♪ ♪♪♪ ♪   ♪♪ ♪♪♪ ♪   ♪♪ ♪♪♪ ♪

"What the fuck?" Tiffany uttered as she wondered, who would choose a time like this to whistle the tune to "Whistle while you work."

Her question was answered when she heard what sounded like a cannon going off. Her jaw dropped when she saw her ape like accomplice spin around. He screamed in pain. His arm seemed to dangle from his shoulder.

It was then; Marcus emerged from behind a large bulldozer, yielding a large, chrome plated, .50 caliber handgun. The big man groaned in agony as he attempted to reach, with his good arm, for the weapon he had dropped.

Marcus looked at Tiffany, who sat frozen. He cracked a smile showing off his fronts; then, with the wink of an eye, he began to whistle again.

♪♪ ♪♪♪ ♪   ♪♪ ♪♪♪ ♪   ♪♪ ♪♪♪ ♪

The big man got within inches of his gun. Marcus raised his weapon, swiftly; letting off a single round that left the big mans other arm dangling at the elbow.

♪♪ ♪♪♪ ♪   ♪♪ ♪♪♪ ♪   ♪♪ ♪♪♪ ♪

Marcus stopped whistling, long enough to smile, at the sight of the big man, cursing and screaming, as he fell to his knees.

Turning his attention towards Rhameek and his opponent, who both lay on the ground wrestling for the gun, Marcus

raised his weapon and was about to let off a shot when
Champ darted from the side, running head on with
Rhameek's attacker.

The tall man let out a loud cry, as he and the large dog went
rolling across the ground.

"Get him boy!" Rhameek yelled, as the dog found a grip and
locked his jaws on the tall man's neck.

"Shake him!"

Within seconds, the slim man's screams became no more
than a gurgling moan, as Champ shook his head, violently,
from side to side, until the man went limp.

♪♪ ♪♪♪ ♪   Tiffany snapped out of her trance as
Marcus moved within point blank range of the, already
wounded, big man and pointed his gun at his chest.

♪♪ ♪♪♪ ♪   Just as Marcus was about to let off the
finishing shot, a flurry of gunfire came from his left.

Cutting his eyes to the side, he saw three men running his
way, from a distance, letting off rounds at him.

Marcus turned and dove behind the bulldozer, leaving the
big man to suffer. Rhameek snatched up Slim's gun and
headed for cover, behind his truck, with Champ following
close behind.

Tiffany was glad she had thought to bring the extra help
with her. But, she decided she would wait till later to pat
herself on the back.

Darting from behind the Expedition, she ran towards the big
man who lay dead on the ground, with the straps on the
duffle bag still attached to his shoulder.

As if all of the shooting, going on around her, wasn't
enough to shake her up; Tiffany almost shit on herself,
literally, when she reached for the large bag, and it started to
move.

"What the fu ..." Tiffany's words were cut short, when a

hole exploded from the side of the bag. She felt her face heat up as the bullet whizzed past her, missing her by inches.

Tiffany grabbed her face, and ran for the Expedition. Had she looked back, she would've seen the big blade poke out through the bag and rip down the side.

"You mean to tell me Shawt Change ain't good enuff for you?" Shawt Change cackled, as he burst from the large duffle bag. "Just like a broad, always bout the big money!" He mumbled to himself, as he raised his .45 and fired a shot in Tiffany's direction.

Tiffany screamed at the sound of the bullet hitting the door as she was opening it. Wasting no time, she jumped in the truck, crank it up, and sped off.

"Would you please shut the fuck up!" Shawt Change barked, as he spun around, facing the dead gorilla's twin brother, who still lay on the ground, maimed and screaming in pain.

Shawt Change shook his head in disgust. Then, he approached the man, letting off round after round into his body, until he no longer moved.

"Marcus would you stop that God damn whistling!" Rhameek screamed, as he ducked behind his truck.

The whistling ceased, but only long enough for Marcus to crack a smile at his friend. Then, dropping the empty clip from his gun, he popped in a fresh one and resumed.

" Whistling"

Rhameek shook his head then let off a flurry of shots, pinning down the three remaining aggressors behind a pile of rocks.

Marcus took the opportunity to step out, from behind the bulldozer, and took aim at Tiffany, in the Expedition.

"Whistling"

Tiffany heard a loud bang. Her front tire exploded, causing

the Expedition to swerve aggressively, until, she lost the
wheel and the truck began to tumble, throwing up a cloud of
dust as it rolled end over end.
♪♪ ♪♪♪ ♪   "I'm out of bullets!" Rhameek screamed, as
Shawt Change began letting off a flurry of his own, keeping
the three men pinned down.
♪♪ ♪♪♪ ♪   Marcus continued to whistle, as he signaled
for Shawt Change to cease firing.

The three men, assuming that their adversaries had run out
of ammo, took the opportunity to rise up and return fire.

"Shit!" One of the men cursed, when three loud shot's rang
out, simultaneously, causing them to duck back behind the
pile.

"I knew we shouldn't have fucked wit that Bitch!" The
short, chubby man cursed, as he looked to the right, towards
his partner.

"What the fuck's wrong wit you?" The chubby man asked,
noticing the grim look on his friend's face. His friend had a
sickly look on his face, as he stared over the chubby man's
shoulder.

The chubby man turned to see what had his friend's
attention.

"Oh shit!" He screamed, at the sight of his accomplice
laying on the ground, with a chunk missing from the top of
his head.

"Motha fucka" he cursed, as he leaned into his remaining
friend, and began kicking at the dead corpse, as if it was
trying to bite him.

"That motha fucka killed Ace ... what the fuck we done got
ourselves into ... damn!" He cried out to his friend, who still
sat frozen in a state of shock.

"And why that motha fucka keep whistling?" His voice
cracked, filled with panic.
♪♪ ♪♪♪ ♪

"Nigga, I told you this was the mufuckin spot" G-Lo cursed,

as he, Ron and Fly, crept behind an old storage building.

"Nigga we would've been got here if yo ass wouldn't have been givin us the wrong directions!" Ron snapped back.

"Would ya'll shut the fuck up", Fly cursed at a low whisper "we here now; and it sounds like we too late."

"How the fuck it sound like we too late and mufuckas is still shootin?" G-Lo cursed.

"Yeah mufucka, sounds to me like we right on time." Ron added.

"Stop talkin so fuckin loud." Fly demanded.

"Who the fuck you talkin too?" G-Lo and Ron retorted.

"Shhh" Fly gestured, with his finger to his lips, as he began to point at the window on the small shed.

Ron and G-Lo looked up and spotted what had caught Fly's attention.

All three of them ducked down and began to whisper.

"It's just two of em" Fly uttered.

"Why the fuck they hidin in here?" G-Lo questioned.

Ron sucked his teeth. "Nigga, they ain't hidin out of fear!" Ron shook his head in disgust. "They waitin to ambush a mufucka!"

"Which is exactly why we was spose to be here on time!" G-Lo added smartly.

"Better late than never" Ron replied, as he began to creep, at a low crouch, towards the rear entrance of the shed.

"Move yo scary ass!" G-Lo stated, nudging Fly forward.

Fly resisted. "Nigga I'ma make sure don't nobody creep up on us."

G-Lo frowned and eased his way around Fly, following Ron's lead.

"Don't you think we need to go out and help?" The slim guy, standing by the window, asked.

His partner in crime, who sat on a crate to the left of him, nonchalantly picking out his Afro, as he enjoyed the view of the events outside, responded.

"Hell nah! ... we gonna let those mufuckers kill each other, then we'll finish off whoever's left, and take the money."

"You'ze a grimy ass nigga dawg" the slim man stated.

Afro began to laugh, then all of a sudden; he straightened up and tried to reach for his gun, as he spotted Ron and G-Lo out of the corner of his eye.

"Too late!" Ron barked, as he let off a shot, knocking Afro off the crate.

G-Lo followed suit. Letting off a round, he hit Slim in the shoulder before he could react.

"Aaagh ... motherfucka!" Slim cried out in pain.

"Shut up nigga!" G-Lo spat, as Ron checked Afro, to make sure he was dead.

"One gone!" Ron stated, confirming that Afro was down for the count.

"Quit whining nigga!" G-Lo said to Slim, who was still holding his shoulder, moaning.

Slim straightened up and gritted his teeth, poking his chest out like a soldier, ready to die.

"Fuck you nigga!" He stated.

"What?" G-Lo spat, as Ron broke out into a fit of laughter.

"He said, fuck you, nigga!" Ron instigated, holding his side, as he continued to laugh.

"Oh, you a tough nigga?" G-Lo spat, with a look of anger on his face.

"Fly, get yo scared ass in here!" G-Lo yelled.

Fly bent the corner and cringed at the sight of the dead man on the floor.

"Hold this! Wit yo soft ass." G-Lo snapped, passing Fly his gun.

"Nigga I ain't soft; I just prefer Bitches over gunplay!" Fly replied, grabbing the gun in his grip.

Ron continued to laugh, making G-Lo angrier.

"What you say nigga?" G-Lo asked again, getting nose to nose with the slim guy.

"Nigga I said fu ..."

G-Lo cut his words short with a hard right to the jaw, causing him to stumble into the wall.

Before he could recover, G-Lo grabbed him by the collar and looked him eye to eye.

"Nah nigga ... I ain't gone kill you yet!"

Tiffany crawled through the shattered windshield of the truck. Her head was bleeding and she was a little shaken, but happy to be alive.

Shots continued to ring out, as she took advantage of the moment to stagger away from the scene.

Shawt Change began to open fire at the pile of rocks once again. Holding the remaining two men at bay, as Marcus moved in closer, at a slow walk.

"Man fuck this shit!" The chubby man screamed to his partner, who was still staring at their dead accomplices exposed skull.

Marcus waved for Rhameek to follow, then he signaled for Shawt Change to cease fire, everything became quiet.

"They outta bullets, I think" The chubby man's partner stated, finally breaking his silence.

The two men gave each other an approving nod, then jumped up, with their weapons raised, only to come face to face with the barrels of Marcus and Rhameek's guns.

The two men were in no position to react; instead, they both dropped their weapons and put their hands up.

"Dumb ass niggas! Mines ain't even loaded!" Rhameek chuckled, as he smashed the chubby man across the jaw, with his empty pistol.

Ron had tears in his eyes, from laughing so hard, as G-Lo picked Slim up off the ground.

"How long you plan on beatin this niggas ass?" Fly asked, getting tired of Ron's laughter and G-Lo's antics.

"Nigga shut up! What, you feel sorry for him or somein?"

G-Lo snapped.

Fly waved him off, then glanced out the window of the shed.

"I think everything's straight now", he stated, seeing that Marcus and Rhameek had two men at gunpoint. "Do what you gone do, and lets go."

G-Lo smiled, and looked at Ron, before hitting the slim man in the gut, causing him to fold over.

"This one's for you nigga!" He stated, to Ron, as he tucked Slim's head under his arm, in a headlock position.

G-Lo let his whole body drop to the floor, pulling the man's head with him on the way down. The maneuver, he had seen many times on wrestling, caused the man's head to make a cracking sound as it hit the floor with deadly force.

"Now that's how you D.D.T. a mufucka!" G-Lo screamed, as he got up off the ground, dusting himself off.

"You call dat a D.D.T.?" Ron mocked "nigga, if it was me; I would've picked his skinny ass up and power drivered him!"

"Its pile driver, mufucka, not power driver!" G-Lo argued, as the three of them headed for the door.

"It's power driver nigga!" Ron replied.

"Pile driver!" G-Lo repeated.

"Nigga I watch RAW every Friday, how you gonna tell me!" Ron snapped.

"Nigga, RAW come on Monday. You be watching Smack down!" G-Lo countered.

"Nigga how the fuck you gonna tell me what I've been watchin? ... Its RAW!"

"SMACKDOWN!" G-Lo insisted.

"Nigga I'll smack you down!" Ron threatened. Fly threw his hands up in submission, getting tired of G-Lo and Ron's bickering.

"Nigga I'd like to see you do it!" G-Lo challenged, bumping chest with Ron.

"Oh yeah?" Ron replied as he grabbed G-Lo in a headlock and they both fell to the ground and began to tussle.

"Look at these niggas!" Rhameek said as he, Shawt Change and Marcus lead the two unarmed men towards the shed.

"Ya'll cut that bullshit out!" Rhameek yelled "I can't believe these mufucka's!"

"Where ya'll been?" Shawt Change barked, as the two of them let each other go and got to their feet.

"This nigga got us lost!" G-Lo snapped.

"Bullshit!" Ron cursed.

Rhameek turned his attention towards Fly. Fly was about to open his mouth, but changed his mind when he saw G-Lo and Ron glaring at him.

Fly threw his arms out and shrugged his shoulders, deciding it would be best for him if he didn't place blame on either one.

Rhameek shook his head "ya'll some confused niggas" he remarked, before turning his attention to the two hostages. "So, which one of ya'll gone tell us where Felicia is?" Rhameek questioned.

"Man we don't know where the Bitch at!" Chubby man responded.

"Champ!" Rhameek called out. Champ, busy sniffing on one of the ape twins corpse, raised his head at the sound of his masters' voice, and came running to Rhameek's side.

"WATCH him boy!" Rhameek said, in a low tone.

Champ crouched low and began to growl, as the hairs on his back spiked up, and his tail stiffened.

"She at the hotel! They left her at the hotel, tied up!" The chubby man's partner blurted out.

Rhameek slapped himself on the forehead and cursed. "That's what she was doin there." He said out loud.

"What you talkin bout?" Marcus inquired.

"Nothin bruh; I know where she is!" Rhameek hesitated, then looked at the chubby man. "Well, I almost know!"

Chubby man immediately gave up the room number, without hesitation.

"Lets go" Rhameek stated, wasting no time, he ran for his

truck.

"What about them?" Shawt Change asked, pointing at the two captives.

Marcus looked at G-Lo and Ron, who looked at each other and smiled.

"Ya'll take care of em" Marcus stated.

"Whoooo!" Ron yelled at the top of his lungs, doing his best impression of Rick Flair, while imitating his favorite wrestlers signature walk.

"Let's get ready to rumble!" G-Lo yelled out like a ring announcer.

"I gotta see this!" Shawt Change commented, nudging the two men into the shed.

Fly shook his head, and stated, "Ya'll some sick mufuckas!" As Marcus took off in the direction where he had parked his motorcycle.

"Where you think they going?" Mike said, as he and Peabo sat in the car, in an inconspicuous spot.

They had arrived, within seconds, after the shooting had began.

Mike was eager to get out of the car but, just as he had reached for the door handle, Peabo had grabbed him by the shoulder.

"Let's see what those niggas is made of!" Peabo had commented, with an icy grin.

The whole time, Mike was fidgeting, anxious for some action. But, Peabo sat, stroking his beard as he watched the scene intently, as if he were at home watching an action movie.

They both had sat in the car in silence, until, Peabo popped in his "Scarface" CD and commented.

"Action ain't action without a lil good background music!"

Mike smiled and relaxed as they watched the episode play out.

"I don't know where they goin", Peabo replied as he opened the car door "but we bout to find out, and when we do, we gone send them on a lil detour down a One Way Road!"

"A Dead End Road!" Mike added, cracking his knuckles, before stepping out of the car as well.

"You next, fat boy!" G-Lo screamed, as he stood on a stack of crates, pointing at the chubby man whom Shawt Change held in the corner, at gunpoint.

"Hold dat nigga, right there, Ron!" G-Lo yelled.

Ron held the chubby mans partner in a back breaker position. The chubby man dropped his head, feeling sorry for his partner, who lay limp, with blood running from his nose and mouth; and a pleading look on his face.

"Dusty Rhodes!" G-Lo yelled, diving off of the crates, dropping an elbow across the mans face.

His body cut half a flip as he tumbled off of Ron's shoulders.

"Yeah!" Ron screamed "did ya'll see that shit?"

Fly waved Ron's attempt at a high five off. He was about to comment, when his words were interrupted by the sounds of a gun clicking.

"Don't move mufucka!" Peabo barked, catching everyone's attention.

They all froze at the sight of Peabo and Mike, standing beside Shawt Change, with their guns held to his head.

"Muu ... tha ... fucka!" Shawt Change cursed under his breath.

"Don't even think about it!" Mike warned. He saw G-Lo and Ron looking towards their weapons, which they had carelessly left laying on a crate, on the opposite side of the room.

All Fly could do was drop his head into his palms, as he wondered, why in the hell he had even came along with them in the first place.

Fly coined himself as a ladies man. Gunplay wasn't his

forte. And now, here he was caught in the midst of more drama than he'd ever seen in a lifetime.

"Get yall's ass over here!" Mike barked. Fly and the others put their hands up and began to walk towards Peabo and Mike.

"Nah; not ya'll two" Mike stated, pointing Ron and G-Lo out, before passing his gun to Peabo and removing his shirt.

"So ya'll niggas like to wrestle?" Mike said with a huge grin on his face, while flexing his massive chest.

"I got these two Peabo; them niggas can tell you where they boys was headed, while I play wit these niggas." He said, twisting his head from right to left, making his neck crack.

"I ain't tellin you shit!" Shawt Change blurted out.

"That means you useless to me!" Peabo replied coldly, as he let off a shot that sent Shawt Change into a world of darkness, where the guns echo would haunt him for infinity.

G-Lo and Ron reacted immediately, rushing Mike, who returned the gesture by meeting them both head on. Arms spread wide, he knocked them both off of their feet, bulldozing them to the floor.

"Now, how bout you start talking!" Peabo snarled, pointing the gun at Fly.

G-Lo and Ron both were dizzy from the blow. Using each other for support, they glared in Mike's direction, as he stood, with his back to them, bouncing around as if he were a wrestler, pumping his fans up for the big finish.

The eyeballs, tattooed on the back of Mike's head, seemed to stare at them both as they staggered to their feet.

"That's all you got?" Ron slurred, with blood dripping from his mouth.

Mike only replied with a flex of his wide back. Then flexing his biceps, he pointed at the large tattoo that read I.C.U. with his thumbs.

G-Lo and Ron looked at the huge tattoo then looked at each other, as if having a subliminal conversation. Then, they both looked towards Fly, with disappointment on their faces, as he spilled the beans.

"Bitch ass nigga!" G-Lo spat. Then, he and Ron turned their attention back to Mike, who was now facing them, with a grin on his face.

"And now for the grand finale!" Mike barked, saliva flying from his mouth, as he beat his chest like a rabid gorilla.

Ron and G-Lo gave each other an approving nod, then stood, with their chest out. They both rushed Mike, letting out a battle cry like warriors from the days of old.

Mike side stepped as the two approached, catching G-Lo with a hard over hand right to the nose. The blow echoed throughout the large supply shed, stopping G-Lo dead in his tracks.

Ron only a few steps behind, went low and made an attempt to scoop the big man. He was met with an elbow to the back of the neck, that brought him crumbling to his knees.

Mike caught Ron's head, between his kneecaps, and lifted his feet off the ground.

Ron squirmed around, trying to free his head from the vice like grip between Mike's legs. It was useless, Ron felt his legs go into the air as he began to get light headed and lose his breath.

"Pile Driver!" Mike yelled at the top of his lungs.

It was then, at that last moment, that Ron used his last breath to utter the words.

"Its 'POWER' driver mothafucka." Then came blackness.

Rhameek and Marcus burst into the hotel room, waving their guns around.

The room appeared to be empty, until, they heard a muffled cry, coming from the bedroom in the huge suite.

Approaching the door carefully, they swung it open, guns poised.

They both breathed a sigh of relief at the sight of Felicia, laying on the bed, tied up and gagged.

Marcus checked the bathroom, as Rhameek removed the

gag from her mouth.

"It's clear dawg!" Marcus stated, as he came from the bathroom, finding Felicia with her arms wrapped around Rhameek's neck, in a death lock.

"I thought they was gonna kill me." She cried.

"Its o.k. baby, its o.k." Rhameek whispered, as he stroked Felicia's hair, then kissed her, gently, on the lips.

"Who dat is!" Marcus yelled, with a grin on his face.

Felicia looked at Marcus and wiped the tears from her face, then, looking Rhameek in the eyes she replied.

"Dat's just my baby daddy!" Then, leaning forward, she kissed him passionately.

"Let's get outta here!" Marcus said, with a broad smile on his face.

Candy was filled with joy as Marcus informed her that Felicia was safe.

"Let me talk to her" Candy said with tears in her eyes.

"They not wit me. Her and Rah went home. They got some catchin up to do!" Marcus replied.

Candy ran her fingers through her frizzled hair and exhaled deeply.

"Okay ... I won't bother her right now ... I'm just glad she's o.k." She said as she looked at her fingers.

Noticing, for the first time, she had chewed all of her nails off, in the midst of all her worrying and pacing.

"Marcus, hurry home, please."

"I'm on the way" he responded before hanging up.

"Marcus, I know I been acti ..." Candy began, then stopped; realizing Marcus had hung up.

"I love you too." She mumbled, to herself, as she made her way to the bathroom, and looked in the mirror.

She was a mess. All of the drama, and worrying, had taken its toll on her.

"Too much in one night!" She thought out loud, while turning the shower on.

Just as she was about to undress, the doorbell rang.

"Who is this?" She wondered. Walking to the front door, she looked through the peephole.

The morning sun shined brightly. The sounds of birds chirping filled the air as she opened the door.

"What's up boy!" She teased. "What you doing over here this early?" She said, with a smile on her face.

Fly dropped his head and her smile faded.

"Fly, what's wrong?"

CHAPTER 24

Marcus pulled into the driveway. He found himself feeling extremely tired. Removing his helmet, he looked up at the sky.

He began to wonder if any of this had been worth the trouble he had brought upon himself.

All he wanted to do now was put it all behind him. Maybe leave the state, give himself a change of scenery.

But for now, all he wanted to do was go inside and make love to Candy.

The episode with Felicia had made him realize, anything could happen, at any time.

He thought, it was due time, he and Candy learned to appreciate each other more.

"No time like the present!" He said to himself, as he stepped off of his bike, and entered the house.

Marcus smiled when he entered the living room and heard the stereo playing Candy's favorite Mary J. Blige CD.

Even over the loud music, he could hear the shower running down the hall. His smile widened. Removing his shirt, he headed down the hallway.

Upon entering the bedroom, he could see the steam coming from the shower.

Marcus removed his jeans and was about to sneak up on Candy in the shower, when he thought about something.

"Ice Cream!" He said to himself.

"I scream, you scream, we all scream for ice cream!" He chanted, deciding he would get Candy nice and sticky after they finished their shower.

He slipped his sneakers back on; laughing to himself, due to the fact, he knew Candy would have something to say about him walking around in sneakers and boxers in the house.

"Why do you do that?" He said, imitating her, under his breath, as he walked down the hallway, heading for the kitchen.

Marcus bobbed his head, to the sounds of Mary J., as he dug in the freezer for the ice cream.

"I hope you like Pralines and Cream on dat ass!" He yelled as he pulled the box of ice cream from the freezer and closed the door,

"I like Butter Pecan myself."

Marcus looked up and dropped the box of ice cream upon seeing Mike standing in his kitchen, with an apple in his hand, blocking Marcus off from the living room.

Marcus swung immediately, but missed. Mike ducked under the punch and delivered a hard blow to the gut.

Marcus folded from the blow, but recovered quickly. He backed up, leaving a small space between him and Mike.

"Where's Candy?" Marcus spat.

Mike laughed, then bit a chunk out of the apple, before replying.

"Ain't no need in coming home, cause Peabo done got yo girl and gone!"

Marcus charged him aggressively, ramming Mike with his shoulder. It felt like he had ran into a brick wall, but he managed to make Mike stumble back a few steps.

Mike looked like a defensive blocker on the football field as he found his footing and shoved Marcus back with his forearm; leaving a gap in between them.

Mike smiled arrogantly, and took another bite from the apple, as he and Marcus locked eyes.

Marcus wiped the saliva from the corner of his mouth, with his forearm. He began to pace, from left to right, looking for an opening to get around Mike.

Mike smiled; his eyes followed Marcus' movements,

waiting for him to rush towards him again.

"You know I was the man in high school; ain't seen a nigga yet who could get past me when I'm on that line!"

"Where's my motherfuckin girl!" Marcus hissed, as he became immobile, his sneakers gripping the kitchen floor as he poised himself for combat. "I swear ... if ya'll hurt her!"

Mike laughed out loud, sounding like the villain in a movie "don't worry we gone take nice care of her for you" he paused, embracing the tension in the air.

"Shiiit, Peabo probably got those pretty lil legs throwed up in the air, as we speak, and after I kill you ... I'm gone go have a lil fun wit her myself."

Mike smiled, and nodded in approval, when he saw Marcus' jaw tighten.

"Yeah, get mad nigga!" Mike said, becoming hyped "that's what I'm talking bout!"

Mike looked like a madman, as he took one bite from the apple, then crouched low. His arms spread wide, he began to chant under his breath.

"Defense! Defense! Defense! Defense!"

The veins in Marcus' arms began to rise to the surface as he clenched his fist. The veins extended all the way from his forearms to his neck, rising until the point, they looked like serpentine cables running through his body.

He could feel his whole body tensing up as the adrenaline began to pump throughout every part of him, causing his temples to throb on beat with his heart.

"Defense! Defense! Defense! Defense!" Mike uttered. His eyes got wider and foam began to build up in the corner of his mouth.

Marcus could feel his blood boiling as he thought of Candy, then, he thought of the things Mike had said were happening to her.

"Come on Bitch! What you waitin for!" Mike barked as he beat his chest, with his right hand, while bringing his left hand towards his mouth, to take another bite from the apple.

Marcus' body reacted like a rubber band that had been stretched to capacity and released spontaneously. All of the tension left his body, instantly, as he felt himself become like fluid.

Mike didn't have a chance to react; Marcus struck with the swiftness of a Cobra.

Grabbing Mike's wrist, just as he was about to bite the apple, he followed through with a hard right, that jammed the apple into Mike's mouth. Mike could feel his teeth shatter as the entire apple lodged itself into his throat, cutting off his wind.

Stumbling backwards, Mike grabbed his throat and desperately tried to cough up the core that was jammed in his mouth, like a cork in a Champagne bottle.

"Why go around you, when I can go through you!" Marcus stated coldly as he watched the big man buckle to his knees, gasping for air.

Mike took short quick breaths, through his nostrils, as he felt himself becoming dizzy.

"Oh you still tryna breathe!" Marcus spat as he stood over Mike.

Lifting Mike's chin up, he looked him eye to eye, then brought the bottom side of his fist down on the bridge of his nose, like a hammer, cutting off his remaining air supply.

Marcus took a step back, and felt his knees get weak. Reality hit him, Candy was still gone, and he had no way of finding her.

Tears welled up in his eyes as he staggered into the wall and slid to the floor, where he sat in a daze, staring at Mike's limp body.

KARMA IS A CHAMELEON

Marcus wasn't sure how long he had been sitting there on the kitchen floor. Time had come to a stand still. Nothing moved and the house was silent. Mary J. had sang her last song, and Marcus had sat there staring at Mike's motionless body, waiting for him to wake up and give him an answer to the question that repeated itself over and over in his head.

"Where is Candy" but deep down inside, Marcus knew Mike wasn't going to wake up, and he wasn't going to get an answer.

"Coo Coo - Coo Coo" Marcus raised his head at the sound of the Coo Coo clock, signaling the top of the hour. The clock came to a halt and Marcus was about to fall back into his trance, when the doorbell rang, snapping him back to reality.

Marcus' body felt like it was weighted down by a ball and chain, as he rose to his feet, and stepped over Mike's body on his way to the door.

He heard Rhameek and Felicia's voices, on the other side, so he wasted no time opening the door.

"Where my girl at ..." Felicia began, then cut herself off, when she saw the expression on Marcus' face.

Her jaw dropped when she looked over Marcus' shoulder and saw Mike sprawled out on the floor.

Pushing past Marcus, Rhameek pulled Felicia into the house and shut the door behind them.

"What the fuck happened?" Rhameek questioned "Where's Candy?"

Marcus dropped his head, a look of defeat on his face, as Rhameek's phone began to ring.

Rhameek snatched his phone from his pocket and flipped it open.

"Yeah! ... what's up Rah Rah"?

Rhameek listened for a second then smiled "Oh yeah?"

Peabo stood in his bedroom, smiling, as he studied Candy's curvaceous frame.

Candy lay in his bed, with her hands binded to the bedpost, and her mouth gagged. Her eyes were puffy from crying. She had cried from the time Peabo and Mike had burst into her home.

She couldn't believe Fly would betray Marcus in such a way. She didn't have a chance to so much as let out a scream, when the two big men had rushed in behind Fly.

Peabo had slapped her so hard it had left her feeling drunk.

She had thought she was going to die, right there in her own home, but instead, she had found herself being gagged and forced into Peabo's car.

His intentions were clear to her, when she heard him tell Mike "you stay here, and when that nigga get home; kill him." Then, he had turned his attention towards Fly and stated "you get yo punk ass outta here; only reason I'ma let you live, is so you can spread the word ... don't fuck wit Peabo!"

Fly couldn't even look her in the eye. He simply exited the house, and didn't look back.

Candy had been crying for the past hour, not only due to the fact that Peabo had fondled her continuously, but out of fear that Marcus was possibly dead by now.

She sat on the bed squirming, as Peabo stared at her with hungry eyes. He had taken his time to strip her down to her panties, and bra, as he kissed all over her body.

Candy knew Peabo had to be sadistic, from the way he spoke to her, as if she were his girlfriend.

He had even brought her out to his large home on Lake Norman, speaking to her in a gentle tone as he tugged her inside.

"You like this baby?" He had asked. Then, when they had entered his home, he even gave her a formal introduction to some girl he had introduced as Rhonda.

"Rhonda baby, this is Candy. She's gonna be spendin a little time wit us ... I'm bout to show her to the bedroom ... you're welcome to join us."

Candy was shocked when the girl had looked at her, as if it were normal for him to bring a girl home tied and gagged, then stated. "Be glad to!"

She had even helped Peabo undress her. Then stepping out of the room, she had told Peabo "you go head and get her comfy, I'm bout to go 'n' get us some whip cream!"

Candy felt like she was living a nightmare, but this was no dream, it was all 100% real.

"You see, it was never about the money." Peabo stated, while removing his shirt. "It's the principle; yo nigga took from me ... now I gotta take from him."

Candy's eye's produced more tears, as Peabo removed his pants, and then his boxers. He smiled at her, as he stroked his beard, with one hand, and his manhood with the other.

"You gone fight it at first, and I ain't gone lie, its gone hurt a little" he said, as his shaft began to fill with blood and stand straight. "Well maybe it'll hurt a lot ... but, I promise you, its gonna get good to you. Then I'm gonna remove yo gag, then, you gone tell me you want more. Then, eventually, you'll realize this is where you wanna be ... and that's when I'll untie you. So you can embrace the new life you bout to have."

Candy began squirming, while trying to scream through the gag.

"Shhh ... shhh" Peabo shushed her as he unsnapped her bra,

exposing her breast. "It's o.k. baby ...Peabo gone take care of you." He uttered, while spreading her legs.

Peabo was so strong that her efforts to resist were futile.

Positioning himself between her legs, he began nibbling on her breast as he pushed his fingers inside of her, parting her lips.

Candy grunted, then began to cry when he raised up, holding his throbbing flesh in his hand, and began to ease towards the passage to her womanhood.

Candy turned her head to the side, trying to look away, and spotted the girl coming back into the room, with a smile on her face.

Candy's eyes grew big as Peabo pressed the head of his swollen flesh against her outer walls.

"Mind if I cut in!"

Candy tried to scream as the blood splattered her face.

"What the ..." Peabo screamed as he rolled off of Candy, holding his neck.

A look of shock covered his face, when he saw Rhonda holding the hawk billed blade in her hand; covered in blood.

"Rhonda?" Peabo's words sounded as if he were speaking underwater as his throat filled with blood.

Rhonda smiled a cold smile. Peabo felt himself getting weaker and weaker. All he could do was try to use the bed to hold himself on his knees.

The knife had cut him in a line parallel to the huge scar he already had, running from his neck to his chest.

"Last time I ain't go deep enuff!" Rhonda hissed "but I think I got it right this time."

Candy continued to squirm, in a state of panic; until, she saw a familiar face.

"One thing bout a woman ... she don't forget nothing!" Zone said, as he entered the room.

Peabo was so disoriented, he thought he was dreaming when he saw Zone enter the room, with "Jah Jah" behind him.

Zone laughed at the look of recognition in Peabo's eyes. "I

see you remember Janice here" Zone laughed "or should I say Jah Jah."

Peabo fell back into the dresser, sitting flat on his ass and looked from Janice to Rhonda.

"I see you've met Rah Rah too!" Zone laughed.

"Yeah nigga, it took me a while to clean ole Janice up. And Rah Rah here ... never did get over that shit ya'll did."

Zone shook his head then kneeled in front of Peabo, being careful not to get any blood on his suit, as Rah Rah began cutting Candy loose.

"See ... I dropped by here in the wee hours of the morning, but you was out on bizness, so I decided, I might as well go get ole Janice here and let her enjoy your demise, first hand." Zone said, with a smirk, before he stood up and nudged Peabo to the floor, with his foot.

The last thing Peabo witnessed was Zone unzipping his pants. Then, he felt not only the moisture from the blood oozing out of him, but, he also felt what he guessed was piss falling all over his face as the world around him faded to black.

"Its over baby girl" Zone said, giving Candy a fatherly hug, as they walked towards the car. At that moment, Rhameek's truck came flying down the driveway.

"Candy!" Marcus yelled, as he hopped out of the truck and ran to check on her.

Zone smiled at the two as they embraced.

Rhameek exited the truck, and met Zone with a firm handshake.

"It's taken care of" Zone stated flatly, turning his attention to Candy and Marcus. "Ya'll go get ya'll a room; I heard you left a lil mess back home, on the rug" Zone stated, tipping his hat to Marcus. "I got a few friends that own a carpet cleaning company!" He winked "they owe me a lil favor; I'll have em clean it up for you."

"Ya'll bounce." Rhameek said, handing his keys to Marcus.

"I'll ride wit them."

Marcus nodded, taking the keys; he wasted no time helping Candy into the truck.

As Marcus made his way around the truck towards the driver's side, he saw Rah Rah, looking him in the eye, she mouthed the words. "You owe me" as she rubbed herself between the thighs.

Marcus couldn't help but smile. Shaking his head, he jumped into the truck and pulled off.

CHAPTER 25

Candy was at the counter, inside the Petro Express, purchasing three Tropicana Twisters.

She had insisted that Marcus stop. She was dying of thirst; being gagged had taken its toll on her. She was tired and ready to get to a room, so she could rest and try her best to forget everything that had happened to her.

The past few days had made her realize how much Marcus meant to her. The thought of losing him had tortured her internally. All she wanted to do was lay back with her man, and show him how much she really loved him.

Marcus sat in the truck, fumbling through Rhameek's CD case, as Candy exited the store; he didn't even notice Tamika pulling up behind him at the gas pump.

Candy stopped in her tracks, upon spotting Tamika. There was no doubt; this was the girl whom Marcus was all up on, in the club."

Tamika smiled as she got out of her car and walked towards Candy.

"Don't I know you?" Candy commented. Tamika didn't have a chance to respond. "Oh yeah. I know ... you the hoe who was all up on my man!" Candy spat.

Tamika gave her a smug look, then stated. "And who might 'yo man' be?"

"Don't play dumb!" Candy stated, pointing towards Rhameek's truck.

Tamika looked towards the truck and smiled when she saw Marcus, who was still looking down at the CD case.

Tamika smirked, then replied "a lil advice ... from now on ...

before you go dashing drinks on yo man and attacking him ... make sho he doin somein wrong!"

Candy's blood began to boil. But, she had been through enough for the day, and didn't have time to "beat a Bitch down." Yet, she did want to make herself clear.

"Listen, I've heard all about you. I heard you done ran through half the niggas in the club and bout 40% of the niggas in the city ... Sonny told me all about you. But let's get this clear ..."

"Hold up!" Tamika interrupted "first of all, the night you saw me was my first time in that club, or any other club in this city. Second of all, I've only been livin here a few weeks. So don't nah nigga in this city know me." Tamika replied, as she pulled her Texas I.D. from her purse, and held it inches from Candy's face.

"Which brings us to our next question" Tamika continued "who the hell is Sonny?"

"Uh, that would be me!"

Candy and Tamika spun around.

"What's up Candy?" Sonny remarked, as he limped closer to Candy. "Oh, don't look surprised!" He spat.

Tamika stepped back, wondering what was going on.

"What the hell takin her so long?" Marcus said to himself. He, finally, looked up from the CD case, his heart dropped as he looked in his rearview and spotted Candy and Tamika, standing within feet of each other.

"Ain't this a Bitch!" He cursed as he opened the door; unable to see Sonny, due to the fact, he was blocked from Marcus' line of sight.

Marcus could hear a male, raising his voice, as he came around the back of the truck.

"So that's how you get down Candy? Fuck a nigga, then get him fucked up!"

"Sonny I ..." Candy began, as Marcus bent the corner, causing her mouth to get stuck in midsentence. She realized

Marcus had heard Sonny's last comment.

"What the fu ..." Marcus began, as Sonny reached under his shirt, and pulled out a large revolver.

"No!" Candy screamed. The juice fell from her hands. Time seemed to slow down, as Tamika jumped out of the way, and Candy made an attempt to grab Sonny's arm.

"You like to set mufuckas up, Bitch?" Sonny spat, as he knocked Candy off her feet, and opened fire on Marcus.

Candy and Tamika both screamed Marcus' name, as Sonny left the scene with haste.

"No!" Candy cried, repeatedly, as Marcus' eyes began to roll back in his head.

Tamika stood to the side, with her hands over her mouth, in shock, as she watched the blood pour through Marcus' shirt.

"Baby, please don't leave me!" Candy cried "Marcus baby, I love you, I need you!" She screamed.

"Somebody get help" Tamika cried out, as Candy lifted his shirt to see where he was hit.

Candy froze when she lifted the shirt. But it wasn't the sight of the blood that had her in awe; it was the huge tattoo that covered his left side.

It was her name in large letters, going across his ribcage, and from her name there were large lines, that appeared to be veins, that lead to a life-like tattoo. It was a vivid picture of a human heart; beating.

"Marcus baby I'm so sorry!" Candy cried, realizing that the specks of blood she had spotted on his shirt, the previous day, were nothing more than, the results of a bleeding tattoo.

"Oh my God!" She whaled, realizing the mistake she had made.

"Marcus talk to me baby!" She cried "please baby, please!"

Marcus wanted to speak. He wanted to say so many things. But, his mouth overflowed with blood, and his muscles began to twitch, as he felt himself getting cold.

His eyes danced around in his head, as he caught glimpses of Candy's face, and Tamika's face, simultaneously.

And, as he faded to black, Sonny's last words replayed themselves, over and over, in his head.

"That's how you get down ... fuck a nigga then get him fucked up ... fuck a nigga then get him fucked up ... fuck a nigga ... fuck a nigga ... fuck a nigga ..."

"Marcus, Nooo!" He heard Candy cry out, one last time, before blackness engulfed him, and all became silent.

Jealousy and Assumption
lead to the consumption of
destruction ....

Candy and Flowers

EPILOGUE

"He's stabilizing now, Miss Brown." The doctor replied, as he and Candy sat in the I.C.U. waiting room. "He's had a traumatic experience, but I think he's gonna pull through." The doctor paused to make sure his words were sinking in.

He reached out and grasped Candy's hand. "The best thing you can do now is, go home and come back tomorrow ... hopefully he'll be awake when you come back." The doctor said with a reassuring smile.

The doctor gave her a pat on the shoulder then walked off. Candy hesitated, then decided to take his advice; she walked down the hallway towards the elevator.

She was so shaken; she hadn't even called Rhameek to tell him what had happened. She decided she would call him and inform him, as soon as she got to the car.

She felt as if she were about to pass out, from lack of sleep, as she stepped onto the elevator. Just as the door was closing, she heard a voice yell "hold the elevator!"

It was too late, the door had closed and the elevator had already began its descent to the lobby.

"DAMMIT!" Tiffany cursed, as she reached the elevator, a second too late.

Irritated and angry, she decided to take the stairs. She was ready to get back to Peabo's house, and take the doctor's advice, and get some rest.

The doctor's told her that if she had called the paramedics a

minute later, Peabo probably would've been dead by now.
He had lost a lot of blood but the doctor's were able to patch
him up.

"Come back tomorrow and hopefully he'll wake up again."
They told her.

Tiffany was glad she had come home and found Peabo when
she did, but she found herself irritated, due to the fact, the
doctor's told her he had awakened once, in I.C.U., and called
out the last name she would've expected him to call out.

"Rhonda!"

'Yes, may I help you" the receptionist downstairs said, with
a big smile on her face.

"Yes, can you tell me what room a Mr. Marcus Flowers is
in?" Tamika said, as she smiled back at the receptionist.

"One moment please" the receptionist said, as she focused
on her computer, neither her nor Tamika seeing a distraught
looking Candy walking past, as she headed for the exit.